THE MIDWIFE'S PROMISE

ELIZA GRAHAM

Storm

Ebook ISBN: 978-1-80508-288-0
Paperback ISBN: 978-1-80508-290-3

Cover design: Sarah Whittaker
Cover images: Arcangel, Shutterstock

Published by Storm Publishing.
For further information, visit:
www.stormpublishing.co

ALSO BY ELIZA GRAHAM

The Girl in Lifeboat Six

For Isla

ONE

It's my ninetieth birthday, they keep telling me, so I can do anything, have anything I want. *Within reason,* I imagine they add silently. As I grow older, I become more frivolous. I'm half-tempted to ask for a horse-drawn sleigh ride. It's been a good year for snow in New England and even in late March it's clinging on in the mountains. I'd love to go up in a ski lift one last time, but there's not a chance in hell anyone would take me. So I simply specify Pol Roger and a particular cake you can only get from a particular Viennese bakery charging eye-watering amounts. My daughter-in-law puts these on her list. My ninetieth birthday has added several more inserts and pull-outs to her already bulging Filofax.

I order a new dress, in the style the dressmaker has made up for me for over a decade, but in a more luxurious silk-jersey blend. My regular hairdresser offers to come to the house before the event to do my hair, but why miss out on the salon with its snippets of gossip and its young women coming and going, bringing with them news of love affairs, weddings, pregnancies and new babies?

Ninety. Sometimes I still think an extra decade's been

added on in error, but it's the age I really am. And the cards pouring into the apartment reiterate the truth. 'If it's on your birth certificate, it must be true,' my son tells me, folding paper napkins at the table next to me. There's a lot I could say about birth certificates, but I hold my tongue. I've written everything down; eventually he'll find out. He's been fussing around with party canapés, glasses and crockery for later, but now I need him to leave so I'm not tempted to blurt everything out.

I distract myself by looking at the envelopes on the side table next to me. There's one with a South African postmark I haven't opened yet. 'Melissa will hand-deliver her card later.' Paul chuckles. 'She can't wait until this evening. She's spent hours on it. Pretend you're thrilled.'

There's nothing six-year-old Melissa – Milly, I call her privately – could do that wouldn't thrill me. I have a present for her, too. If I'm ninety, I can give presents at my birthday party, I reckon.

An envelope with South African stamps on it. I open it to find a birthday card with an illustration of Cape flowers.

I'm catching you up in relative age terms, it says. *Thank you for my 85th birthday card. Lottie and the family are still over from London. We're all having fun. Do you remember the fritillaries on the plateau? I haven't seen anything like them here, but you would love the South African flowers. Have a wonderful day,* liebe *Sophie. You know what I'd like to add, but you can ignore my advice as you usually do and just accept my fondest love. Erich.*

There's the old twinge of regret at what might have been: all of us in the sunshine in South Africa. Or Erich here in Boston with me. He'd love the city. But all in all, I still can't see a way it could have worked out any better for everyone than this. Me here. Him there.

Erich and I hold my secret between us. Each year makes it weigh heavier and the guilt harder to bear. He couldn't have expected, when we first started working together, that he'd be bound to me like this.

Paul is looking edgy. 'What is it?' I ask. 'You don't think we've got enough champagne glasses?'

'You always have enough glasses. And plates.'

I've always liked being ready for a big party.

'Melissa was hoping to put up some kind of board for you, with photos of you as a child. You don't seem to have many?'

I do actually have a few more pictures of myself as a baby and small child, but they're in albums with photographs of other people, many of them taken in the decades before Paul's birth. 'I only have a few downstairs,' I lie. 'The albums are stored... Not sure where.'

'Probably buried in a trunk up in the attic. It'll only take me a second to have a look.'

'Oh, I wouldn't want you to risk that lovely pullover in all those cobwebs. And I'm not sure exactly which trunk they're in.'

I stand up. 'Let me fetch the photos I do have down here.' Refusing his counter-suggestion that I sit down and let him fetch them, I retrieve the pictures from the desk in my bedroom. It's good for me to walk. Everything I need has been brought down to the same floor now. 'There you are.' I hand him a few pictures of me as a baby and small child in Holland. There are a few of Paul as an infant, too, including one taken in the Cévennes. He's lying in a wicker basket on a sunny terrace, smiling up at the mulberry trees while I crouch beside him, my hair tied back in a silk scarf.

'It's not the most cheerful photograph of you I've ever seen,' he says, looking closely at it.

'I was probably just hungry. We all were, all the time.'

And scared, mourning and guilty, too. At least, I was. 'This one is more cheerful.'

Paul and I on Tybee Island, Georgia. Our first beach holiday after our arrival in the States, both smiling broadly. I remember a kind passer-by taking the photograph for me on my Box Brownie.

'You look as if you need to rest, Mum.' I nod as though this is true. 'You sure you're not too tired to see Melissa before the party?'

'I wouldn't miss her for the world.'

'She just wants to give you her card after school, before you have your hair done.'

'I'll have a nap beforehand so I'm fresh for her.'

When he leaves, I walk to the apartment window and watch him walk away, as I always do. I'm not going to rest, I'm going back to my desk to write a little more about what went on in the weeks and months before the photograph of him on the sunny terrace was taken.

One day he'll pull out all the pictures in the attic and chances are I won't be around to answer the questions they bring up.

There's someone else with me as I move slowly into my bedroom to return to the past. A gentle ghost, an girl who never ages.

She's just behind me. If I turn quickly enough, I'll catch a glimpse of Camille, asking why her image is to be banished from Melissa's board.

'I'm sorry,' I whisper to her. 'I know I have to make it right.'

TWO

CAMILLE, FRENCH RIVIERA, JULY 1942

The Italian soldier grinned at the girls, stepping aside to let them walk up the steps ahead of him. 'The Italians aren't too bad,' Laure told Camille under her breath. 'The fishermen don't like them because they stop them going out in their boats when they want. But they're not brutes like the Germans.'

'Nobody could be like the Germans.' All the same, Camille shivered as she felt the Italian soldier's eyes on her back. They mightn't be Nazi occupiers, but they didn't belong here: along this beautiful stretch of French Mediterranean coast. She felt the rush of nausea she'd experienced when the first news films of the Nazis marching down the Champs-Élysées in Paris was shown in the Lyon cinemas. But she was safe here, Camille reminded herself.

Once on the café terrace, they ordered *citron pressés*. Camille put on her dark glasses and let the scent of jasmine and myrtle wash over her. She could almost relax and pretend the war, the carving up of France by occupiers, wasn't happening. But then thoughts of her father popped into her mind and she felt the heavy grief creep over her as it did at unexpected moments. She swallowed.

Thankfully, Laure was examining her wristwatch and not looking at her. 'Good, we're early. Since Jean-Luc came back from America, he's become obsessed with efficiency and time and motion.'

'Time and what?'

'Something to do with the American automobile manufac-turers he visited. Though what motor cars have to do with silk production, I do not know.'

Dedication to industrial efficiency must be the reason why Laure's cousin was allowed to carry on weaving silk in Lyon instead of being sent to work in Germany on his return to France. Most of the boys Camille knew were now propping up the German economy, the price for the French surrender two years ago. If she'd been Jean-Luc, she'd have stayed out of France, joined the Allied fight, done all she could to drive them out of the countries they and their allies had occupied.

She sipped her *citron pressé*, enjoying the tangy lemon, feeling herself relax. The Mediterranean glimmered azure in the distance from this hilltop village, still an elevating sight, even if barbed wire garlanded many of the beaches. Apparently, the Italians worried about Allied raids on the coast.

'Here he is!' Laure waved.

The young man moving swiftly but elegantly up the steps took off his hat and kissed his cousin on both cheeks, before shaking hands with Camille. He was dressed in a light sports jacket and white trousers, perfectly pressed. It had been such a long time since she'd seen someone his age dressed like this: not in a uniform, marching glumly towards a prisoner-of-war camp, or wounded, dressed shabbily, queuing for food. He was tall and the well-cut jacket hinted at an athletic physique.

Laure must have briefed Jean-Luc on Camille's recent bereavement because he managed to convey unspoken and gentle sympathy mixed with the same light, slightly teasing manner he showed his cousin. Once or twice, Laure batted him on the hand with her little wicker bag. 'Stop. Or I'll tell your big sisters.'

'Don't tell Vivienne. She's still in Lyon and she can be very fierce.'

'Nearly as fierce as *Tante* Véronique.'

'Where do you think she learned it?' He leant towards Camille. 'My mother's got a certain reputation for liking people and things to be just so. Actually, she's soft as a kitten when you get to know her.'

Camille thought of her own mother: never fierce, but never one to back down if she believed herself right. Yet Papa had often won a heated debate by defusing it with a joke, reducing Maman to exasperated laughter. She felt a lump in her throat and picked up her glass. Empty.

Jean-Luc nodded at the passing waiter. 'Another for mademoiselle.' She was going to tell him she'd had enough but something in his dark-brown eyes told her he was giving her a moment to recover.

'The serious business of the day needs resolving.' He steepled his long fingers. 'What time should we play tennis this evening?'

Camille sipped her drink, letting the two of them debate timings and the best itinerary for a drive up into the hills later in the week. When they stood up to leave, he pressed her hand. 'I felt lost when my father died a few years ago. The worst of it passes even if you always miss them. It was very sudden, I gather? That always makes it harder.'

'His appendix.' Such a small part of the body, but if it burst the infection could fell even a strong man like Papa, who walked so fast you couldn't keep up with him and who had a heart like an ox.

'He's kind, your cousin,' she told Laure as they walked back to the villa.

'Makes up a bit for the fact he didn't head somewhere he

could join the Free French to take on the *Boches*.' Laure's face hardened. 'Business always comes first for my cousins.'

Jean-Luc's family had been weaving silk in Lyon for two centuries, Laure told her. The looms meant more to them than France itself. Véronique had had two daughters before giving birth to the much-longed-for son and heir to the business.

'I suppose he feels it's worth keeping the silk business going for... after?'

'When the Germans and Italians leave?' Laure sighed. 'Let's sit under the canopy. I need some shade.'

At least the Germans weren't occupying Lyon. For now. Papa had always warned that they'd certainly advance south. He'd moved Maman and Camille out of Paris in the June of 1940. They'd already abandoned Berlin when Hitler came to power in 1933. Only a week or so before he died, he'd been regretting the fact he hadn't pushed for American visas when they'd still been in the States and had good contacts. He'd relaxed too much in the Phony War, he said, the quiet period before Hitler started invading western Europe. Neither of her parents were Jewish, but Papa was German and the Nazis hadn't liked his journalism. His name was almost certainly on a list of people to be arrested and detained. Maman and Camille might be at risk by association, too. The French state still protected its citizens to a degree, but those who weren't French, well, they had to take their chances with the Germans. Papa had talked about moving on to neutral Portugal, putting even more distance between them and the Germans. Camille hadn't wanted to leave Lyon where she had good friends. Especially Laure.

She and Maman should have felt less vulnerable now Papa was gone. Except that Camille suspected Maman, a nurse and midwife, was quietly helping refugees from all over Europe who'd rushed south to escape the Nazis. Most of them were in the city unofficially at best. More likely illegally.

Anyway, whatever Maman was up to, Camille would have swapped years of safety for more time with her father, hearing his booming laugh or enjoying one of his tirades against the tobacconist who passed off cigarettes he claimed were actually tea leaves wrapped in lavatory paper, or French industrialists who'd do anything to line their pockets. Maman had been just as fierce in her condemnation of the latter group.

'They are detestable.' Maman's blue eyes had flashed with scorn. 'Some of us have long memories.'

Camille thought of Jean-Luc and shifted on the cushioned deck chair, feeling suddenly uncomfortable.

One night, while the three of them were admiring the scent of mimosa at the top of the small hilltop village, Laure excused herself to take a photograph of the moon over the valley. Jean-Luc took Camille's hand. 'Do you mind?' he asked.

She gave a slight shake of her head, barely able to look at him. After a moment, he'd raised her hand to his lips, before squeezing it. Then he let go of the hand. Hardly a declaration of great passion. Did she really mind that his overtures seemed merely those of a friend, someone trying to express sympathy? She found she was a little piqued. Nobody wanted to be just an object of sympathy after all.

'He really likes you,' Laure insisted later on.

'He's just being kind.'

'I've seen Jean-Luc being kind. This isn't it.'

Camille felt a little rush of joy.

'Tomorrow morning it'll be flowers or chocolate, perhaps even a book.' Laure was almost clucking like a mother hen.

Sure enough, a bunch of roses and a Raymond Chandler novel, in English, smelling crisp and new, arrived with Jean-Luc. 'I know your English is perfect, Camille,' he said, smiling. 'I thought you might like to read something distracting.'

'I do!' She hadn't even realised that was just what she wanted, to lose herself in an American detective novel, forget about the Nazis being in Paris, Papa dying, the increased food shortages back in Lyon, all of it.

'He's serious about you,' Laure told her later, when they were alone again and trying out a nail polish Laure had found in a drawer.

'But—' She felt herself blush.

'But what? You don't think he's a catch? Jean-Luc? Half the girls in Lyon have been batting their eyes at him since he started at *lycée*.'

'Even if he's not fighting with the Free French?'

Laure grimaced. 'I'd prefer it if he was. But perhaps keeping his looms operating isn't entirely selfish.'

Camille looked at her inquiringly.

'He keeps his workers from being sent to labour camps in Germany.'

It was a fair point.

Laure rolled her eyes. 'Anyway, far more intriguing than boring old factories is what's to happen next between you two?'

'Probably nothing.' This was just a holiday, after all, time off from the harshness of real life.

'Camille, he's very, very smitten.'

'Not sure how you can tell that from a few very kind presents.'

'I've known the man since he was in short trousers, bossing me around like a little Napoleon.'

'He's too tall to be a Napoleon.'

Laure grinned. 'Yes, he is tall, isn't he? And not exactly plain, either.'

Camille's cheeks flushed.

'He'll ask you out for dinner. Probably that restaurant with the jasmine terrace and the view of the sea. You can still get decent food there, if you're Jean-Luc.' She looked at Camille's

nails and made a face. 'Yours look so much neater than mine.'
Camille held out her hand for the little bottle.

'Let me finish them for you.'

As predicted, the next evening Camille found herself seated
at a table with a canopy of scented flowers twined above them.
The menu wasn't extensive, but the fish was fresh and the wine
beautifully chilled.

After they'd eaten, they went for a walk before curfew,
Jean-Luc tucking her arm under his. 'When we reach that pine,
I'm going to kiss you,' he said. '*Ça va?*'

She laughed. 'It sounds very organised.'

'That's me, organised.' He tightened his grip on her arm.

'Why that tree in particular?'

'Would you prefer the bougainvillea on the other side? That
Italian private on the corner might be an interested observer.
The Italians love a bit of *amore*.'

'Let's stick to the pine.'

Her skin was tingling all over in anticipation of the kiss, the
amore. Delaying the moment made it seem more exciting. Too
exciting. She half wanted to break away, but something kept her
walking with him. As they reached the tree, he turned to her
with a murmur. His restraint was gone. His mouth was on hers,
fierce, insistent. She'd kissed boys before, once or twice, but he
wasn't a boy and none of them had ever made her shiver the
way Jean-Luc did.

There were other kisses under trees, on balconies and in
gardens over the next week. Laure found herself mysteriously
busy with an elderly great-aunt who lived nearby.

On the night before the girls were to return to the city,
when the two of them were alone, Jean-Luc pushed Camille
gently back onto the sofa and they went further than they had
before, stroking skin beneath clothing, finding places to kiss that
had been hidden before.

'I'm only stopping because something needs to be said first.'

He sat up, brushing down the front of his shirt, looking shaken. 'I'm not playing around, Camille. I'm serious. May I speak to your mother when you're back in Lyon?'

'No.' The word was instinctive and emphatic.

He looked surprised.

'Maman... She would think that strange.' Maman and Jean-Luc meeting couldn't happen. Maman was so vehement about the Germans, about French businessmen who were using the Occupation to their advantage.

'If your father had still been with us, I'd ask him for permission to court you.'

'Court me?'

'With a view to proposing.'

'Proposing? Marrying me?' Her mouth was hanging open. 'What?'

He took her hand. 'Of course.'

'I ... I didn't...' Despite all Laure had said, she hadn't thought of him being serious like this. It was so quick, so sudden. 'You don't know me.' She wasn't sure about this. And the insistence on needing to talk to a parent – did he think she was too immature to know her own mind? 'I come from a different kind of background to yours.' She didn't want to say too much about her family, had simply told him Papa had written books about history, left it like that, not even talking about Maman's work. Like some of her old schoolmates he might be shocked that her mother went into all kinds of apartments, caring for all kinds of women.

'I know enough. And the fact you're not the same kind of girl I've been playing tennis with, whose mothers go to the same spa as my mother does, well it makes you all the more alluring.'

'All the same, we haven't known one another long.'

'Things move quickly nowadays.' A pause. A note of uncertainty in his voice. 'You do want to be with me, don't you, Camille?'

To her own surprise she found that she wanted it very much. She buttoned up her blouse. 'You don't need to ask anyone's permission.' She put a hand out to his hair, pushing a chestnut lock back off his brow. 'My parents brought me up to know my own mind, to make my own decisions.'

She was only nineteen. Camille tried to recollect the law about marriage. Did she still need parental permission if she was under twenty-one?

'When my brothers-in-law proposed to my sisters, they talked to my father first.' He was looking at her, still puzzled. 'You're very independent.'

'As you say, it's wartime.'

'Your mother won't try to stop us?'

'No. She'll think it's happened too quickly, though.' It was easier to use this as the reason for any lack of enthusiasm than to give the real one. 'Anyway, will *your* mother approve? She doesn't know me.'

'She trusts me to make wise decisions. Not just for myself, but for the whole family.'

Camille had only known Jean-Luc for weeks, but it was clear that he saw himself as the family figurehead. He carried these responsibilities lightly, but he was obviously the adored only son in a very traditional family. Rather different from her own family.

'They're going to adore you.' He stroked her hair. 'You're perfect.'

'Am I?'

'You're beautiful and accomplished.'

'You're just saying that because we beat Laure and that friend of hers in doubles?' She had to make a joke of it, she felt so overwhelmed.

'That elegant but ruthless backhand of yours clinched it for me.' His eyes sparkled. 'Seriously, I've never met another girl like you. I just want to look after you.'

Maman and Papa had valued education above everything. Maman was still expecting that she'd continue with her studies after school. Camille had expected to continue, too. Until now. Papa was gone. The war grew uglier by the week.

'You'll be joining a clan, Camille. They'll all adore you.'

She'd never had brothers or sisters. Her cousins were vague memories. They'd moved from Germany after her birth and then she'd lived in France and America and briefly in Britain, too, before they'd come back to France. So many of her friends in Lyon had been scattered in the last few years. Even Laure was talking about taking up a position as companion to the elderly great-aunt down here. The thought of kinship was like a warm blanket to Camille.

'So, will you agree to an engagement?' His smile was half-confident, half-uncertain. The uncertain part made him look younger. 'A quiet and extended one, if that makes it easier? I just want to look after you, give you some fun.'

The way he was looking at her made her feel safe in a way she hadn't for some years now. Maman and Papa would have laid down their lives for her, but Jean-Luc was offering something different: a secure position within French society.

Her answer was to press her body against his and push his lips open with hers.

On the train home, she sat feeling stunned, almost relieved to be away from the dazzling Mediterranean light, the scents, the presence of Jean-Luc, which seemed to flood her body with sensation, knocking out her ability to reason. Her stomach churned at the thought of the conversation with her mother to come.

She couldn't tell her she was marrying a man from the kind of family Maman despised. She'd write to Jean-Luc, call it off. No, that was cowardly. She'd ask him to meet her somewhere neutral. She was rushing into a commitment she'd never have made in other circumstances. The cells inside her body seemed to scream at her. Memories of how she'd felt when Jean-Luc was caressing her flooded her. She'd been alive again, full of longing.

She couldn't give up Jean-Luc. He was more than just a safe harbour in a storm. Surely the body knew its own truth?

Camille set her chin, preparing for battle with Maman.

'We'd wait until next summer for the actual wedding.' Camille said it as though that would reconcile Maman to the marriage.

Maman was still silent, something that rarely happened. Their undrunk *tisanes* sat in cups in front of them. Maman had just come in from dressing an old man's ulcer. Before that she'd delivered a baby. Keeping busy helped her through her grief, apparently.

'I know it's all very quick.' Camille fiddled with the teacup handle.

'You've only known this man for a few weeks.'

'That's why we're not having an official engagement just yet. Jean-Luc thinks we should spend more time together before we announce it to everyone.'

Maman reached for her cigarette case. 'His family work closely with the Vichy regime.' After the invasion in 1940, the Germans had left the southern sector of France apart from the area bordering Italy and including the city of Lyon, to run its own affairs, technically unoccupied, but with a puppet government operating from the old spa town of Vichy. Basing itself in a genteel and picturesque setting didn't mean the new regime was a benign one, though. Vichy France might be technically unoccupied, but it danced to Berlin's tune.

'One of the sisters is married to a politician here, a sub-prefect,' Maman went on. 'He's quite the enthusiast.' She lit a cigarette but didn't put it to her mouth.

'Jean-Luc's not like that.' All the same, Camille hadn't known about the brother-in-law's tendencies. To be fair, they hadn't exactly talked much about the war. Those wonderful Mediterranean days had been spent in another world, in a bubble. 'He's not a Nazi supporter, Maman.'

'Maybe not.' Maman was trying to be fair. 'But you don't think this is a reaction to losing your father? We've suffered a sudden bereavement. It might make you more... susceptible.'

It was exactly what Camille had wondered herself on the train, but she couldn't let herself admit it now. 'He's not some adventurer taking advantage of me, Maman. He's a good, kind man.'

Maman stubbed out the cigarette. 'You had plans for your life. You wanted to carry on with your studies.' She sounded sad.

'They just don't seem as important now. Some married women go to university, it's not unheard of.'

'It's much harder once you're not a free agent. Do you think marriage to Jean-Luc will give you the freedom you need?'

'What does freedom actually mean these days?'

Maman couldn't argue with that point.

'I just want not to be thinking sad things all the time. When I'm with Jean-Luc, it feels... normal. As though there's something to look forward to again. Silly things, perhaps, meals out, trips, flowers.'

Maman's face softened. 'I only want you to be happy.'

'You'll give us your blessing? You know I can't marry if you refuse.'

Maman's sigh was so gentle she could hardly hear it.

'On condition you do as you promise and keep the engagement to yourselves for at least a few months.'

· · ·

Yet from that moment onwards Maman politely avoided opportunities to meet Jean-Luc, even when the engagement was officially announced at the end of October.

'I can't go to the party. Tell them I'm out of town or indisposed, *liefje*.'

'You're still disappointed in me.' Camille was just back from the *coiffeuse*, who'd done something wonderful with her hair. Maman expressed admiration while obviously longing to return to the midwifery journal from England she'd somehow managed to acquire. Camille felt a lump in her throat.

Her mother's answer was to put down the magazine, pull her into her arms and stroke her hair.

'Never.'

Someone banged on the door. The concierge. 'Madame? There's a lad downstairs says his sister's gone into labour.'

Maman released her and grabbed her brown leather bag. It was always the same, always had been. Maman's work as a nurse and midwife came first. How many times in the past had family life been interrupted? 'Sorry, but if that's who I think it is, it might be a complicated labour.'

'A Jewish refugee?' Maman didn't seem to have heard. So yes, probably yet another unfortunate who'd fled the occupied northern zone, possibly after already having left a home in Germany or Belgium.

'Don't wait up for me. We'll talk tomorrow.'

Things would settle down, Camille told herself. Maman would agree to meet Jean-Luc. She'd see how lovely he was. She might yet be persuaded to come to the engagement dinner they were planning.

Two days later, on the tenth of November, the Germans marched over the demarcation line and into the southern sector of France. Just as Papa had predicted, Vichy France's unoccupied status had only lasted a few years.

German black-and-red flags hung over Lyon's public buildings. Their boots tramped over the cobbles. Camille felt the same churning sickness she'd experienced in June 1940, when the Germans had occupied Paris. 'It doesn't change anything,' Jean-Luc told Camille. 'We'll announce the engagement as we planned, even if we have to postpone the dinner itself. We can have champagne with close friends and family.'

He might claim nothing had changed. But it had. The arrival of the Germans meant Maman's work became far more dangerous with the dispossessed and frightened refugees in the city at more risk of deportation. Camille found herself spending more time at Jean-Luc's house during the day, distracting herself with talk of wedding gowns and flowers with Véronique.

The gap between mother and daughter seemed to widen by the day.

THREE

SOPHIE, JULY 1943

The French gendarme looked sharply at the small boy sitting next to Sophie. They'd hoped there wouldn't be a spot check on identity papers. They'd been unlucky. When the train stopped at a small town ten or so kilometres outside Lyon, this policeman and his plain-clothes German over-seer had boarded, demanding to see the passengers' identity papers and travel permits. 'And that's his mother?' The gendarme nodded at the sleeping pregnant woman on the seat opposite.

The boy looked up at Sophie, frowning. He found it hard to stick to their cover story and was probably about to blurt out a correction.

Sophie nodded. 'At least Anton avoided serious injury in the attack. It left his mother, Madame Barnard there, in a dreadful state. In her condition, too. That's why she employed me.'

'You're a nurse?'

'And midwife. Looking after her until the birth.'

'A Resistance attack again?' His lips pursed.

Sophie gave what she hoped was a nonchalant shrug. 'I only know the two of them were on a train derailed by explosives.'

She looked nervously out of the window; that part wasn't put on. Her hands wanted to tremble.

The gendarme looked at Ida Barnard, brow creased. If he insisted on questioning her, Ida's thick Polish Yiddish accent would give her away. He was probably wondering if he should summon his German supervisor. Sophie felt her stomach turn. 'Madame Barnard's husband was killed in the attack. Such a tragedy. A decorated naval officer who'd suffered terrible injury earlier in the war.' She'd learned the cover story thoroughly.

The gendarme stood taller. 'An outrage.' He handed back their papers. 'Your patient is lucky to have a midwife to accompany her.'

Sophie managed a grateful smile. Anton was still looking mutinous. 'But she's not my *maman*,' he said.

The gendarme turned back. Sophie thought quickly. 'He thinks you're saying I'm his mother.' She smiled at the boy. 'Travelling by train again brings back bad memories. Because of what happened last time, you know.' She put a hand on Anton's shoulder, hoping to convey the need for silence. If the boy insisted that neither of the women were his real mother, everything would fall apart. They'd be dragged off the train for further questioning, Anton's false identity would be pulled apart. He and Ida would be revealed as unrelated Jews from Poland. She shuddered to think what would happen to him then. And to her. And there were other groups of Jewish children and their helpers on this train, who might be uncovered, too. Most of the other boys and girls lacked fluency in French, unlike Anton, who spoke without an accent because he'd been in the country since infancy. Interrogating them would unravel the whole operation.

She pulled herself together. 'It's all been so confusing for poor Anton. His mother hasn't been... the same since the bomb.' She tapped her temple.

'Shows you who the real enemies of French children are.

The Allies. And their treacherous Resistance spies.' A curious frown covered the man's brow. 'Is that the hint of a foreign accent? Where are you from originally, madame?'

She worried about the children's accents, but it was her own damn accent, faint but still there, that would give them away. 'Holland.' She willed herself to look relaxed. *The risks are greater for you, you're not a French citizen, you have less protection*, she'd been warned when she agreed to take Jewish children to the Swiss border from where they'd be smuggled over into safety.

He looked her up and down. Sweat beaded Sophie's brow. Was he about to ask what had brought a Dutchwoman to France? Unlike Ida and Anton, she was travelling under her own name with genuine identity papers and proof of her profession. If this policeman knew what she'd been doing in Lyon, helping illegal Jewish refugees, he would pull her off the train for interrogation. She forced herself to sit up straight. With a final nod, he walked on.

'Why did you tell that policeman a lie?' the little boy asked again. 'Madame Barnard's not my mother. I haven't seen my *maman* for ages.' Sophie's neck beaded with perspiration as she looked around, but nobody seemed to have heard him.

She bent down to him. 'Remember how we told you we were going to be actors?'

He nodded.

'We just have to pretend for a bit longer. As if we're in a play. Now, let me tell you about the picnics we're going to have when we reach Annemasse.' Hunger fought puzzlement in his face. 'You know they have raspberries? And I heard there are sometimes peaches, too.'

She dared not look down the carriage to see if the rest of the party were being similarly interrogated, their identities questioned, weaknesses in their stories exposed. It only took one child to utter one artless comment and it would all come crum-

bling down. Anton was their weakest link. Trauma or separation from his parents, who'd both been arrested, meant he
struggled to remember even simple instructions. You had to
remind him again and again what to do, what to say. He'd only
be safe out of France.

'Can I have another story?' Anton asked.

Sophie reached inside her midwife's bag for his book. Ida
opened her eyes. Sophie shook her head at her. 'Another minute
for them to move on,' she said quietly, just in case the gendarme
turned round and saw Ida awake and decided to commiserate
with her on the terrible loss she'd suffered.

She'd been warned that involving herself in this trip would
be dangerous, Sophie reminded herself. She didn't have to be
here, on this train, helping smuggle Jewish children out of
France into Switzerland. She'd chosen to do it.

The risks had been made clear when Pastor Lefroy had come to
her apartment in Lyon a week earlier.

'I hate to ask you after all you've been doing for us, Madame
Hansen.' He'd pushed his spectacles up his nose and smiled at
her sorrowfully. 'But the convent isn't safe for the children any
more. There's a pregnant woman we'd very much like to get to
safety, too.'

'It does me good to help.' A year on, Bernhardt's death still
made this apartment feel so empty. Camille was often out these
days, planning for her wedding.

'The risk is greater for you than for a French citizen. We
still have a little more legal protection from the Nazis.'

As a foreign national, an alien, Sophie could be deported.
Back to the Netherlands, if she was very lucky. If not, to some
camp where harsh punishment would be doled out for helping
Jewish fugitives.

Sophie had met the pastor a few times now on his trips to

Lyon and identified families in the city she knew might be brave enough to take in Jewish children temporarily. On one occasion, weeks ago, she'd delivered a baby in an apartment lacking running water or heat, where she knew the mother's name, but where the woman, following the safe delivery, took her hand, looking into her eyes with almost unbearable intensity, the gratitude clear to see. She'd left mother and baby with the unnamed middle-aged woman who would take them on to their next hiding place when the mother was fit to travel.

Now the Germans were increasing their effort to arrest and deport non-French Jews, the stakes were higher. Some said they were transported east to certain death. Others said it was just hard labour. Hard labour for infants? It didn't make sense.

'How dangerous is it really, pastor?'

The route over the Swiss border at Annemasse was an established one, he told her. Their group had researched the plan thoroughly before taking the first group of children out. They used a playing field adjoining the border fence, slipping them through the wire a few at a time at the end of the day.

'There are more Gestapo at the Swiss border, even though it's in the Italian occupation zone and they aren't supposed to interfere. And our own French police are helping the Germans, too.'

'I'll do it.'

The expression on his face mixed relief and anxiety. 'You have a daughter, though?'

'Camille's fiancé is popular with the occupiers.' She could hear the tone of her own words. Another, more pressing thought struck her. She'd miss Camille's wedding if she went to the Swiss border with the children.

After a pause he nodded. 'Go up to the convent to meet Hélène, the young woman organising the... expedition to the Swiss border.' He rose. 'I'll tell them to expect you tomorrow evening.' He put on his hat. 'And Madame Hansen, Sophie, if

Lyon becomes too dangerous for you, there's refuge for you in my village up in the Cévennes. We always need midwives and nurses there.'

But it would surely only be a few weeks before she'd be back in this apartment, admiring Camille's wedding photographs and seeing her daughter wearing the gold pendant she'd bought her as a present for her marriage.

Sitting on the train now, Sophie tried to put thoughts of Camille out of her mind. This was no time for daydreaming. She should concentrate on her role – a nurse taking a pregnant woman and her small son to a holiday camp on the Swiss border for fresh air and relaxation after a terrible experience.

Further down the carriage she could just make out Hélène, who could only be Camille's age. She sat with a boy and a girl, both travelling under false names. The gendarme and the German had checked their identity papers with little interest. It would have been reassuring to exchange a smile with Hélène, but the girl had been clear when she'd briefed Sophie up at the convent near Lyon's basilica. 'Nothing must connect us to one another. It's unfortunate we all have to travel on the same trains, but it's not safe for us to stay here with the nuns any longer and we've run out of time to organise another group out of Lyon. We'll split into small groups, sitting as far away from one another as possible.'

This route to Annemasse had been chosen because it used a series of slower, local trains supposedly less likely to be subjected to identity checks. So much for that.

'People have been talking about the children the nuns have taken in,' Hélène had added. 'The man who repairs their boiler was asking questions. We're worried the police or Gestapo will come sniffing around the convent.'

Sophie'd only met Hélène on that one occasion before

today, but the girl's composure and organisational ability had impressed her deeply.

She looked at her watch. They were due to change train at the next stop, Bourg-en-Bresse. Transfers were the danger spots. The children would be tempted to wave at one another. Sophie closed the book. 'Do you remember what happens when we change trains?' she asked quietly. 'We go to the lavatories first, before any of the others. We do not look at the other children. We don't call out to them or wave at them.'

'Don't look at the children,' Anton whispered. 'Don't wave at them.'

The train was slowing. 'Time to wake up.' Sophie touched Ida Bernard's knee. Ida opened her eyes, which never seemed to lose their anxious expression. 'Pull your hat brim down, Ida,' Sophie whispered.

Further down the carriage the two children with Hélène were replacing their books in their satchels. Were the boy and girl too quiet, too well-behaved, Sophie worried? Would that draw suspicion? The French expected decorum from all ages in public but children of seven and eight would naturally be expected to chatter and laugh occasionally.

Making this trip to the Swiss border was opening up another world of danger. She could have been safe back in the comfortable apartment, surrounded by the books she and Bernhardt had brought with them when they'd left Paris.

Anton slipped his hand into hers as they stood up. He smiled at her and she knew the risk was worth everything.

FOUR

CAMILLE

Only five days until Camille's wedding. The last fitting for the dress was this morning. 'Your mother isn't with you?' The dressmaker frowned.

'She can't be here today.'

The dressmaker gave the sympathetic half shrug that so many people used nowadays to express feelings about the war, the Occupation, the difficulty of travelling anywhere. Camille had spent the last few nights at Jean-Luc's house so she and Véronique could confer on wedding plans. She'd rung the apartment at Les Brotteaux to remind Maman about the fitting, in case she changed her mind about coming, but Maman had been out. Babies came when babies came, so that wasn't unexpected. Camille just hoped it was a woman in labour that was keeping her mother away rather than something more dangerous.

The dressmaker ran an appreciative hand down the satin length of Camille's gown. 'So generous of your bridegroom's mother to give you this to use.'

Véronique's wedding dress had been cut from exquisite satin and lace in the lower-waisted fashion of her youth, but now taken apart and re-designed to suit a wartime wedding. It would sit just above Camille's ankles as there wasn't enough fabric to lower the hem to her toes, but the dressmaker had fitted it tightly around her waist and bust in keeping with contemporary fashion. She shook her head with admiration. 'Almost a shame to unpick this gown, it was a masterpiece of couture. You won't find cloth this quality these days. Shame your husband's looms don't produce silk for clothes.'

It *had* been generous of Véronique. She could surprise Camille like that: be so judgemental, so sharp, but then sacrificing her own wedding dress.

The dressmaker knelt on the floor, checking the hem was even. 'You have the perfect figure, Mademoiselle Hansen. Your groom is a fortunate man.'

In the mirror, Camille saw the satin ripple like early morning mist. It would have meant more had it been Maman's wedding dress that was being adapted into Camille's. Maman had laughed when Camille had asked her if she knew where her dress was. 'I can't remember seeing it since we left Berlin in 1933.'

A book about obstetrics or childhood disease – that would have been guarded with Maman's life, lugged from city to city, country to country.

Véronique's wedding dress had been stored in tissue paper, protected by moth balls. When unwrapped, the fabric looked as fresh and uncreased as it would have done on her wedding day.

Camille had begged the dressmaker to let her take the sketches she'd made of the new design to show Maman. But when Camille had unlocked the apartment door a few days previously, she'd realised Maman was still out. The rooms had smelled unaired, as if nobody had been home for a while.

There was a note on the small kitchen table.

Brief trip away for a week, perhaps longer. I'm sorry, chérie, *I won't make the dress fitting or wedding. When I'm back in Lyon*

*I look forward to seeing the photographs and hearing all about
your special day and, of course, about your new husband. This
present comes with all my love. Maman xx*

A velvet jeweller's box, wrapped in a white satin ribbon, sat
on the table. Camille had opened it. A pendant not much bigger
than the tip of her thumb, gold, with tiny diamonds, *Camille,
with love always, Maman*, inscribed on the back.

Her own mother wasn't coming to her wedding. Camille
had stood staring at the locket until her eyes were too blurred
with tears to see it properly.

The dressmaker was asking her something. Camille blinked
herself back into the present. 'Sorry, yes, I'll be using my
mother-in-law's veil. It's ivory, too, and quite long. And I'll be
wearing a gold pendant that comes down to here.' She placed a
hand on her breastbone. Something of her parents would be
with her on her wedding day.

FIVE

SOPHIE

The stress of the train journey and the task of settling the children into the holiday camp at Annemasse meant Camille's fast-approaching marriage often slipped Sophie's mind. Camille would be going to her final dress fitting, packing up her possessions for her new home, dealing with her wedding nerves. All without either of her parents to support her. *Other people's children matter more than me.* Words of Camille's thrown at her years ago when she'd failed to turn up for an important tennis match, echoed in Sophie's mind.

'It's not bad, is it?' Hélène said, the first morning, when they went outside with the children after breakfast. The girl seemed to have recovered from the strain of the train journey here. 'I thought I'd be sick when I saw that gendarme and the German get on the train,' she admitted. 'I heard what Anton said. You handled him well, Sophie.'

'My heart was pounding. It's a relief just to be here.' The holiday camp had been built before the war for city children to outdoor breaks in the sunshine. Its playing field stretched right up to the border fence with Switzerland. Now, at the end of every afternoon, the Jewish children played with a group of

local children from the town, throwing a ball in the direction of
the border fence and sending one another in turn to retrieve it.
At dusk, when the time came to slip under the wire, the guards
on each side would hopefully believe nothing out of the ordinary was happening – the children were just playing their usual
ball game. Just enough time would pass between patrols for
them and Ida to slip under the fence.

Sophie felt herself forget why they were here as she ran
after balls and acted as referee. Once or twice, a couple of
Italian soldiers strolled by, nodding a greeting.

Spending so much time outdoors meant she slept well for
the first time since Bernhardt had died.

'Sometimes I think we should just stay here with the children,' Hélène said. 'But look.' She gave a backward nod of her
head towards the road behind them, where a black car cruised
slowly along. 'Germans. Again. Just watching. Worrying that
too many Jews escaping into Switzerland makes them look
inept.'

Sophie pulled her cardigan sleeves down even though there
was no cloud passing over the sun. The car wasn't stopping, it
accelerated again. She held her breath until it had gone.

'Isn't there anywhere else in southern France to hide the
children?'

Hélène shook her head. 'There's a village in the Cévennes
that we sometimes use.'

The pastor's home village, Sophie thought.

'But these children are on a register of Jewish aliens. The
local police and the Germans know they missed their deportation dates from Lyon. They're actively hunting them.' Hélène
looked much older than her years as she spoke. 'They can't stay
in France.'

The days were long this time of year. Summer wasn't as safe
as autumn for border crossings. Sophie and Hélène served a
picnic of bread, cheese and sausage each evening to make it look

normal for them to stay out on the field as the shadows lengthened.

As dusk fell and the local children went home, the guards patrolling the fence regarded those remaining on the field with near boredom: just another group of city kids and their teachers and assistants taking in every last minute of healthy fresh air. Nobody seemed to be counting how many children left the field at the end of each day, but if they had, the first two nights would have shown that everyone returned to the hostel in the evening.

Discreetly, while they organised games, acted as referees and wiped noses, Sophie and Hélène kept a close eye on the guards on both sides of the border. They observed the pattern of their patrols, the time it took each to cover the perimeter, the short window when both patrols were away from the section bordering the playing field. On the fourth day, Hélène made a decision. 'We'll go tonight. There's no moon. There's not as much time to cut the wire between patrols as I hoped for, so we'll have to move quickly.'

The smaller children could have squeezed under the fence. But Ida would need the wire lifted and cut. 'I've timed it. It's very tight. But we should get everyone safely into no-man's land at least.'

Once they were there, if caught by the Swiss guards, the children were told to weep and say nothing at all. With luck, this would mean they'd eventually be sent on to Geneva, to be safely retrieved by the charity workers there. If, as hoped, they managed to penetrate further into Swiss territory, a young Swiss man would be waiting to take them directly on to Geneva.

At lunchtime they told Ida the crossing was on. She closed her eyes briefly, before quietly thanking them in her accented French. Hélène and Sophie told the older children what was going to happen. They could be trusted to say nothing to their local playmates. The rucksack Hélène took out with her contained warm clothes. Even in July, the air could grow chilly at dusk so close to the mountains. Sophie brought her midwife's bag onto the field, as she had each day. Wherever you had a group of children playing outside, you had bruises, scrapes and blisters. Hélène had smiled the first morning. 'You're never without that bag?'

'My husband had this long strap made for it so I can wear it like a satchel if I need my hands to be free.' She put it down by the bench they used as their base.

Her bag was part of her.

They started the ballgame at the usual time in the afternoon, at first sending the children to retrieve the ball and return and then, at a nod from Hélène, running in pairs along the fence towards a clump of trees where they were to wait until everyone was assembled. Sophie went over and over the plan with Anton until she was sure he understood. 'Don't go off until Lia takes your hand.' He nodded.

Hélène said something to the local children. They left the field in dribs and drabs, looking casual.

'They've been well briefed,' Sophie said, watching them with the two other women.

Hélène raised a hand in farewell. 'Their parents are all friends of our cause.'

Ida put a hand to her mouth, muttering under her breath. 'What is it?' Sophie asked.

'Nausea. My stomach hurts. And I feel a little faint.'

'Perhaps it's nerves.' Hélène looked worried. 'You can rest once you're over the border. It won't be long now.'

'Let me examine her quickly,' Sophie whispered. Nausea could mean the start of labour.

'There's not time.'

'If she's going into labour, you won't want it happening in no-man's land.' She led Ida back to a bench. 'Take off your jacket,' she told Hélène. 'Hold it open to screen her.' If Ida was having contractions she'd have to take her back to the hostel and look after her there, which would mean Hélène going on alone with all the children. No time to open the midwife's bag to retrieve the blood pressure monitor.

'We really need to go.' Hélène, normally so calm, was looking around, anxious.

Sophie felt Ida's abdomen. No sign of a contraction just at this particular moment, but really she'd need longer to know for sure whether Ida was going into premature labour. 'Any pains?'

Ida shook her head.

'Probably the liver pâté at lunchtime,' Sophie said. 'We're not used to rich food like that. Sit up now.' She took Ida's pulse, looking at her watch. A little raised, but given the circumstances, that was normal.

Hélène was looking at her own watch, too. The window had shrunk. 'We haven't got enough time to get them all through the fence before the patrols come round again.' She frowned. 'And we can't stay here, doing nothing as it gets dark. It's too obvious that we're waiting for them to move on. We should abort.'

Ida, having drunk some more water from Sophie's bottle, said she was feeling better and could continue. The children showed little sign of weariness as they waited obediently by the trees. Even Anton knew not to talk, not to complain.

The conjunction of a moonless night with fair weather might take months to recur. Sophie looked at her watch again. They'd lost about seven minutes. Each of them mattered. 'We can still get through before the French patrol is back. The small ones can squeeze through the bottom of the fence and make a dash for it.'

'It's the patrol on the Swiss side that's worrying me.' Hélène was squinting in that direction. 'If they reappear just half a minute ahead of time, we're in trouble.'

'The children know what to do if the Swiss soldiers catch them.'

Hélène glanced at Ida. Crying and not talking wouldn't

work for her. But she nodded. '*Bon.*' Sophie helped the woman stand up. They walked over to the children.

'In a few minutes you'll be the safe side of that fence.' Sophie heard the confidence in her voice.

They crept forward towards the wire fence. 'Little ones, get ready to wriggle under like worms,' Hélène said in a low voice. 'Remember, keep going until you meet the kind man in the black hat with the feather in it. Madame Ida will follow you, but don't wait for her.' She smiled at the pregnant woman, the smile not quite reaching her eyes, which still scanned the fence.

Sophie and Hélène tugged at the bottom wire, lifting it up so that the first four children could squeeze underneath.

Anton was one of them. He glanced back at Sophie. She smiled at him. 'Look out for the cuckoo clocks.'

He made a cuckoo sound. She put a finger to her lips. Hélène took her cutters and tackled the lower strands so the woman and the older children could pass through, swearing under her breath. 'It's all taking too long.'

'The little ones will be scared by themselves.'

Hélène turned back to the wire, working away with the cutters.

Sophie heard something. Boots. A group approaching along the French side of the fence. Hélène looked over her shoulder and pulled the cut strands of wire back. 'Come on.' The older children were through now. Sophie passed the baby to her brother. He darted forward, holding her tightly. 'Quickly,' Hélène whispered. All the children were away, vanishing into the evening mist.

They helped Ida lower herself under the fence so she could push herself through the gap on her back and shoulders. She stood up, breathing heavily, thanking them in a low voice, and grabbing the bag they shoved after her.

The boots were coming closer now. Voices rang out.

Sophie was still watching Ida, willing her to move faster.

'Sophie.' Hélène was pulling at her jacket sleeve, finger to lip. Something moved on the Swiss side. A guard? A deer? If they shouted a warning at Ida, they'd alert the approaching French guards to their presence here at the cut fence. They'd summon the Gestapo. Sophie felt cold. All their careful planning was going to be for nothing.

'Let's split up,' she whispered. 'I'll pull the Swiss patrol away from here. Can you do the same with the French one?'

Hélène nodded briefly. 'Wait for me at the cemetery, I'll head there via the hostel – I need to check we haven't left anything incriminating there.' The cemetery on the outskirts of town was the rendezvous they'd agreed on in an emergency. Sophie picked up her bag, slinging it around her chest, grabbed the wire cutters from Hélène and shot off along the fence. If she could distract the Swiss patrol away from the children as they entered no-man's land, they could still make it.

Sophie was already metres away when she heard the roar of a motorcycle engine. She'd heard bike engines that rumbled like that, in Lyon, ridden by German enforcers, often the SS. Was Hélène well clear now? 'We've lost the kids,' a male voice said, in German. 'Forget about them. Let's flush out the two bitches we saw on this side.'

Sophie tasted bile in her mouth. No time to panic, she was closer to the hostel than they were. With luck she might reach it in time to warn Hélène. She turned to run.

'Cuckoo.' The child's voice came from the other side of the fence.

'Anton?' He appeared from the trees, smiling.

'*Cheri,* you need to run after the others now, quickly.'

'I tripped on my lace.' She noticed the dirt on his knees. 'Lia and the others didn't notice I'd fallen over. I can't see them now.'

'Ida's through now.' She pointed in the direction Ida would be running. 'See if you can catch her up.'

If Sophie sprinted, she could still warn Hélène, but that would mean leaving Anton by himself. 'Run, Anton. Back the way you came.' She pointed towards the trees. Anton blinked, trotting along the fence, towards the cut wire. 'Not that way, *chéri*. Into the trees.'

He stopped and turned, face bewildered. He was only four. How could he be expected to understand what he was supposed to be doing? Raised men's voices told her that now the French gendarmes had arrived at the cut wire.

If they spotted Anton, they might bully him into squeezing back under the wire into French territory. 'Come here.' She pushed her fingers through the wire. He ran back to her and reached out his hand to touch them. 'We'll stay here for a moment. Very quietly.'

She probably still had time to intercept Hélène before the motorcycle reached the hostel. But if she left Anton alone here, there was no way he'd make his way alone through the trees to safety.

A twig crackled. Ida appeared in the trees. 'Anton?' She held out her hand. 'Come on.'

'Go with madame,' Sophie hissed at him. 'She'll look after you. Go and find those cuckoo clocks.'

He seemed to have lost his fear, turning and running to Ida. '*Bon courage,*' Ida whispered as she pulled him into the trees, further into no-man's land and into Switzerland.

Sophie ran away from the fence, skirting the side of the field where trees gave some cover.

The motorcycle had pulled up in front of the hostel, alongside a black Simca, often driven by the *gendarmerie*: the one Hélène had pointed out to her before. She crouched down so that she was below eye level. *Go straight to the cemetery.* The instruction flashed through her mind. Two gendarmes and an SS officer stormed through the front door of the hostel.

It would be empty now. The women who'd cooked for the

children would have returned home. Hélène wouldn't have left anything incriminating – lists, names, addresses – in the hostel. Sophie had only known her for a short period, but she already knew how meticulous she was.

If Hélène was still in the hostel, where would she hide? Sophie thought of her curled up under a bunk, squeezed into a cupboard. But they'd find her. They always did. Perhaps Hélène had already fled. There was still a chance.

The hostel door flung open; the gendarmes held Hélène between them. Her head was up; she didn't look frightened. Her eyes scanned the field, perhaps checking that nobody else had been caught. The German followed, shouting something at Hélène, who shook her head. He asked again. Sophie saw her lips form 'Just me. Nobody else.'

The German shouted at Hélène, pushing her hard. 'You can't have done all this by yourself. Who helped you?'

Even with the gendarmes holding her, Hélène stumbled, nearly falling. They pulled her up and this time the German hit her hard around the face. But she said nothing.

The rules the pastor set the group were always clear: if anyone was captured, the others were to escape. No rescue attempt.

Hélène was eighteen. She wanted to study veterinary medicine.

Examining Ida, who'd only been suffering nerves or the after-effects of a rich meal, had cost precious minutes, the difference between safety and capture. Sophie should have agreed that they abort this evening's crossing. She'd been too much the midwife.

SIX

CAMILLE

Camille didn't see her mother again until a week after the wedding. They met in a café tucked away in a side street near the garage, a place where they were not known and where clean tables and unchipped coffee cups were distant memories. Maman had sent an anonymous note to Camille's new marital home in La Croix-Rousse. Half-eleven – it meant cancelling a game of tennis with the wife of one of Jean-Luc's business contacts.

Maman had grey circles under her eyes, her usually bright skin looked sallow. When Camille greeted her as Maman, she shook her head. 'Best not to look as though we're close.' Was she using a false identity now?

After kissing her briefly on the cheeks and holding her close, Maman seemed to move into a detached mode. 'It's going to be safer for me to stay hidden away for a bit.' Maman stirred the brown liquid in her coffee cup, seeming to give all her attention to the task. The teaspoon trembled in her hand. If she'd taken off her kid gloves, it might have been easier for her. What was she doing wearing gloves in summer anyway? It was most unlike Maman to worry about developing sunspots. 'You can always get a message to me, if you're careful. Leave it in the paint pot in the garage.'

'You're not going to tell me anything, are you?' Camille sighed. 'Jean-Luc's not a monster, you know.'

'For everyone's sake, it's better this way.'

'You've never even met him.'

'I will do, one day.'

'I missed you at my wedding.' She knew she was being unreasonable, childish, but tears pricked at Camille's eyes. All her life she'd been planning her wedding and she'd never imagined it without her parents being there. Papa was dead. And Maman had stayed away because of this 'trip'. She hadn't even asked how the day had gone, how married life was going for Camille. Other people had mattered more than her only child, and now Maman's freedom, possibly her life, were at stake.

'Probably best for everyone that I wasn't there.' Maman's eyes softened. 'Do you have pictures?'

Camille pulled them out of her bag. Maman looked at the photographs and blinked hard. 'You're as beautiful as I knew you would be. Radiant.' Maman put a hand to her throat. 'That dress was perfect. Your father would have been so proud of you.' When she looked up, her eyes were welling.

'I felt Papa was there in spirit.' Camille gulped. 'That photo is for you.' She struggled to regain her composure. Maman looked down again. 'And what about Jean-Luc? You can see how kind he is, it's in his eyes.'

'He certainly seems to adore you.'

'He does.' She said it vehemently. 'So what now? I just don't see you anymore, Maman? You just leave?'

Maman leant forward, looking almost fierce. 'I will always come to you if you need me, *liefje*. But I can't stay in this city for now.' She lifted her eyes to Camille and the burning emotion in them made Camille blink.

'Where did you go? I worried myself to death when I found your note.'

'The Swiss border.' Maman said it so quietly Camille barely heard the words.

Sinking back into the uncomfortable chair, Camille stared at her mother. 'Oh God. Were you...?'

'Best not say more.'

'Smuggling Jewish children over?' Camille whispered. Maman looked at her blankly, as though she didn't comprehend. 'You'll get yourself—' She couldn't finish the sentence, couldn't even let herself think about what would happen if Maman were caught.

'One day we'll look back at these times and all will be well.' Maman's voice was steady.

'I wish it wasn't like this.' The words burst out of Camille's mouth. 'I know you don't approve of Jean-Luc, but I... I just...'

Her mother's hand covered hers. 'We never have to apologise for who we love. One day perhaps it won't matter.'

'He doesn't like the Nazis.' She blushed, knowing that wasn't saying much.

'They aren't the only ones we should dislike.'

Maman had never openly called Jean-Luc a collaborator. It was probably what she was thinking. And by association, Camille would be a collaborator, too.

There was no point in debating it. *Besides*, a painful little voice inside Camille said, *Jean-Luc is doing rather well from the Occupation, isn't he? And you do like having a few more comforts than you would otherwise enjoy?*

Camille shuffled on her chair. 'I could go over to Les Brotteaux, take some of your things to Jean—to our house, so they're safe?'

'No.' Maman's eyes flashed a warning. 'Stay away from Les Brotteaux. My things will just have to stay where they are, for now.' She glanced around the café. 'I don't want to remind people you're anything to do with me. You're Jean-Luc's wife now.'

Camille was being pushed away again. Because she was untrustworthy now? But she looked at her mother and saw only concern for her on Maman's face.

'I've already dropped my suitcase at the left luggage at the station, I'm going straight there. By this evening I should be somewhere safe.'

'But—'

'It won't be for long, things will change.'

'I suppose you can't even tell me where you're going?'

'Up into the hills. One day soon, you can come and see for yourself. We'll make a holiday of it.'

Always so hopeful, Maman. Nothing that had happened to them in the last few years seemed to dent her certainty that everything would work out. Papa had died so suddenly. One day, joking that he was malingering, the next, collapsed and writhing on the pavement outside their apartment, dying hours later from the perforated appendix. How Camille missed that roaring laugh of his. If he'd lived, would Papa have joined Maman in this dangerous work of hers?

Camille looked over her shoulder, too, making sure they couldn't be overheard. Her voice was so low Maman had to move so their heads were almost touching. 'Did the children get over—'

Her mother's warning shake of the head stopped her asking more. 'As far as we know, but...' She suddenly looked every year of her age. 'Someone was picked up on our side. A girl about your age.'

Camille leant back in her chair. 'Sometimes I feel so inadequate.' The words came bursting out.

'You've helped, too, Camille.' The words were spoken gently, as though her mother could read her guilty conscience.

'I didn't do anything.'

'You took the provisions to the safe place.'

A few months back, Maman had asked her to bring a basket of food and clothes to a garage in some distant suburb. She hadn't told her anything more: who needed the things, where they were hiding, nothing. Camille hadn't asked. Nor had she offered to help anyone in trouble since then, even though she'd seen people picked up off the streets, the look on their faces haunting her. She'd always been too scared to say a word in protest.

The conversation was making her feel so uncomfortable. It was the last time she'd see her mother for an indefinite period. They needed to end on a happy note.

'I love the locket you gave me.' She pointed at her neck.

Maman really did smile properly now. 'It looks beautiful on you, *liefje.* I should have said something when I first saw you.'

Papa would have noticed she was wearing the pendant and commented.

'I wore it on my wedding day, even though Véronique wanted me in pearls.'

Maman nodded, looking down again at the photograph Camille had given her. 'It looked just right with the wedding dress. Thank you for this.' She put the photograph into her handbag and looked at her wristwatch.

'I hope you don't mind me asking, but wasn't the pendant terribly expensive, Maman? You're not going without yourself?'

Maman smiled. 'Your father had a couple of old signet rings he never wore but kept because they'd been his father's. I found someone to melt them down and make the pendant. The little diamonds came in part-exchange for some of the gold.'

'So I'm wearing something that was Papa's?' Camille touched the locket.

'I thought it was a way of keeping him with you.' Maman looked at her watch again. 'If I miss the train, I mightn't squeeze onto the next one.'

'When will I see you again?' Camille felt tears threatening her.

'When I know I'm not bringing danger with me.'

'The girl who...?'

'Hélène?'

'You were fond of her?'

'I only knew her a little. But she was admirable, yes.' Maman put a hand to her mouth. 'I saw her face,' she whispered. 'As they dragged her away.' She stopped, pulling shoulders straight. 'You don't need to know all this. Go and enjoy newly married life, *liefje*.'

She kissed Camille again, quickly, and was walking away before there was even time to say goodbye.

This girl Hélène had probably given up her freedom, possibly her life. And all the time Camille had been fussing about the lace detail on her wedding gown bodice.

As she stood up and left the café, Camille reflected that her mother must regard her as frivolous. Shameful, perhaps.

Perhaps it was true. She'd always enjoyed the good things in life: pleasant surroundings, interesting places. And Jean-Luc offered her all this and so much more. She'd only been married for weeks but could already tell it was the best thing she'd ever done.

SEVEN

SOPHIE, 1992

'There's this old television show,' Milly tells me, solemnly. 'It's called *This is Your Life*.'

I act as though I've never heard of the show. 'I wanted to do it for you, Grandma. Friends who've known you since you were young come and tell the audience all about you when you were young, too. And when my dad was a baby.'

I freeze, then force myself to reply calmly. 'They'd have to be very, very old people, *liefje,* to have known me in my youth.'

'Hmm.' She looks disapproving. 'That's a shame. And Daddy said you don't have many old photos of when you were married and when he was a baby.' She makes it sound like a moral failing.

'I've given him what I could put my hands on. And I've told you my stories about skating on the frozen rivers when I was your age. And the Christmas markets. And what it was like when Daddy and I came to Georgia when he was little.'

'You had a peach tree in the yard. You and Daddy used to go swimming in a lake. It's just the middle bit that's missing, when you were in France.' A sigh. 'I'll just have to do the best I can, Grandma.'

'I can't wait to see it.'

My own account of what I did in those middle years of my life is now almost complete, written out in longhand. I have a word processor, but writing it down in ink seemed to connect me with my deepest secrets in a way the plastic keyboard couldn't. A lot of what I've written wouldn't be words I'd want a six-year-old to read at a party.

Family history's becoming a growing obsession with Americans. I can never be reassured that the itch to track down documents won't afflict Paul, too. I blame the TV for encouraging people to go nosing around in archives. That programme, *Roots*, about the descendant of slaves tracking down his ancestors, caught everyone's imagination.

'I made this for you.' She opens her backpack and pulls out a large white envelope, which I open. The card's front is made up of painted flags. German, Dutch and French as well as the Stars and Stripes. 'All the countries you lived in.'

She's done a beautiful job, detailed beyond her years. I can imagine Melissa, head down, biting her lip, concentrating hard on colouring in the flags without crossing lines. The image reminds me of another young girl, decades earlier. I blink. The air in the apartment is too dry this afternoon. 'I don't think I've ever had a card like this before.'

'Do you like it?'

'It's my favourite card ever.' I open it up and read her greeting: *To Grandma with lots of love on your 90th birthday from MELISSA...* Her handwriting is meticulously formed, too. I think my heart might break. I shouldn't be reading this. 'Do you think you can stand it on the table for me, darling? Right in the middle because it's the most important card.' Milly beams at me and does as I ask. It gives me a moment to recover.

'Dad says we have to wait until this evening to give you your present.' She looks at me, head tilted.

'I can wait. I have a present for you, too,' I tell her. 'You'll have to wait as well.'

Her eyes light up. And now I'm worried because the present isn't anything she can probably use for some years. But by the time she's old enough, I'll be gone, and I want to see her wear it.

Her father finishes doing whatever he's up to, chilling champagne in my small kitchen, polishing glasses. 'Come on, munchkin, time for us to go home. And your grandma has a hair appointment.' He twinkles at me and I think I spot my husband in him. It's hard to tell whether you're seeing what you want to see in someone, though.

When they're gone, I go to my jewellery drawer and take out the box wrapped in tissue paper. I still regard the contents as something I probably shouldn't have taken. Giving it to Milly will make everything right. It will be another step in doing what Erich has been urging me to do for years: explaining myself.

Excusing myself. Craving forgiveness.

EIGHT

CAMILLE, APRIL 1944

In the maternity clinic waiting room, Camille examined her sewing, frowning. No flaw in her stitches. Each small, almost invisible, identical to those next to it. The baby's nightdress was going to be perfect. Even Véronique would be unable to find fault in it.

She'd always been good at needlecraft. At the convent school in Paris, the nuns had put her work on display when the bishop visited or rich parents came to look around. She'd been honoured with requests to help with vestments and altar coverings, distinguishing her from the other girls. In Lyon, she'd attended a non-religious school, leaving with excellent results, to her parents' pride.

They weren't like Véronique, with her belief in traditional values for women. It was still awkward explaining to her husband and mother-in-law why they hadn't yet met her mother more than eight months after the wedding. Camille found herself implying that Maman had some vague malaise, sometimes requiring convalescence out of town. Recalling how her mother hurled herself around Lyon on her bicycle made this seem a ridiculous thought.

'For some women, losing a husband so suddenly takes some time to recover from.' Véronique had nodded. 'Ideally, your mother would take a cure in a spa, but, regrettably, that's not easy these days.'

Camille thought of Maman in a robe, subjecting herself to massages and strange diets, scoffing at the evidence behind the treatments. None of Jean-Luc's family knew her mother's profession. They'd almost certainly regard being a nurse-midwife as *déclassé*. Camille felt a little ashamed of how much this bothered her.

When the Germans had marched over the demarcation line and into the southern part of France, Camille had wondered whether Jean-Luc's family would feel less socially assured. But they shrugged off the situation. 'Ghastly flags, those boorish soldiers everywhere. But while the Allies threaten the Germans, what can you expect?' Véronique said. 'France is paying for all those years we let things slip.'

What about the people being pulled off the streets? Camille had wanted to ask.

Jean-Luc skirted questions about Vivienne's husband, the sub-prefect, high up in local administration. 'We don't see him much. He's kept busy at work.' She'd met them at the wedding, of course. He'd been a cheerful, attentive guest, admiring her appearance, congratulating Jean-Luc on his good fortune. When the pregnancy was announced, Vivienne arrived in a taxi with boxes of tissue-wrapped baby clothes and equipment. She'd seemed genuinely concerned at Camille's early sickness, going into the kitchen to make tisanes.

The waiting room clock struck the hour. The consulting room door opened. Camille started to pack away her needlework.

'Madame Garnier?'

The woman who'd arrived fifteen minutes after Camille stood up.

Camille stretched each leg out, trying to ignore the receptionist's raised eyebrows. Maman said movement stimulated a
pregnant woman's circulatory system, giving the baby more
nourishment. Healthy pregnant women shouldn't sit for long
periods. At the last appointment, the doctor had insisted that
exercise was to be limited to gentle walks only, close to home.
She'd paced out the courtyard garden so many times this spring
that she could have done it blindfolded. Except for the risk of
tripping.

The maid visited the market so Camille had no reason to go
out shopping and there wasn't much to buy anyway. She could
walk up and down the boulevard and look at the empty shop
windows or head to a church to light a candle for some vague
intention: the Germans to leave, suddenly, peacefully? For all
the prisoners of war and exiles to come home? For those hunted
and persecuted to feel free?

The consulting room door opened again. Madame Garnier
came out.

She sat down again and picked up the needlework.
Véronique probably wouldn't approve of her doing this in
public. She should have brought a book with her, but it would
have been heavy in her handbag and she wanted to walk home
rather than taking the tram, enjoy the fresh air and sunshine.

Camille's pregnancy had gone well to start with, though
she'd been alarmed by her early sickness and the ease with
which she'd put on weight.

'You're a textbook case,' the doctor had told her at her early
appointments. 'A healthy young woman who'll have a healthy
baby.' They were keen on women having babies in Vichy
France. The government claimed that many of France's problems had resulted from the failure to reproduce quickly enough
after the last war when so many Frenchmen had fallen. Pregnant women were treated with respect – large families were
smiled upon, featured in propaganda posters: the children rosy

cheeked, the mother radiant. Camille had to admit she enjoyed the positive attention from pedestrians who stepped aside to let her along narrow pavements ahead of them, or stood up promptly on the tram to give her a seat.

The door opened again. At last the doctor came out and called her into his consulting room, making chitchat as he took her blood pressure at his desk. 'A little raised, but not too much. Do you have a sample for me?'

'The receptionist said there were no glass bottles or tubes.'

He tutted. 'We'll do it next time. Up on to the couch please.'

She did as she was told, feeling herself so ungainly now, wincing as the bump inside her shifted. The doctor didn't wash his hands before he examined her. Maman wouldn't have approved. His palms were cold on her belly. He frowned and swallowed. 'You can get dressed now.' He pushed his glasses up his nose.

'What's wrong?' The words came out in a rush.

'The baby seems to be lying in what we might call a sub-optimal position.'

'It's grinding against me. At times it's really uncomfortable. I knew it wasn't right.' Previously, he'd dismissed her as inexperienced, her body adjusting to a first pregnancy.

But she hadn't been imagining it, something wasn't right.

'What will happen?' she asked.

'Get dressed.' She pulled on her underwear and skirt. When she pushed the curtains open, he motioned to her to sit up and moved behind his desk, as though seeking a barrier between the two of them. 'We will wait and see.' He looked down at the file.

'See what?'

'The baby may yet move into a more favourable position.'

'And if it doesn't?'

'It's still early. There are... things that can be tried.' He wrote something on her notes as he said it.

'It should be head down now, shouldn't it? But it's not. I can feel a head here.' She put a hand on her abdomen.

'Could be a head, could be a posterior. No way of knowing.'

'Would an x-ray—'

'Madame, we are a city under occupation. Our hospitals are short of equipment and staff.'

'Could we try to turn the baby?'

He looked irritated. 'We'll discuss that at the next appointment. Don't go far from home. Pack a bag. Have your husband call me on this number if you go into labour in the meantime.' He handed her a card.

'Is it serious?'

He stood up. 'No, no. You young first-time mothers worry too much.' He sounded irritated at her questions.

As she walked out of the consulting room, the baby seemed to grind against a nerve somewhere in her pelvis and she winced.

Things that could be tried? What things? Back at home that afternoon, her mind would not stop racing.

'Can you feel how strangely the baby is lying?' When he came home in the evening she took Jean-Luc's hand and placed it on her abdomen. He looked at her as though she'd suggested something indecent.

'The doctor will examine you again in due course, *chérie*.'

'I thought you might like to feel him.' She smiled. 'Or her.' She remembered how tactile her father had been with Maman, always putting an arm around her waist, stroking an arm, if he passed her. Jean-Luc was affectionate, but somewhat more constrained about touching her belly now. He'd been so thrilled by her announcement of the pregnancy.

'He,' Jean-Luc said. 'Our first-born will be a boy. You look even more beautiful now. That's a known sign of a male baby.'

They were sitting on the sofa in the salon, with its elegant, shuttered windows and antique furniture. She nestled into him. 'You think that's how it works? M—' She'd been about to say 'Maman' but stopped in time. 'Most doctors say it's the husband who decides the sex of the baby.' Maman had explained the role of sperm and egg without a scintilla of embarrassment. 'And you think it's just through sheer willpower?'

'Beautiful women have sons, it's a known fact.' He stroked her cheek and tucked a lose lock of hair behind her ear. They placed a value on appearance, this family. How you looked, how you presented yourself, it mattered a lot. Even in her fifties Véronique was probably still one of the most feted beauties in the town, dressing with care. If wartime meant she couldn't buy all her usual expensive creams and cosmetics, her face was still immaculate. Jean-Luc's sister Vivienne was also frighteningly well turned out. Trying to meet the standard set by her in-laws, Camille now paid more attention to how she presented herself than the nuns or her mother would have approved of. Sophie had always loved buying clothes, when it had been possible, but had never fussed over her appearance.

Objectively, Maman was probably more beautiful than any of Jean-Luc's family, with a striking combination of height, blue eyes and blond hair; rare among the French. But she appeared totally indifferent to what others thought about her. Her way of dressing had a certain charm to it: she often went out with a headscarf twisted around her light hair and a man's shirt worn over a pair of breeches, as though she were working on a farm. She said it was easier to ride a bicycle in trousers and they were warmer in the winter. Camille had seen photographs of the American actress, Katharine Hepburn, in her trousers and recognised something of her mother's easy elegance.

Camille had found a photograph her father had taken of Maman wearing a rare evening dress to celebrate their wedding anniversary. She was proud of her mother's tall, shapely figure and high-cheeked face and had shown it to Jean-Luc before their marriage.

'That face, that smile, she's almost as lovely as you, except bigger and with fair hair. It's such a shame she couldn't come to our wedding.'

She wondered whether her husband found her undesirable now she was the size of a hippo. She oughtn't to make a fuss – men didn't like that. She was just a nervous first-time mother. When Jean-Luc was with her, she felt relaxed. She wished they could stay together in the salon, that he didn't have to go back to the factory. Jean-Luc sometimes shook his head and said he wished the family had made the move to the more fashionable Sixth Arrondissement with its elegant apartments, but this house in Croix-Rousse with its rare and good-sized private courtyard garden, planted with raised beds of flowers and herbs was perfect. She could step outside whenever she wanted to smell a spray of lilac or admire a tulip. In the early days of their marriage, she'd almost stopped worrying about the Occupation, the war and Maman, who, she reassured herself, must be safe up in the hills. She tried to reconnect with those feelings of optimism, smiling as Jean-Luc rose and wishing him a productive afternoon.

Camille hoped the baby might have turned overnight, but next morning the bump seemed just as awkwardly positioned as ever. Should she try lying on the floor with her legs up on the bed? Would gravity help move the infant? Maman would know. If only she were here. Camille dared not try anything herself. Suppose she made the position even worse or damaged the child?

She was half-tempted to take the tram and return to the apartment, see if Maman had left any midwifery books behind that might enlighten her, but that would be madness. Maman

had been right to advise cutting herself off from her former
identity as the daughter of Madame Sophie Hansen, the tall
Dutch midwife who assisted Jewish refugees.

She dressed and ate a single piece of dry bread and a
scraping of *confiture* for breakfast and tried to lose herself in her
needlework for the rest of the morning. By eleven, she gave up.
Without letting herself think too much about what she was
doing, she made her way up to the box room where her old
things from before the marriage were stored. She found an old
exercise book and a pencil. What she was doing was dangerous.
She was connecting her mother with the world outside her
remote hideaway. Camille paused. The baby shifted inside her.
Heart pumping, she wrote a few words.

Véronique was out today, lunching with Vivienne. Jeanne,
once the *femme de confiance*, the housekeeper, and now more
of a general maid and cook, was visiting her sick mother and had
left the meal in the stove. Nobody would know where Camille
was going, or what she was doing. The key was still in an old
sock she'd rolled up at the back of her lingerie drawer.

The tram ride and walk to the garage took some time and
people gave her curious glances. She should have worn older
clothes. She looked over her shoulder once or twice. Nobody
was following, nobody was going to demand to know what on
earth a girl like her was doing in an area like this. The same
heavy padlock opened to her key, but the garage door felt even
heavier than last time. With an effort, she pulled it open,
grimacing as it creaked. Inside, it smelled of old rusting metal
and oil. Something rustled in the tarpaulins piled up in one
corner. Camille shuddered. She'd forgotten to bring a torch, but
enough daylight permeated the interior for her to be sure
nobody was sleeping in here. Just mice. Probably. She placed
her folded note in the empty paint tin and left without looking
back, almost dropping the key in her haste to re-lock the
padlock. On the way back to the tram stop, she had to force

herself not to hurry, not to do anything that would draw attention.

She had cobwebs on her coat sleeve. Sitting on the tram she pulled them off, taking long deep breaths. Out of the corner of one eye she saw field-grey uniforms sitting behind her. Normally, they wouldn't pay adverse attention to a middle-class, respectable woman in her condition, but she'd witnessed an 'incident' just a few days ago. Germans had boarded a tram. A man, late middle-age, unremarkable, respectably dressed, had been dragged off. She'd tried not to look, wishing she had the courage to object. He'd said something in protest, and she heard the crack of his head hitting the pavement.

Everyone was jumpy now. Camille looked down at her leather-gloved hands until she reached her stop. What had she done?

NINE

SOPHIE

The woman in labour wanted to cry out. Her mouth was drawn into a grimace, her wrists clenched into white knuckles. Beads of perspiration ran down her brow.

Sophie stroked her arm. 'You don't have to stay quiet.' The woman's dark eyes seemed to lose some of the anguish as she let out a small gasp. 'Breathe,' Sophie said. 'Don't try to fight it. You're doing well, Marta.'

When the pain passed, the woman sighed. 'When I had my last baby, the midwife told me off for making a noise.' She pushed a lock of hair off her brow. 'But as soon as you told me I didn't have to hold the pain in, I didn't even need to scream after all.'

Sophie squeezed the woman's hand briefly before picking up the Pinard horn to check the baby's heartbeat. The horn looked like a little trumpet. Sophie placed it gently on the mother's pelvis and listened to the beat, holding her watch in her other hand, nodding. One hundred and thirty beats a minute. Good. 'Trust your body, Marta. This baby's doing well. May I examine you again?'

Marta nodded. 'Last time, the midwife never even asked.

She just tied my legs up and open, and groped around... inside me whenever she wanted.'

Sophie's mouth twisted into a scowl. She washed her hands again before gently examining Marta. 'Fully dilated. Excellent. When the contractions start again, you can push. Quick little breaths, like I showed you. Don't strain.'

She always wanted to avoid tears and stitching. Marta's body tightened again. 'Oh God, I can't bear this.' The words were almost shrieked. Sophie bent down.

'I can see the crown.' She'd attended to so many mothers in labour, but the thrill was always the same and she heard it in her voice. 'Your baby is nearly here.' A second-time mother, Marta should be able to do this last bit smoothly. The baby's presentation was as it should be. Sophie watched, waiting to catch the child. A pause. Another contraction, a long groan from Marta, and more of the head appeared. She saw something, blinked, looked again. The cord, wrapped around the neck. It appeared to be only loosely looped. If Marta delivered the baby quickly, Sophie could unwrap it before the child suffered any problems. But if Marta pushed hard and pulled it tighter, blood flow to the baby might be cut. The heartbeat had been fine just minutes ago. The cord was pulsating so the supply was still good. Things could change very suddenly, though. Scenarios flashed through Sophie's mind.

She could see the baby's shoulders now. 'Monsieur le Docteur,' she said calmly to the man standing behind her. 'Please could you find me a clamp and my scissors.'

'What's wrong?' Marta called out between gasps.

'Nothing.' Sophie met Marta's gaze steadily – there was no need for panic, even if adrenaline was pumping through her.

She heard Erich Meyer move over to her midwife's bag and search for the instruments. Pulling gently at what she could see of the cord she found it was tighter now. Erich was waiting at her side.

'Push again, Marta,' she said firmly. They needed to hurry now.

A gasp from Marta and the infant fell into her hands. She pulled the cord loose. A boy, pink, with good muscles tone. He let out a cross squawk at his entry into the world. She tied the cord but waited a moment before cutting it, feeling as she always did that there was something significant about severing this link to his mother's body and that the last of the precious nutrients should go to the baby. Then it was cut. The boy was fully his own person.

Rubbing his body with a towel, she smiled at Marta. 'A healthy son. I'm just going to weigh him. Then he's yours to hold.'

She had a set of simple scales and wrapped the boy in a napkin. Talking gently to him, she hooked the napkin with the baby in it to the scale. He stopped crying, looking up at her. Hers wasn't the face he craved, though.

'Very good, 3.3 kilograms, accounting for the weight of the napkin.' Dr Meyer sounded impressed.

Sophie felt a rush of relief as she wrapped the child in a light blanket. Keeping Marta adequately fed during her pregnancy had required endless foraging, bartering and sometimes outright black marketeering. She handed him to his mother.

'The cord?' Dr Meyer asked, when she was out of Marta's earshot. 'You seemed very calm about it?'

'I'd checked the heartbeat just before. The best plan was still to deliver him quickly. It's just... experience.'

He nodded solemnly. 'In the hospital where I trained, they tended to cut first and ask questions afterwards.'

A riposte came to Sophie's mind. But Dr Meyer was a good man, a skilled German doctor who observed and only intervened when he had a question or when she asked for his advice.

Sophie's attention moved back to Marta and ensuring that

the placenta came out. She massaged her abdomen gently. 'If you encourage him to feed, that will help.'

The placenta was delivered without it causing much discomfort to Marta, who appeared distracted by the new baby. Sophie checked it. Complete. Good. Dr Meyer took it downstairs to dispose of, working like a ward auxiliary rather than the paediatrician he'd been in Berlin. Sophie returned to her patient to wash her.

'And now to find you something to eat,' she told her. Dr Meyer was already coming back upstairs with a plate of bread and liver pâté, and a glass of red wine diluted with water. 'No after-pains yet?'

Marta shook her head. 'It was the same last time – the moment the baby was born I was just ravenous.'

How were they to keep Marta nourished enough to feed her new child? Sophie tried not to worry now. Let the celebratory mood continue. She filled in the certificate for the baby's birth. Not that the Jewish Marta would be taking him down to the *mairie* for registration while she and her children were in hiding from the French authorities, who'd almost certainly hand them over to the Germans.

Marta's older child, a girl of two, came upstairs with the farmer's wife who had taken them in. Sophie knew the woman well. She'd look after mother and child. The little girl ran to her mother, peering up at the baby, eyes bright. Even in the worst of times, a new life always made Sophie feel normal, human happiness. 'What'll you call your son?' she asked.

'Franz, after his father.' Marta blinked and looked away. Franz had been picked up on the streets of Lyon six months earlier and deported. Nobody had heard from him since. The family had fled first Germany and then the Netherlands for southern France, but even that hadn't been far enough to run. Franz might never have known he had a healthy new son.

Sophie changed the sheet on the bed and helped Marta into fresh nightclothes.

'I'll leave you now,' she told Marta. *'Félicitations* on your beautiful Franz.' She bent down to the older sister. 'Look after your maman and little brother.' The child nodded solemnly.

'Send for me any time if you are worried,' she told the farmer's wife, a mother of five and grandmother of three. 'Though there's not much you don't know about looking after newly delivered women and newborns.' She put on her jacket, pulling her thick plait of hair over the collar.

'Bless you, madame, for coming out at this hour.' The woman stood at the front door, waving them off. Sophie wished they'd had more to give her for her troubles apart from a rubber sheet to protect the bed and a tin of haricot beans.

'I always learn a lot from you, Madame Hansen,' Dr Meyer said as they walked along the track towards the village. 'In the hospital I only saw complicated labours.'

'I learn from you, too. We make a good team, Monsieur le Docteur.'

He gave her his quick, shy smile.

Most nights, the group of refugees hiding out up here on a lonely plateau in the Cévennes went to bed with growling stomachs. Everyday essentials like soap were few. Fear kept them awake when they needed sleep. But thrown together, the group shared knowledge and experience. This village was a little university. Sophie would glean all she could from the experience, do her best to become a true *sage-femme*, a midwife, but more literally, a wise woman, and the best nurse possible. One day, things would be better. She'd return to Lyon, to Camille. Everything she'd learned here would be used elsewhere.

On bad nights, when there were no house calls and she lay sleepless in her cold bed, all she'd lost felt like a grey fog oozing into every cell of her body. Nine months since she'd left Lyon. She hadn't heard from Camille and she'd resisted her longing to write to her daughter. Better for everyone if Sophie Hansen just vanished off the face of the earth. She had a false ID stored safely away in case the gendarmes or Gestapo ever came up here, hunting down the Jewish children and other refugees hiding away.

Tonight she felt healthily tired yet exhilarated, rather than afraid. 'Was the night sky always so bright?' Dr Meyer asked. 'Perhaps I just notice it more than before.'

Before. The word expressing everything they'd lost. In the east a faint band of violet dusted the sky. Sophie yawned. At least she'd have a few hours' sleep before the day started.

Through the broken shutter slat a chink of light fell on Sophie's face, waking her. Seconds of delight at the birdsong filled her senses before everyday concerns broke through. She fought to cling to the light. April. Not even the Nazis could prevent it being spring, the start of everything fresh and new, Easter Sunday just a few days past, and a healthy new baby just born up the mountain.

Her stomach rumbled. She placed a hand underneath her navel, feeling her lawn nightdress, soft and worn. No need to worry about a thickening, middle-aged figure now.

She got up and pushed one of the shutters back to allow in more light, yawning and stretching. As always, she silently wished Camille's wedding photograph on the chest of drawers good morning. Camille smiled that smile of hers – simultaneously demure and wise, as though sharing a secret with you. Sophie tried not to look at the bridegroom more than necessary.

She washed with water from the jug, gasping at the cold smart of the liquid on her skin. Her wafer-thin sliver of soap barely lathered any more. Apart from during a brief time in the West Virginia Appalachians, until now she'd lived with hot water available at the turn of a tap, cakes of soap stored in drawers and piles of thick towels. Sophie undid her plait of hair and combed it out. It was still thick, which was pleasing at a time of reduced rations, but she sighed at the time it took to make the hair presentable. Perhaps she should cut it shorter. But Bernhardt had loved it. She left it loose, just pinned back on each side, as she wouldn't be examining anyone today.

Her housemate Nina had already laid out the bread on the table and was pouring the brown liquid they called coffee into bowls. In a cracked old jug, she'd arranged sprigs of cherry blossom. Last autumn, Nina had lived in hope of finding an apple or pear tree in fruit, but apparently it was too exposed up here in winter. Cherries could sometimes endure the long months of snow. They'd finished their last jar of cherry preserve only yesterday, looking at one another with regret as Sophie scraped the last of it out.

'Still no eggs from the hens,' Nina said, sitting down. 'I'm sorry there isn't more for you after your busy night. How was it?' They always spoke French together, even though they could just as easily have spoken in German or Dutch – all part of blending into their surroundings.

'Mother and son doing well.' Sophie yawned. 'I'll check on them both this afternoon.'

There was milk in the jug for the coffee. Goats' milk. The pasture up here was too thin for cows. She'd never yet managed to enjoy it in a hot drink.

'I'm no nurse, but I know you need the protein from that milk. And someone left it on the doorstep this morning, still warm from milking.' Nina stood up and brought over a small glass, pouring Sophie's half into it. She screwed up a face, but, this fresh, the milk didn't taste too bad.

In the valley, a gun cracked. The women started, caught one another's eyes and looked away again. 'Just a hunter,' Nina said, busy wiping an invisible drop of milk off the table, her voice studiously casual.

What was there left to hunt in this valley? They hadn't even seen rabbits recently. Only a few days ago Sophie had seen a man, rifle slung over shoulder, disappearing into the gloom, the beret on his head identifying him as a member of the local pro-German Milice. She'd fallen back into the shadows, heart thumping. The people sheltering in this village high upon the plateau were still safer here than almost anywhere else in France, but nobody took anything, or anyone, for granted. The Milice could be every bit as vicious as the Germans, whose fascist views they shared, sometimes even more extremely. If they discovered Jewish children and adults and those who'd hidden them, they would be ruthless.

Footsteps ran up to the door. The women held their breath, no time to hide themselves, but the feet were light. 'Just a child,' Sophie whispered to Nina. Whoever it was rapped on the door.

'Telegram for Madame Sophie!'

'Telegram?' There hadn't been one of those for a while. In fact, what the boy's grubby fist handed over was no more than a note, written on a single sheet of paper and folded over several times. Sophie handed the lad the heel of the loaf in exchange.

'*Merci.*' He gave a wide smile.

Her first glimpse of the handwriting as she unfolded it made her sink down onto a chair. It had been written on what looked like a sheet from an old school exercise book. There was no name or address on the front of the paper. It had probably been passed along by hand, with only verbal directions: *Give this to Monsieur X in Y. Tell him to take it with him on the train and pass it on to Mademoiselle A in Saint-Étienne to hand to her mother when she visits her up on the plateau*, and so on and so on. Sophie opened it. The words were written in pencil, elegantly penned. Only someone familiar with this handwriting would know that the note had been written quickly, in the heat of the moment. She scanned the note once, hastily, and then again, heart pumping.

*I'm having a baby in a month's time, perhaps less. They say it's
lying in a difficult position. I don't trust my doctor, he thinks I'm
just a silly girl. You're the only person who can help me. Please
come to me.*

No signature at the bottom, only a date, four days earlier.

'Camille?' Nina asked. There was no need to reply – confir-
mation was written all over Sophie's face.

'She wants me to go to her.' She explained about the baby.

Nina's face, usually so expressive of her optimism, fell into a
watchful wariness. 'Sophie? You know it's too dangerous? You
were lucky to get away from Annemasse.'

'If I don't go and she...' The words wouldn't come out,
couldn't be spoken in case they took form as reality. 'If the
child's large or lying transverse or a footling breech or the
placenta's in the wrong place... If Camille...' She could be so
calm, so composed, when tending to a pregnant woman, but
when it came to thinking about her own daughter, her ratio-
nality dissolved. Everything had been bearable, manageable, as
long as Camille was safe.

Nina grunted and leant over to squeeze her arm. 'They do
still have maternity clinics and doctors in Lyon, you know. It's
the second-largest city in France. If that husband of hers is that
important, surely they can find a good obstetrician?'

'Camille doesn't trust the doctors.' Sophie handed the letter
to Nina and looked down at her own hands, trying to regain her
composure. She had long, flexible fingers rising from slender,
but strong palms. The skin was dry from lack of hand lotion.
She'd always regarded her hands as her best feature: strong,
sensitive, good at coaxing a baby into the right position and out
of its mother into life. As well as Marta's last night, she'd
attended several dangerous pregnancies since she'd retreated up
here: the shepherd's wife whose first baby had become
awkwardly wedged during labour. The grocer's eldest daughter,

whose blood pressure had caused such anxiety during her first pregnancy. Helping these women and their babies had sent a rush of satisfaction through Sophie's veins. She was still the person she'd once been. She wasn't just a refugee, just another victim of war, washed away from normal life. She still had agency, professional skill. She was needed. And now her daughter needed her.

'Does Camille have any idea how dangerous going back to Lyon would be for you now? And for her, too?' Nina placed the note on the table, sounding fierce. 'Your fake identity wouldn't stand up to questioning, Sophie.' The name on Sophie's papers – Mireille Leclerc – was invented. Enough to pass a quick inspection, but not a more rigorous examination. She'd been given the new identity when she'd fled up here last summer.

'They don't have anything on Camille.' Thank God. Camille had only brought the provisions to the empty garage in the city, just that once, weeks before Sophie had gone to Annemasse, nothing more. And yet, a little voice inside her whispered, just doing that could be enough to be arrested. Even if Camille's husband was such a friend to the Vichy regime and their German overlords, he mightn't be able to protect her.

'When has that ever stopped the Gestapo? Or even the French police. If they pick you up in Lyon, they'll work out who you are, what you did last year.'

'Jean-Luc shields Camille.' Every time he invited a visiting German wife to look around the factory and choose a length of material otherwise unobtainable, he probably became even more indispensable to the occupiers.

Sophie looked down at the piece of paper in her hand, imagining how much it had cost Camille to pick up the pencil and write those words to her mother in the old exercise book, possibly one she'd had at school, not so many years ago.

Nina shuddered. 'I can't believe you'd think of going back there.' Since the summer, there'd been even more raids on homes and offices in the city. The Germans, aided by some French officials and police, were hunting out Jews and anyone who helped them. The trickle of Jewish children up here to the remote plateau had become more of a flood.

'The logging train down to Saint-Étienne is still safe. I wouldn't use the mainline train onto Lyon from there.' Sophie was thinking aloud.

'So what would you do?'

Bicycle, perhaps. Or maybe a series of buses, interspersed with long walks.

Nina looked at her watch. 'Look at the time. Don't answer this message now, Sophie. Let's talk it through later.'

But Camille hadn't even asked Sophie for an answer because she knew there could only be one: her mother would come to her.

By many people's standards, Sophie had been a poor wife and mother at times. Often preoccupied by her work, she'd tried to make her family the priority when they needed her. Not always successfully. As she cleaned her teeth outside by the garden pump, she could hear Camille's voice as clearly as if she was calling to her across the orchard.

I need you, Maman. Only you can help me.

TEN

CAMILLE

'Public morality and work ethics needed a shake-up.' Véronique took a mouthful of coffee. 'And the new youth organisations for boys are doing good work. Better for them to be out of cities, enjoying some fresh air and exercise. More wholesome.'

'It doesn't all look that wholesome,' Camille said. 'Some of those boys' groups seem to train boys up for the Milice. It's just like the Hitler Youth.' The Milice seemed to base itself on Nazi ideals of patriotism. Lots of talk of enemies of the state and French family values.

Véronique shifted on her chair. Had Camille been too outspoken again?

'Most of those boys just want the comradeship and outdoor activity.' Jean-Luc looked at his watch. 'I'm not sure I'll have time for lunch today.' Even on the busiest days, Jean-Luc would return for the midday meal.

Véronique looked scandalised. 'But it's pork. And I'm lunching with the Daughters of the Sacred Heart today. Camille will be alone.'

'Do you have large orders to meet?' Camille asked, almost

shyly. She still knew so little about the silk business. Jean-Luc regarded any interest she showed in the factory with a mixture of pride and something close to surprise.

'We have a few delays. Spare parts coming on a train from the north have been held up.'

'Another Allied raid on the railway?' Véronique tutted. The British and their American allies bombed ports, strategic rail links, airfields and factories. Thousands of French civilians had already died.

'They say it was the Resistance.'

'I'm afraid that just makes the case for the Milice. The Resistance simply provoke them, blowing up railway lines, endangering civilians, helping foreign forces.'

Sometimes Camille could hear her father's questioning voice in her head: *Aren't you going to challenge Véronique on that point, Cami?* But arguing with his mother would distress Jean-Luc. She loved him so much and he was such a loyal son. Family mattered most, he said. Which was what you wanted of a husband and soon-to-be father. Making an enemy of her mother-in-law would be a mistake when they were starting their own family.

Another pelvic twinge made Camille bite her lip. Something was wrong with this pregnancy. But she couldn't run away from it. There was no way of changing her mind and returning the baby to sender. Nothing, not even war, could stop women having children, it seemed. Perhaps Jean-Luc read her mind. 'I'm sure I can come back briefly at lunchtime,' he said, kissing her good-bye at the door.

'Not if the factory needs you.'

'You don't have to worry about the factory.' Véronique gave him a sidelong look as he said this. Did she think that Camille should show more or less curiosity about the family business? Sometimes Camille felt she could never behave in the correct way.

If only she could distract herself with something that wasn't the war, the pregnancy or this household. She seemed to have no concentration for reading. Even needlework seemed an effort this morning. She gave up after a few hours.

Before her pregnancy became uncomfortable, she'd loved to stroll along Lyon's two rivers. At this time of the year, there was blossom on the trees. She could sit watching the barges on the river as they travelled upstream to the Vosges mountains along the Saône, or to the Swiss glaciers along the Rhône. Jean-Luc had told her how the silk trade had operated along the waterway for centuries, linking this city to Europe and the wider world. It sounded so romantic.

She went upstairs. Jean-Luc's father had been a keen book collector and she found it relaxing to flick through the volumes of travel books in his old study, reminding herself of where she had travelled as a child. The time passed in a haze of memories.

Camille looked at her watch. In ten minutes, Jean-Luc would be home for lunch. Camille had set the table herself, placing a small vase of primroses in the middle. Ordinarily, Jeanne wouldn't let her touch a thing in the kitchen, which was a shame as she'd enjoyed standing with Maman in the cramped kitchen of the apartment in Les Brotteaux and helping her cook.

Why was she thinking about Maman all the time now? She'd left that foolish little note in the garage in a moment of panic after the appointment with the obstetrician. She'd felt so alone, but now she regretted sending it so much. Maman would be worried sick, but it was too dangerous for her to come back to the city. Perhaps the note was still in the garage. They – whoever Maman's contacts were – probably didn't check it every day. Even if the note had been collected it might never arrive in Maman's village. So many people would be involved in passing it on, and the unaddressed note could easily be lost or forgotten. Camille half-hoped this would happen.

A foot inside her kicked. She put a hand on her dress. The

bump felt as it had the previous day, but her pelvis ached. Surely the baby should be head down by now? Those old midwifery books of Maman's she'd flicked through as a child when she was bored and had nothing else to read said that babies turned themselves by this stage. Could they turn back again? Perhaps she really ought to try elevating her legs. Or even standing on her head. The thought of her mother-in-law's face if she saw Camille doing this made her laugh. She felt momentarily better.

The front door opened. Jeanne was back from her shopping and came out to greet Jean-Luc, taking his hat. Camille felt the familiar flutter in her heart when he returned. That was something, wasn't it, to be married for nine months and still feel that excitement at the return of her husband after just five hours?

She smoothed down the front of her dress and went out to greet him, trying not to grimace as she walked and the baby ground itself on a hip bone. A proper Frenchwoman didn't make a song and dance about it in front of her husband. She turned the grimace into a smile as she entered the tiled foyer. '*Mon amour.*' They embraced and she rested her forehead on his suit jacket. The weather was warm now and he'd switched to a lightweight fabric, but his outline was as elegant as ever.

He kissed her on the brow. 'And what have you been up to this morning? No more tearing around the city, I trust?' He pulled back from the embrace to examine her carefully.

'The layette is still a preoccupation.' She groaned. 'One nightdress made. Still plenty of others to go.'

'But you're so good at needlework.'

'I like it, but I wish I could excel at something less pedestrian.'

'What would you prefer?' His eyes twinkled at her. 'Figure skating?'

She stroked his cheek, peachy-smooth. He took trouble over

shaving. For all his air of nonchalance, he took trouble over everything.

'A buffalo figure skating would be more elegant just at the moment.'

'You could never look inelegant. When the baby's here and you're feeling yourself again, let's think of something you can do to keep fit in the fresh air. I hate to think of you being cooped up.'

An image of herself walking docilely around the park pushing the perambulator flitted through her mind.

'You loved tennis before. And I thought perhaps riding?' he said. 'You told me you used to enjoy it as a child?'

'Oh, I'd love to ride again.' Her heart leapt with pleasure at the memory of the breeze on her cheeks as she pressed her horse into a canter and then a gallop, the smell of the tack and the warm animal.

'Have you thought more about a *bonne d'enfant* for the baby?' He released her. 'I don't want you doing all the work. You'll need time for yourself, too.'

'They sent me details of the nursemaids on their books. They were not what I...' Camille shrugged.

She'd imagined a kindly, rosy-cheeked girl from some large rural family, who'd sing to the baby. Or a soft-figured grand-motherly type. The women on the books of the agency were mainly middle-aged, thin-lipped, severe in features. Of course, it was important that a baby was introduced to regular habits from the moment of birth. Her own childhood would perhaps have been the better for more routine. But surely there must be a happy medium between being slapdash and a kind of prison guard?

She was relieved when Jeanne called them into the dining room. The pork smelled even better as she lifted the lids and served them both. A business contact of Jean-Luc's had sent the small loin to them and it had been carefully parcelled up into portions for each of them, Véronique's put aside for her. Jeanne would have hers in the kitchen. Véronique might be severe, but she made sure Jeanne received her fair share of food.

'Maman would be delighted to help find someone suitable to help with the baby,' Jean-Luc said. 'It would be no trouble for her.'

Camille could imagine the kind of person Véronique would consider appropriate. She swallowed. 'I don't want to put your mother to the trouble, I'll try another agency,' she said.

She ate with appetite. The portions were the size of match-boxes, accompanied with carrots in parsley – no butter today – and a few early potatoes each. Jeanne had left out a small piece of Saint-Marcellin cheese for afterwards. France was a fertile country, but there were few men left to harvest and farm. Much of what was produced headed straight to Germany. But Jean-Luc's connections still handed him food parcels.

Jean-Luc watched her as she cut a second sliver of Saint-Marcellin, so thin it was almost translucent. 'You're hungry?'

'Ravenous, today.'

Did he think she was eating too much? The doctor had told her to be careful not to put on too much weight, though it would be hard to do that with food shortages. Nobody could claim Camille was working a hard job, sitting in these comfortable rooms, watching the hours pass until the baby was born, worrying because something was wrong and she wasn't just being a neurotic first-time mother.

'We could try a specialist in Paris,' Jean-Luc said, frowning at her. 'I know you're very anxious about the baby. It's just such a business getting there on the train these days.'

Since the Germans had occupied the southern part of France and abolished the internal border last November, it should have been simpler to travel to the north. But trains were shunted into sidings to prioritise German military transports. Points were sabotaged. And of course there were the air-raids.

She gave him a brave smile. 'I thought everything in Lyon was better than everything in Paris?'

He grinned. 'Most of the time that is undoubtedly the case. But perhaps not in terms of specialists.' He leant forward and took her hand in his. 'I just worry about you having to sit on a train, *mon ange*, perhaps with delays, or... other unpleasantness.'

People being dragged off trains, perhaps. The kind of people desperate to reach places of refuge like Maman's village.

'We could stay with Martine? She would know a good obstetrician.'

Martine had two children, apparently delivered without fuss or loss of her figure. Camille could picture Martine flicking through an address book with a manicured finger and finding a Paris telephone number for Jean-Luc. At least telephone calls from one zone of the country to the other were now allowed again, assuming saboteurs hadn't damaged the lines.

'Let me think about it.'

He looked at his watch. 'There's a meeting. I shouldn't be late.'

'Still having to persuade the Germans that you need every one of your workers?'

He grimaced. 'It's proving a challenge, but I'll do what I have to.'

The Germans were offering a mixture of bribes and threats to extract French workers to the Fatherland. Jean-Luc was equally desperate to retain his trained loom workers.

'Some of them... well, I've known them for a while. I feel I have to do all I can, Camille.'

She could understand that. Skilled workers would be impossible to replace. And he obviously felt a bond with his employees.

As she stood up to walk out of the dining room with him, the nerves in her pelvis emitted another protest. The pain seemed to run down to her left thigh. She rubbed it, wincing. Just as she did, Jean-Luc said something else about the workers. '*Désolée,*' she said. 'I didn't hear that?'

He looked as though he was about to repeat it but stopped. 'It can wait. I want you to rest now.' He rubbed the back of his neck. Perhaps the cotton was fraying. She'd turn the collar for him this evening. Véronique couldn't say she wasn't good at looking after Jean-Luc's linen.

Camille kissed her husband, hiding her discomfort behind a smile. As the salon door closed behind him, she thought again about what they might do to her and the baby. Forceps tugging him or her out, hurting the fragile head? A Caesarean? Such a major operation, with a risk of haemorrhage or suffering some terrible infection. And even if it went well, she'd be left with a vertical scar down her lower abdomen. What would Jean-Luc think about that? Would he regard it as witness to the life of their child, something done for the best reason, or would he regard it as a mark on her otherwise flawless body that made her less desirable? There was something else about Jean-Luc pressing on her subconscious. Once or twice she'd had the feeling he wanted to say something but had stopped himself at the last minute, just as he had now.

She heard Véronique coming in from her lunch. Jean-Luc said something to his mother in the hallway. 'That's twenty now.'

'Too many.' Véronique sounded sharp. She claimed that the operation of the looms was men's business but could probably have numbered every silk thread in the factory.

Too many what? Silk bales? Was it something to do with what Jean-Luc had started to tell her just as she'd felt the pain? Gifts to Germans or to government officials to keep them happy?

She felt too sleepy to even think about it. This wretched pregnancy was supposed to be a source of delight, and it was. But it was drawing so much of her energy away from the rest of life. If she just knew all was really well, she could concentrate properly.

Once again, she longed for Maman.

ELEVEN

SOPHIE

'You'll go to Camille whatever I say, won't you, Sophie?'

Pastor Lefroy gave her his kind, slightly mischievous smile.

'She needs me.'

'Sometimes we best protect those we love by staying away from them.' Outside in the garden, some of the children he and his wife fostered played tag, squealing as they caught one another. The race of the 'orphans' they took in was never openly discussed in the village. Pastor Jacques's records were hidden away in the garden of his cousin's house miles away down in Valence. Everyone knew they were Jewish. Some of them had seen their parents dragged away at a station or from their home. Others had been purposefully sent away for their own safety by parents anticipating deportation to the east.

Small children. Helpless. Just like Anton had been that night on the Swiss border. Camille was a grown woman. Sophie's sacrifice, cutting herself off from her only adult child, staying away from her to keep her safe, was nothing in comparison to that of these Jewish parents. But Sophie still felt a fierce blood call to protect her daughter.

'I truly believe I'm the best person to help Camille and her baby through a dangerous birth.'

She'd stopped mothers from being ripped open between the legs by over-zealous doctors. Picked up on the hint of the placenta sitting on the opening of the womb, meaning the baby's exit was blocked and the woman was in danger of haemorrhaging to death when she went into labour. She'd been scrupulous about checking for signs of infection during and after delivery. She'd revived infants who'd arrived silent in the world. As a nurse, she'd looked after people with diphtheria, kidney infections, bronchitis and measles.

'Dr Meyer certainly respects you. He says he's no more than your assistant at births.'

She smiled. 'Dr Meyer is generous. I've learned a lot from him.' Was the pastor trying to persuade her she was indispensable? For all his goodness, Jacques might not be above flattery. Sophie sat straighter. 'I will be absent for a month, perhaps six weeks. If you need my room to house someone else, I will understand.'

'Your room is your room, Sophie. It will await your return.' The warmth of his expression made her feel guilty. 'Are you sure your understandable concern about Camille isn't causing you to act rashly, though?'

He sounded like Bernhardt had in the past when cautioning her. But Bernhardt would want her to go to their child, wouldn't he?

'I know my daughter.' Camille had been a hardy child, rarely complaining if she hurt herself or felt unwell. As a five-year-old, she'd fallen off a swing and broken her arm. She hadn't even cried. *It doesn't hurt that much, Maman.*

'*Oui.*' The pastor's sigh was long and heartfelt. 'Nobody could be better placed to assist Camille than you.' He leant forwards, hands clasped. 'But here's a question for you, Sophie.

How would your arrest and deportation, perhaps worse, affect your daughter's health?'

Sophie sighed, too. Just as Bernhardt had, Jacques had the knack of drawing honest answers out of her. 'I could be picked up and thrown into a cell or stinking railway wagon on the way to Poland. And the effect of that on Camille would be terrible.' She looked him squarely in the face. 'I know that if I was tortured, I'd endanger everyone here and elsewhere.'

Many of those involved in the rescue of children had families themselves. Pull one thread out and the whole piece of lace would fray. The network was already weakened. 'What happened last summer...' She couldn't even name Annemasse, as though just saying the word aloud would bring down misfortune.

'You know that wasn't your fault.'

She'd scurried up here to hide and they'd taken her in, never a word of reproach about the loss of Hélène.

She still couldn't stop her mind replaying what had happened: the choice she'd made between Anton and the girl. If she'd been sterner with Anton, if she'd left him, chanced that he would eventually drift back into the trees, there might have been time to reach Hélène, to have saved her. If, if, if... She'd been lucky herself, she needed to be grateful for that, at least. She needed to forget the night she'd spent after Hélène had been dragged off, her nervousness on the train back to Lyon.

A rubber ball bounced against the window. Jacques stood up. 'They need to move away from that glass or Marie will be on the warpath.' He waved gently at the boy who'd thrown the rubber ball and the group moved away. Jacques and Marie had their own children and grandchildren, but their loyalty to these children of strangers was immense. But how would they react if asked to choose between their own flesh and blood and these children?

As they reminded themselves frequently: *Don't expect*

*anyone will hold out against the Gestapo if their family is threat-
ened with arrest or execution.*

'I can't even tell you that women here need you, Sophie.' He
sounded resigned now. 'Nobody's expecting a baby in the next
few months, are they? And we don't seem to have any more
than the usual outbreaks?'

'A few local women are in early pregnancy – second and
third babies.' These were usually the safest pregnancies, the
women's bodies having learned what to do in the first confinement. 'I've examined them in the last few days and they're
doing well. Their notes are written up.' The locals concerned
were robust, healthy women. 'I'll ask Dr Meyer to visit Marta
Goldblum and her new baby every day for the next four or five
days. We're through the worst of the early spring infections
now.'

'You'll want to avoid the mainline train up to Lyon if you
can,' Jacques said after a moment. 'Too many checks on ID now.
You know your fictional alter ego won't stand up to close
scrutiny.'

But since last summer travelling in her own name was too
risky so she'd have to travel as Mireille Leclerc.

'Be careful accepting lifts.' The pastor's eyes twinkled and
then grew more serious. Women jumping into trucks or cars
with strangers risked men's hands wandering onto a thigh or
breast. Usually, a stern word was enough to make the driver
desist. Sometimes it took a slap. Sophie had treated a young
woman who'd had to undo the passenger door of a truck and
jump out, scraping her legs on the gritty road surface.

Jacques went over to his desk, removing an old and tattered
map from the drawer and unfolding it on the desk. They bent
their heads over the map, discussing the best route. If it hadn't
been for the concern gnawing away at her, Sophie would have
felt a stirring of excitement at the prospect of a journey, a
change.

'And once you're at your daughter's? You said her husband was someone you were avoiding? He's in the Milice, is he?'

'No.' She shuddered. 'Just an industrialist who likes to keep in with the occupiers.'

He looked startled at her tone.

'Jean-Luc's energies are all given to his silk factories. He seems to court anyone who can keep the looms running. One brother-in-law is a sub-prefect. Before I left Lyon I heard rumours that he was very attentive to his political duties. Every Jew accounted for, that kind of attentiveness.'

'If you come to stay with them, Jean-Luc will want to know all about you, won't he? I certainly would, if my *belle-mère* came to visit.'

Sophie realised she had made a decision. 'I'll interact with my daughter as Mireille, not as her mother.'

The pastor sat bolt upright. 'You want your daughter to use an assumed name for you, to pretend you aren't her mother?'

'I will be the midwife and maternity nurse recommended for her confinement.'

'You can maintain that role while your own child is going through labour pains?'

'Yes.' If it would save Camille's life and that of the child, of course she could. 'It may be that I simply have to accompany her to the maternity clinic and hold her hand.'

He looked as though he was struggling for words. 'And you think Camille can remember that you are just her midwife?'

'I think she can, yes.'

Jacques looked unconvinced. She shuffled on her chair. 'It'll be hard, but I'll only stay in Lyon until the baby is born and both are safe.'

'You lived there for, what... two and a half years? A neighbour might remember you?'

'I'm not going near Les Brotteaux. If I can't stay with Camille, I'll find somewhere discreet.'

'The convent isn't safe anymore.'

Sophie looked down at her skirt. She wanted to ask what the pastor had heard about the convent. It wouldn't be news that would make her feel better about going to Lyon, so what was the point?

As she and Nina prepared their evening meal, Sophie told Nina that she'd made her decision. 'I'm leaving as soon as possible. Tomorrow, hopefully, if Marta and her baby are well when I visit first thing in the morning.'

'Dr Meyer will look after your mothers and babies.' Nina handed her a gnarly carrot to peel.

'Why are you looking at me like that?' Nina had a little smile on her face.

'Dr Meyer will be very happy to assist you. And very sorry that you're going away.'

Sophie stared at her.

'He likes you, Sophie. Haven't you noticed?'

She hadn't noticed anything more than professional courtesy between the two of them. 'We just have a good working relationship—'

'Bah, Erich Meyer's definitely thinking of other kinds of relationship.' Nina took the carrot from her. 'I've forgotten something.' She went over to the wicker basket she took everywhere with her on the off chance of finding something edible. 'A can of anchovies.' Sophie's mouth dropped open at the sight of the small tin, with its bright design of sea and fish, a souvenir of a previous, happier age.

'I haven't seen one of those for such a long time.' She took the tin from Nina to admire it, wondering how Nina had acquired it. Sometimes it was best not to ask questions.

'We can fry a couple of anchovies in the pan and add the

carrots when they're boiled, give them some flavour and protein.'

'Carrot and anchovy fricassee. What a delicacy.' She handed it back.

'*La spécialité de la maison*. Might help with our dry skin.' Nina was unwinding the tin of anchovies as carefully as if she were defusing a bomb, so none of the olive oil was wasted. Whatever they didn't use tonight could be saved for a future meal. 'I'm going to put some of them in whatever bread I can find overnight. Wrap it tight in muslin and weigh it down. For your journey tomorrow. I'll find you some other things, too.'

'I'm not taking all the food.'

'You can't make that long journey on an empty stomach.' Despite Nina being younger, she often stood in as a stern mother. 'I'll miss you,' she said, matter-of-factly. 'So will everyone.'

'Nobody's irreplaceable.'

Nina shook her head. 'As a friend, you are. Even if you're worrying me to death with the risk you're taking.'

Sophie made a *pfft* noise. 'I'm much steadier these days. You should have known me in America.'

'When you went off with the horseback midwives for weeks?'

'Or in London.'

'When you managed to sneak into a lecture for eminent obstetricians?'

All men, of course. Sophie had squeezed into a row at the back, wearing trousers and an overcoat, her hair up under a trilby, which she hadn't removed. The lecture had been very informative, even if she hadn't agreed with all the points made. Being in a lecture hall with a male professor lecturing all-male doctors about women in labour had felt wrong.

'Returning to a city swarming with SS and Gestapo where you are known makes those look like schoolgirl pranks,' Nina said. 'Can't you wait a few days until we can find some hair dye?' She eyed Sophie's tresses. 'I asked in the pharmacy this afternoon – very discreetly, for my own roots. But it was a no. We could ask in the *coiffeuse*?'

'The hairdresser's been using all kinds of things to dye her clients' hair. If she makes a mistake, I could end up orange and I'd stand out like a carrot.' Sophie pulled up a strand of her hair and examined it. 'More grey hairs than I had last summer. That'll help.'

'Don't fool yourself, you don't look nearly old enough to be becoming a grandmother.' Nina let out a long sigh. 'I can't say anything to make you change your mind, can I?'

Many people in Sophie Hansen's life had tried to persuade her out of doing what she set her heart on. Few had succeeded.

Nina crouched down and opened a cupboard. 'We should have a shot of this. Toast your safe arrival.' She pulled out an old bottle of jenever, a traditional gin-like spirit familiar to anyone from Belgium or the Netherlands. The two of them seldom acknowledged their roots in the Low Countries, but there were times when it was comforting to remind yourself where you came from.

Nina poured two small measures and handed one to Sophie. '*Santé*. And good luck.'

TWELVE

The little train down to Saint-Étienne bearing its resinous load of logs almost lulled Sophie into pretending she was making an ordinary trip. She breathed in the scent coming through the carriage, almost able to imagine she was off to a midwifery conference. Or enjoying a short break to take in a concert or play.

She'd been sniffy about Lyon before the war, thinking of it as a backwater after Paris and New York and, some years back, Berlin. But during her time there with Bernhardt and Camille, she'd grown to love France's second city. When Camille was on school holidays, they'd explored the old quarters, lapping up the history and architecture and the views of red-tiled buildings over the two rivers: Saône and Rhône.

They'd spent their family life travelling. Sophie herself had been born on the Dutch-German border, Bernhardt not many kilometres away on the German side. Their daughter had taken her first breath in Berlin, moving with her parents to Paris at the age of four. They'd lived there long enough for Camille to be completely French in her accent, manners, tastes and even her dress, to the amusement of her mother, before returning to

Berlin again. They'd left Germany in haste in 1933, like so many others, for an eight-month trip to New York, followed by brief spells in the Netherlands and London before returning to France. Camille had seen the arrival of packing cases as a normal part of childhood. The departure from Paris in June 1940 had been hurried, though. No meticulous lists produced by Sophie indicating which possessions were in which crate. They'd packed what they could in suitcases and driven down crowded, chaotic roads on the way south. Bernhardt had been glued to the wireless during the last few weeks, sitting with an open map while listening to the news and telling them a good five days before the Germans entered Paris it was time to go. They'd managed to get ahead of most of the Parisian exodus.

When they'd reached southern France and it had become clear the Germans wouldn't occupy this part of the country, he'd relaxed. 'They won't come any further, not for a while,' he'd said. 'Let's enjoy ourselves here while we can.'

They'd explored the countryside whenever they found petrol or could buy train tickets, but they'd never been to the industrialised belt south of Lyon running towards Saint-Étienne, with its mines and foundries. Bernhardt would have been fascinated by the contrast between the remote rural plateau where his wife now lived and this zone. He'd have puzzled over who exactly was carrying out all the heavy labour now that the Germans were sending Frenchmen to their own country. Polish prisoners of war? Russians? Half of Europe seemed to be living and working, or enslaved, in the other half. Sophie frequently thanked her *geluksterren*, her lucky stars, that her earlier life had prepared her for living and working almost anywhere.

The Germans were on the platform at Saint-Étienne when the train pulled in. Sophie forced herself to calm down, to collect her bicycle from the guard's van and wheel it to the exit as though the Germans were a minor inconvenience. She tried not to say much but had to answer when asked where she was travelling to. Being non-French these days always made you an object of suspicion, someone who might be on the run.

'A foreign accent, Madame Leclerc?' the German said, looking up from her ID card for Mireille Leclerc and frowning. 'Dutch, is it?'

'My parents blamed the native staff in the house we lived in in Martinique. Those Blacks couldn't pronounce the language properly. The times my mother slapped my wrists to correct me!' Sophie rolled her eyes. The German gave a wry smile.

'The *untermenschen*, eh? You should hear the Poles mangling the language of Goethe.' He handed back her papers. 'A long cycle to Lyon for you?' He nodded at the bicycle.

'My husband says it's good for my figure.' She gave a flirtatious smile.

Stupid thing to say. If he asked her where her husband was and what he did, it would push her ID for Mireille to its limits.

'What takes you to the city?'

'A sick relative.'

'Open the bags, please.'

In the rucksack on her back she carried clothes and toiletries, enough to last her through a few weeks. He barely looked at them. The instruments in her midwife's bag didn't interest him. 'No morphine?' He held up the empty bottle.

'I haven't been able to restock my drugs.' She badly lacked all kinds of things now. Perhaps she could restock in Lyon, if she was discreet, staying away from the pharmacies and dispensers she'd used before.

He sniffed, prodding at Nina's anchovy sandwich, which emitted a piquant aroma. 'My lunch,' she said.

'You're a nurse?'

'Nurse-midwife. I don't work as much these days, but my niece needs some care in her pregnancy.' Near enough to the truth for her to sound convincing, she hoped.

The German guffawed. 'A whiff of that sandwich will bring on premature labour.' He waved her through. Nina would laugh when she told her the anchovies had scared him off. A shared sense of humour was probably why the two of them got along so well. Camille had often complained that her mother laughed at silly things, blaming her foreignness for her over-developed sense of the ridiculous. Her daughter would soon become aware that childbirth and early motherhood were some-times best handled with a sense of the absurd. Sophie took her midwifery and nursing duties as seriously as she took breathing, but knowing when to smile, when to make a gentle joke, had probably helped keep an anxious mother calm.

Coming down here to Saint-Étienne felt like landing on a different planet after the months in the mountains. The slag heaps and chimneys were a gloomy counterpoint to the spring air. The route through the town took Sophie through run-down streets where children scowled at her and looked as though they might have thrown stones, if it hadn't been for the German patrols. At a junction, a sergeant put up a hand to stop her. She showed the Mireille ID and he nodded her through. Twice lucky, but she hadn't expected to be stopped so often already.

The valley's shape meant the main road out of the town was the only way she could cycle north-east towards the Rhône and from there north to Lyon. She still hoped to reach the city by night, but there were fifty kilometres to cover. She was a fit woman and unworried by the distance. All the same, the prospect of cycling alone in the dark wasn't one she was looking forward to, although it might mean fewer patrols. She'd be breaking curfew, but this wasn't her main concern. Bands of armed men moved around at night: some Resistance groups whose members were desperate men she was wary of. A far more frightening prospect was the Milice catching her out during curfew. Some of those men in the regime's militia had their own ways of disciplining women they didn't approve of.

Before leaving Lyon, Sophie had assisted a pregnant sixteen-year-old who'd been raped by a group of men for having a brother in the Resistance. It had been both a sadness and a small mercy that the girl had gone through labour three months early to a stillborn child.

She pedalled hard to eat into the kilometres between her and the city. The clouds passed over. It grew chillier. She stopped to pull her mackintosh out of her rucksack. With only the dim cycle lamps to guide her, she would be very likely to part company with the bicycle on any sharp downhill bend.

Petrol was almost impossible to acquire for most people now. For the next few miles, the traffic was mainly German trucks and industrial vehicles serving mines and foundries, occasionally interspersed with cars and trucks adapted to use wood gas, complete with tanks on their roofs. The German soldiers in the trucks passed her, looking at her curiously. Perhaps the bus would be less conspicuous. They'd usually let you jam your bicycle in if there was space. At the next settlement Sophie pulled off the road and asked a woman pushing a pram when the next bus would arrive. The woman eyed her suspiciously. Sophie pointed at the bag in her basket. 'I'm a *sage-femme*, there's a woman I need to see, but I lost time at a German roadblock.' A smile covered the woman's face, disappearing when she told Sophie there would be no further buses until later in the evening.

'My husband's delivering logs,' she said. 'Only twenty kilometres or so to the north, but it would get you part-way to the city, non?' She beckoned Sophie on to her house and insisted on pouring her a glass of water and cutting her a slice of bread. Outside, the small patch of garden was given over to vegetable growing, as was usually the case, but a lilac tree wafted its scent through the open door. The bread was fresh; she hadn't eaten anything like it for weeks. Sophie breathed in the lilac and the yeasty bread and felt herself relax. These moments of sensory enjoyment gave her strength. 'Your work is so important, madame. Do you know the midwife here?' her hostess asked. 'She delivered my son.' She beamed proudly in the direction of the perambulator.

'I'm fairly new to the area,' she said in answer.

'Ah, the war.' The woman sighed, taking the baby out of the perambulator. 'It has displaced so many people.'

Sophie admired the little boy, glad for the distraction away from other topics. The husband arrived soon after, casting a suspicious look at Sophie until his wife explained that she was a *sage-femme*. He lifted her bicycle into the back of his Citroen truck, on top of the logs. He was older than his wife, probably why he wasn't working in Germany. To her relief, he wasn't as chatty as his wife. Sophie even managed to doze briefly, her head slumping down onto her chest. When he braked and she was jolted awake, she hoped she hadn't been sleeping with her mouth open or snoring. When they reached his destination, he lowered her bicycle down for her. She thanked him and cycled on, refreshed by the rest, even though it had started to rain. The drops felt grimy, probably picking up black coal dust. She felt dampness seep into the pores of her skin.

A little less than twenty-five km to Camille's marital home. A flash of excitement made her disregard the rain and the growing awareness that there was a rip in the shoulder seam of her mackintosh, perhaps worn out by the rucksack strap, and that damp was spreading down her body, making her shiver as the temperature dropped. She found temporary shelter under a poplar and ate Nina's anchovy sandwich, which tasted better than its fierce aroma suggested.

Sophie looked at her watch. It was growing late. It was still wanted to press on to Lyon, but it was probably still another two and a half hours away. She hadn't a fixed plan for what she'd do when she reached Lyon – no midwife would make a house call so late at night outside an emergency. She'd considered finding a hotel somewhere near Camille for a single night. But hotels were dangerous. ID papers were taken at the reception, Germans carried out spot checks and the local police were sometimes keen to investigate strangers, especially single women. She'd heard of people spending the night in railway station waiting rooms, taking cover if necessary. Not ideal, but possibly safer.

She still had her key to their former home, tucked away in a pocket of her bag. A longing for the apartment in Les Brotteaux swept over Sophie. Clean sheets. The books she and Bernhardt had squeezed into the car when they left Paris. But Mireille Leclerc didn't belong in that apartment, with its views over red-tiled roofs and its small balcony.

Turning up anywhere late at night in Lyon would draw the worst kind of attention to her. She couldn't afford to dawdle on this journey. Better to speed up and arrive in the city as quickly as she could. She remounted the bicycle.

The rain became more of a problem, turning the road into a slippery rink and thwarting her efforts to pick up her pace. The wet air seemed to be full of grime from the metal works and factories producing bricks and tiles, she felt it on her skin. Falling off the bicycle or arriving soaked and frozen in the city would help nobody. She needed to find shelter until the weather eased. The landscape along the road was peppered with industrial plants and workers' accommodation, but occasionally a patch of countryside opened up into fields and farm buildings, a little window into the agricultural past.

Someone was running down the road in front of her – a small figure, a child. She skidded to a halt. He looked at the bag on her bicycle. 'Madame, are you the nurse?'

His face was pale.

'We've been trying to reach you for hours. My mother's really ill.' His face crumpled.

'A message?' Her blood went cold. But he couldn't possibly have known she was coming along this road.

'Come now.'

She followed him off a track leading towards a farm, with barns and outhouses. Five o'clock now. Smoke curled from the farmhouse chimney.

'You can put your bicycle there, it will stay dry.' He pointed at an old tarpaulin covering a stack of silage. She hid the bicycle under the tarpaulin and, taking her rucksack and midwife's bag, walked cautiously around the edge of the outhouses with the boy.

'She's here, Oncle Ernst!' the boy cried, grabbing her hand. 'Hurry up, madame.'

A German officer came out to meet them. Nowhere to run to, no way to avoid him. Sophie felt every muscle grow tense and her stomach churn. '*Gott sei dank*, we were giving up hope, nobody could find you. She needs you badly.'

THIRTEEN

Sophie did not often find words failing her. *Your tongue is never at a loss,* Bernhardt used to say, grinning.

She'd learned to hold that same tongue over the last years. Her brain ticked over as she followed the German officer and the small boy. Someone had been summoned to this house. Nurse? Midwife? Doctor? Might this person appear at any moment? Not if they hadn't been able to track them down. Was there even a telephone in the farmhouse? She looked around as they led her through and couldn't see one. The place looked run-down, if reasonably clean, the windows patched with news-paper, the tiles on the kitchen floor cracked. She could attend to whatever was happening here, forget about sheltering for the night and hasten on to another refuge.

'She's up here,' the German said, taking her up a worn wooden staircase. They passed a room in which a pair of uniform boots stood upright by a small desk, a cap on top of them. So, he was the lodger.

The woman, in her mid-twenties, lay on the bed, two bolsters propping her up and a towel underneath her, which was fast turning crimson. Early miscarriage? She wasn't showing yet, so was probably less than twelve weeks. At the sight of the woman, Sophie found herself switching mode. This was her sphere, this was what she did. 'What's your name?' she asked the woman gently.

'Marianne.'

'I must wash my hands,' Sophie told the German. 'Bring me a basin and soap, please.'

It felt good, even now, to issue instructions to an occupier. Man and boy disappeared. 'How many weeks, Marianne?' she asked, gently.

The woman looked down at her clenched hands. 'Twelve. Or so. Not sure.'

The German brought in a bowl of water and soap – a new cake, Sophie noted. It must have been his own as no civilian had seen a fresh bar for months and months. He'd found what looked like a clean towel. Some of the anxiety had left his face. 'The three of us were all unwell, fever, sore throats, sore limbs,' he said. 'But it didn't seem serious.'

She washed her hands, up to the elbows, the water turning grey and put on gloves and apron. Sophie took Marianne's wrist and checked her pulse against the second hand of her wrist watch. Raised. She put a hand to her brow. Feverish. 'I'll examine you properly now,' she told the woman. 'Leave us please,' she added to the German, who nodded obligingly.

'Marianne, I'm going to feel your abdomen.' Marianne had already removed her underwear, probably because it was soaked with blood, now rolled up on the wooden floor. Gently, Sophie's hands ran over her lower pelvis, which was slightly rounded. Hard to tell what was happening. 'Have you passed anything other than blood?'

'No. Can't you listen for a heartbeat?'

'It's probably too early in the pregnancy.'

'Please.' Marianne sat up straighter. 'I just have to know.'

It would do her no harm, so Sophie nodded, removing the

Pinard horn from her bag. 'This will feel cold,' she warned Marianne.

She placed the end of the horn onto Marianne's pelvis and listened, moving it around. Nothing. But she'd never expected there would be. Marianne watched her, expressionless.

'That's your son out there?' Sophie asked, helping her to sit up against the bolsters.

Marianne smiled. 'My *beau-fils*. Luc's mother was my husband's first wife. She died soon after he was born. He's a good boy.'

'Where's your husband?' Sophie asked gently.

'He died, too. Before Christmas.' Sophie had no need to make the calculations. Marianne touched her shoulder, face tense.

'I have sinned, I know. But I haven't done anything truly wicked, madame. I was tempted. I was scared, but I would not do... that.' Vichy France regarded termination as an abhorrence, so Marianne was understandably scared of being accused of doing this to herself deliberately.

Sophie placed her hand on the younger woman's. 'Miscarriage for natural reasons is not uncommon. Who knows about the pregnancy?'

'Not a soul. I didn't want Ernst to go to the neighbours for help. Or the doctor or the local nurse. He left messages, but he didn't think they'd pass them on.' She swallowed. 'Because he's a Boche.'

'You aren't German, though? Would your neighbours not wish to help you?'

'They wouldn't think like that. Anyway, I thought I'd be fine at first. But then you came.'

'You must forget you saw me.' Sophie said it almost coldly. 'I never met you.' So much for her plan to slip into Lyon without drawing attention to herself – she was leaving a trail behind her.

The truck-driver's wife. Now the German and Marianne and the little boy.

'Oh.' Marianne gave a gasp. 'Something's... happening.' From her bag Sophie quickly removed an enamel bowl, which she placed between Marianne's legs.

Just in time. Marianne groaned. Sophie tilted the bowl to catch most of the tissue, which appeared to be that of a roughly ten-week pregnancy.

'There are some old sheets in the chest,' Marianne said faintly. 'We can cut them up and wrap it up in them.'

She sounded neutral, almost relieved. Sophie found the sheet and took out her scissors from the bag. She examined the foetus again, beside the oil lamp on the dresser. Leaving any tissues inside the woman could lead to infection, if there wasn't already one. She waited, massaging Marianne's pelvis again for a few minutes to be sure. 'That's everything now,' she said. 'You were very brave. It hurt, I know.'

'Nothing more than I deserve.'

'No woman deserves pain.'

Marianne's pulse, when she checked it, had dropped. Her blood pressure was good. Still a touch of fever, but it would take longer for the temperature to drop. 'How long have you been ill?' she asked.

'Luc was poorly last week. Ernst and I started to feel bad two days later.'

'Probably the sickness caused this.' She looked at Marianne. 'Nature has been kind, perhaps?'

Marianne let out a sigh. 'I care for Ernst. But I couldn't have his baby. The locals would punish me for it.'

Sophie helped Marianne sit up and changed the towel underneath her for a clean one, threadbare and faded before finding fresh undergarments in her chest of drawers. Sophie helped her with them before taking out the aspirin bottle. She poured a glass of water and handed one to Marianne. 'Do

nothing around the farm tonight or tomorrow,' she warned.
'Stay in bed. Do you have help?'

'Ernst is off duty today and tomorrow morning. He'll put
the chickens in and milk the cow. There's not much left on the
farm now. The Germans took most of it.'

Sophie looked out of the window. The rain had stopped. It
had cleared some of the greyness from the air. She could
continue her journey, perhaps find a hotel on the outskirts of
Lyon, knock on Camille's door in the morning. She could still
escape, but leaving Marianne like this? The bleeding might
return or the fever persist. Every professional cell in her body
told Sophie that she could not entrust Marianne to a young
member of the occupying army and a small boy. She didn't like
to leave any woman, any patient, alone like this. But Camille...
She felt a near-pain in her heart at the thought of a delay.

'I will need to stay here tonight,' Sophie found herself
saying. 'To keep an eye on you.' Spending a night in a house
with a German? Suppose he questioned her about who she was,
where she lived, why she was going to Lyon? Would her identity hold up?

She gave herself a shake. The three adults were one another's insurance. Each would want tonight's events to go unnoticed by anyone else. She prayed whoever it was that Ernst had
tried to rouse to help Marianne had never got the message and
wouldn't appear at the farm tonight. But the little boy...

'Luc'll hold his tongue,' Marianne said, seeming to guess at
what was going on in Sophie's head. 'I was so lonely when his
father died,' she went on. 'I wanted to go back to the factory. It's
what I did before I married. But we had this place to run. I
missed my husband so much, madame. It's only been a few
times that Ernst and I...' She bowed her head.

A few times was all it took, sometimes just the once. How
often had Sophie heard the same sad old story from a tearful
girl? All she could offer was a kind ear and a promise to make

the pregnancy as physically easy as possible. Vichy France forbade midwives from mentioning family planning techniques, even to married women whose bodies were crumbling as a result of multiple pregnancies, even if it might kill them to have another baby. All the state would offer Marianne was scorn and harshness for sleeping with one of the occupiers.

Sophie picked up the basin and the bloodied sheet. 'We'll need to burn these.'

'The stove should still be lit in the kitchen,' Marianne said. 'If it's gone out, Luc knows how to get it going again.'

'Best to keep him away from... this.'

Marianne nodded, looking suddenly weary. Of course, she did: she'd had both an infection and a miscarriage. 'When did you last eat?' Sophie asked. 'What can I bring you?'

'There's cold rabbit on a plate. Bread. Milk, in the jug.'

Sophie found the stove still alight. She riddled it and topped it up with the coal in the scuttle, allowing it to burn fiercely before she placed the bundle and contents of the enamel bowl into it. Let everything be reduced to ashes. If Marianne was lucky, she could recover quickly and quietly without anyone else ever knowing about the forbidden relationship and the pregnancy.

'You were lucky,' she told Marianne, returning with a tray. 'But your lodger needs to move on.'

'He has been kind. He helps us.'

In place of Ernst, Marianne might find someone else billeted on her who was harsher, not so good with Luc. But it would stop the rumours. Almost certainly locals had noticed the young German with the gentle way and pondered how he might be getting along with the recently widowed young woman.

Outside, Ernst and Luc were walking out towards the farm-yard. Perhaps to put the chickens in. The boy chatted away to the man. The lad would miss this male companion who'd perhaps made the absence of his father more bearable. Sophie pulled the shutters closed, feeling inside her the familiar despairing pang. This Occupation turned anything that might be bearable – kindly – into something tawdry. She wondered whether Marianne would tell Ernst to leave or whether she'd cling on to him, to hell with the risks. When the war ended it would be the Mariannes who were blamed and punished: vulnerable, lonely girls who'd taken comfort from an amiable soldier in the wrong uniform.

Sometimes, life made Sophie so furious that she had to take slow, deep breaths, just to stop herself from yelling out. *Calm yourself*, Bernhardt said in her head. *Keep your wits about you.*

FOURTEEN

The little boy, Luc, showed her into a room at the back of the house, simply furnished with a battered iron-framed bed made up in frayed, yellowing sheets and old blankets. He came back with a bowl of warm water for her to wash with. Sophie sat on the edge of the bed and took her notebook out of the bag. As always, she would write up the case. As was often the case there would be no names, no addresses. Once her notes were complete, she shook up the stained and lumpy bolster and hoped she wouldn't be bitten by anything living in the bed. Nina and Sophie sometimes fantasised about what they'd tell a fairy godmother who promised them each one luxury. Nina always chose a bed made up with crisp linen sheets and pillow-cases, topped with cashmere blankets and silk quilts. She'd made a good choice.

'You must eat, madame,' Marianne called from her bedroom. 'Ernst will serve you something.'

The thought of sitting down at the kitchen table with a German made Sophie feel almost dizzy, but when she went down, Ernst merely nodded at the table, muttering about seeing to the chickens. He'd provided a generous plate of the rabbit

leftovers, a hunk of cheese and a not-too-withered apple. Luc
ate with her, watching her with large, solemn eyes. She stood up
and made to wash the plates, but the boy shook his head.
'Maman told me to do that.'

The old farmhouse creaked around her as it settled for the
night. Sophie found herself making the best of the situation.
She'd leave at dawn. The night's delay had probably made no
difference to Camille. Staying here was probably safer than
staying in a hotel where the Gestapo might burst in.

Ernst's feet pounded the stairs and passed along the
corridor towards the back of the house. He wasn't going into
Marianne's room tonight. Good.

Sophie woke just before dawn to the crowing of a cockerel, and
half longed to creep out of the house in the dark, without seeing
any of the other three. Her professional inner voice told her she
had to examine Marianne again and take her temperature.

When she went downstairs, Marianne was already in the
kitchen, poking at the stove embers to get it going again. The
young woman looked brighter this morning. She insisted on
making Sophie coffee, the real version, taking out a small
package from a cupboard. Ernst again, probably. Sophie drank
it, half relishing every drop, half longing to be on her way before
this situation could detain her any longer. She asked Marianne
to go upstairs for another examination. The bleeding had
slowed. Marianne's pelvis was less tender and her temperature
was normal.

'No heavy work on the farm,' Sophie warned her again,
knowing she was asking for the impossible. 'Rest.' She pulled
out her notebook and added to her notes. Catching sight of
Marianne's concerned face, she reassured her. 'No names. No
addresses.'

'What good is writing it all down then?'

It was a good question. 'Each time I'm with a woman, I learn something new and that might help the next woman I see.'

'I hope I help someone.' Marianne said it very quietly. 'Before the Germans came, I wasn't wicked.'

'You weren't wicked, you were human. But you'll be foolish if you don't ask him to leave now before anyone gets wind of this.'

Leaving Luc and Ernst still sleeping, they crept downstairs again and out of the door into the farmyard. Sophie removed her bicycle from underneath the tarpaulin. 'I can't pay you.' Marianne flushed.

It had been some time since actual money had been handed to Sophie. 'You don't need to pay me.'

'It feels wrong.'

'Perhaps one day someone will come to the door and need your help, Marianne.'

Marianne nodded, looking solemn and murmuring *merci* as Sophie cycled off. Did she know how vulnerable she was? People judged women harshly. Sophie shivered in the morning air, thinking of Camille, respectably married, bourgeois. Would she too be judged one day for marrying into a family who'd made such a success of the German occupation?

Sophie felt the city growing closer now, the traffic building up as trucks loaded with food, livestock and raw materials passed her. She wondered how much of the food would find its way to Lyon's markets and shops and how much loaded onto trains heading to Germany. In the town of Givors, the road met the main route heading north towards Lyon from Valence and Avignon in the south and crossed the Rhône. Sophie was heading due north now.

A kilometre or so out of Givors, the traffic slowed and stopped in front of her. Yet another German checkpoint. She cursed under her breath. In front of her, a delivery of chickens was inspected, each crate removed from the truck and examined by the guards. Two of the crates were taken aside, the driver waved back into his cab to carry on his way.

Perhaps helping themselves to the chickens sated the curiosity of the soldiers. They nodded Sophie through with barely a glance.

Spring was a real presence in this part of the Rhône valley. Now she was through the roadblock and further away from Marianne and Ernst, Sophie couldn't help but feel the warm air and breeze from the river lift her spirits. She'd always responded strongly to the changing of the seasons. 'There's something of the primitive in you, my love,' Bernhardt had told her as she rushed to throw open windows and shutters on the first sunny morning of the year or to throw on a warm coat on the first autumnal day. 'You embrace the new season, each change, with such greed.'

Was that still true of her? Not all changes were welcome. Most of the ones coming her way in the last three years had been sad, unpleasant or frightening. And Bernhardt was no longer here to guide her through them. *'You allowed yourself to be pulled into that situation at the farm,'* his voice told her now, sounding sorrowful.

'I had to help. I'm obliged to use my professional skills where they are needed.'

'That German soldier at the farm now knows you're a midwife. He seemed reasonable, but you can't be sure he won't talk to someone about you.'

But there must be plenty of midwives in the area. Nobody would connect her to the midwife who'd fled from the town of Annemasse, miles and miles away on the Swiss border last summer, would they?

Inside her head her husband's voice went quiet.

The traffic slowed. Another roadblock. But the delay wasn't caused by identity checks. The soldiers were clustered around something on the ground.

Sophie wove her way through the stationary vehicles to the front.

A young private was having a fit, lying on the ground, legs and arms spasming.

The corporal kneeling beside him turned round and frowned at Sophie. 'You. Is that a medical bag?'

'I'm a nurse.'

'What are you waiting for?'

She propped the bicycle up and took her bag out of the basket.

'Hurry up.'

She knelt down on the tarmac, checked the young man. Sometimes, people liked to stick things into mouths to stop those fitting biting their tongues. She'd never been convinced by this. 'Give me something to put under his head,' she said, forgetting to sound anything other than authoritative. The corporal stared at her. 'We don't want him to injure it.'

Reluctantly, he shouted at another young soldier to remove his jacket. Sophie folded it and placed it under the soldier's head and loosened his collar. 'Has he had fits before?' Emotions jostled inside her: anger at being ordered to treat this man, professional concern, and something else – dismay that a boy this age was here on this checkpoint in the first place.

'In the barracks, last week, sir.' One of the soldier's comrades proffered the information, looking nervous. Sophie kept her eyes on the fitting man. At least he wasn't wetting himself in front of his fellow soldiers.

His limbs stopped thrashing and his breath came in rhythmic pants. 'Get him up,' the corporal barked.

'He needs a moment more.' She'd spoken instinctively, with her usual authority. The corporal scowled at her. Once again, she'd brought attention to herself, but what else could she do when someone needed treatment?

'I want him out of the way.' The corporal nodded at two soldiers. 'You two, pull him to the side.' Sophie bit her lip.

'Gently,' she told them, following them. 'It'll take him some time to recover.'

They propped him up against a tree trunk. The young man blinked, looking up at her. 'You had a fit,' she told him in German, immediately wanting to take the words back. She was travelling as Mireille, not Sophie, as far as the Germans were concerned. Why would Mireille speak German? The other soldiers didn't seem to have heard. 'You'll be fine now,' she carried on, in French, rolling him onto his side. 'Don't try to stand up just yet.'

She turned to the other two. 'Make sure a doctor sees him. He probably won't remember anything about this.'

The soldier was rubbing his head, putting a hand to his lips. 'If your mouth is sore, saltwater is the best thing,' she told him.

'Do what she says,' the corporal snapped at the soldiers. 'You, what's your name?'

'Mireille Leclerc.' She felt herself go cold.

'Wait here until we're sure you're not needed.' He stood aside.

Just what she wanted, to linger in sight of a group of German soldiers, giving them more opportunity to note her unusual hair and height. She'd filled her water bottle at the farmhouse and pulled it out of her rucksack now. Might as well take a drink while she waited for them to let her through. Her hands shook as she took the top off. She found a chunk of sausage, wrapped in paper in the rucksack. Marianne must have slipped it in when she wasn't looking. Presumably the sausage was one of Ernst's household contributions. She pulled a chunk off, but her stomach was lurching and she had to force herself to swallow it. Sophie felt eyes on her. Looking up, she met the gaze of a small boy sitting on a wagon next to an elderly man. She pulled a bigger chunk of sausage off, beckoning him over. He jumped down, mumbling a thank you and the elderly man tipped his beret at her. There were still moments when people were kind, civil, to one another. Her need to get to Camille was burning through her, but she must stay calm.

Her German patient was trying to make eye contact with her, nodding a thanks. She gave him the briefest nod and turned her back.

The corporal beckoned her through the checkpoint impatiently. He switched his attention to the bus behind her and waved it through as well, before turning to the man and the boy on the wagon, shouting at them to get down and remove the empty crates from the back.

'Madame?' A woman's voice made her turn around. A nun, standing in the door of the bus. 'You're going to Lyon?'

She nodded.

'Bring your bicycle onto the bus.'

'I don't mind cycling, sister.'

'You'll be less noticeable in a crowd.'

But less able to jump off the road and hide from patrols?

Sophie realised she was still shaking. She nodded. The bicycle seemed very heavy. A younger woman helped her lift it up, shrugging when Sophie apologised for taking up space. The passengers clasped rucksacks and duffle bags to themselves. On the floor of the bus, boxes were crammed in underneath seats. Food-hunters, Sophie thought. Returning to the city with whatever they'd found in the country. Many of the bags and boxes would be empty but for a few dried mushrooms and chestnuts.

'Quick,' the nun said.

Sophie sat down beside her.

The bus groaned back into life and edged forward.

'Whereabouts in Lyon are you travelling to?' the nun asked.

'Croix-Rousse.' If only she could warn the nun not to talk to her, not to pay her too much attention, not to place herself in danger by associating with her. The habit this nun wore was identical to those other nuns she knew, those endangered by what had happened at Annemasse.

As they picked up speed, putting a few kilometres between them and the roadblock, motorcycles and a black car screeched past them, going in the opposite direction.

'They're very twitchy today,' the nun said, in a low voice. 'I hear rumours of possible reprisals for a shooting near here last night.'

'I helped the soldier. They won't be interested in me.' But she remembered how she'd spoken to the young soldier in German, making her more memorable.

'And I watched you as you gave your name to his superior, madame, and then when you stood up again. Your shoulders and back were tense. You spilled your water.'

If the nun had noticed, others might have done, too.

'Nobody likes giving their name to the Germans. Or waiting at roadblocks.' She said it as casually as she could.

'A single woman of striking appearance on a bicycle is more noticeable than she is sitting on a full bus,' the nun went on.

'Perhaps.'

'When we get off the bus, you might like to come with me to the convent, madame.' She smiled. 'Your face is very dusty, my dear, and I fear your clothes have dirt on them.'

Sophie glanced down at her jacket, smeared with oily dirt. Her hair would be falling out of its pins, too.

Her heart sank. She'd tried so hard to wear an outfit that wouldn't shame Camille. The evening at the farmhouse and now this... both events had conspired to make her turn up on Camille's doorstep looking disreputable.

'I can't come to the convent.' Sophie looked the nun directly in the eye.

'Why is that?'

'I'm known in Lyon.' She'd dropped her voice. 'It isn't safe for you.'

'The convent has many entrances. And exits.'

A few minutes to clean herself up? If she was recognised going back there, those whose warm water and soap she was borrowing would be at risk, but the thought of being somewhere inside, hidden, for even half an hour was enticing. And the convent up by the basilica wasn't too far out of her way. But was she bringing danger to the nuns?

'I can also offer you bread and soup.'

When Sophie was still silent, the nun put her hand on her arm. 'You are anxious, but you needn't be on our behalf.' Her eyes were kind but shrewd.

Lyon absorbed them. The city felt different. It had only been nine months since she'd last been here, even though the basilica on the hill still stood proud and white. More sullenness in the faces of the pedestrians? Clothes even drabber than they had been last year? Through the open windows of the bus, the aroma of drains and the exhaust spewed by gas-burning cars drifted in.

'This is our stop,' the nun said. Sophie realised she hadn't paid for her bus fare. A detail like that could make the driver remember you. She reached into her pocket and found a coin as she took her bicycle off the bus. He shook his head as she offered it.

'Before you helped that private, they were about to tear the bus to pieces looking for something or someone.'

Others didn't share the driver's logic. As she lowered her bicycle down onto the road, a female passenger came behind and whispered a few words. Something landed on Sophie's neck, moist and warm. Spittle.

'Boche-helper, *sale conne.*'

Sophie turned around to glare at her.

'We fight each other as much as the occupier,' the nun said, sighing, as they walked away. 'I am Sister—' Sophie raised a hand.

'Please, no names.' She tried to soften the reply with a smile.

The nun's eyes were shrewd, understanding. She was younger than Sophie had thought at first, her skin still clear and supple. 'Not far to go.' They walked down a street of respectable houses and apartments. Sophie didn't know this southern suburb well. A modest presbytery stood next to a nine-teenth-century church.

'The priest will still be saying mass,' the nun said. 'Wait a moment for me to collect my bicycle.'

Sophie waited, looking around, noting pedestrians, vehicles, just in case anyone was following them. The nun appeared with a black bicycle, complete with chain guard to protect her habit. 'Our clothing wasn't designed for cycling.' She mounted the bicycle with grace. 'When I have further to go, as I did this morning, I use the bus.'

Sophie got onto her own bicycle, noticing the blackened knees of her stockings and blushed. She should have followed her own instinct and made the journey bare-legged instead of trying to present herself as a respectable woman.

'You're working as a nurse in the city?' the nun asked.

'Just one case, with a complication.' Sophie and the nun were cycling side by side now.

'You're worried about drawing... attention to yourself.' It was said as a statement.

'You're helping me. I think you need me to do something in return, sister?' Was this what it had come to, always suspecting kindness to be transactional?

'I need someone medically trained to look at one of our patients. She's just given birth.'

Another detour. When all she wanted was to get to Camille, to hold her in her arms, to look her over, to use her hands gently on her daughter to see what was wrong. The nun was waiting. 'Before I explain what we need at the convent, why don't you tell me more. No names, no details.'

Sophie gave her a long look, meeting the shrewd gaze. 'The patient is my daughter. She's pregnant.'

'You're a midwife, too?'

Sophie felt her blood pulse through her veins. 'Yes. My son-in-law is the problem.' Briefly, without naming him, she explained Jean-Luc's position in Lyon's business community, his family's support for the Vichy regime. 'He's been a good husband to my daughter, but I don't want him asking questions, which he will naturally do when he meets me for the first time.'

'You want to be anonymous?' The nun slowed down at a junction, waiting for a convoy of German trucks carrying soldiers to drive past. 'You worry about him prising out of you details which may put others or yourself at risk? It is a fear we all have if we choose any kind of... opposition.' She met Sophie's stare with a steady gaze. Opposition. They both knew what that word meant and how dangerous it was. 'Now, let me tell you exactly why I need your help.'

FIFTEEN

The road grew narrower and busier. When they could cycle abreast again, the nun continued. 'As you'll perhaps know, we take in a small number of expectant mothers and occasional sick people who... can't always find medical help.'

While she'd still been in Lyon, Sophie had heard the pastor talk in veiled terms about the convent's small sanatorium and how it would take in patients nobody else would touch. At her one visit to the convent to meet Hélène, she'd been ushered into a small reception room and had seen nobody other than the girl herself. She felt herself slump over the bicycle handles at the thought of Hélène. Perhaps the sorrow and guilt would never leave her.

'There's a girl in our convent, a *tsigane*, a Romani.' She lowered her voice as she said the last word. 'She escaped from one of the camps. I'm ashamed to say she'd been rounded up some time ago by our own people before the Germans even marched in. She was emaciated and heavily pregnant and had her baby two days ago. Mother and child both seem well.'

Sophie looked at her, eyebrows raised, waiting.

'Our sisters are experienced, but I'm now the only one left

with nursing qualifications. I feel the lack of second opinions and guidance.'

'I'm sure your judgment is sound, sister.'

'I fear it isn't so.' She sounded almost ashamed. 'A woman we assisted in labour a few days ago developed an infection.' She faltered, looking suddenly less sure of herself. 'The doctor who looks in on us can sadly no longer help.'

He'd probably been arrested or scared into staying away from the convent. They came to another junction and stopped to let a horse-drawn wagon pass.

'Post-delivery infections can set in very suddenly. It's easy to miss them in a patient who's undernourished or suffering other conditions,' Sophie said.

'We had an autoclave steriliser, and we were very careful about hygiene. But that was obviously not enough.'

'The mother probably already had the infection before she went into labour.' She thought of Marta and prayed that Dr Meyer was watching her carefully up on the plateau. 'There were no complications during birth?'

'None. She's fully recovered, God be thanked. They've left us now. But I worry about this new young mother. She was so thin when she came to us.' The nun nodded at Sophie to cross over the junction and they pedalled on. 'I worry I might have missed something. Apart from the malnutrition, she must have been exposed to so much disease in that terrible camp. I'd be so grateful for a second opinion.' They'd turned towards the Rhône now. In a moment, they'd approach the bridge over to the Presqu'île, the near-island that sat on the confluence of the Rhône and Saône. From here, Fourvière lay across yet another bridge across the Saône, on the west side of Lyon.

'What will happen to her?'

'We'll keep them as long as we can. We might have to look into adoption for the baby then. It might be... safer for them both.'

Tsiganes, gypsies or nomads, as the government chose to call them, were still imprisoned in France. Some were also deported to God knows where. An infant would probably not survive either prospect.

'I'm a risk to you and those you help,' Sophie said, bluntly, braking. Part of her wanted to cycle off before they reached the convent, but the mention of a newly delivered mother in need of help had made it impossible. 'My identity papers are good, but not perfect. And they could recognise me from... something that went wrong some months ago. I've been to the convent before.'

'Last summer?'

Sophie nodded.

'Ah, yes.' A shadow passed over the other woman's face. 'That was a time of grave danger for us.'

'Did they...? The sisters who helped the children, were they picked up?' Other than Hélène, had more people been arrested as a result of what had happened at Annemasse? She'd asked the pastor, but he hadn't heard. Sophie felt nauseous.

'One was. The other, we managed to get out of Lyon.' She nodded at Sophie to push the bicycles up off the cobbled road. It was quiet and nobody was looking at them. Sophie felt herself needing to talk.

'What happened to the one who was arrested?'

The nun sighed. 'For a while, we had messages from her.'

'Was she the other trained nurse?'

A nod.

'You can blame me for her arrest.' Sophie's words came out harshly. 'I was with the party going over the Swiss border last summer. Hel—the other person involved wanted to abort. I said we should go on, even though we had lost valuable time.'

The nun looked unsurprised. Sophie wondered how long it had taken her to work out who she was. 'Our contacts on the border say it was all down to ill luck. A newly arrived

Gestapo officer throwing his weight around in the Italian zone.'

'I still feel guilty.'

'Yes, I do see a soul indulging itself in guilt. I wonder why you distract yourself like this?'

'Distract myself?'

'Oh, we all do it. The world, the war, the Occupation, it's all too much to comprehend. So we obsess about what would have happened if we'd done this or that. If I'd taken a closer look at the newly delivered woman who actually had an infection.'

Sophie found herself lacking words. She felt almost absolved, although she'd need a priest, not a nun, for that, and she wasn't even a believer. 'If anyone is watching and they see me going into the convent, you're in danger again.' She realised she'd agreed to help.

The nun nodded. 'I can bring you inside without a soul seeing you enter.'

Sophie looked at her quizzically.

'We opened up an old tunnel. It allows us to come and go without being noticed through the old passageways the Germans don't know about.' She put a hand on Sophie's. 'We shouldn't be lingering out on the street like this.'

To help a woman and a newborn was her professional duty. But Camille was waiting for her, wondering when her mother would appear, worrying that she wouldn't come at all, that she was too concerned for her own safety. Or that Sophie disapproved so much of her marriage that she couldn't bring herself to come. 'Sometimes I wonder when the sacrifices will end.' The nun sounded weary. Sophie looked at her properly: a woman in her early forties, with dark, thoughtful eyes, the faint lines around them suggesting humour, not anxiety, was her usual response to life.

'The sooner we go, the sooner I can be with my daughter,' Sophie said, keeping her eyes on the bridge.

SIXTEEN

Seemingly unnoticed by the soldiers, they crossed the Saône into Vieux Lyon, the old part of the city. A woman with a medical bag and a nun – perhaps they were invisible. They turned right sharply and pushed the bicycles through a passageway cutting away from the river into the next street. 'You know about the old tunnels, the *traboules*?' the nun asked.

'Just that centuries ago residents used them for fetching water and transporting their silk and other goods up and down the hill.' Bernhardt had been fascinated by the *traboules*.

'And for more nefarious purposes, I'm told. And now they have yet another use.' The nun's eyes glinted. 'Useful for throwing off eyes one doesn't wish to have on one.' They came out into the street again.

'The funicular is the quickest way up the hill,' the nun said. Sophie had used the funicular on happier occasions in the past with Bernhardt and felt a swift pang at the memory. 'My dear, we said no names, but I am Sister Marie-Claude.'

'Mireille Leclerc is what it says on my identity card.'

Sister Marie-Claude nodded. 'If the right people are on duty, they will let us bring the bicycles up on the funicular,

Madame Leclerc. Otherwise, we can leave them in an alleyway here to be collected.'

The right people were on duty and waved both women and bicycles onto the funicular, scowling at passengers who objected. No Germans. A uniformed man who was wearing a Milice beret. At the sight of Sister Marie-Claude, he turned his attention to his newspaper. The stone walls of the tunnel were covered with Vichy government posters, threatening and cajoling its citizens into family values, anti-Communism and regular baths, promising fulfilling jobs in Germany. At the top of the funicular, the uniformed man acted as a conductor, holding back the other passengers so the two of them could disembark first, and receiving a warm smile from the nun.

'The regime has brought in a remarkable respect for the Catholic church among a section of the population,' Sister Marie-Claude said when they were out of earshot. 'I exploit it to the full. I may be married to Our Lord, but if doing his work means I have to smile at some of his lesser male creatures, I do.'

'Even the Milice?'

'Sometimes. Much as I loathe what they stand for.'

Even wheeling her bicycle and wearing a heavy habit, she moved with grace and authority. At the top of the hill they walked away from the basilica, but not before Sophie glimpsed Lyon's red roofs glowing soft in the April afternoon light and the rivers sparkling beneath them. Tired, anxious and impatient as she was, her heart gave a flutter at the sight.

'We have our own version of a *traboule*,' her companion told her, propping her bicycle up against the wall and taking a key out of her habit pocket. She unlocked a gate that was barely noticeable in an unremarkable wall and beckoned Sophie through. A passageway led into a courtyard. At its far end, a second door was set in a stone frame. Marie-Claude produced a second key from her pocket and opened it. They bumped the bicycles down stone steps. Marie-Claude seemed to relax.

'Only a few of us know about this,' she said. 'It's not really a *traboule* as it's only about seventy years old. We only discovered it a few months ago. It takes us into a convent cellar without us needing to go through the main gates.'

Nobody could see her coming into the convent. They pushed the bicycles on for another minute or so.

'We're right underneath the drive, close to the main building. We'll come out behind it in a moment.'

Just as Sophie was convinced the passage would become so tight she wouldn't be able to push her bicycle through, a rectangle of light appeared in front of them. Sister Marie-Claude produced another, newer-looking key and opened the door. A single step brought them up into a room lined with shelves containing jars of preserved fruits and vegetables. 'We can leave the bicycles here.'

Sophie leant hers up against one of the shelves. She looked at her watch. Half-one. The day already seemed to have lasted an eternity. Had it only been this morning she'd woken at the farmhouse? She put a hand to her brow.

'You must be hungry.'

She hadn't actually eaten much today, Sophie realised, except for the sausage shared with the boy at the side of the road.

'Before we see the patient, I'm finding you something to eat.' She shook her head at Sophie's half-hearted refusal.

A couple of steps led to the ground floor of an outbuilding. They exited onto a courtyard leading to the main building. Sophie felt her feet slow. Was this really sensible, coming here again, even through the dark passageway? Suppose there was another raid on the convent while she was here? The Jewish children she'd helped into Switzerland certainly weren't the only group the convent had helped. Some of the children up on the plateau might well have passed through its doors, too. Religious institutions were still respected by the authorities, but respect only went so far where helping Jews was suspected. If the police or Germans thought there were fugitives here, they'd burst through the door to tear the place apart.

'You won't be here long, Madame Leclerc,' Sister Marie-Claude said, seeming to read her mind. 'You'll soon be on your way to your daughter.'

They passed through an open door into the main building, seeing nobody. In the kitchen, a young nun in a simpler habit was chopping carrots at the table. Asked to serve Sophie something to eat, she nodded silently, producing a bowl of soup and slice of bread. Sophie washed her hands and face in the sink while this was served.

The soup had shreds of what looked like chicken in it and the bread was fresh. She hoped she didn't seem too greedy as she scraped the bowl clean. The young nun poured her a glass of thin red wine, mixed with water.

Almost immediately she felt more like herself again.

Sister Marie-Claude was watching her. 'You were so pale and drawn as we pushed our bicycles into the tunnel. Now you look completely revived.'

'Food and rest always work miracles for me.' Feeling revived, she thanked the young nun for the meal and they walked out across a tiled floor to the sanatorium, now more of a miniature hospital, with curtained cubicles. Some of the curtains had been pulled back to reveal women, lying in bed or sitting quietly on the simple wooden chairs, some of them holding babies, some knitting, others reading tattered books. 'Mainly maternity cases, but some patients come to us where they are not acute enough for the hospital but have nowhere else to go.' She lowered her voice. 'Or where they are safer hiding out under the veil of infection.' Her eyes gave that glint. 'The fear of catching typhus can keep the Germans away. For now.'

'You have typhus here?'

Sister Marie-Claude's eyes widened and she looked as innocent as a newborn. 'How could I rule it out for certain? I'm not a doctor.'

'Are they all women?'

'We take in the occasional male, too.'

She took Sophie to a basin and gave her soap and a clean towel. 'I will find you an apron, too.' There was a small mirror. Sophie found her comb in a pocket and tidied her hair, taking out the pins and replacing them.

Feeling more professional in her apron Sophie accompanied her to a small side room leading off the main ward. 'Rosa, may we enter, child?' Marie-Claude asked.

A hand pulled back the curtain to reveal a girl of about seventeen, holding her baby in her arms. Her eyes, dark and wary, took in her visitors. 'I told you we were looking for a midwife to examine you and your baby,' Sister Marie-Claude said. 'This is Madame Leclerc.'

'There's nothing wrong with him.' Her voice was almost accentless, but suggested French wasn't her first language. Perhaps she was one of the Romani who'd found themselves rounded up by the French before the Germans had marched in. Or her family might have fled across the Pyrenees before the war started, escaping the civil conflict in Spain.

'He looks very lively,' Sophie said, smiling at the baby, who was trying to wriggle his legs free of the blanket. 'Have you named him?'

'Patrin.'

'What does that mean?'

'Leaf. My people lived among the trees. Before.' Her eyes flashed as she said the last word.

'Giving him that name is a fine way to connect your son with them,' Sophie said. 'May I?'

She held out her arms. After a moment, Rosa handed Patrin to her. Sister Marie-Claude took a folded muslin cloth from the

locker and placed it on the bed. Carefully, Sophie laid the baby
on the cloth and undressed him. He watched her with bright
eyes, moving his legs and arms. She examined his small body.
The umbilical cord had been cut correctly. His skin was a good
colour and his body was perfect. No question that the legs
kicking up and down had good muscle tone. She was about to
say as much when a squirt of liquid from the baby caught the
top of her apron.

She laughed and saw Rosa relax, too. 'If I had a franc for
every time a baby boy has done that to me, I'd be a wealthy
woman.' She replaced his napkin and clothes and handed the
infant to Marie-Claude. 'May I examine you quickly, too, Rosa?'
She took off the soiled apron and rolled it up.

Rosa's uncertainty had returned. She looked down at the
floor. 'I understand your people may have particular rules about
modesty. I just want to be sure that you're healed up and the
placenta has come away completely.' Rosa nodded and lay
down. Sister Marie-Claude pulled the curtain around the bed.
Rosa still looked as though she might spring up at any moment
as she removed her lower garments.

Sophie put on gloves, before asking her about her bleeding,
which had ceased. Gently, she examined the perineum, which
was untorn. She palpated Rosa's lower abdomen. 'Why are you
doing that?' the girl asked.

'I'm checking that your womb is going back to its pre-preg-
nancy size, and you're recovering properly.'

'Am I?'

'Indeed, you are.'

Finally, she checked Rosa's blood pressure and temperature.
'Everything's fine,' she told Rosa. 'You're much too thin, but I
can tell you've taken care of yourself.' The girl's skin was clear
of any infection and her hair was clean, tied back in a plait.

'You thought I'd be dirty because of who I am?' She glared
at Sophie.

'I mean you've managed better than most people when they lack basic sanitation. May I ask if you suffered any illnesses while you were in the camp?'

The girl's eyes flashed again. 'It would have been a miracle not to catch something. I had dysentery a few times. We tried to keep clean, but the water was contaminated, even when we boiled it.'

Sophie could imagine.

'I had some kind of infection in my throat, too.'

'We looked at Rosa's throat,' Sister Marie-Claude said. 'It's clear. No scarring. No neck glands up.'

'May I check the rest of your glands?'

'Where?' Rosa's eyes narrowed.

'Your head and neck, underarm, knee and groin areas.' After a moment's uncertainty, the girl nodded.

No abnormal swellings. She checked the insides of Rosa's eyes. 'I can't see anything that's cause for ongoing concern. Rosa. You're probably anaemic, but that's not surprising.' She turned to smile at Sister Marie-Claude, and the nun let out a long breath.

'*Merci beaucoup.* I just worried I might have missed something. I know iron deficiency is likely. It's a problem for so many of our mothers. But one of our benefactors has promised me a delivery of ox liver.'

'They look after me well here.' Rosa looked down at her shirt front and grimaced. 'I must feed Patrin again. The milk, it just comes and comes.'

'Rosa is blessed with a good supply,' Marie-Claude said.

'Patrin is a lucky boy,' Sophie said. 'No wonder he's doing so well.'

'Nobody can say I don't look after him. But they say I may have to give him up.' Rosa shot a look at the nun. 'If anyone will take a half-gypsy baby.' She sounded defiant, but Sophie noted the downward cast of her eyes.

Sophie wondered who the father was. A German soldier? A Frenchman, Jewish or Gentile, imprisoned in the same camp?

'Patrin is very beautiful,' she said, trying to rebuild trust with the girl.

'Rosa was starved when she came here,' Marie-Claude said. 'But her constitution is robust. Your family fed you well, Rosa, I think, when you were a child yourself?'

'My mother never let us go to bed without full stomachs.'

'Tell madame how long you were in the internment camp.'

'Two years.'

Even now, at this stage in the war, Sophie could be shocked – a young girl like this, locked up like a criminal for so long.

'My younger brother and sister both died in the camp when we got dysentery. My mother's still there. Unless they've shipped her out somewhere even worse.' Rosa looked as though she wanted to spit on the clean linoleum floor. 'My mother bribed a guard to get me out. I didn't want to leave her there. She said she'd go mad if I was locked up for longer. Can I go now, please?' she asked, suddenly looking smaller and wilder. The nun took her hand and stroked it.

'Where would you go, child, with such a small baby? The city is not safe.'

'It's spring. I can get out of Lyon, find some of my people hiding out in the forests. They'll look after me.'

France was blessed with deep forests where people could disappear. But food – there was always the food issue. Everyone was desperate for it now. Hunters went into the forests more deeply, more ruthlessly in pursuit of game. If they, or the Milice, came across a girl like Rosa, Sophie shuddered to think what might happen. Many French people didn't like the *tsiganes*. The Germans hadn't created dislike – it had existed in some communities here for generations.

'Things have changed,' Sophie said, trying to make her voice gentle. 'I live up in the wilds of the Cévennes. Food is short. Conditions are harsh.'

'The Germans don't know that area like we do. And there are Resistance groups out there now.'

'And Milice, roaming the hills, shooting anyone they don't like the look of.'

'I can hide myself and Patrin.' Her chin jutted up.

'How would you feed him, once he's bigger?' Sophie asked, as gently as she could. 'Even trapping a rabbit is a rare thing these days.' She'd seen the men in her village coming back from the traps with empty sacks, shoulders slumped, knowing they'd face hungry children.

'We always need help here,' Sister Marie-Claude said. 'In the sanatorium and kitchens, out in the grounds. In summer we grow much of the food we need. And you'd have your baby here with you, Rosa. Things may become easier—'

'You don't know when the Germans will go, sister, nobody does.' She spoke with a flat defiance.

Rosa reminded Sophie of Camille, usually a biddable child but occasionally capable of stubbornness. If you gave her time to think it over, Camille would usually come round to wearing a woollen hat and scarf on a morning the frost lay hard on the ground.

She stood up. 'For Patrin's sake, stay here for a few more weeks and eat your liver, Rosa. Wait until you're both through the most vulnerable stages before you move on.'

'Is this iron thing what made me tired sometimes when I was carrying Patrin?'

'Yes. Lack of iron means your red blood cells dropped, that's anaemia. They couldn't transport as much oxygen round your body to give you energy.'

Rosa considered the information with interest.

Sophie looked at Sister Marie-Claude. 'And now I must go.'

The longing for Camille was so powerful now she could almost feel it pulsing through the stone walls of the sanatorium.

Sister Marie-Claude handed the baby back to Rosa. 'Asleep, bless his soul. You should rest yourself while you can.'

'I don't need rest, sister. Let me do the sterilising?'

Romani kept their caravans pristine, Sophie knew, from her visits to a camp in the Netherlands years ago where she'd provided basic antenatal care to women.

Sister Marie-Claude gave a long sigh. 'Sadly, we've lost the steam steriliser, the autoclave.'

Sophie looked at her, puzzled.

'In my absence it had to be given to... someone.' She looked down at the floor. 'The man who serviced our plumbing threatened to report us to the authorities.'

The plumber Hélène had mentioned last summer. He'd probably sold the steriliser on the black market to some clinic where they didn't ask questions. Sophie felt a chill. People knew about this convent, about the secrets it held, about the children hidden here until they could be moved out of Lyon. Secrets could be used to blackmail.

'I'll boil the instruments then,' Rosa said. 'For thirty minutes.' She sounded proud of her knowledge. She placed her baby gently in the bassinet. 'Thank you, Madame Leclerc.' She spoke gruffly.

Sophie nodded. 'I'll visit you again soon.' It would surely be possible for her to sneak back to the convent sanatorium at some stage as discreetly as she had entered today. Even so, the thought of returning made her feel cold.

Sister Marie-Claude led her out of the ward, past the cubicles with mothers and babies. 'The war goes on, but still the babies come,' Marie-Claude said. 'It makes us happy to see, although finding food for labouring and nursing mothers is a constant worry.'

She stopped at the doorway to the outhouse, holding

Sophie's arm. 'I can perhaps make entry into your daughter's home easier?'

Sophie looked at her.

'Let me come with you. A visit from a midwife accompanied by a religious sister is the most respectable thing in the world.'

'But you have so much work?'

'We work for women and their children. Visiting your daughter counts. And you have helped us. You're clearly very experienced and well qualified.'

Sophie thought again about Dr Meyer up on the Plateau. 'I accompany a doctor on his rounds. He's taught me so much about infection and disease... before.' A pang for Erich Meyer's calm watchfulness hit her, the reassurance of him standing close by her shoulder. The pang was replaced by guilt, remembering Bernhardt.

They returned through the tunnel. When they emerged into daylight, they bumped gently down the cobbled streets on the bicycles, towards the Saône. Sophie had never visited Camille's house but knew exactly where it was.

Mid-afternoon now, the streets busier after the lunchtime break, the people of Lyon going about their business, paler-faced, heads more bowed than Sophie remembered. The Germans were even more of a presence now, their flags hanging on civic buildings, their uniforms crowding the street. As she cycled behind Sister Marie-Claude, she felt herself tighten up inside, hoping her fear didn't show. They crossed the Saône to the neighbourhood of La Croix-Rousse.

A maze of smaller streets led them onto the boulevard and to the five-storeyed house with well-maintained pale-rose walls and stucco and wrought-iron balustrades. It stood proudly but not ostentatiously on the boulevard, quietly proclaiming its family wealth and status. This was her daughter's home now.

Sophie's heart was going to burst out of her chest.

SEVENTEEN

CAMILLE

Camille laid out the garments she'd stitched for her baby on a sheet on the nursery floor. She'd knitted cardigans and matinee jackets, too. She'd never been as good at knitting as sewing. Every stitch had cost her much in patience. Please God, let this be sufficient for the baby. Thank goodness for Vivienne's loan of baby clothes. She'd hoped there'd be a chance to get to know her sister-in-law, but there always seemed reasons why they couldn't invite her and her husband to dinner or Sunday lunch. And anyway, it would have meant spending more time with Vivienne's husband. Camille knew she'd disagree with his politics. He worked closely with the occupiers. Even Véronique didn't talk much about him now.

There was hardly anything new to buy in the shops these days. She'd asked Jean-Luc if any of the silks from the factory would be suitable for baby clothes and he'd laughed. They were furnishing fabrics, he'd told her, ruffling the front of her hair, not finely enough woven for infants' garments. And not easy to wash. She'd flushed, feeling silly.

'But I'll look at the lining fabrics, good idea,' he said. 'We never produced them ourselves, but we bought in a few rolls to make up curtains to show commercial customers. There may be some finer cottons tucked away in a back office out of sight of any visiting Germans.'

He was more openly critical of the Germans, she noticed. Mainly because their demand for French workers meant that some of Jean-Luc's workers had fled the city, probably hiding out in the hills with the Resistance. Still, she thought that sometimes he wanted to tell her more. Maybe he worried about making her even more anxious. Pregnancy certainly was making her cautious, inward-looking. She wasn't much of a support to her husband.

Camille folded the baby clothes carefully and placed them in the drawers she'd lined with lavender-scented paper. Once again, she counted the towelling napkins she'd bought. A large perambulator sat downstairs, ready for its trips outside. To the courtyard garden first, and then further afield. Vivienne had lent them the pram because even Jean-Luc with all his business connections couldn't find a new baby carriage. Perhaps all the perambulators in France were heading for Germany. When they'd been in New York years ago, Maman had once taken her on a trip to a reservation upstate, where she'd seen women carrying swaddled babies on cradleboards on their backs. Maman had thought this completely practical and natural. Camille almost laughed aloud at the thought of her mother-in-law's face witnessing Camille walking up and down the boulevards of Lyon with an infant strapped to her back.

Véronique was at home for lunch today, her friends having all inconsiderately conspired to be otherwise occupied. Food restrictions were simply making it too awkward for people to continue their social lives in the old way. Vouchers, rations, general shortages: it wasn't worth it. Camille hadn't seen any of her own friends for weeks now. Laure sent letters, but her great-aunt in the country kept her busy and she didn't plan to return to Lyon anytime soon.

A wave of loneliness and longing for her friend washed over Camille. She hadn't imagined she'd be approaching the birth of her first child feeling so isolated, even in the middle of a large city. She'd feel so much better if she could sit in a café with Laure and laugh over something trivial: a German soldier with a face like a pug, or a gas-fuelled car that made rude explosive noises. Camille stood up and walked to the window, grimacing as a grinding sensation worked its way around her pelvis. When would her mother get here? Half of her still regretted her note. It had been a mistake and would bring danger to Sophie. But Sophie was shrewd: she wouldn't just march up to the front door and—

Camille blinked. Coming up to the entrance was a nun pushing a bicycle. Behind the nun was her mother, also wheeling a cycle, her midwife's bag visible in the basket. This couldn't be real, she must be imagining it. She wanted to run downstairs and open the door before Jeanne could reach it and warn Maman that Véronique was at home. Maman was glancing up at the windows, as though aware of Camille. She smiled, the calm professional visiting a client. The nun motioned to her to leave the bicycles propped up in the passageway between the house and its neighbour; just as well or else Véronique would be complaining about lowering the tone.

They were to play the roles of midwife and first-time mother? Walking into the bedroom she shared with Jean-Luc, Camille applied lipstick to her mouth and tidied her hair.

The doorbell rang. Jeanne's heels clattered across the parquet to open the door. '...expecting us earlier... apologise... brought the midwife for madame as I promised.'

Camille descended, one hand on the banister, a slight smile fixed to her face, feeling as though she was on stage. She greeted the nun politely, trying not to look at her mother, trying to think.

'Bonjour, madame, I am Madame Leclerc.' Maman

extended a hand. Camille took it, feeling the familiar warm strength.

'I needn't detain you further,' Sister Marie-Claude, as she'd introduced herself, said. 'As I made the recommendation, I thought I should present Madame Leclerc myself.'

'I'm grateful for you taking the trouble, sister.' Camille's heart was pumping, her voice coming out as a squeak. She hadn't seen her mother since the previous summer and now she was here, in the house, and she couldn't do more than politely shake her proffered hand. She wanted to cling on to it but let go. 'May I offer you a tisane before you leave?'

Sister Marie-Claude shook her head. 'I must go. Madame Leclerc may return to the convent at any time whenever she isn't needed.' She looked at Camille with an unblinking gaze and slight smile, as though urging her to be calm.

'Shall I show Madame Leclerc upstairs, Madame Camille?' Jeanne asked. 'Forgive me, I didn't know you were expected to be in residence this week, madame. The room is ready, but I haven't opened the shutters to air it.'

Maman smiled disarmingly. 'My last lady delivered ahead of her due date. In view of the discomfort madame has suffered, it seemed prudent to come straight here.'

'Very unusual.' They all turned. Véronique stood in the door to the salon. 'A *sage-femme* living in the house for weeks until your confinement, Camille?'

'I must do what I feel is best for the baby.' Camille spoke with more authority than she normally used with Véronique. 'Jean-Luc will be happy I have found someone to help me. I would like you to stay here tonight, Madame Leclerc. Possibly longer, depending on how I feel.' She still couldn't look her mother in the eye. Her face would give her away.

Véronique huffed. 'Neither Martine nor Vivienne thought this kind of arrangement necessary. And you have your doctor's appointments, Camille.'

'That so-called specialist tells me there is something wrong but doesn't seem to have a clue how he can help me. Last time he couldn't even find a glass tube at the clinic to test my urine.'

Véronique looked aghast at the last word.

'Shall I examine you now, madame?' Maman asked gently. 'We can let Sister Marie-Claude return to the convent, non?'

'Of course.' Camille extended a hand towards the staircase. 'Thank you for helping—' – she'd been about to say 'Maman' – 'Madame Leclerc find me, sister.'

Sister Marie-Claude nodded a polite farewell.

Camille led her mother upstairs, keeping her back as straight as she could with her sore pelvis and stiff back, knowing Véronique would be watching her, scowling. They went into the bedroom Camille had just left.

Camille closed the door. Her arms were round her mother's neck a second later, as though she was a little girl again. She felt safe. At last.

'It's hard to get too close because of the bump,' Maman said, releasing herself to kiss Camille on the forehead, just as she had when Camille had been a small child and she'd returned from a day at work. She smelled vaguely herbal as she always had, probably from washing her hair in some concoction made from plants. She stood back, looking Camille over, eyes sharp and gentle, both at the same time.

'It feels as if the baby enters the room five minutes before I do.' She felt herself smiling, weeping, both at the same time. 'I think I'm having an elephant.'

'I came as quickly as I could, *liefje*.' Maman grimaced, seeming to realize she shouldn't use the old Dutch endearment.

'I'm sorry. I know it's so dangerous for you. I don't know what I was thinking, writing to you.' Camille glanced quickly round to make sure the door was still closed. 'Véronique creeps around the house.' She felt a pang. Véronique was her husband's mother, not an enemy. She was excited about Jean-Luc's first child arriving and that was to be encouraged.

'Let me examine you, hop up on the bed.'

Camille snorted. 'Not much hopping going on here. I move like a buffalo these days.'

Her mother washed her hands at the basin, drying them carefully, clearly enjoying the feel of the soap. 'What a luxury running hot water is.' She put on a pair of gloves.

'I can't imagine what it must have been like living up there during winter.'

'There's a pump. We heat water on a stove, even fill a tin tub occasionally if there's enough wood.'

'You look well on it, Maman. Thin, but well.'

'I've probably never been fitter. More food would be welcome, but you know how I hated my hips and stomach before the war. We do better than most in France.'

'And still you help the Jewish children?'

Sophie turned slowly from the washbasin and looked purposefully at the door.

'Sorry.' Camille flushed. 'I'm doing exactly what I said we shouldn't do.'

'The children come up to the plateau for us to hide,' Sophie said softly. 'More of them as things here become worse. Sometimes, if they're particularly at risk, people still try to move them into Switzerland, but not me, not since—'

She stopped, returning to the bed. Camille knew not to ask any more. Maman pulled up Camille's blouse gently, running her hands over the bump. She stopped, blinked, moved one hand and then another, looked down, stopped again. 'I'm going to listen to the baby's heartbeat.' She turned to her bag and took out the horn Camille recognised from a childhood watching her mother tidy her midwife's bag, cleaning her implements, checking everything was in place, preparing for an unexpected call in the night. 'What did you do to your hand?' Camille asked, spotting a small, thin, white scar.

'Caught it on a wire fence. It's not serious.' Maman placed the trumpet on the bump to listen to the heartbeat.

That was why Maman had been wearing the kid gloves when they'd met that last time at the café, before she'd left the city. She'd hurt the hand while smuggling the children over to Switzerland.

'Very good,' she said, after a minute. She moved the horn along a hand's width or two and listened again.

'What are you doing? I thought you said—' Maman silenced Camille with her spare hand. Seconds passed. She moved the trumpet back to where she'd first heard the heartbeat. Maman raised her head with an expression on her face Camille couldn't read.

'The reason for your discomfort is quite clear, *chérie*.'

'Something's wrong, isn't it?' Camille sank back on the pillow. 'I knew it.'

Maman smiled at her. 'Not wrong. Just... more complicated.'

'Complicated?'

'You're having twins.'

'What?' She sat up, pulling down her blouse, wincing as she felt the weight of the bump. 'I can't be. Are you absolutely certain?'

'I've just listened to two separate heartbeats, going at slightly different rates. That's why you feel so uncomfortable. Carrying two babies instead of one puts more pressure on your joints and muscles. And on your respiratory system. You must feel fatigued a lot of the time.' She replaced the horn in the bag and took out a notebook, writing something down.

'That's why I feel hands and feet all over the place.' Camille shook her head. 'And why something's grinding against me most of the time. How did that doctor not notice?'

'It's not uncommon for twins to be missed. I've been in deliveries myself where we thought everything was over and then another little head appeared.' Maman took out a tape. 'I'm going to measure you, but with twins, it doesn't mean as much. When did you think your due date was?'

'I thought there were about three weeks to go.' Camille tugged her blouse out again so her mother could measure vertically up from her pubic bone to the highest point of her womb.

'Seems roughly what I'd expect. Sometimes twins come early, though.' Maman took out her blood pressure monitor – sphygmomanometer, Camille remembered it was called.

'You said your urine wasn't tested last time?' Maman sniffed. 'I can test for sugar and albumin –a protein that shouldn't be present.'

'Is that when you heat it up on a burner? I used to watch you do that when I came to the clinics with you.' Camille wrinkled her nose. 'Smelled bad.'

'That's right. First, I'll need to scour the local pharmacies for supplies.' She helped Camille sit up, placing pillows under her arm so to raise it to the level of her heart, before taking the pressure.

Maman removed the cuff. 'I'm going to take another measurement in a moment.' She busied herself tidying up her bag.

'Is the pressure elevated? Last time, the doctor said I was probably a bit nervous coming to see him and that's why it was up a little.'

After a minute, Maman retook the measurement. 'Better, but still a little above what it should be.'

'I remember you telling me about toxaemia of pregnancy. Is that what I've got?' She heard the tremor in her own voice.

'I'll rule it out when we test the sample.' Maman ran her hands over her lower shins and ankles. 'Not too bad. Headaches?'

Camille shook her head.

'Nausea?'

'Only in the first few weeks.' She grimaced, remembering. 'Jean-Luc found someone who could supply eels. Jeanne made these stews...' She gulped, putting a hand to her throat. 'It was wasteful when the eels were so nourishing.'

'The smell of herring on a particular Berlin market stall made me retch when I was expecting you.'

A shadow passed beneath the bedroom door. Véronique, hovering outside. Camille put a finger to her lips. Maman nodded. 'Do please get dressed again, madame, I have finished my examination.' Maman's voice had taken on a cool, professional note. It was if her mother had pushed her away. Camille blinked hard. Her mother must have seen something of her emotion on her face because she smiled, looking like a mischievous girl. Maman's face could change from serious to comic in a flash. Mobile, that's what Papa had called it. He'd always told Camille that she, by contrast, would have made a good poker player.

The shadow under the door passed on and Camille heard Véronique's bedroom door open and close.

'She listens in to conversations,' she said quietly.

'Is she kind to you?'

Camille tried to be fair. 'She's been very welcoming and generous, having clothes made for me when we could still buy fabric, taking me out for lunch with her friends, when the restaurants still served something decent.'

'And Jean-Luc?' Maman's voice was very soft.

'Treats me like a piece of Limoges porcelain. Almost to a fault.'

'It's right he should feel protective. And when you tell him the news, he will have even more cause to feel like that.'

'Are twin births still dangerous? I remember the stories of when you rode up to some remote village in the Appalachians with another midwife and delivered twins in a cabin, with just oil lamps and a water pump outside.'

Maman smiled. 'To be honest, it's worse for some women in European slums these days. The woman in the log cabin kept it spotless and prepared everything beautifully ahead of time.'

'You hadn't ridden for years, but the midwives went everywhere on horseback, didn't they?'

'Fortunately, the horse was more experienced than I was. Even so, I couldn't sit down for weeks after that ride up to the cabin. The mother was tough and the twins were, too. They all survived. I learned more that night than I ever did working in the fanciest maternity hospital.'

'If we'd stayed over there in America, we'd have missed all this.' She nodded towards the window.

Maman sighed. 'Perhaps. But we've had less to fear than many.'

Camille reminded herself that she wasn't like the scared runaway women with their thin children in terror of the French camps or those in the east, from where nobody returned. Her twins wouldn't be like those children her mother helped to hide and feed up on the Plateau or took on the dangerous journey to the Swiss border. She felt a sense of strength flow through her. Her mother was with her now, everything was going to be fine.

'I'll show you to your room. You are going to stay, Maman, aren't you?'

'As your mother-in-law says, it is a little unconventional for a *sage-femme* to live in before labour has started.'

'I could say I've been having pains. Women sometimes do have false alarms late in pregnancy, don't they?'

'Braxton Hicks contractions. He was a physician in England last century.' Maman was looking doubtful. It meant a lot to her that she was always truthful with her patients. 'I could honestly say I want to keep an eye on the blood pressure overnight until I can carry out the urine test. I'll stay up here, out of the way.'

'It would be strange having you eat dinner with the three of us without acknowledging who you really are.' Camille knew she'd slip up, call her mother Maman, instead of Madame Leclerc.

'What will happen,' Maman asked mischievously, 'when the war is over and you have to introduce the midwife to your husband as your mother?'

'I'll tell him I was protecting him as much as you. What he doesn't know can't harm him.' Yet she knew Jean-Luc would not like the deception. She felt a stab in her heart at the thought of not being open with him about such an important personal matter.

'I'll go back to the convent tomorrow,' Maman said. 'Spending too much time here may not be sensible. And I'd like to refill my midwife's bag and buy anything else I can find. There's not much in the dispensary shelves at home.'

Camille winced at the last word and hoped Maman didn't notice.

'There's a wonderful doctor from Frankfurt who's been teaching me all kinds of things.' There was an enthusiasm in her voice that made Camille smile, feeling the discomfort slip away.

Maman looked at her, brow creased.

'It's just good to hear.'

'Hear what?'

'Your passion for your work. After all that's happened, you still find such interest in it.' There was a wistful note to her words, she noticed, flushing.

'Your father dying was a terrible blow. I've been fortunate to have my work to keep me going. We must find a passion for you, too.' Maman sounded casual, but Camille could tell she hadn't missed the wistful tone.

'Oh, I'll have plenty to do.' She patted her abdomen. 'Espe-

cially if there're going to be two of them.' She thought of her
knitting and sewing. She wouldn't have enough clothes, even if
she worked her fingers to the bone. Oh well, plenty of children
in Europe were wearing rags. Her babies would be fine. Seeing
her resourceful, practical mother had given her courage.

Maman turned to her bag, replacing the blood pressure
monitor and the horn. 'One day the little ones will be grown-up
and following their own dreams. It is good to have your own
interests. Your father always encouraged me in my work.' Her
fingers passed lovingly over the tools of her trade.

As a little girl, Camille had helped her pack the bag, very
carefully so that she didn't break the glass bottles. She wasn't
allowed to touch the vials of morphine and Maman, ordinarily
so relaxed about discipline, in comparison with her friends'
mothers, at least, had threatened her with severe punishment if
she ever disobeyed this rule. Camille had filled her school
satchel with whatever she could find, carrying it around to help
her dolls deliver their imaginary babies. By the time she was ten,
she knew many of the medical terms most women didn't even
learn until they were expecting their first baby. She'd kept her
knowledge to herself after some girls' mothers complained
about their daughters learning too much about reproduction
and childbirth. Camille needed to fit in with her schoolmates, so
she'd been more careful about saying anything that would
expose just how different Sophie was from all the other
mothers.

All this reminded her now that Véronique would pick up
Maman's faint Dutch accent. Would she remember that
Camille's mother was also Dutch and note the coincidence? She
only had one photograph of Maman in the house, the one she'd
shown Jean-Luc, and she'd put it away in her lingerie drawer
when Maman had fled Lyon.

Véronique had already asked plenty of questions about
Camille's parents. Camille had glossed over the political nature

of Papa's writing. The fact he was dead meant Véronique had been respectful, perhaps believing it was grief alone that made her unwilling to talk about her father. Camille had been vague about Maman, saying she lived a quiet life now, moving between friends who lived in distant countryside. Jean-Luc had steered his mother away from the subject.

Maman had only been in this house for forty minutes and already Camille felt a pull between longing to keep her mother close and worrying that everything she'd built up could be toppled by a careless word.

EIGHTEEN

SOPHIE

Camille showed Sophie into a guest bedroom, furnished with silk curtains and bed coverings – presumably woven on the family looms. Sophie stroked the jacquard patterns, marvelling at the intricacy and softness of the threads. The room had its own basin. An uncracked cake of soap sat on a porcelain dish. Despite the shortages, Jean-Luc and Camille kept a good house. Or perhaps it was the mother-in-law, whose shadow under the door had caused Camille to flinch, who kept the rooms immaculate. Sophie was curious to meet Véronique properly, almost as curious as she was to clap eyes on her son-in-law. Jean-Luc was a handsome man, she knew, from the wedding photograph Camille had given her, but seeing him in the flesh would tell her more.

Sophie was wearier than she realised, partly because of the journey and partly because of the worry about Camille. She could relax a little on the latter score. Camille didn't seem to have signs of toxaemia, that terrifying condition. Once she'd obtained test tubes and a burner, she'd confirm this. Her daughter simply needed someone to watch over her and reassure her. Someone to accompany her to the next appointment and ensure the twin pregnancy was officially noted so the doctors would be ready for any complications. That was the role of Camille's mother.

She would encourage Camille to go to the maternity clinic for the births. Apart from anything, she had no form of pain relief with her other than the bottle of aspirin. She could not deliver twins herself unassisted. Even delivering a single baby in an uncomplicated pregnancy could be challenging if labour took an unexpected turn. She was always grateful for the presence of a sensible mother or sister, or more particularly, for the presence of Erich Meyer. She wished he was here now, but that was just selfish. A German Jew caught by the police or Gestapo was an unthinkable prospect.

No, Camille would be better off in a maternity clinic unless another midwife could be found. And bringing in anyone else would present its own risks. Sister Marie-Claude would agree to help, if she could be spared from the sanatorium. Presumably Jean-Luc would make a generous donation to convent funds in appreciation.

Mulling all this over, Sophie lay back on the bed and dropped off, waking a few hours later, mouth open, hoping she hadn't snored. She had time to wash at the basin and change her blouse for the one she'd packed in her rucksack before Camille knocked at the door and came in. 'Véronique has a migraine and will take some soup in her room this evening. Jean-Luc has been detained at work for another hour. Or so he says. Probably more like two hours.' She smiled conspiratorially. 'Come downstairs, Maman. We only eat lightly at night, but Jeanne managed to get hold of some fresh bread and we have a decent piece of cheese. She's got the evening off to visit her sister.'

Sophie felt like a wicked schoolgirl, creeping downstairs with Camille. They went down the parqueted corridor into the kitchen. The window looking out on the courtyard garden was open as the evening was still warm. The scent of camellias wafted in, lilac adding an extra sweetness. Sophie longed to explore. There wasn't a garden in the world that didn't draw her to itself, but it was probably best to stay indoors, out of sight.

As her immediate hunger left her, she told Camille about life on the plateau, how they spent their time foraging and bartering for food, distracting the children, watching out for patrols. Camille was frowning. 'In the city, we hear of people going out into the country-side to forage. I had no idea it was so hard for you, Maman. I could have sent you food parcels. We don't have much, but we manage.'

'Many of those we take in don't have ration cards. Or if they do, there's nothing to buy in the shops. The farmers help when they can. And it'll be easier in summer when the vegetables come in.'

'I'm going to run you a bath. We've been careful with fuel all week so there should be enough to have a soak. I have some expensive bath salts Jean-Luc bought me.' She frowned. 'Why are you smiling, Maman?'

'I came here to look after you, *chérie*. Not the other way round.'

'We can look after each other. But we need to watch out for Véronique. If she sees too much of us together, she'll guess. I'm shorter and darker, but we both have these full lips.' Camille pursed them together. 'And the small nose.'

'As a child I fretted my nose would mean I could never aspire to heroism,' Sophie said. 'When did you ever see a small-nosed woman who wasn't depicted as being sweet and unde-manding?'

Camille snorted. 'Papa certainly wouldn't have said you were undemanding when you scolded him for not chasing up a newspaper editor who owed him a fee.' She smiled fondly. 'I was only about eight, but I remember him scuttling off to that office in Berlin and coming back with the money.' She sighed. 'That must have been just before Hitler was elected.'

Sophie sighed, too. 'Ah, your papa. What I wouldn't give to have him here with us now.' Sitting here with Camille brought a yearning for Bernhard, his booming laugh, his twinkling eyes, such a contrast to the stereotype of the German male. Camille reached across and squeezed her hand.

She lowered her voice even though they were alone. 'You really are safe up there, Maman?'

'It's a tolerant and courageous community. We look out for one another.'

'Lyon isn't like that,' Camille said. 'Though perhaps people are finally realising what the Germans are really like. You'd have to be blind not to see what's going on.'

'And Jean-Luc?' Sophie tried to keep her tone neutral. 'He sees them for what they are?'

'He hates them trying to take his workers. Dictating what his looms produce. Buying his silks for pretty well nothing.'

'You must be excited about telling him your news.'

'I just hope I'm still awake when he comes home. I tried telephoning the factory earlier on this evening, but nobody answered. Sometimes he goes straight out to meetings.'

She swallowed. 'If I go into labour, I'm worried I mightn't get hold of him.'

Sophie took her hand. 'You won't be alone. I'll make sure he knows. Even if I have to send his mother to find him.'

'Véronique likes to feel important.' Camille's face lightened and then grew more sombre again. 'You really think it might come to surgery, Maman?'

No point in being untruthful. 'Sometimes – if the presentation of one or both twins is not optimal. Or if the mother's or babies' interests are not served by a lengthy labour.' She heard her own words, so cold, so dispassionate, like a textbook. 'In a modern hospital, with good physicians and a good operating theatre, it makes sense.' Erich had told her of how the hospital he'd worked in had kept babies alive she'd never have been able to save.

'Of course, lots of twins are born at home, as I said. When I worked in Berlin, there must have been something in the water because we had five sets of twins in one month and they were all born at home.' Most of these twins hadn't been first babies, though. And they'd been born in areas where taxis to hospitals could be summoned if needed. Perhaps Jean-Luc could get hold of an *ausweis*, a permit, for them to break curfew, if necessary? One of the twins in Berlin hadn't survived, she now recalled.

She composed her face. Camille shouldn't see a hint of fear. 'Once you go into labour, I'll come to the maternity clinic with you. But they may not allow me in.' Sophie couldn't show them any professional accreditation matching her faked identity as Mireille Leclerc. Would the clinic check her credentials or accept her unquestioningly as Camille's *sage-femme*?

Camille's face fell. 'If you're not there, I'll be terrified.'

She tried to reassure her. 'If they're as short staffed as most hospitals and clinics, they won't be particular about checking the paperwork.'

Camille was looking at her as though greedy for reassurance.

'You're a healthy young woman, fit and as well fed as anyone could be. I'm going to be keeping an eye on you. You'll go into that clinic knowing everything has been monitored.'

Everything could be monitored. Nothing could be guaranteed.

'In my rucksack upstairs I have dried camomile.' Sophie stood up. 'I'm going to make us both an infusion. It will settle your nerves.'

A bell rang on the wall. Camille stood up, too. 'Véronique has finished her soup and needs the bowl collecting.'

It went against the grain for Sophie to allow a heavily pregnant woman to go upstairs while she just sat there.

Camille returned with the tray. 'Véronique would like a tisane, too.'

Sophie wanted to ask Camille more about Véronique, but something stopped her. Camille had chosen to live here. She'd have to find her own way to make the domestic arrangements work. When the war was over, Sophie would be on hand to help. She dared to think of herself, her daughter and the twins walking in a park, playing in a garden, perhaps going to the Mediterranean to play on the beaches.

As she crept upstairs to fetch the herbs from her rucksack, Sophie thought, for the first time in months, about the future. She still owned the house in a suburb of Paris, bought with Bernhardt. Last she'd heard, it had been commandeered by a German officer. She'd be able to prove it was legally hers, wouldn't she? She'd rebuild a life that would include Camille's children. There'd be Christmases and birthday parties. In time, First Holy Communion celebrations would follow, not that she held religious ceremonies in great respect, but parties of any kind always filled her with delight. Bedtime stories would be read. Traditional Dutch gingerbread baked. Perhaps she could buy her grandchildren their first bicycles.

She was tempting fate even thinking about it. As she opened her bedroom door quietly, she told herself to concentrate on the next hour, the next day, just as she had from the moment she'd arrived on the plateau last July: frightened, exhausted, carrying a suitcase she'd hurriedly packed in her apartment.

She picked up the blood pressure monitor. A good idea to check Camille's blood pressure before she had her tea while she was sitting down, relaxed.

Downstairs, she found that Camille's blood pressure had indeed dropped. Now that Camille knew that nothing was actually wrong with her pregnancy, her body was relaxing. It had been worth coming to Lyon just to do that much for her daughter.

In companionable silence, the two of them made the infusions and Camille brought one up to her mother-in-law. That done, they sat drinking the tea. 'I still like camomile,' Sophie said. 'Lime blossom tea is too much of a good thing now. It, and chestnuts, over-feature in our repertoire, my housemate feels.' She told Camille about Nina, her ability to find something flowering to arrange in a jug on the table, her clucking over Sophie when she returned from a night call.

At nine, Sophie went upstairs. 'I'll be gone before you have breakfast,' she told Camille. 'Back after lunch.'

'Eat something here before you go. They probably don't have much to spare in the convent? You see the bread bag,' Camille nodded at it hanging on the peg.

'I'm a tough old bird.'

'Not so old.'

Most days, she felt the same age as her daughter. Tonight, she felt every year of her forty-two years. 'Save your bread for yourself and those two little people we will meet soon.' She put her hands on each side of Camille's face and kissed her on the brow. '*Prends soin de toi.*'

'You take care of yourself, too, Maman. Run that bath now.'

The water was almost hot in a way bathwater had once been before the war. Camille's bath essence sat in a glass bottle on the side. Sophie added a small drop. To her dismay, the water turned grey as she lay in it. She and Nina had grimly washed in cold water most days, removing the overcoats they wore indoors and pulling up layers of clothing to clean themselves. Nothing was as good as total immersion in a tub.

When they could, the women went to the public baths in the village to soak themselves and scrub at their bodies with the meagre wafers of soap handed out. Nina and Sophie enjoyed reading out the posters encouraging hygiene to one another in the pompous tones of an imaginary civil servant.

She scrubbed off the deeper layers of sweat and grime she'd acquired on the road to Lyon. Nina would have liked this tiled bathroom – the geranium bath salts, the soft towels. She should try to find a present for Nina. A new hairbrush. A second-hand silk blouse for summer that still had a bit of life in it. Possibly another small jug or vase for her flowers, if she could carry it on the bicycle.

Sophie was drifting off into the fantasy of buying gifts at will, as though there were no occupation, no war, no shortages. She forced herself to pull the plug and get out of the bathtub.

Lying in the guest bed, in clean, soft linen, sleep claimed her swiftly.

Camille found sleep tugging at her as soon as she lay down in their lavender-scented sheets. Perhaps because her mother was close at hand now, under the same roof, her anxiety about the pregnancy had ebbed. Twins, she thought, drifting away, unable to make the concept stick in her mind. Two babies at once. Yes, it was riskier, but perhaps they could sneak Maman into the clinic to help with the delivery, after all.

She struggled to stay awake for Jean-Luc's return, dropping off for half an hour and awakening to the sound of the bedroom door opening.

Her husband looked drained. His face, which ordinarily retained a tan through the winter and spring, was pale. 'Jean-Luc? Is everything all right?'

He brightened at her voice. 'I woke you? I'm sorry.' He came over to the bed and embraced her. 'I thought I'd have missed you tonight; this is a lovely surprise, even though you should be sleeping.'

'Is there a problem at the factory?'

'No, no, nothing wrong at the factory.' Something in his voice made her wonder what else it could be.

'But—'

'Just a long day with obdurate officials and demanding Germans. It's good to leave it all behind me for the night. Tell me about your day.'

She sat up, unable to keep the smile from her face.

'Camille?' He took her hand.

'You always sounded as though you wanted this baby to the first of several?'

'*Bien sûr*. Of course, if God's willing and if it healthy for you, *chérie*.'

'You're getting your wish come true.' He looked at her quizzically. 'Perhaps a little more quickly than you thought.' She couldn't help laughing. 'I'm not just fat and greedy.'

'You've never been either of those things. You're beautiful.'

'I'm expecting twins.'

His eyes opened wide. 'But the doctor never said this before. You didn't see him today, did you?'

'The *sage-femme* visited. She found two babies' heartbeats when she listened with her little trumpet.'

Jean-Luc flopped back against the pillows, his arm still around her. '*Mon dieu*. She's sure? Two babies?'

'She's sure.'

He laughed. 'Twins! That's wonderful.' He squeezed her. 'How on earth are we going to manage?' He shook his head. 'I can't even think about that now. Two babies.' He turned to her. 'But is it safe? For you, I mean? Is it riskier? And the babies, too?'

'The *sage-femme* will keep a close eye on me. And she'll try to attend at the clinic, too, if I go in.'

'Whatever your midwife needs to keep you and the babies well, she'll get.' Jean-Luc was shaking his head. 'I can't believe it.' He kissed her cheek. 'You're just astounding, Camille. I can almost forget—'

'Forget what?' She nestled closer to him.

'About the war, the Occupation. Everything that matters is in this room.'

She fell asleep again, still resting against him.

NINETEEN

SOPHIE

In the convent next morning, Rosa greeted Sophie with a fleeting smile. She was wearing a neat navy dress and grey apron, a broom in her hand. 'People will keep tramping inside with mud on their shoes.' Sophie remembered the pristine interiors of the Romani caravans she'd once visited.

'You've been given liver to eat?' she asked.

Rosa made a face but nodded.

'And Patrin?'

'Outside in a pram, with the other babies.'

'Don't work too hard.'

'I told you, I'm strong.'

'I wish all the new mothers I saw had your constitution.'

The girl seemed placated. 'And how...' She looked down. 'I don't want to be indiscreet... the lady you visited, she is well?'

'She is, but...' Sophie sighed. 'I have some concerns about her pregnancy.' Rosa's look was enquiring. 'She's having twins. And her blood pressure was elevated. It can be dangerous, although it seems to have settled.'

'Blood pressure means how the blood vessels are working?'

'Sometimes increases mean there are problems.' Rosa was

looking genuinely interested, so she continued. 'The relationship between the placenta and the mother's blood circulation and kidneys is important. If it goes wrong, it can be bad for baby and mother.'

'As if their two bodies aren't speaking the same language?'

'Indeed.'

'There was a lady here who was having her second child. She had problems first time, but everything was fine with her blood pressure this time, Sister Marie-Claude said.'

'Often with a second pregnancy, the mother's body has learned what to do.' She would like to have lingered with Rosa, who seemed genuinely interested, but felt she should go to find Sister Marie-Claude in the sanatorium. The nun greeted her cheerfully, asking after Sophie's patient.

'I have concerns.' She walked to the basin to wash her hands. 'I need to keep myself busy so I don't fret. What can I do for you here, sister?'

'Are you any good with boils?'

'I've lanced a few in my time.' Sophie smiled. 'Nothing like skin infections to keep one in the present moment.'

'We recommend saying the Rosary for similar purposes, but perhaps boils are as useful.'

Sophie found an apron and went with her into the general ward. 'We try to admit only women and children, but we found this poor soul living in a cemetery early this morning. I didn't like to ask Rosa, as she's not married.'

Rosa had survived God knows what in the internment camp and had given birth to a son, but her modesty was to be protected. It touched Sophie.

The man in the bed was of indeterminate age, his skin crusted. The aroma he gave off made Sophie swallow. 'He needs bathing first,' she said quietly. 'Tell me where the basins and cloths are kept.'

Scabies, she noted, removing his clothes. Ringworm? No.

And fortunately no impetigo, which was so infectious she would fear bringing it back to Camille. He put a hand out to stop her removing his drawers. She shook it off gently. 'I've seen it all before, monsieur.'

Much of the smell was coming from his clothes rather than his body. She tossed them onto the floor for burning. They'd been good quality once. This man came from a prosperous background. He was younger than she'd thought at first, his muscle tone good. He seemed to have most of his teeth. When she listened to his chest, it was clear. If they could only feed him up, he'd recover his health quickly. The boil was easily lanced and he gave a grunt of relief and thanked her in an educated voice. Perhaps he'd escaped from a deportation train or a camp. Someone's husband or son? Someone who hadn't been heard of for a long time but who was missed, longed for? He was probably Jewish, she knew from helping him wash below his waist. The old habits learned on the plateau forbade her from asking any questions.

'I'll leave as soon as I can stand up,' he said.

Where would he go? He didn't look strong enough to reach a mountain refuge like the one she'd just left. 'They'll want to feed you up for a few days.'

He blinked hard and turned his head away, muttering a thanks.

Lunch was served in the refectory, a thin gruel and some bread. She ate sparingly, aware that she'd eaten well with Camille the previous evening. Sister Marie-Claude caught her looking at her watch. 'You must want to return to your patient across the river?' she asked quietly.

Sophie blushed. 'Forgive me.'

'What is there to forgive?'

'I'd like to come back here this evening, if that's all right? I can take another look at your male patient and make up a bed on the floor for myself—'

'You'll have a bed. If you're sure your patient can spare you?'

'I'm reassured now I've seen her that she doesn't need me in the house overnight. Not for now.'

In the afternoon, Sister Marie-Claude insisted that, rather than attempting to purchase them, Sophie take a burner, test tubes and solutions from the infirmary for testing Camille's sample. As she made her way by bicycle back to La Croix-Rousse, Sophie reflected on Marie-Claude's earlier words. *You'll want to return to your patient across the river.* Her daughter had become her patient.

She hadn't always been a good mother to her only child. She'd jumped at the chance to go off with the horseback midwives when the opportunity arose. Camille had just recovered from measles and was still lethargic. When Sophie returned to New York, it was to find a nurse sitting with Camille in their apartment. 'Your daughter's fever came back,' the nurse said. 'Your husband didn't want to leave her, but he had a meeting.' The woman said it neutrally, no reproach intended, but a flush had covered Sophie's face. She'd helped other women's babies and left her own child and it hadn't been just that once. From now on she'd always put her daughter and grandchildren first.

This afternoon, the house was quiet. Camille herself let her in, pointing up the stairs to indicate that her mother-in-law was resting. 'I told Jean-Luc that I'm having twins.' She was smiling. 'I could barely keep my eyes open. He's so excited. And this morning he said it was double the joy.' She looked radiant herself.

'As long as he realises your lives will be very busy when they are born.' As was the case for most men Jean-Luc would probably regard the twins as his wife's concern. But two newborns in a house would inevitably affect everyone's life, even with nursemaids and maid to assist. And he would no longer be his wife's sole focus.

'Why are you smiling?' Camille asked.

'Ask me in a year's time.'

They went up to Camille's room and Camille lay on the bed. 'They aren't moving as much,' she said. 'Perhaps because there's less space inside me.'

Sophie washed her hands and waited for her daughter to pull up her blouse and unfasten her skirt before answering. 'Sometimes that's a sign that labour isn't far off. I'll listen to the heartbeats.'

She was pleased with what she heard through the stethoscope. When she took Camille's blood pressure, it was still normal, too. Camille had provided a sample and watched, nose wrinkling, as her mother lit the burner to heat it.

Tests complete, she turned to Camille. 'No toxaemia. No sign of diabetes.'

'That's a relief.' Camille let out a sigh.

A knock on the door. 'Camille?' Véronique.

'I'm just with Madame Leclerc.'

'There are questions I'd like to ask her myself.'

Camille looked at Sophie.

'Are you comfortable with her coming in?' Sophie asked in a whisper.

'Is it usual?'

'I don't often have the *belle-mère* sitting in at appointments, but it isn't unheard of. I could put a mask on, I have one in my bag, but of course she did see me briefly yesterday.' Up on the plateau, Sophie had visited the nervous young wife of the shepherd, who clutched the hand of her mother-in-law, a woman of few words who sat nodding, conveying a sense of reassurance. Sophie wished she could borrow the woman for all her appointments with nervous mothers. She had the feeling kindly approval wasn't Véronique's style.

Camille sighed. 'Let's not risk it.'

Sophie nodded. 'Bonjour, madame. Please ask your questions through the door. My client is *déshabillée* at the moment.'

An audible sniff. 'I've seen two daughters through four pregnancies.'

'Your daughter-in-law is a very modest young lady, madame.'

'Far be it from me to push myself in where I am not wanted.'

Camille raised her head. 'Forgive me for being a little old-fashioned. The nuns, you know... Please do ask questions. I'm just a novice at all this baby business, after all.'

Another sniff but this one sounded more gracious. 'Are we going to make an appointment with the specialist to confirm this rumour of twins?'

Sophie's cheeks flushed a little. Camille looked from her to the door. 'I am due to see him again this week. I'm sure he will confirm. Madame Leclerc did hear two heartbeats again today, after all.'

'Perhaps the baby moved and that was why she thought there were two of them?'

Camille laughed. 'There's not much room for anyone to move anywhere inside me.'

'And does Madame Leclerc have any insights as to the date of arrival of the baby or *babies*?'

'I think we could be within a week of labour starting,' Sophie said. 'The babies are not as active as madame remembers them being.'

A chuckle. 'My daughter-in-law is inexperienced, as she herself admits. The doctor will tell us all we need to know. I shall wait until we have his opinion.' Her footsteps moved away.

Camille muttered something she certainly hadn't picked up

at the convent and then bit her tongue. 'She is good to me, but sometimes I feel as if she's judging me against Jean-Luc's sisters. I know I'm young and inexperienced.'

Sophie bit back the retort she wanted to give. Everyone had to stay calm. 'You're as good as any of them. Look how well you did at school.' Sophie took her daughter's hand. 'When the babies are born, you and Véronique will have something to bond over.'

Or the relationship could be even more strained as Véronique offered advice. Or, more likely, decrees. 'You'll be a wonderful mother. She'll respect you for that.' Camille still looked unconvinced. 'I remember your father's mother, Ottoline. A statuesque German lady who loved climbing mountains and attending Wagnerian festivals. She had a booming voice and terrified me.' Camille smiled. 'And your father, too.'

'I've never seen you terrified by anyone, Maman.' She was laughing now.

'Believe me, there are plenty who scare me these days.' But Sophie didn't want to dampen the lighter mood. 'When I was pregnant, Ottoline interrogated me as to the exact hours you'd spend outdoors in your perambulator, the age you'd be weaned. The age I planned to place you over the pot after feeding you. And she was insistent I shouldn't pick you up too often. It would spoil you.'

'I can't wait to hold my babies.'

'Good for them and good for you. As long as you don't enslave yourself.' She packed away her instruments. 'Twins may sometimes have to wait in their cots a bit longer. But they'll have one another, too, and I think they'll find that a comfort. You'll employ a *bonne d'enfant*, won't you?' She didn't want Camille's life to be one long domestic slog. Babies could be fascinating, but a lot of their daily routine was, frankly, repetitive and sometimes not very interesting. Camille would need a nursemaid to make time for herself.

'I've spoken to some agencies. None of them seem to have the kind of person I'm looking for. Most of them seem like Ottoline.' Camille looked very young, sitting up on the bed. She rolled her eyes. 'Enough of my moaning.' She winced. 'Oh.'

'What?'

'This cramping pain.'

'Probably a Braxton Hicks.'

Camille bit her lip.

'Try standing and moving gently. Sometimes that eases it.' She helped Camille to her feet and leant her gently over the dressing table, showing her how to rock her pelvis backwards and forward and side to side. 'And practise breathing through it. Like this.' She breathed in and out slowly. Camille was still obviously feeling discomfort. Her daughter, if she gave birth in the maternity clinic, would probably be confined to a bed. A shame. Up in the mountains she'd seen women move around during labour, sometimes delivering in the hands-and-knees position.

'It's gone.' Camille looked at her watch. 'Just as well. I must make sure everything's in order for dinner. Jean-Luc has a guest we have to make a fuss of, apparently. Though how we're expected to lay on a feast these days, I don't know.'

'I will leave you.' Feeling a sudden pang that she could not stay and dine with her daughter, Sophie packed up her bag. A gasp from Camille made her put it down again and look at her.

'They're quite strong, these practice contractions.'

'Where do you feel them, *chérie*?'

Camille pointed to the front of her abdomen. 'My back hurts a bit, too, though.'

'I'm going to wait with you and see if another one comes along.'

Camille looked at the watch again. 'I must go down to the kitchen.'

'Just wait a few more minutes.'

Nothing more happened. After ten minutes Camille insisted on getting up.

'I think I should stay,' Sophie said. 'They're probably just a dress rehearsal, but if you needed to call me back, it might mean breaking curfew. May I sit quietly in the room I was in last night?'

'Of course you can.' Camille looked shocked. 'You're my mo —' She glanced at the bedroom door just in time. 'I want you to stay. I wish you could eat with us.'

'One of these days it's going to be very confusing to explain who I really am.' Perhaps her son-in-law would never forgive them for the deception.

'I'll bring you up something to eat,' Camille said. 'There are shelves of books in the study down the corridor. Perhaps you could find something to read that might make it less boring? Véronique never goes in there, she's not a reader. If you're quiet, nobody will know you're there.'

Sophie felt a rush of joy at the prospect of books. There were some up on the plateau, but she'd read most of them by now. Sometimes, she'd longed for a shot of Zola or Balzac. Or even some romance or detective novel one might read by the seaside. Anything to distract her away from reality.

'I thought that would cheer you up,' Camille said, smiling. 'Jean-Luc's father was quite a reader in his spare time. He read in German and English as well as French.'

Someone rapped on the door. 'Camille, you are aware that Jean-Luc and our guest will be with us within a few hours?'

'I'm on my way downstairs,' Camille said.

'Leave that to me. I was thinking of what you're planning to wear. Your midnight velvet dress would be appropriate. If it still fits. With the pearls. To draw the eye up to your face and away from, well, it would be flattering, non?'

'I'll need to try it on.'

A sigh from outside the door. 'My girls and I were lucky not to exceed *la limite* during our confinements. But we'll worry about how you're going to lose the weight another time.'

Sophie bit her lip hard.

'I try hard not to eat too much,' Camille said as the footsteps receded, sounding crushed. 'There isn't much anyway. But I do feel hungry.'

'You're eating for three people.' Sophie shot a venomous look at the bedroom door in the direction of Véronique. 'Make sure you get a good share of whatever's on the table tonight.'

Left alone in the guest room, Sophie washed her hands and face, forcing herself to take long, even breaths, in and out, almost as she had instructed Camille to do. It was probably as well that she was not going to be face-to-face with Véronique tonight. She might be tempted to say something extremely rude. Why had her daughter chosen this constricted life, in this prison of a home with its beautiful furnishings and antiques?

The promise of fresh books drew her out of the guest room. She crept down the corridor and opened the study door. The room smelled of old leather bindings. Sophie's heart leapt. She closed the door behind her quietly. Jean-Luc's father had indeed been a wide reader. The shelves housed antiquarian titles, which she dared not remove. To her relief, there was also a case of nineteenth-century fiction, including her old friends Zola and Balzac. He'd travelled widely – there was a shelf of guidebooks. Somewhat to her surprise she found herself picking up an old Baedeker guide to Switzerland, in German, too. She and Bernhardt had spent their honeymoon touring the country, admiring mountains that seemed too perfect for this world. At night they dined by lakes, sampling local wines. For half an hour, Sophie was back in the past, the weeks full of walking through meadows of wildflowers, lovemaking and laughter and the sense that the worst was in the past, the First World War behind them, Europe at peace and the future sparkling like alpine streams.

Sudden rage made her slam the book shut. Why had all the promise of the twenties turned to dust? Why was she creeping around her daughter's home using an assumed identity? She hadn't harmed a soul last year and had only wanted to save children's lives.

She replaced the Baedeker on the shelf. As she did, she caught a closer glimpse of the photograph in the silver frame. A woman, early thirties, beautifully dressed, on the arm of a man in a suit that shouted of expensive tailoring. They stood in what looked like an automobile showroom, the light bouncing off shiny chrome and glass. Just out of focus, to the right of the woman, a man in German uniform raised a glass of champagne. One of Jean-Luc's sisters? She certainly resembled him. This looked like a Parisian showroom and the man holding her arm must be the dealer in expensive automobiles, happy to sell to anyone who could afford them, obviously. Even if they wore that uniform. Was Jean-Luc so very different from his sisters?

She forced herself to breathe out. If you allowed fear or anger to overpower you, you just wasted energy. She'd come here to protect her daughter. She couldn't do that unless she remained calm and watchful. She opened the Baedeker again and found herself flicking through the pages to the map showing the western borders with France, with rail links and crossings shown. She knew them well: she'd memorised maps last summer. Her eye caught the name of the town of Annemasse itself. She looked away, stomach turning. Now was not the time to think about that night again.

TWENTY

CAMILLE

Knowing Maman was sitting quietly upstairs, in the study or the guest bedroom, gave Camille courage as she finished arranging spring flowers on the dinner table and checked that the wine glasses were shining. The napkins weren't as crisply white as they should be but that couldn't be helped at a time when laundry soap and bleach were running short at the *blanchisserie*. It would be dark anyway. They'd rely on candlelight and gas lamps to supplement the electric wall light, which might fail if there was a power cut tonight. Nobody would notice that the table linen looked drab. Camille moved a fork handle so that it was exactly parallel to the table mat. She liked things to look exactly as they should do. It was possibly the one trait she shared with her mother-in-law: love of a well-set table, a properly arranged *salon*, a hostess dressed with attention, ready with witty conversation on books and art exhibitions.

'I wondered whether you'd notice that fork.' Véronique had entered the room so silently, Camille jumped at the sound of her voice. Another little test for her to pass or fail?

She smiled at her mother-in-law and said nothing, which,

she was learning, was often the best way of dealing with her comments. 'I must go up and change now.'

'You look tired.' From anyone else it might have been concern, but from Véronique it sounded like an accusation. But perhaps that was Camille reading into a comment something that hadn't been intended.

'I'll be sitting down soon enough, and I'll feel better then.' She hoped she would, anyway. Her stomach felt a little peculiar now. Leaning over the table to adjust the settings had made her lower back ache. She stood up straight and gave it an absent rub.

'Put your feet up when you've finished dressing.' Véronique sounded softer. 'I'll handle things down here. I know a little about Jean-Luc's guest.'

'Who is he?'

'A Herr Gruber.'

'A German? I thought...' Camille had assumed they'd be wooing yet another Vichy official. Jean-Luc dined with Germans, but he'd never yet brought one home. She felt even queasier.

'He owns a rayon manufacturing plant near Cologne.' Véronique's face conveyed the slightest hint of distaste.

Why were they dealing with an enemy competitor? Let alone entertaining him.

'I believe there was talk of some kind of cooperation contract.'

'What?'

'We send workers to Cologne with the promise they'll be decently paid and well treated and it will only be for six months.'

Camille must have looked puzzled. 'That sounds very generous by German standards?'

Véronique hesitated before continuing, looking as though every word she spoke was hurting her. 'Jean-Luc and Herr

Gruber would sign a contract transferring half the German plant to us.'

Pregnancy was obviously draining her intelligence, because Camille couldn't see why a German manufacturer would do this. Véronique nodded and left the room. Camille pulled out one of the dining room chairs and sat down, her legs feeling heavy, still thinking about Herr Gruber.

The Germans never countenanced any other outcome than ultimate victory. Yet they must know that one day the Allies would land in Europe and sweep them out. Papa had always said that the Soviet Union and America both joining the Allied cause in 1941 meant that Hitler's defeat was inevitable. And then what would happen to the factories in Germany belonging to those who'd pillaged subjugated nations? The Allies would confiscate them. But if half the assets in Cologne were owned by Jean-Luc in Lyon, well, perhaps the entire German business couldn't be taken in reparations? No doubt the contract Herr Gruber was drawing up would arrange for Jean-Luc's share to be transferred back to him at some point in the future when he was safe from Allied demands. It was just as well Maman wasn't taking her blood pressure just now because Camille could feel anger boiling inside her.

Was Jean-Luc going to agree to this travesty? Surely not. And yet why would he have the German here if he wasn't planning to sign the contract? She needed to talk to him about this. She recalled the snippet of conversation she'd overheard between Jean-Luc and his mother, something about twenty being too many. Twenty employees going to Herr Gruber's factory in Cologne? Her brain felt full of cotton wool.

She went up to wash and change. Each stair seemed like a climb in its own right. When she reached the bedroom, she was breathless. Before her pregnancy, she'd taken Lyon's steep hills in her stride. She'd been a fit and active young woman: a skier, tennis player. But it would soon be over, this exhausting pregnancy.

Her head was aching. She had aspirin in the room and took a couple. Slipping off the comfortable flat heels she wore indoors, she searched her underwear drawer for a fresh pair of stockings. Camille looked at her calves. They didn't seem too swollen, but ached.

She lay down for a moment. The headache was clearing but she found she needed to make a dash, or the closest to it she could still make, to the lavatory. Something she'd eaten hadn't agreed with her insides. Sometimes, Jeanne kept meat a day or two longer than she liked, shaking her head as she served it. The food always tasted good, though.

Camille washed her hands and looked at her watch. The guest would be here in thirty or forty minutes. It would take her every bit of that to finish dressing and arrange her hair. In pregnancy it had grown almost as thick as Maman's, which was pleasing, but it took her longer to manage. Jean-Luc had bought her a set of pearl-encrusted hairpins as a wedding present, which she planned to wear tonight. The lustre of the pearls would be flattering, help soften the weariness on her face. She'd wear Maman's gold pendant, despite Véronique's advice to wear the string of pearls. It was graceful and discreet and wouldn't detract from the combs. Thankfully, she still had a lipstick that was more than a worn-down remnant of pigment. She was staring at it, unable to focus on grooming herself, irritated by the effort it all took.

Another pain made her catch her breath and lean forward while it lasted. When it finished, she lay down on her bed, feeling distracted, as though there were things she needed to sort out, things that had nothing to do with this dinner. She'd already checked the baby clothes again this afternoon. All the same, she felt an urge to go into the nursery and open the drawers and count every garment, rearrange the little blankets on the wicker bassinet. Where were they going to put the second baby? Would the twins be able to share for the first week or so – head to toe, perhaps? She thought of birds in the spring, fussing over twigs in the nest. If only she was a mother bird high up in a tree, with no loathed guests to entertain.

Sighing, Camille lowered her legs and picked up her stockings, gazing at them as though they were unknown objects. If only something would require Herr Gruber to cancel his appearance.

Could she just absent herself from the meal? When even Véronique seemed ruffled by the prospect of dining with the German, surely her condition gave her the perfect excuse to opt out?

The pains stopped. She bent down and pulled up a stocking, puffing with the exertion. She would do her duty tonight for her husband's sake. In return, she'd insist that no more Germans should ever be entertained in this house. And she'd ask Jean-Luc what on earth was going on with this contract. He might be her husband, the head of the family and director of the business, but as the soon-to-be mother of his child, children even, she had a voice in this house.

She blinked. Was impending motherhood making her fierce in a way she hadn't been before? Camille smiled briefly at herself.

TWENTY-ONE

SOPHIE

Sophie wrote up her notes on Camille, trying to do so as an objective professional rather than concerned mother. Only a few days until Camille saw her doctor again. She noted the urine test results and dated them. Surely the doctor would agree with Sophie about the twins? But she knew of cases where the babies had moved and finding two heartbeats again was harder than it had previously been. Sometimes, clinics x-rayed pregnant women to be sure, but this seemed like an unlikely option in a city where every kind of medical equipment was running short.

From downstairs she heard occasional footsteps and doors opening and closing. Her heart ached for her daughter having to sit through a formal-sounding dinner when she probably longed to be eating something on a tray, feet propped up, the wireless tuned to some light entertainment programme. But she could only advise, as Camille's midwife; she had no power to insist on this. She noted Camille's contractions in her notes, saying that they were probably Braxton Hicks or false labour as they hadn't settled into a regular pattern. She would ask her further questions later on in the evening. Assuming she could get her daughter alone.

The maid, Jeanne, knocked on the door and handed over a tray of supper with a smile. 'Is Madame Camille doing well?' Her face was knotted into concern.

'We just need to watch her for the next week.'

'My sister looked the same at the end of her first confinement. Her *sage-femme* said she was not to be troubled with domestic problems and must be allowed to rest.'

'She was right. Madame will need someone keeping an eye on her.'

Jeanne nodded. 'The young madame is kind to me. She worries there is too much for me to do now it is just me in the house.'

'It's a big place to look after, with all these floors.'

'A woman comes in to clean twice a week. So I mainly do the cooking and organise the laundry. But finding food takes up so much time nowadays. Madame Camille used to like going to the market for me, but they don't like her walking far now with heavy bags.' Jeanne opened the door. 'I'll watch her when you are not here.'

Sophie felt tears prick at her eyes. Strange how, for all her talents and achievements, it was mention of Camille's kindness that moved her most.

The meal, though meagre in size, was delicious. A thin sliver of chicken breast cooked in some kind of wine sauce, with early potatoes. A dish of carrots. A slice of soft-rind cheese with half a pear. A glass of what tasted like white burgundy. Sophie hoped Camille's portion of chicken would be larger than this one, delicious though it was.

Downstairs, the front door was opened. Male voices rang out. Jean-Luc and someone older, with a strong, guttural accent. The business contact from Germany, Sophie guessed.

Curiosity overcame her. She hadn't yet seen her son-in-law

in the flesh, only in the wedding photograph. Opening the bedroom door, she crept along the landing to stand out of sight at the top of the stairs. She could only really see Jean-Luc's legs, in a well-cut pair of suit trousers. The German was in civilian clothes, too. She couldn't see his face, either.

He stepped forward to hand his hat to Jeanne and she saw him in profile. Frowning, Sophie moved a step closer and looked down at him, at the tortoise-shell-rimmed spectacles, at the little fuzz of hair above his upper lip. The hat he was handing to the maid, with the little feather in its band, looking as if it had been bought in the Tyrol – all these were familiar.

Bile filled her mouth. She clutched the balustrade. Camille was coming out to greet the men, the warmth in her voice as she kissed her husband marked in comparison to her cool *bonsoir* to the German. Camille glanced up as she stepped forward to shake the latter's hand and Sophie darted back to avoid being spotted. Jean-Luc told his wife that their visitor had decided he'd stay the night and he assumed the guest room was ready?

'I'll go upstairs shortly myself and ensure all is in order.'

'Let my mother do it? You know she likes to help.'

Sophie peeped round the top of the staircase. '*Non.*' Camille smiled at her husband. 'I would like to check myself. In a moment.'

She said the last words more loudly, perhaps hoping that Sophie would hear and prepare herself to move.

'My wife is very particular about our guest arrangements, Herr Gruber,' Jean-Luc said. Herr Gruber said something about housewives and pride in domesticity that sounded like a line straight from the German Nazi newspaper, the Völkischer Beobachter. They walked down the hall, presumably to have aperitifs with Véronique who'd be acting as lady of the house, sitting down and waiting for the guests to be presented to her.

Sophie went back to the bedroom and tried to eat the last of her pear, although it no longer tasted as sweet. She was overreacting. The guest downstairs, Herr Gruber, had no reason to remember her. They could spend the night under the same roof without coming across one another. Even if they did bump into one another, why would he make the connection? She was here as the midwife, Madame Leclerc, not Sophie Hansen, mother of Camille, after all.

A sudden recollection chilled her. When she'd first encountered Gruber nine months earlier on the train leaving Annemasse after the disaster with Hélène, she'd told him she was a midwife. She'd been exhausted, grieving.

Sophie had circled the town, wary of each sound. It was well past curfew by the time she found the cemetery. She slept the night in the recessed entrance to a family tomb that provided partial shelter, knees pulled into her chest, shivering, dropping off for minutes at a time, only to awaken with a start, alert to every sound.

In the morning, she did her best to tidy herself up. She had no mirror but a hasty rummage through her jacket pockets yielded an old comb and an even older lipstick, along with her ticket and identity papers. Her midwife's bag was still strapped over her chest. Thank God for Bernhardt's extra strap. When the bag was full, the strap dug into her shoulder and so she preferred holding it by the handle, but last night it meant she hadn't lost the bag. Her clothes would still be in the hostel, lost to her.

She walked briskly through the town towards the station, finding the streets mercifully quiet. At the station, she darted into the ladies' and attempted to comb her hair into place with shaking hands and apply the crumbly old lipstick. The beret she'd worn had been lost somewhere along the border, no time to shop for something else to cover her head, even if shops still sold clothes.

She reminded herself over and over of the story prepared in advance for the return journey to Lyon. She'd taken a few days' vacation in the town, walking and enjoying the views of the Alps. As a widow, she'd travelled alone. She knew nobody in Annemasse but had wanted a change of scene for a few days. Now she was returning to Lyon.

But she'd been seen out on that field with Hélène and the children. Had the Gestapo already tortured Hélène into telling them the name of the woman who'd helped her smuggle the group into Switzerland? The thought of the girl being mistreated, abused, made her want to vomit. Would Hélène's parents have received the news yet? Sophie wanted to cover her face with her hands. It felt cowardly to run away from this town and leave Hélène to face it all alone, but the rational voice inside her said that her arrest wouldn't help Hélène now and would only endanger the pastor and the rest of the group. And Camille. Sophie's blood ran cold. Jean-Luc would offer some protection to his new bride, but Lyon mightn't be safe for Camille if her mother was arrested.

She'd have to leave the city and go somewhere she wasn't known. They'd already run from Berlin, and then Paris and now she'd run again, even if it meant separating herself from Camille.

There was no extra guard at the station, no indication that anything was out of the ordinary. Sophie showed her return ticket and walked onto the platform. The train was on time. She found her carriage and sat down, wishing she had something to read, to distract herself with. Carrying an everyday basket or string bag would have made her look more of a day-to-day traveller. A woman with the uncovered, thick blonde hair needed to do all she could to blend in. If only she had a headscarf. Too late now, even if she could have found a shop still selling such a thing.

The German man with the Tyrolean hat got into the

carriage just as the whistle was blown, nodding at her and wishing her *Bonjour, madame* in accented French. He wore a Nazi party pin in his jacket lapel and carried a briefcase. She nodded back and sat looking out of the window, as though sadly saying goodbye to a holiday.

He was looking at her. She could see his reflection in the window, his pale eyes observing her through tortoise-shell spectacles. The irises were very blue. What would an innocent person do if they knew they were being observed? Look back quizzically? Pretend they hadn't noticed? Sophie decided to yawn, raising a hand to her mouth and settling back in the seat. Her eyes were almost closed, but open just enough to see what he was doing now. He seemed to be looking at her left hand. She must have scraped it on the wire fence last night as she pushed Ida through.

Was the cut bleeding? She dared not look. The train gathered speed and she let her head nod backwards and forwards with its motion. Though perhaps this was suspicious? At nine in the morning would a healthy woman be so sleepy? On the other hand, alone in a carriage with a German, perhaps it would seem like a normal response to avoid eye contact or conversation.

She needed to do something that looked perfectly normal, but her wits seemed to have deserted her. Write a shopping list? Trying not to look flustered, she searched her inside jacket pockets, discovering a piece of writing paper and a pencil. She scanned the paper quickly, making sure there were no names on it.

It was an old list from years ago when they were still in Paris. *Oranges, 1 lemon, butter, eggs, coffee.*

She might as well have written caviar, gold bars and diamonds. Nobody would take her shopping list seriously. She crossed out the original items and added cooking oil. Carrots. Shirt buttons. Sewing needles.

'You have no basket, madame,' her companion said, making

her jump. Obviously, those glasses were doing a good job with his eyesight. 'And that bag looks pretty full already.' He smiled as though they were sharing a joke. Did he think she was smuggling in illegally acquired food from Switzerland?

She nodded politely.

'Your hand looks painful.'

She looked down at it as though noticing it for the first time.

'How did you do that?'

'Must have been the broken wire netting on my friend's rabbit hutch,' she said.

'You should mend the wire and dress the cut. There's a risk of infection.'

She nodded demurely.

'Do you have a clean handkerchief?'

'I have something in here, monsieur.' Without thinking she patted the bag again. 'I'll attend to it in a moment.' He peered at it short-sightedly.

'Oh, I didn't notice. It's a medical bag? You can't be a doctor, madame?' He laughed.

'A nurse and midwife.'

'A midwife?' He nodded. 'One hears that the birth rate in France is increasing. Marshal Pétain has done well there.'

He meant the falling birth rate since the first war, something the puppet French prime minister was devoted to halting. But Sophie wasn't thinking about population statistics now. She was cursing herself. Why give him extra details about herself he hadn't needed to know? She should have said the bag had belonged to her brother or father and she used it for travel purposes.

She felt her heart rate increase as she waited for him to ask where she was travelling to, but he had turned his attention to the briefcase beside him on the seat, taking out fabric samples, laying them out on his lap, holding them up to the light.

TWENTY-TWO

CAMILLE

Camille knocked on the door of the spare room. Maman was reading in the chair, or pretending to. She explained about Herr Gruber staying in the house tonight. Maman stood up immediately, very wary. She straightened the bedcover and plumped up the pillows. It looked as though nobody had been in here. Jeanne knew, of course. She'd have a word with her, make it sound a matter of no consequence that the *sage-femme* had been moved into the lesser spare bedroom with its view onto a side street.

'I'm sorry, Maman,' Camille said. 'We weren't expecting him to spend the night here. It makes me furious to think of him sleeping in this room instead of you.' She looked around at the delicate silk furnishing fabrics: the best the factory produced, the antique furniture. Véronique had a good eye for interior design, she had to admit. Having her mother stay in the house under an assumed identity had initially knotted Camille up inside, but there'd been deep pleasure knowing she was sleeping in this room, close by, in comfort – luxury, some might say, after the difficult conditions up on the plateau. 'It actually makes me

sick having someone like Herr Gruber anywhere in the house.'
Come to think of it, she actually did feel nauseous again.

'I should go back to the convent. It might be best.' Maman's
face was white.

'What's wrong?' It wasn't like Maman to show such fear of
the Germans.

'That man.'

'What about him?'

'We've encountered one another before.'

'Oh God.' Camille felt herself sink into the chair. 'He saw
you at Annemasse?' Her voice lowered even more as she spoke
the town's name.

'On the train. Leaving the following morning. But he asked
questions. He knows I'm a midwife. He saw the cut on my
wrist. He remarked on it while we were on the train. I said I'd
cut it on rabbit-hutch wire.'

'Are you sure it's him?'

'Those glasses. And the Tyrolean hat.'

Camille had also noticed a Nazi party pin on the guest's
lapel. He might be wearing it because that's what every businessman had to wear in the Reich to flourish. But he was in
France now. No, the man was dangerous, even more than she'd
first thought.

'But he didn't actually see you at the border?'

Sophie shook her head. 'But the police and Gestapo in the
town know I was involved. I'd been observed out on the field
with Hélène in the days before. I'm a tall Dutchwoman with
this—' She pointed at her hair. 'And like a fool I told him I was a
midwife when he asked me oh-so-innocent questions on the
train. If he sees me here again, he'll remember. And if he has
contacts in the Gestapo or SS and they talk about what's been
happening with child smuggling into Switzerland, well, you can
see why I'm concerned.'

Another twinge in her pelvis grabbed at Camille, making it

impossible to talk. The twinge became more purposeful, muscular, as if someone was clenching her, strong enough to make her swallow hard. It seemed to form a band around her pelvis and lower back and down to her thighs.

Maman was watching her. The contraction was still making it impossible to talk.

'They've started again?' Maman said. 'Breathe like I showed you.' All fear seemed to drop from her shoulders; she was back in command of herself, the calm midwife with a first-time mother. Camille breathed out slowly. The grip on her abdomen stopped.

'It's gone. I must get dressed.'

'Can you not tell that husband of yours you're indisposed? That he must send the guest away?' The words came out more curtly than perhaps Maman had intended. She started to apologise, but Camille held up a hand.

'Jean-Luc's worried about something at the factory. I can't tell you what and I don't know all the details, but I—' She stopped. It was suddenly starting to make sense, Jean-Luc insisting that Herr Gruber came for a meal, the meetings late at night, the concern about the workers, the muttered conversation with Véronique Camille had overheard. It wasn't all to do with Gruber's factory contract. Of course. 'I think he might be hiding... people who work for him,' she whispered. 'Possibly Resistance or Jewish? And entertaining people like that man is a cover.'

Maman's sharp eyes met hers. 'He hasn't told you anything about it?'

'Once or twice he started to say something. But I was always so tired, so worried about the pregnancy.'

'He was probably hoping that keeping it secret would mean you were safer.'

Camille was feeling a little better now and not just physically. She ought to have been worried about what Jean-Luc had done, but a sense of pride filled her. 'We should move you to the other bedroom.' She opened the door. 'It's clear.'

She led Maman up the staircase. The rooms on the floor above were smaller. Jeanne slept in one of them. Was there even a spare bed made up? She opened the bedroom door opposite Jeanne's, seeing that the room was ready for occupancy, but dusty and tired-looking, the bolsters lumpy, the sheets yellow.

Maman put up a hand to silence her apology. 'If you knew the places we've sent children to sleep in up in the hills, this looks like the Ritz.' She frowned. 'My only issue is being further away from you.'

'I'll tell Jeanne you've moved room,' Camille said. 'She'll get you if the contractions become more regular.'

Maman put a hand on Camille's arm. 'I've noted the time, ten past eight,' she said. 'You must make a mental note of the time of the next one. If it's within the next fifteen minutes or less, make an excuse and ask her to fetch me.'

Camille nodded.

'Go back to your guests. Eat: you'll need the energy later on.'

Camille felt a wave of emotion. She put her arms around her mother and kissed her. 'I'd be so scared if you weren't here.'

'I'm very close, *liefje*. And first babies usually take their time. I'll telephone the clinic when a pattern sets in and tell them we're bringing you in. You should be there in good time, given the circumstances.'

'I want to stay a bit longer.' Her mother looked at her quizzically. 'I need to support Jean-Luc this evening.'

'Well, if you can eat a meal first, so much the better.' She sat down on the bed. Camille closed the door quietly behind her.

As Véronique and Herr Gruber were sitting down, she managed to catch Jean-Luc and motion him out of the dining room. While Véronique asked stiff questions about Herr Gruber's home in Cologne, Camille whispered to Jean-Luc that things seemed to be starting. 'Do you want to retire to the bedroom?' His eyes were wide with concern.

'No.' If what she now suspected about Jean-Luc and his workers was true, she wanted to do all she could for her husband. If that meant helping him with Herr Gruber, she'd do that.

'Shouldn't I drive you straight into the clinic?' He took her hands, looking anxious. 'If we go now, we'll beat the curfew.'

'No, the pains aren't regular. My—the midwife is upstairs, she will tell us when we need to go.'

'I could cancel this dinner.'

'It really matters, doesn't it?'

He tried to tell her the dinner wasn't important. She cut him off. 'I know, Jean-Luc.' She moved around so that her back was to Gruber. 'I've guessed,' she whispered. 'We'll talk about it later. But we have to keep him on side, don't we? He's providing cover?'

He nodded and squeezed her hands, his eyes expressing anguish and love. 'Once or twice I started to tell you what we were doing, but it seemed selfish.'

'Selfish?'

'You're my wife, expecting my first child. Children plural! Why should I lay yet another burden on you?'

'It's exactly because I'm your wife that you should.' She rubbed his hands between hers. 'I hate to think of you carrying this alone.' She remembered Véronique's whispers outside the salon door. 'But of course your mother knows.'

He signed. 'No keeping it from her. She always claims women have no place interfering in business, but she knew something was going on. She meets the foreman's wife at Mass sometimes. The wife said something about... certain workers. Maman worked it out and asked me directly. I hadn't wanted her to know, either. You were both safer knowing nothing.' He shivered, despite the warmth of the spring evening.

'You think the foreman's wife is a blabbermouth?'

'She knows my mother is discreet. I'm hoping she was the only confidante.'

As Camille sat down, she'd told herself she felt fine. No more pains. Perhaps the fear intermittently sweeping her was distracting her body. Jean-Luc had been taking such a heavy risk, all the while putting on a cheerful and supportive face for her benefit. She looked across the dinner table at her husband and felt her eyes prickle. If only they were alone, eating a quiet supper together, talking opening about everything they hoped for and everything they feared. There was so much about her husband she hadn't known, so much she hadn't told him herself. Why had they left it so late? Her eyes prickled again.

She needed to pull herself together, be more her mother's daughter. She put her shoulders back and picked up her cutlery. The *hors d'oeuvre* was a celeriac salad. Jeanne had managed to find olive oil and Dijon mustard to dress it. Herr Gruber, sitting between her and Véronique, praised it. The chicken wasn't a large one, but Jeanne had cooked it so it was buttery tender. Camille hoped eating would stop the guest talking. He'd been so impressed with the factory, with the quality of the fabrics produced, the knowledge of the workers. When the maid had shown him up to his room, he was even more impressed to see examples of the silks made up into the furnishings. This was a beautiful house. And Lyon itself was clearly a city of great culture and history. She nodded and tried to interject the occasional neutral comment, but it all felt a strain. Perhaps it showed. Herr Gruber frowned.

'You seem fatigued, madame? I hope I'm not boring you?'

She gave a quick shake of her head, forced a tight smile and picked up her fork. She was hungry, aware that she needed to eat, but simultaneously too restless to put more than the smallest forkfuls into her mouth. Perhaps a sip of wine... but that wasn't helping either.

Herr Gruber was asking her about her family, whether she'd always lived in Lyon. She told him her father had died and was vague about Maman, saying wartime made it hard to keep in touch with her, diverting the conversation back to Herr Gruber where she could. Had he visited other silk manufacturers in Lyon?

'None as estimable as your husband's.' He all but winked at her. She pictured his plump little hands fingering the silks and salivating. Something of her disgust must have shown on her face – his lips tightened.

But as the plates were cleared and the third course appeared she started to feel strange, her head floating but her body somehow pulled down towards the ground. She wanted to be up and out of the chair, going through the baby things in the nursery again. Sitting here and making small talk felt absurd.

Irritation turned to knowledge that this dinner table was not where she ought to be. Her back was suddenly hurting again, quite insistently, she needed to stand up to relieve the pain. As she rose, she caught the edge of the table and the crockery on her plate rattled. Véronique frowned.

'*Excusez-moi,*' she told Herr Gruber. 'I must just—' Véronique said something to her, but Camille cut her off with a shake of her head. 'I need to check on something with Jeanne.'

Instead of going into the kitchen, she walked up the stairs, taking her time, but feeling an urgent need to visit the lavatory again. This wasn't anything she'd eaten, though.

The contraction grabbed her so forcibly she only just had time to place her hands on her dressing table to support herself. She felt a gush of liquid over her ankles. 'Maman,' she called, before she could stop herself. Fool, fool. Her mother was running lightly down the stairs and through the door in an instant, closing it silently behind her.

'It's all right,' Maman said, 'nobody else heard. I was listening out for you.' She took her by the arm. 'Let's take you to your bed.'

'My waters... the carpet.'

'I'll tidy up in a moment.' Maman opened the bag she'd brought down with her, washed her hands and put on a pair of gloves and a mask. 'I wouldn't normally wear it in a private home, but in case someone comes in.'

Her hands ran gently over Camille's abdomen as she lay down. She helped her remove her underwear and examined her internally. Her back was hurting more now. Maman told her to lie still until she felt stronger and then to try to move around the room between contractions while she could. She went into the bathroom, running taps.

'We should be in the maternity clinic,' Maman said. 'I will go down and tell Jean-Luc.'

'No. This can't be happening. Not with that man in the house. This isn't how it was supposed to be.' Camille felt a wave of pain start in her back and squeeze her. Maman looked at her and took her wrist. 'It feels... different.'

Maman was looking at her watch, timing the pain. When it stopped, Maman examined her again.

She nodded. 'Too late for getting you to the clinic.'

'They're really coming? I thought it would take ages first time.'

'Usually.' Maman washed her hands. 'I'll ask Jeanne to fetch extra help for us.'

'Can't you...?'

'I can't care for one mother and two babies by myself. I'll call the doctor and ask the nuns to send someone. There are some experienced women in the infirmary.' Maman smiled at Camille, looking confident, filling her with the knowledge she could do this. 'I won't be a moment. I won't leave you alone. Give me the doctor's number.'

'It's too early.' Camille heard the panic in her own voice.

'Three weeks isn't too premature. Many twins are early. We're ready for them.' Maman's smile filled Camille with strength.

'The pain is more than I expected.'

Maman shook her head. 'My drug supplies ran out. Your doctor might have something stronger than aspirin, but it may be too late by the time he gets here. You're going to be fine. I'll help you. You aren't alone.'

'But that man is downstairs. He scares me.' Camille moaned again.

Maman looked fierce. 'I won't let him harm you or your babies.'

And Camille knew all would be well because this was what her mother always did: deliver babies safely.

TWENTY-THREE

SOPHIE

It was all happening too quickly with Camille. There were so many reasons why this could be, but no time to delve into them now. Sophie prayed Camille hadn't seen the worry in her eyes.

The door to the dining room was closed as she walked past. Jeanne was in the kitchen, her arms in a bowl of hot water. Quietly, Sophie explained what was happening upstairs, that she needed to call Camille's doctor immediately and tell him a twin delivery was taking place at home. And they needed to send a message to the convent.

Jeanne looked sharply at Sophie. 'They can't hear you telephoning from the dining room. Let me tell monsieur what is happening.'

'*Merci.*'

'You don't want *him* to see you, do you?' She pointed at the mask.

Sophie shook her head. Jeanne looked at her sharply. Could she be trusted?

'Many people in Lyon choose not to see or hear things these days, madame, don't you worry.' She pointed to the stove. 'That pot's just off the boil. The hot water in the bathrooms upstairs runs slow these days. I'll pour it into a jug for you and find you a basin.'

Sophie walked back down the hall to the little foyer, really just a half-cabinet enclosing the telephone. Making calls was all but impossible these days; she half expected the exchange to inform her she could not be connected, but telling them she was a midwife in an emergency seemed to soften the operator's terse tone. After the telephone rang for some time, a sleepy-sounding woman answered and told her that the doctor was on a house visit. She took the number and information Sophie gave her about a twin delivery.

She longed for Erich Meyer, standing quietly at her shoulder, passing equipment, ready to intervene if needed. No time to daydream, would the nuns all be in chapel? She could never remember the times of their services.

But the call was answered and the woman she spoke to promised to pass word to Sister Marie-Claude immediately, double-checking the address. 'The babies will be small, they will need a lot of care,' Sophie told her.

If they both survived.

Would a dash by car to the maternity clinic still be better? With roadblocks and diversions, it mightn't be a quick drive. If Camille gave birth in the car, they might be stranded with a newly delivered mother and frail newborns. It was only April – nights were still cool. Camille was as comfortable as she could be without pain relief, and in warm, familiar surroundings. The doctor would turn up later. Above all, Sophie herself was here. Her experience with twin births must count for something.

Jeanne appeared with the jug and basin, which Sophie took up to Camille. Her daughter was bending over the dressing table, another contraction about to sweep through her. 'Reinforcements are on the way.' Quickly, she pulled sheets and blankets off the bed to cover the mattress with the rubber sheet, adding towels from the bathroom.

'No clinic.' Camille groaned. 'Oh God, this pain's going to kill me.' The last words were gasped out as the full power of the contraction took over. Sophie longed for a mask and nitrous oxide. Some of the hospital liked twilight sleep – a mixture of drugs to knock out a labouring mother. Sophie distrusted the idea, believing women would wake feeling disassociated from the birth, and that the cocktail might affect the baby. At this moment, however, she'd have done anything to spare Camille. The pastor's words echoed in her mind: was she sure she could be objective while looking after her own child?

When the pain eased, Sophie lay Camille down and examined her again. She was dilating very quickly, already six centimetres. Someone knocked on the door. Jean-Luc. 'Camille? Are you all right?'

'It's all happening.' Camille put on a brave tone.

'You mean...? But it's too early.'

'Sorry for interrupting your dinner.' Sophie could see Camille making a real effort between the contractions. 'Is your guest still intending to stay the night with us?'

A sigh from outside the door. 'I told him we'd understand if he made his excuses. But he's absorbed in the *tarte aux pommes*. He says he understands if we're a little distracted.'

The German was going to stay in the house despite the start of Camille's labour? Sophie felt her mouth open in objection. To stop herself speaking out, she poured a glass of water for Camille and handed it to her, still raging. How could that man be so insensitive? But why was she even asking the question after all these years? He was an invader, an occupier, after all. He could do anything he wanted in France. A man who wore a pin like that in his lapel need never feel he should remove himself from any situation in the occupied land. His convenience was all that mattered. Everything else, every courtesy, every social convention owed to a woman in childbirth, was subordinate.

'My mother will manage him. Don't worry.' But a note in Jean-Luc's voice made it clear that he didn't like the situation either. Was he really so desperate to ingratiate himself with Herr Gruber, or, at least, not to antagonise him? But Sophie didn't have time to think about it now. Camille was groaning again, the groan turning into a gasp of pain. Her face was contorted and covered in perspiration. Jean-Luc whispered another endearment from outside the door and his footsteps disappeared.

'Are the babies positioned any better now?' Camille asked when she could talk again.

'I believe I can see the crown of the first baby's head,' Sophie said, kneeling down, feeling a rush of excitement that even her anxiety couldn't diminish. She tried to establish whether the start of labour had repositioned the second child, but Camille winced as her hands moved, puzzling out the position of its head and legs. Another contraction. Sophie held her daughter's hand, quietly encouraging her to breathe through it, telling her she was doing well. Her voice might sound as it always did: calm, confident, but with her own daughter and with twins, she didn't feel as she usually did. She'd have to ask Jeanne or even Véronique to come and assist in a minute. If Véronique had been present at her daughters' confinements, she might actually be useful. Jeanne was clearly a competent and sensible woman.

To her relief, Sophie heard the doorbell ring and Jeanne's footsteps going to open it. The visitors came upstairs and knocked on the door. With relief, she called them in, still absorbed in Camille. 'Help is here,' Sophie said. 'To look after the first baby at least.' She smiled at Camille. 'You're managing so well.'

'I never imagined...' Camille bit her lip as the pain swept her. Nobody could ever accurately convey to a woman what labour pains would feel like. There was a balance between giving women the confidence that they could manage and being realistic about what they might expect. Camille's labour had come on very fast and the contractions were fierce. Did her body have some instinct that the twins should be born now, that the womb that had nurtured them was now failing? Was there something that Sophie had missed? The raised blood pressure yesterday... That reminded her to take the pressure again. When the contraction finished, she wrapped the cuff around Camille's arm. Her heartbeat slowed as she saw that Camille's readings were as she'd expect at this stage in labour, raised, but not dangerously high.

At last she turned around to greet the newcomers. Sister Marie-Claude felt like an old friend. Standing beside her was someone else. 'Rosa?'

'She's spent a lot of time with the other mothers, despite being so newly delivered herself, and proved herself invaluable. We thought you might need two of us if there are two babies.'

'But Patrin?'

'I left milk for him with the sisters.' Rosa shook her head. 'I still seem to have more than I need.'

Marie-Claude was already rolling up her sleeves and heading for the basin. Rosa followed.

'It feels like burning,' Camille said, grimacing.

'That means you're very close now,' Sophie told her. Camille groaned again, more of a scream this time. Now the first baby's head was clearly visible. 'Little breaths,' Sophie said. Camille did as she asked. The baby seemed to fall into Sophie's hands. 'You have a daughter,' she told Camille, looking the child over. Her mind was still that of the midwife's. This was her granddaughter, her first grandchild, but for now she was looking at her almost dispassionately. The girl made a small noise like a kitten. Sophie wrapped her quickly in a towel, checked her mouth was clear and rubbed her arms and legs, trying to encourage her circulation. She was small and pale, but breathing well. Sophie tied the cord in two places with sterile silk thread and cut it in between and handed her to Camille to hold. She washed her hands again before finding the silver nitrate to apply to each of the baby's eyes. 'Enjoy your little girl before I weigh her,' she said, remembering something. 'Where are the napkins and clothes?'

'In the nursery, first door on the right.' Camille didn't lift her eyes from her daughter.

Sister Marie-Claude was already moving towards the door. She returned with a bundle. Rosa weighed the napkin first on the portable scales and then took the baby from Camille, with a gentle whisper of reassurance, wrapping her in the napkin and attaching it to the hook.

When she'd finished the weighing, Rosa frowned at Camille. 'You need to drink some water, madame.' She poured her another glass from the carafe and helped her rearrange her pillows so she could sit up straighter.

Sophie smiled at her. 'You're a natural, Rosa.'

Rosa gave a little shrug, as though she didn't know what to do with praise.

Sophie massaged Camille's abdomen and the first twin's placenta appeared. 'One for each twin?' Rosa peered closely at what was happening.

'Probably means these are non-identical twins,' Sophie told her. 'Or they'd share a placenta.'

'Good.' Camille was absorbed in her daughter. 'I was wondering about that. I think I'd prefer two separate little people who won't be mistaken for one another.'

Sophie checked the placenta in an enamel bowl and beckoned Rosa over, showing her how she examined it. 'Even a small retained piece can cause bleeding or infection.' Rosa focused sharply on what Sophie was showing her, showing no aversion. Any other time, Sophie would have found it interesting to ask Rosa about traditions and rituals among her people at this stage.

She wrapped it up and examined Camille again. 'Pass me the trumpet from my bag, Rosa, please,' she asked. The second twin's heartbeat was in a different place, it had shifted. To her relief, the beat hadn't slowed, the baby wasn't showing distress yet, but it was positioned with its head upwards. Perhaps it had always been this way round, impossible to determine because it was squashed in with its sibling. A breech birth. 'I'll need to examine you again,' she told Camille, who moaned. 'I'll be gentle.' Sister Marie-Claude took the baby.

The second twin's legs were tidily tucked up against the body. Good. Sister Marie-Claude watched her as Sophie stood up again, her eyes sharp, rocking the first twin gently. She nodded at Sophie. 'You'll manage,' she said in a voice so low that nobody else heard. 'And I'll say a decade quickly.'

A decade of the rosary, a sequence of prayers said at times of need or thanks, often before a statue of the Virgin Mary, mother of God. Despite Sophie's religious scepticism, she felt herself gain strength as she heard the prayers.

TWENTY-FOUR

'Get onto all fours, Camille.' Sophie looked at Rosa. 'Can you help me move her, please?'

'Like an animal.' Camille was trying to smile. 'Is this something you saw out in the wilds of the Appalachians, Maman?' Sophie glanced at Rosa – had Sister Marie-Claude told her the true relationship between mother and daughter? Before she could say anything, Rosa placed a hand on Sophie's arm.

'I trusted you with my secret. You can trust me.'

Sister Marie-Claude nodded at Sophie, her steady gaze expressing confidence in Rosa. Sophie felt herself breathe out.

'I do remember a similar case, yes,' she told Camille. A woman in a remote cabin, her first baby, a big child. The older of the midwives Sophie had travelled with had told her that the worst thing was to apply traction with a breech like this one, they should let gravity and the baby do the work. The head would find its way out. Usually. But she wasn't going to think about what would happen if it didn't.

The first twin had been born, Camille had shown she could deliver a baby. The second infant was probably going to be smaller. And there was no time to reach the clinic now.

Fleetingly, she thought back to Marta's labour, when she'd had Erich Meyer with her. Pure indulgence to wish he was here now.

With the next contraction, the baby's buttocks appeared, a tiny boy. Camille yelled that she couldn't go on, it was killing her.

'You're so nearly there,' Sophie told her. 'Your son's legs are uncurling themselves. You'll meet him soon.'

She turned to Rosa. 'Pass me a towel please.' Rosa handed it to her. She wrapped it around the baby's waist.

'Why are you doing that?' Rosa asked.

'So he's not cold. We don't want him to gasp in fluid,' Sister Marie-Claude told her, watching intently.

'The fluid would injure his lungs?'

'Exactly.'

Sophie placed a hand on Camille's pelvis, applying gentle pressure. Too much would risk pulling the baby's head down before the passage was clear for it, risking injury. 'Usually, nature will find the best way out for the baby,' the old Appalachian midwife had told Sophie. 'Hold back, take a breath, watch.'

The watching without acting was the hardest thing for Sophie. She might be rash in other parts of her life, but not here, with her daughter and grandson at risk. *Count to twenty,* Bernhardt said in her head. The baby was turning, she helped him rotate his shoulder. Camille cried out again. 'Oh God, I can't do this.'

'Your baby is so nearly with us, child.' Sister Marie-Claude's calm voice soothed Sophie, too. There was comfort in not being alone here.

'Come on, little one,' she whispered to the boy. Now the other arm could release itself too and it was only the head to come out. Camille, too exhausted to cry out, gave a muted gasp. The baby somehow managed to position himself so both shoul-

ders and then his head were free. Sophie caught him. The cord
was short, compressed around his neck. Quickly, she untied it.
The infant was grey, motionless. She checked his mouth and
nose and rubbed his back. 'Pass me the trumpet,' she asked
Rosa. She placed it gently on the baby's upper chest. A heartbeat. Faint. She lifted his arms up and over his head slowly and
then down again, repeating it, encouraging the lungs to expand
and contract. Sophie paused, watching the chest. It rose and
fell, so slightly that she could barely see it happening. She
waited, putting her fingers on the heart. The beat seemed a little
stronger.

'What's happening?' Camille asked from the bed.

'Your son needs a moment,' Sophie told her. 'He's breathing,
but he's weak. The best thing you can do now is take your
daughter and put her to the breast. She needs you.' She wanted
to distract Camille away from what was happening with the
male infant, who was hovering right on the threshold between
life and death.

'You mustn't let him die, Maman. Please. Save him.'
Camille, now a mother of two, sounded like the little girl who'd
wept when her pet rabbit had died, her words coming out in
sobs. Sophie wrapped the boy in a blanket and held him in her
arms, watching his chest. Still rising and falling. Again she
rubbed his arms and legs again under the blanket. His colour
was better.

'We're going to swap the babies over. Take your son.' She
handed the baby to Camille as Rosa took the girl and helped
Camille hold him to her breast. Sister Marie-Claude covered
them both up with a blanket while Sophie returned to massage
Camille's lower pelvis and apply gentle traction to the cord.
The placenta came away. Good. Sophie inspected it. Complete.

'Now we should weigh the little boy, too.'

Rosa took him from Camille and weighed him, her move-
ments as assured as if she'd been doing it for years.

The stove in this room needed to be stoked. 'We need to keep you warm,' she told her daughter. 'Before I wash you and give you a clean nightdress.' She kissed Camille on her forehead when Rosa and Sister Marie-Claude were tidying up. Even now, when they both knew what the relationship was, she felt she had to be careful not to remind them that she was more than Camille's midwife. 'I'm so proud of you, *liefje*,' she whispered. 'You did magnificently.'

'I thought it was going to kill me.' Camille sat straighter. 'We need to tell Jean-Luc,' Camille said. 'A girl and a boy.' She sounded almost dazed.

Sister Marie-Claude nodded. 'I'll fetch your husband, Madame.'

Sophie wrapped up everything that would need to be burned, washing her hands again and pulling up her mask so as much of her face was covered as possible.

Someone was knocking at the front door. Jeanne was letting them in. The doctor. They came upstairs and knocked on the door. Rosa opened it. Sophie found herself in front of her son-in-law. His wedding photograph had shown him to be a handsome man. In the flesh he was even better looking, though his dark eyes were wide with anxiety. 'Madame,' he said. 'How is my wife?'

She liked him for asking that question before he enquired about the babies. 'Exhausted, but well.'

'There was some message about my patient delivering twins, but perhaps my housekeeper misunderstood?' A middle-aged man, whose tie was loose and whose breath smelled of brandy, bustled into the room ahead of Jean-Luc and Sister Marie-Claude. The doctor.

'A girl and a boy. The boy was an uncomplicated breech, not breathing at first until assistance was given.'

He sighed. 'I suppose you thought you could manage this, madame?'

'My wife was supposed to have her confinement in the maternity clinic with you attending,' Jean-Luc told him. 'I just pray this home delivery hasn't caused damage to the babies.'

Sophie bit her lip. Jean-Luc was worried, of course, probably in shock. But at the sight of Camille, sitting up in bed, the boy in her arms, Rosa beside her holding the girl, the tension seemed to sink out of his shoulders. '*Chérie.*' He went straight to her. 'Are you all right? Do you need anything?'

'I'm fine.' Camille handed him the boy.

'He is too small,' he said, looking at the doctor. 'So light. We must take them to the children's hospital?'

'I'll examine the infant first,' the doctor said. 'If we can keep him very warm here and if madame can feed them adequately, he may do better at home.' The doctor seemed slightly more focused now. Perhaps the effects of the alcohol he'd had were wearing off. He took the boy from Jean-Luc and laid him out on the bed, listening to his heart.

'They're both a little jaundiced,' Sophie said. The doctor looked as though he was about to dismiss the suggestion.

'They have a slight yellowish tint.' Sister Marie-Claude said. The doctor frowned and nodded.

'Perhaps. Sunlight will be the best cure for that. And plenty of milk.' He nodded at Sophie to replace the baby's clothes. 'Can you manage that, do you think, madame? Feeding two babies?'

'I am not sure. It all happened so quickly. I wasn't expecting it to be tonight.'

'You didn't attempt to reach the clinic?' He frowned at Sophie. 'One of my assistants could have looked after your patient while I was, erm, on my way.'

'The contractions quickly became very frequent,' Sophie said. 'I didn't like to risk getting madame into a car and having her deliver there, especially as they were going to be twins, and

probably small. I am well supported, too.' She nodded towards
Sister Marie-Claude.

He grunted, looking pained to agree with her. 'You may
need to find more milk to flush out the jaundice.' He motioned
to Rosa to lay the boy on the bed. 'You recorded both babies'
weights?' he asked Sophie.

She bit her lip beneath the mask. 'Yes, Monsieur le Docteur,
and I've started my notes on—'

He waved a hand. 'I don't need your notes. The girl infant is
stronger. She will almost certainly survive. The boy...' he looked
at Jean-Luc. 'You might want to have him baptised sooner
rather than later, monsieur.'

Camille moaned.

'Finish tidying up,' the doctor told Sophie. 'Make sure the
babies are fed every two or three hours throughout the night.'
He frowned at her mask. 'You are protecting madame from
some illness you have been in contact with?'

'An old habit. From my hospital days. I am perhaps over-
cautious.'

His eyes were still on her. 'Is that an accent I can hear?'

Someone knocked on the door and came in. 'I've been
patient long enough, I need to see my grandchildren.'
Véronique. 'And you, of course, Camille, I'm so relieved to see
you looking well, if tired.'

Distracted, the doctor stepped away from Sophie, heading
downstairs with Jean-Luc.

Had Véronique left the German downstairs? Sophie
checked her mask was pulled up as high as it would go, and
turned towards the pair from the convent, who had moved
outside the room, talking in low voices. 'Thank you both for
coming,' she told them.

'I thought...' Rosa stopped, looking at the nun.

'Rosa wondered if it would help Camille if she left milk for the twins before she goes back to the convent?' Sister Marie-Claude said.

Sophie felt her face relax into a smile. 'Let me ask her.' A look of relief flashed over Camille's face as Sophie passed on Rosa's offer while Jean-Luc and Véronique were fussing over the babies.

'It would be a relief to know I don't have to do all the feeds myself. There are bottles in the nursery. Could you ask Jeanne to feed our helpers, too? They must be tired and hungry.'

Sophie took her glass pump out of the bag and led Rosa down the landing. As they reached the nursery, the door to the spare room opened. Herr Gruber stood in front of them. In her mask and midwife's apron, Sophie felt she had some protection from his gaze, but Rosa flinched. '*Bonsoir*,' Herr Gruber said. Behind the spectacles his eyes narrowed. 'The midwife, I assume. And who is this young lady?'

'My assistant. Excuse me, monsieur.' Sophie gave Rosa a gentle push forwards. 'We need to do something for the newborns.'

He stood back to let them pass. Sophie felt his gaze on her back. She had tied her hair into a plait and pinned it up today. She could only pray that she looked less like the dishevelled woman on the Annemasse train he'd seen that last time, months ago.

'That man,' Rosa said, when they were out of hearing. 'He knows who I am. *What* I am. His type have an extra sense for finding people they think should be locked away or murdered.'

'Do you want to leave? I wouldn't blame you,' Sophie said. Rosa shook her head.

'I said I'd leave the milk for your daughter and I will.' Sophie showed her the bottles and found a glass bowl and towel. The girl sat on the bed in the nursery. Her young, fit body, malnourished as it was, seemed ideally suited to providing nourishment for babies and she used the pump with ease. 'I can bring more over tomorrow if you want?'

'I'm sure Camille would be grateful.'

Rosa nodded. Sophie showed her how to use the pump. When she'd finished expressing the milk, enough for a couple of feeds for the tiny babies, Sophie took the two of them downstairs. 'I'd have struggled without the two of you,' she told them.

'Three lives to care for,' Sister Marie-Claude sighed. 'Quite a challenge, even for an accomplished midwife like you.'

'Come into the kitchen with me now, there's food for you.' At the table, Jeanne was plating up the leftovers. Herr Gruber had eaten a good portion of the tarte, but there was still leftover chicken and cheese, along with bread. Sister Marie-Claude picked at her food. Sophie knew she'd be longing to take it back to the convent hospital instead for her patients. Perhaps Jeanne guessed, because she made up a separate small parcel and pushed it across the table, without a word.

Sophie urged Rosa to eat up. She looked at Jeanne. 'This kind young lady is providing extra milk for Madame Camille.'

'*Dieu vous bénisse*,' Jeanne told Rosa. 'With twins, that will be a help.' She placed a hand on Rosa's. The girl looked amazed. Not used to being treated with such kindness outside the convent, probably. Sophie asked Jeanne for a pan to boil water in so she could sterilise her instruments.

'I will do that for you, madame,' Jeanne said.

Sophie returned upstairs with bread and milk for Camille to find Jean-Luc had set up a small camp bed for her next to Camille and had brought in the bassinet from the nursery. The stove had been filled and the room was warm. 'I didn't want to assume too much, madame, but it would put my mind at rest if you'd sleep in here tonight with my wife and the babies.' He looked at Camille, who'd fallen asleep propped up against the pillows holding both her children. The concern on his face made her warm to her son-in-law. 'The infants can both sleep together in the bassinet, non?'

'They can.' If only she could talk to him as mother-in-law to son-in-law, tell him how proud she was of Camille. How much love she felt for the little souls she'd just delivered. How much she feared for the boy. The Occupation had corrupted a situation that should be uncomplicated and joyous. 'I'll do everything I can for the three of them, monsieur.'

He blinked at the fervour in her voice. Had she overdone it? He was probably puzzled as to why she was still wearing her mask.

'She'll need to feed them during the night, though we do have an extra supply.' Sophie explained about the feeding, and that extra milk had been provided.

'The *tsigane* girl?' Something crossed his face. Distaste about his children receiving milk from her? 'Herr Gruber was asking about her,' he added.

She looked at him. He seemed concerned rather than anything else.

'She's a *tsigane*, yes, but also a young mother who's done nothing wrong, and only wants to help us.'

He looked at her, puzzled, perhaps because she no longer sounded like the *sage-femme* visiting the household as a professional, but someone more involved. But then he turned back to Camille. 'She's warm enough? She doesn't need anything?'

Her heart softened towards him even more. 'For now, there is nothing you can do for them, monsieur. You should sleep, too.'

Jean-Luc kissed Camille on her forehead, as gently as if she was newborn herself, before repeating the gesture with both babies.

'They're so quiet,' he said, as he left the room. 'I thought they'd cry more.'

A baby who could cry loudly enough to tell you he or she

was hungry was a baby you didn't need to worry about, but she didn't tell Jean-Luc this. It was the infant who was too small, too sleepy to wake up and cry who worried her. Gently she removed and swaddled each twin, placing them head to toe in the bassinet. She took off her shoes and lay down on the camp bed, covered with a light blanket. She might doze off, but she would wake in a few hours' time to feed the babies. She knew Camille herself would also wake to look after her new daughter and son.

It was nature. Women stirring in the darkness because a newborn needed care was what had always happened since the world began, regardless of the ugliness outside.

She'd slept with a mother and newborn before, on many occasions where she'd worried they would need help in the night. But before tonight she'd never felt the emotion that was filling her heart now. Sophie fell asleep.

TWENTY-FIVE

First the boy and then immediately afterwards the girl woke, two hours after Sophie had drifted into sleep. Camille and Sophie stirred. 'I'll get the extra milk from the kitchen while you feed one of them,' Sophie told Camille.

Jeanne had left Rosa's donated milk where she stored perishables, sitting the jug on a marble slab *garde-manger* cupboard, which kept meat, dairy and leftovers cool. Sophie poured some of it into a bottle and heated it in a saucepan of water. Jeanne had wrapped the instruments carefully in clean strips of cotton sheet for her, she noted with gratitude.

When she returned to the bedroom, the girl was letting out plaintive bleats, moving her head from side to side. 'I'm feeding the boy first, he seems so tiny,' Camille said, 'but I feel bad about leaving her. Am I doing it properly, Maman?' Sophie helped her make a few adjustments and the baby fed on. Plenty of women nursed twins, but when they were so small and seemed to be developing jaundice, what mattered most was getting precious milk into them. Rosa would be such a help.

'I'll feed her for you, if that's all right?' Sophie picked the girl out of the bassinet and offered her the bottle. She seemed uncertain as what to do at first but settled into the feed. 'You must have names for them?'

'Paul. Or Louise, if the baby was a girl.' Camille laughed. 'We can have both our choices now.'

Paul seemed to be falling asleep again. 'Tickle his toes,' Sophie told Camille. She tried this and he seemed to stir briefly. 'He's so sleepy he probably doesn't know he needs to feed.'

When the babies had been fed and changed, they slept once more for three or so hours, until Louise woke again. Camille seemed remarkably refreshed after each short sleep. Nature was lifting her in a post-delivery wave. She'd probably find it harder in a few days' time when many new mothers seemed to be hit by changing hormones. Sophie planned on staying close to her daughter. Jean-Luc no longer seemed like such a threat. Jean-Luc's mother and Herr Gruber were more of a concern.

In the morning, Sophie went downstairs with the pail of napkins. Jean-Luc was sitting in the kitchen with a bowl of what passed for breakfast coffee in front of him. 'May I go in and see them all?'

'Of course you may.' Her heart softened even more at the yearning in Jean-Luc's voice. Her hand went to her face. Her mask. She wasn't wearing it. In the sleep-deprivation she had forgotten to replace it. She tried to smile. Jean-Luc didn't seem to have noticed. She prayed he hadn't recently looked at any old family photographs with Camille. Turning her back, she busied herself by picking up the wrapped instruments to take back upstairs. 'Perhaps you could bring madame a bowl of coffee and something to eat?'

'I must find real coffee beans somewhere for her. She shouldn't manage on this awful substitute, with all she's been through.' He arranged crockery and cutlery on a tray. 'I saved the fresh bread for her,' he said. 'So that Herr Gruber doesn't eat it. Jeanne left a boiled egg for her.' He found the egg and cut it carefully so that Camille could easily manage it with one free hand.

Sophie smiled to herself. He really was a good man. She'd been in the homes of newly birthed women whose husbands expected them up the next morning to prepare meals for them. Sometimes, the women expected this of themselves, too. She couldn't help remembering Marianne on the farm, who would have paid no heed to the suggestion that she rest after her miscarriage.

You could learn a lot about how a marriage worked by observing a new father adapting, or not, to the changed reality of a home with newborns in it.

Two other voices rang down the stairs. Véronique and Herr Gruber, coming down for their *petit déjeuner*. Sophie's hand went to her uncovered face. Surely Véronique wouldn't bring that man into the kitchen? Her sense of propriety would not allow it.

She would wait for them to move into the dining room.

Something shifted behind her. Her heart jumped. She looked around and saw Rosa, one finger placed on her mouth. Without a sound, the two of them stepped backwards. Rosa closed the door silently. 'I thought the babies might need more milk? Patrin has drunk all he can.' The baby was strapped to her back, dozing. 'Do not worry, he will sleep for at least an hour now.'

'How did you get in?'

'Door from the side-street into the courtyard. The bolt's very old.' Rosa gave a faint smile. 'You learn how to look for ways in and out of places when you're on the run.'

'You're very kind to come back here. Wait until Herr Gruber is safely sitting at the breakfast table.'

'Still expecting his meals served for him?' Rosa's lips curled into distain. 'He should eat off the ground, like the dog he is.'

'I hope he's not eating rations needed for Camille. And for you.' Sophie put a hand on the girl's thin arm.

'I don't need much food.' The slight accent in her voice was more marked this morning. Perhaps she trusted Sophie more and could speak naturally?

'You do. Patrin is doing so well, but you need to look after yourself, too. Especially now you're helping with Camille's babies.'

'Usually, people say my kind are a drain on society.'

Sophie squeezed the girl's arm gently. 'They're wrong if they think that.' She moved back to the kitchen door, ear to the wood. 'I think he's safely in the dining room. Let's go upstairs.' From the dining room came the sound of Herr Gruber exclaiming over the excellent apricot confiture and Véronique stiffly telling him there was no more bread, her *newly delivered* daughter-in-law needed it.

Camille, sitting up as she fed Paul, greeted Rosa with pleasure. The two of them, so different in upbringing and life experience, seemed to have formed a real connection. Louise, lying in the bassinet, opened an eye, moved her head from side to side and started to cry.

'I'll give you milk for her,' Rosa said, removing Patrin from his sling, wrapping him, still sleeping, in her shawl and placing him gently on the foot of the bed. 'Or I can feed her straight from me. But you might not like that?'

'I think Louise would like it very much.' Camille smiled. Louise seemed to approve of the idea because she latched on immediately. Sophie watched the door, conscious that Véronique would probably not approve.

'I'm going to find you something to eat,' Sophie told Rosa. 'Let me just put these instruments in my bag.' Rosa watched her curiously as she replaced them in the canvas wrap. 'To keep them away from bacterial contamination,' she explained.

'In the camp, the doctor couldn't keep his instruments

clean. Eventually, he stopped treating some cases because he said he'd kill people faster than their illnesses. Even finding soap for his hands was a struggle.'

Halfway down the stairs Sophie realised her mask was still upstairs. She stopped, listening. Cutlery still clattered on plates in the dining room. She walked on to the kitchen, where Jeanne found a second boiled egg for Rosa and made up a tray. 'I remember what it was like when my friend had her twins last December. The appetite on her.'

'How did your friend's twins get on?'

Jeanne cast her eyes down at the tray. 'The smaller one died. The doctor said she just wasn't strong enough to feed and my friend was very weak after the labour. He said to give the baby powdered milk, made up with water, using a medicine dropper. But we couldn't find powdered milk. Or any other kind, either.'

Sophie bowed her head. Perhaps the child would have died anyway, but to lose a chance at life for want of something as basic as milk made her furious.

As she walked towards the staircase, Véronique came out of the dining room, biting her lip. Had her table companion proved too disagreeable? She looked quizzically at Sophie. Of course, she hadn't really looked at her face before. Was there something about her that reminded Véronique of Camille? The small nose Camille claimed they both shared? Heart thumping, Sophie murmured a polite greeting, head down, hoping she could reach the safety of Camille's room.

'How are my grandchildren?' Véronique asked.

'The babies are feeding and Camille had a reasonable night.'

'Oh, she's a young girl, she'll manage well at her age.' Sophie bristled at the dismissive tone. 'The smaller infant is my worry.'

Véronique sighed. 'But perhaps Our Lord knows what's best.'

She must have seen that Sophie didn't understand. 'If he takes the boy—'

'Paul,' Sophie said.

'Paul?' She nodded, brow slightly furrowed. 'Not a bad name. If Paul is taken from us, Camille can concentrate on the girl. Build her up. Has Jean-Luc given her a name?'

'Ca— madame would like to call her Louise.'

'Louise?' Véronique nodded. 'Perhaps. In the meantime, I will ask the priest to come and baptise them both. Just in case.'

'We have a wet-nurse,' Sophie said. 'She'll help build them up.'

'A wet-nurse? How very quaint. It's been a while since I've known of people using them, but perhaps in these difficult times it makes sense. Where did you find her?'

'The convent,' Sophie said, making to pass Véronique.

Véronique put out a hand. 'Wait, the *tsigane* who was here last night? I didn't realise that was more than a stopgap.' Her brow was furrowed.

'The girl who looks like a young Carmen?' A male, Germanic voice spoke behind Sophie. Herr Gruber, fresh from the breakfast table, hovering in the doorway. 'I'm surprised. I thought you French disliked the nomads even more than us honest Germans do?'

Véronique looked at Sophie, waiting for her to answer.

'She's a healthy, obliging young woman who can assist at a time when we can no longer buy milk to supplement the children's feeds.'

Because the milk all went east to Germany. The coolness in Sophie's tone had been overdone; Véronique's eyes widened but there was something in them that was less condescending now. Sophie had spoken like her social equal, someone who might have embroidered altar cloths and played bridge.

'*Excusez-moi*, madame, I must take this up.'

'But Camille's already eaten. Oh.' Véronique nodded. 'For the wetnurse?'

'An entire egg?' Herr Gruber said. 'For a gypsy?'

The tray shook slightly in her hands, the knife rattling on the plate. Herr Gruber was looking at something on the tray. No, not the tray, her hand holding it.

He was looking at the scar on the top of the hand, where she'd cut it on the border fence at Annemasse. The cut he'd seen bleeding that morning on the train.

'Madame,' he said, sharply. 'We've met before?'

'I've only been in Lyon a few days.'

'Not here in Lyon.'

She opened her eyes wide and tried to look calmly doubtful. 'I have been to many houses, monsieur. It is my job to travel around.'

'Obviously I didn't mean in your professional capacity.' He was frowning, trying to work it out. 'It's coming back to me now. It was on a train.'

'Monsieur?' She tried to sound politely puzzled.

'Just outside Annemasse, that's where it was. There was an incident reported around the same time, an illegal incursion by some Jews into Switzerland. A young woman was picked up. But there was another woman, too, older. Tall. Striking. Acquaintances of mine were discussing it.'

Contacts of his in the Gestapo? 'I have not made any incursion into Switzerland.' She held her head up and looked him squarely in the eye.

'You don't deny being in Annemasse?'

'As I said, I have travelled widely.'

'Very widely at a time when travel over distances is forbidden?'

'Medical professionals have permission to move around a region.'

'Yes, when we met on the train, you told me you had midwifery equipment in your bag, I remember it now.'

'*Excusez-moi*, I have a newly delivered woman upstairs to attend to.' She nodded at him and walked on to the stairs. Underneath her shirt, perspiration prickled on her skin.

He was just a businessman, she told herself. And she wasn't his concern, he'd forget about her and Rosa when greed for French assets and produce distracted him. Yet instinct screamed at her to leave, to get out of Lyon before she brought the attention of the German authorities onto Camille and her newborns.

TWENTY-SIX

SOPHIE, 1992

If Camille had gone into labour just twelve hours later, my path and Gruber's wouldn't have crossed again. I'd have remained in the dusty bedroom at the top of the house in La Croix-Rousse or returned to the convent until he'd left.

But babies come when babies come.

I still have the scar on my hand from the barbed wire in Annemasse.

Perhaps the mask and gloves I wore to deliver the babies would have protected me from Gruber's sharp eyes, but of course, I wasn't wearing either. In any case, they would have appeared strange while I was simply collecting a tray of food from a kitchen in a private home. If Gruber hadn't come out of the dining room at that particular moment, he might not have seen me again before he left the house. But he did. If he hadn't remembered my scar, he might have remembered my mop of hair. Or my voice, my slight accent. My this, my that.

It comes down to the fact that I was in Camille's house that morning when arguably it would have been better for everyone if I hadn't been.

Melissa's present is wrapped. I should have something for

her father, too, but I can't think what to give him that would fully express what I need to say to him. I've practised what I'm going to say tonight, when the guests are all assembled, but now it feels like skating over the truth. It misses out too much.

I pause, the present in my hand, thinking. If I give the combs to Melissa, I'll have to explain where they came from, which will lead to questions. But I've told her she's getting a present. I can't renege on that. Is there still time to make a dash to a toyshop?

I could do with some guidance here. For all my confident manner, I was never good without a counterweight in my life.

But already I'm distracting myself. The past is pulling me back into itself. My eyes are full of the past now, of Camille, sitting up in bed the morning after she'd given birth, exhausted yet radiant, the pearl combs still in her hair because, in all the drama of the previous night, there'd been no time to remove them.

My daughter, looking more beautiful than she'd ever looked before, gazing at her children in a way that made the war, the Occupation, that German in the house, seem bearable. The future, offering hope.

TWENTY-SEVEN

CAMILLE

She was still wearing the pearl-encrusted hair combs she'd put on for dinner. Camille smiled – until now she hadn't even noticed they were still in her hair. This morning, while both babies were sleeping, she was taking the opportunity of washing properly, brushing out her hair, putting on a fresh nightgown and housecoat on top so she looked almost presentable. She replaced the combs. Why not keep them in? She was celebrating, after all. Even if little Paul was so frail. She could keep her son alive, she knew she could.

Maman was asleep on the camp bed, having finally given in and agreeing she should rest. Rosa had gone back to the convent with Patrin, having left more milk, and promising to return when she'd rested for a few hours. They'd sent her back to the nuns with a tin of ham. Jean-Luc would make a handsome donation to the convent.

Camille looked over to the bassinet. Louise and Paul lay with hands touching. Maman had relented and turned them so they were both the same way up, saying that identical twins would often show real distress at being parted while they slept. These two were fraternal, of course, hadn't shared the same closeness in the womb. But they liked lying close to one another, their mouths slightly open, breathing so gently she could barely see their tiny chests rising and falling.

Maman had warned her that Paul would need the doctor to check him over again today. He did look a little jaundiced. She'd put them both in the pram in the square of courtyard where the morning sun first fell. It would help the jaundice.

Camille hesitated, wandering how best to convey them both downstairs when she still felt sore and a little weak. Jean-Luc had taken Herr Gruber to the factory. Jeanne was busy in the kitchen. Maman needed to sleep. Only Véronique was available to help. She knocked on her mother-in-law's door and explained.

'*Naturellement*, the infants should be placed outdoors in their pram at this time of the morning.' She came out of the door. 'The *sage-femme* is not doing this?'

'She's sleeping.'

'Ah. You've swaddled them properly? Let's see if we can take them downstairs without waking them.' Véronique walked into the room and cast an amused glance down at Maman. 'Did you have her prior approval for this little excursion?' The sarcasm was clear.

'M—Madame Leclerc said sunlight would be good for the jaundice. She's very experienced, has worked in many different countries.'

'Oh well, if it's good enough for the experienced Madame Leclerc. I'll take Paul.' Camille lifted out Louise. She was so tiny it felt dangerous to even touch her, and yet she was the heavier of the twins. 'She'll be fine,' Véronique said firmly. 'You can't break her.'

They went downstairs to the hall, where the perambulator stood, Camille clinging to the stair-rail, concerned at tripping, to the hallway, relieved she was well padded and her bleeding wouldn't be obvious. 'When Vivienne lent us this, I never thought there'd be two of them to fit in like this,' she said.

Véronique tucked the top blanket in. 'Nature does as nature wills. I'm still going to call the priest.'

'You think Paul isn't going to live?'

Véronique looked at her more softly. 'Paul has a mountain to climb, but he has all of us caring for him. Even that *tsigane*.'

Camille wheeled the pram through the door to the court-yard. The sun felt soothing on her face. She found the warmest part and put on the perambulator brake. Véronique looked amused. 'Just as well Herr Gruber isn't here to see you outdoors so *déshabillée*.'

Camille looked down at her housecoat, a pre-war silk creation, with embroidered flowers on it, almost like a dress. 'The pearl hairpins give you an air of respectability,' Véronique said in a softer voice, 'though perhaps they aren't quite morning wear. But much can be forgiven of a woman who gave birth only hours ago.' She pulled one of the wrought-iron chairs out from under the table and motioned to Camille to sit down.

For her mother-in-law, she would never be good enough. But she was not going to let Véronique dominate her anymore.

'Nobody will see me.' She pulled back the cot blanket a bit. 'The sun needs to touch as much of their bodies as it can.' Camille unswaddled their arms.

'You'll wake them,' Véronique cautioned. 'Though the crying will be good for their lungs, clear out anything remaining from the birth.' As though understanding this, Louise started to cry.

Camille rocked the pram gently.

'You'll spoil her. She can't be hungry if you've just fed them,' Véronique said. 'I'd go somewhere you can't hear them and have a rest.'

'She's so small. I don't like to leave her.' She'd only known these tiny humans for a matter of hours but already the thought of separation from them, even for a short period, felt wrong.

'She's got her brother.' Véronique smiled, looking kinder again. 'And I'll stay with them, if you want.'

'I like being outside again. It's been less than a day, but I feel as if I've been in the bedroom for weeks.'

'Your life has changed,' Véronique said. 'And you'll never be the same again. Your body feels battered and torn. Mine did, each time. Nobody can really explain beforehand exactly what it will feel like to have a baby. Or two.'

Camille glanced at her, surprised by the softness in her mother-in-law. 'Do you remember the days immediately after your three were born?'

'I most certainly do. Especially where that husband of yours is concerned. I've never known such a ravenous baby. And the temper on him if he wasn't fed when he thought he should be.'

Camille laughed.

'I tried my best to stick to the schedule, but I found it hard.' She shot Camille a guilty little glance.

'You're making me feel better.'

Véronique smiled at her again. 'You're already a good mother, *chérie*.' Her expression grew more sombre. 'Don't get too attached to that little boy, *le pauvre*. God tests us severely sometimes.'

God could be something of a monster at times, Maman had once commented. Camille tried not to let the thought show on her face.

Véronique went inside. Camille continued rocking the pram. Both twins fell asleep. She heard humming and realised it was coming from her.

Raised voices inside startled her. She stood up. 'Jean-Luc? What on earth's going on?' She went inside, walking carefully because her lower body still felt raw.

He was speaking with Véronique, face pale. 'It's worse than that, I tell you.'

'They got away in time?'

'Yes, down the fire escape at the back. But they knew exactly where to find them.'

'Did someone let something slip to Gruber?'

'No. But he was suspicious as soon as we reached the factory. He said there were too few people working the looms to account for our production, it was impossible, even efficient German factories couldn't do it.'

A scoffing sound from Véronique.

'He wanted access to all the personnel files, every single person.'

'I thought they weren't on any records?'

'They aren't. But he's been talking to Georges.'

Georges was the factory foreman.

'Gruber managed to get out of him that there are some workers who are off the books.'

Véronique said something under her breath. 'Georges never was the sharpest.'

'He was scared. His daughter's an invalid, if he's... taken away, she won't receive the medical care she needs. Herr Gruber says he'll come back with the Gestapo if necessary to conduct a full search of the factory and any other related premises, as he put it. Someone's bound to talk eventually. I have to go to the warehouse, Maman, I have to warn them to leave Lyon.'

'Warn who?' Camille looked from one to the other. 'What's going on, Jean-Luc?'

He shook his head. 'Best you don't know any more than you've already guessed.'

Véronique sighed. 'Jean-Luc warned me you were too clever not to ask questions, Camille. We kept things from you, child. For your own sake. While you were *enceinte*.'

'I'm not a child,' Camille said. 'I'm an adult, a mother. Jean-Luc has already told me about what's been happening.'

Véronique bowed her head. 'As is your right as his wife. The subterfuge was done out of love, though.'

'It won't just be the factory workers Herr Gruber's friends at the Gestapo will interrogate. It will be you, Jean-Luc.' His silence confirmed Camille's suspicion.

'Those in hiding have families or elderly parents,' he said at last. 'But if I don't provide the information, they'll threaten...' He looked at Camille.

Maman was coming into the room now, unmasked, probably awoken by the anxious voices downstairs. 'Trouble?' she asked. Of course, Maman would know all about this kind of trouble.

Jean-Luc nodded without speaking.

Maman looked at Camille, sorrow in her eyes.

'You're even at more risk now,' Camille said. 'It's not safe for you to stay here.'

'How does this affect Madame Leclerc?' Jean-Luc asked, distractedly. 'You can stay here in the house with my wife, non?'

Camille was shaking her head. 'Madame Leclerc needs to leave. She is at particular risk.'

'Madame Leclerc, indeed.' Véronique snorted. 'You think I was born the same time as those tiny innocents in their perambulator? She may be taller and blonde, but she has the look of you, Camille: those large eyes, that nose. I've seen the way you look at one another, you're her daughter. And you're right, Gruber suspects her of something.'

'Madame Leclerc is your mother? The mother you said couldn't travel to our wedding?' Jean-Luc's eyes were wide.

Camille nodded. 'I'm sorry. I deceived you.'

'Don't blame Camille,' Maman said. 'She was protecting me. And you.'

'It seems everyone is protecting everyone else and indirectly putting others and themselves at risk.' Véronique extended a hand. 'If you are Camille's mother, you are family.' The two women shook hands.

'Why couldn't you tell us who you really were?' Jean-Luc frowned at her.

'I'm known to the Germans for something I did last year. I didn't want to bring trouble with me.'

'He was asking about you when we left for the factory. Obviously I couldn't tell him anything more than I knew.'

Maman laughed, but it wasn't a happy sound. 'Unfortunately by then he'd already recognised me. I should leave the house.'

'No.' Camille wanted to grab her mother. They were all on the same side now. The situation was dangerous, but there was comfort in knowing that all of them in this room felt the same way about the field-grey uniforms on the streets, the red-and-black flags, the cruelty and injustice. While they were together, she felt safe. But that was delusional, she knew. Families had survived the last years by splitting up as needed. Those children Maman helped, some of them had parents who had let them go to strangers. She thought of the twins and her eyes prickled.

'Gruber recognised you, madame?' Jean-Luc sounded puzzled. 'What do you mean?'

'I met him on a train last summer,' Maman said. 'Just after I'd... there'd been trouble I was involved in.'

'What kind of trouble?' Véronique narrowed her eyes. 'Actually, best not to tell us. I can probably guess.'

'I got away without him being too suspicious then. But when he saw me here again, it seemed to reignite something in his memory—'

The telephone rang in the lobby. The four of them started.

'I should take that.' They followed Jean-Luc to the lobby. He said very little to the caller. At the end of the conversation he muttered, '*Bon courage*' and hung up.

'What is it,' Camille asked. Her legs felt shaky, she clutched at Jean-Luc's arm. 'What's happened?'

'Someone must have talked. The Gestapo arrested one of the people we were... talking about. He was on the street, looking for a pharmacy that would sell him aspirin for his wife's fever.' He took Camille's hand. 'I have to leave, Camille. He'll talk under interrogation. I need to warn the others.'

'Leave? But surely Herr Gruber will have to speak up for you? He seemed very keen to involve you in his plans last night?' Last night felt like last century. This time yesterday she hadn't even started going into labour.

'Removing me will expedite his plans for our factory.' Jean-Luc was rallying – his smile was almost the usual broad and confident one. 'He can seize it immediately, merge it with his production centre in Germany, put in a French puppet as director, make it seem like a French operation.'

Véronique's eyes narrowed. 'And he stayed under our roof when we were so worried about Camille. We gave him food she needed. If I met that man, I'd stab him.'

Jean-Luc looked at his mother. 'Can you help me pack a bag quickly, Maman?'

'I'll do that.' Camille pulled her shoulders back. She might be just out of her bed –

possibly too soon, her legs really were very wobbly and her bleeding seemed heavier – but she was the one who should pack her husband's things. The room spun. Maman caught her.

'You need to sit down, *chérie*.' At least they didn't have to hide their relationship now.

Véronique was already running upstairs to pack Jean-Luc's bag, showing remarkable energy for a woman who normally left the physical side of managing the household to Jeanne.

Maman was helping her upstairs, too. Jean-Luc coming behind. 'Where will you go?' Camille asked him.

He shook his head. 'You can truthfully say you don't know.'

'Everyone's leaving me.' Camille heard the quiver in her voice. 'You, Maman?'

'We should all leave Lyon,' Maman said, as they reached the bedroom. 'Véronique, Camille, the babies. Once they have one member of a family in their sights, everyone's at risk.'

In Jean-Luc and Camille's bedroom, Véronique was going through drawers and cupboards, packing a grip for Jean-Luc, rushing into the bathroom to collect what she could grab. She broke off and turned around. 'Go? Whatever do you mean, Madame Hansen? I'm certainly not letting that awful Gruber drive me from my house.'

'Where would you go?' Jean-Luc asked.

'Better not to give details,' Maman said. 'The remote village where I live. Up in the Cévennes. I think all of us would be safer out of the city for a while.' She sounded calm, as though she was giving maternity advice.

'But Camille shouldn't even be out of bed. The babies are so weak.'

'It's not ideal and it's certainly not what I would normally suggest.' Maman was sounding more decisive. 'You have a car. The drive wouldn't be too long and we can stop on the way to rest.'

Jean-Luc studied Maman's face for a moment.

He nodded. 'Take the Peugeot. Camille knows how to drive, but she shouldn't—'

'I shall drive the Peugeot,' Véronique said firmly. 'It's been a while, but your father said I was a natural when he taught me. And at least we don't yet have one of those appalling gas burner objects so the engine still fires as I remember it.' Véronique spoke as if she were planning a fashionable picnic outing, but her hands trembled slightly. 'I must find my driving hat.' She was doing her best to keep everyone calm. Camille felt a rush of affection for her mother-in-law.

Even now, Jean-Luc managed a wink at Camille. 'I kept

some fuel back for emergencies. Just don't let her drive too fast,' he said. 'Papa actually said she was a natural driver for Le Mans, not normal roads.' He pressed her hands between his. 'How can I stay in touch with you all? I need to know how the babies are doing.' He glanced at Maman.

'Messages reach me through the convent. Rosa—' Maman stopped.

'The *tsigane*?' Jean-Luc asked. 'She should keep her distance from us, too. Herr Gruber was asking questions about her on the way to the factory.'

'Too late,' Maman said. 'She'll be on her way here to do another feed.'

'Rosa should come with us.' Camille looked at her mother. 'She'll be safe where we're going, won't she, Maman?'

Maman nodded.

'You're the expert, but is Camille really up to a drive?' Véronique asked Maman quietly. 'I'm asking you as a professional, not as a mother and grandmother. Are the babies strong enough? Paul should be in a children's hospital.'

'I am actually in the room, and I can answer for myself. Yes, I think I can manage.' Camille tried to ignore the fact that her body felt battered and still bled and she just wanted to lie down and sleep for hours. 'It's the babies I worry about.'

This couldn't be happening. Everything had changed so utterly within a single day. Only yesterday she'd felt as if the pregnancy would never end. Now she was worrying that her baby son wouldn't even survive and that Jean-Luc and Maman, possibly all of them, could be arrested. And then, God knows what would happen. She wanted to scream, but it was like being in a nightmare, where you were paralysed.

'We can be up in...' Maman stopped. 'Where I live by nightfall. If we're pulled over, we say I'm taking a newly delivered mother and her babies up to the Cévennes for clean air.'

'Women usually stay where they are when they've given

birth,' Véronique said. 'I'm no internationally qualified midwife, but even I know that.'

'The doctor said our house wasn't safe for me and the babies. The water supply, or the drains, a possible outbreak of something. An infection risk.' Camille said the words as they came to her. Véronique frowned, obviously offended by the suggestion of inadequate plumbing, but then sighed agreement.

'We'll stop as often as we need.' Maman nodded to herself. 'If we take Rosa with us, we'll have more milk for the babies, though we'll need to insist she eats whatever we can find. She'll be safer up there, at least.' She looked at Véronique. 'We'll need bottles of water and as much food as Jeanne can provide.'

'She'll need to lock up the house as soon as we've gone and go back to her sister. I'll arrange for her to be paid as normal.' Véronique was like a tornado, dashing away to do all this.

'How long do we have to pack up?' Camille asked. There seemed an impossible amount to be done and she still felt as if she was powerless, in a terrible dream.

'You should be out of here within half an hour.' Jean-Luc came to her, putting his arm around her. 'I'm so sorry that this is happening to you at such a time as this, when you should be resting and enjoying the babies.'

'Half an hour?' It felt as though it would take Camille that long to get washed and dressed. Assuming neither baby needed changing or feeding. Changing. They'd need napkins, fresh clothes. How many sets? How long would they be up on the plateau?

He gave a half-smile. 'We left some employee work cards in the filing cabinet with fictional addresses. When Gruber's friends in uniform realise they've been misdirected, they'll come straight here for me.' He squeezed her shoulder and let her go. 'I'll bring the car around from the garage.'

'Let's get you ready,' Maman told Camille. 'Warm clothes, coats, blankets. It can be cold early in the season where I live.'

Camille tried to rouse herself and think what she would need over the next weeks or longer. And what would fit her. She made herself stand up and go to the chest of drawers. Nightdresses. A jumper because it would be cold in the hills for a while yet. Hairbrush. Undergarments. Toothbrush and paste. Soap. The cloth pads she would need for a while longer until her body recovered from the birth. Her thick jacket from the wardrobe. She dressed herself in a skirt that still fastened with a loose-fitting blouse on top. Her mind seemed to be working through a fog. Was this what happened when you'd given birth, this disassociation from everything that wasn't the babies? She put on her gold pendant, the little diamonds catching the sunlight. Her engagement ring had stopped fitting over the last weeks of the pregnancy, but she found it and strung it on to the pendant chain.

Maman returned to the room with a small suitcase as well as her own midwife's bag and rucksack.

'I've packed enough baby things to last. I'll see if Jeanne has laundry soap. It's been impossible to get hold of in the village.'

Only last night Camille had still been pregnant, preparing for the dinner. Now she was a mother of twins, fleeing her home.

The sound of the Peugeot's engine outside on the street roused her. Jean-Luc was back. 'Let me take that.' Maman had come back upstairs and took her suitcase down, Camille following.

Véronique wheeled the babies' pram inside. She and Camille transferred the still-sleeping twins and their bedding into the bassinet. It was a good-sized car, thankfully.

'It's Jean-Luc's second car,' Véronique told Maman proudly. 'He has a Delahaye for leisure, not that we use either of them these days.' When they'd first met, Jean-Luc had driven her everywhere in the sports car. Camille had felt like a film star.

Now she was grateful to see the Peugeot, with its still-elegant but sedate outline. It gave her a sense of security.

A prickling in her breasts reminded her the twins would need feeding again soon and by then, they'd be in the car. How was she going to manage, even with the others to help her? The sight of her husband coming indoors caused a pang to run through her. When would she see Jean-Luc again? He'd miss these early days with his new family. He might have to hide from the Germans for months and months. He probably wouldn't say where he was going. She wondered if he'd tell Véronique. A pique of jealousy struck her. They'd kept so much from her. She understood why but it still hurt to have been shut out.

No time to dwell on that now – they had to go. Jean-Luc carried the cases out to the car and placed them in the boot. Véronique was fussing over a hat box. 'We can squeeze it in.'

'Maman.' Jean-Luc took it from her and looked at his watch. 'The time for a choice of hats is passed.' But he pushed it in beside the suitcases. Camille didn't think her own mother even possessed such a thing as a hat box. Her mind couldn't process what was happening and was distracting her with trivia.

Jeanne came to the door with a basket, wiping her eyes with her apron. 'I can honestly say I don't know where you've gone if they come here before I've locked up and left.'

Camille went to Jeanne and gave her a quick embrace, thanking her for her help.

'Madame Camille, you should not be travelling. You should be upstairs in bed, resting. Stay here with the babies. I will look after you all.'

'It isn't safe for any of us to be here now,' Camille said. Jeanne looked at Maman, who had wheeled her bicycle up from the side of the house but was looking doubtfully at the car.

'I'll try to arrange for the bicycle to be sent up to you

discreetly once it's safe for you to forward on an address,' Jean-Luc told Maman. 'But you need to leave. Now.'

'You too.' Camille embraced him. 'While I'm strong enough to send you away, while you can still get away.'

His lips found hers. 'We'll be together again very soon, probably before you even miss me,' he said when they parted lips, arms still around one another. 'Before those two are much bigger.'

'I already miss you.'

'And we're calling them Louise and Paul?'

'If you're happy?'

'So happy. And proud. A son and a daughter, what could be better? This is the best day of my life, even though I won't see you for a while.'

He released himself gently and went to the car, kissing his fingers and placing them on each baby's forehead, muttering what sounded like a blessing, briefly kissing his mother on each cheek as she came to him.

'I wish we'd managed to tell your sisters about the babies before we left.' Véronique sounded wistful.

With a final wave, Camille's husband walked away and vanished down a side street before she could blink the tears out of her eyes. She put a hand to her mouth to stop herself shouting at him to come back, to stay with her because she couldn't manage without him. But all across France women had waved off their menfolk. Why should Camille be exempt from pain? She was a mother now, no longer just a new bride to be cosseted. And it mightn't be for long, anyway. Perhaps Jean-Luc could find a way of getting up to Maman's refuge, too.

'Where's Rosa? We need to go now.' Véronique frowned.

'Look.' Maman nodded across the boulevard. Rosa was crossing the road, Patrin strapped around her chest.

As she approached, Rosa stared at the loaded car without asking questions.

'We have to leave the city. Come with us.' Maman said it quietly but urgently. 'That man who was there last night.'

Rosa swallowed. 'The sisters will think I've run away with Patrin. I promised I wouldn't.'

'We'll get a message to them as soon as we can. We need you and I think you need us, Rosa. We can shelter you both.'

Rosa shook her head. 'I said I'd help at the convent, I—'

'Herr Gruber's friends in the Gestapo are probably coming for everyone in this household, Rosa.'

Rosa's eyes half closed. She nodded, looking down at Patrin. 'But I look like a *tsigane*. If they stop us, they'll know what I am.' It was true: Rosa didn't look like a family member or even a local servant. Her hair was very dark, her face olive, her clothes, although spotless, faded and threadbare.

Camille's hand went to her hair. 'Put these on.' She pulled out her combs. Véronique looked at her, frowning. 'Pearls always look respectable, that's what you told me.'

Rosa took them, looking uncertain. 'They'll think I stole them.'

'Put them on,' Camille told her again, the firmness in her voice remarkable to her own ears even now. Rosa did what she was told, placing one comb above each of her ears and pulling her hair back off her face. The combs made her look older, more middle class, less wild, somehow.

'*Voilà.*' Camille nodded approvingly, looking at Véronique.

'Possibly not quite what one should wear for a drive to the countryside, but remarkable what good jewellery can do,' her mother-in-law said.

'I know what the sisters will say when I don't come back for lunch,' Rosa looked along the boulevard the way she'd come, sounding tearful. 'They'll say I couldn't be trusted, just like all gypsies.' Any moment now she'd change her mind.

Jeanne was still standing by the door and stepped forward.

'I'll find a way to tell the sisters without saying too much, don't worry.'

'*Merci*, madame.' Rosa swallowed.

'Now, *dépêchez-vous!*' Véronique opened the driver's door. 'We must be going.'

TWENTY-EIGHT

SOPHIE

Rosa sat beside Camille in the back of the Peugeot, Patrin in her arms, the wicker bassinet wedged between them and the front seats. Paul and Louise slept, undisturbed by the hasty departure, facing one another. Sophie sat in the front so she could direct Véronique once they were up in the hills. Her midwife's bag and rucksack were tucked at her feet. A feeling of guilt washed her. Their possessions took up so much space, while Rosa travelled with nothing except a small basket and her son in her arms – probably all she owned in the world. She seemed almost serene now, her wariness when Sophie had first met her now completely gone. Rosa trusted them – not only with herself, but with her son. A bond had been forged between her and a family she hadn't even met until the previous day.

Véronique drove down to the bridge across the Rhône with only a few crashings of the gears and the odd genteel, muttered '*Nom de Dieu!*' as she regained her driving skills. Sophie scanned the streets ahead for roadblocks. The first few guards they encountered waved them on: a carful of women and infants obviously unworthy of their attention. Soon, possibly by now, the Gestapo would visit the house and realise the family had fled and, depending on how quickly they got the word out, things mightn't be as easy. Sophie resisted the temptation to look over her shoulder or crank her neck to reach the rear-view mirror to check that nobody was coming after them. Each time she heard another motor engine behind them, her stomach lurched. 'A drive out to the countryside, recommended by the doctor, for two new mothers who can't stay in a house with a contaminated water supply.' Véronique sounded confident, even if Sophie had some doubts. Not many private citizens still had fuel for such non-essential outings – cause for suspicion to start with. If Jean-Claude was on the run, alerts would have gone out for his family to be apprehended. This often happened rapidly. She'd heard of family running from their home and being picked up within hours.

Perhaps they'd be lucky, though. Occasionally, Germans cast a curious look at them. But maybe the sight of Véronique in her smartly angled driving hat at the wheel was enough to give them an air of respectability. Nobody stopped them.

As they headed further out of the city centre, Sophie felt herself relax a little. The leaves on the trees had come out even more in the days she'd been in the city and this morning the sunshine was bright. A few tulips still bloomed up in neglected municipal beds or window boxes. Trees waved cherry-blossomed boughs in the light breeze: a perfect spring day. Even now, she could find some hope. She had new grandchildren, a daughter she was so proud of for her courage in delivering them. Food was scarce on the plateau, but there would be shelter for everyone. They'd be among people who'd keep them safe. Nina had already mapped out the vegetable patch this year, but perhaps it wasn't too late to expand it further. She could trade vegetables and lettuces for more hens so their egg supply increased. Her bicycle had been lost to her, but she could borrow someone else's.

She glanced back at the twins, still both asleep in the wicker bassinet. Nearly two and a half hours since their last feed. They'd need another one soon, but best to wait until they were further out of the city before pulling over.

'I have a bottle in my basket,' Rosa said, seeming to read her mind. 'We don't want to let it get much warmer.' Rosa seemed to understand the importance of hygiene when it came to feeding babies.

'As soon as we're a bit further south, we'll stop. Are the babies warm enough?'

Rosa placed a hand under Patrin's wool cardigan and felt under his arm. Camille watched her and then did the same with the twins. Yet again, the runaway girl was acting as mentor. 'They're all fine,' Rosa said.

Camille herself looked pale, probably still bleeding. She needed to lie down again, at least for an hour, to rest. Sophie tried to think of somewhere they could pull over but couldn't think of anywhere safe on this part of the journey. Perhaps when they headed west to Saint-Étienne and then up to the hills, they might find somewhere to break the journey so Camille could lie down flat on the back seat. Even an hour could make a difference to how she'd feel.

Jeanne had thrust a package into the car as they left – bread and what looked like cold meat. 'The two of you should eat and drink now. You need to make sure you're well nourished,' Sophie told the young women, turning to hand it to Camille.

'I don't need anything,' Rosa said.

'You do. We ask a lot of you. You need iron, remember?'

'I can't manage without you, Rosa. My babies certainly can't. Please take something to eat.' The warmth in Camille's voice was clear. The paper rustled as she undid the parcel. Sophie was relieved to hear them eating and drinking. Three new lives were reliant on these two young women keeping their strength up.

The car drove on.

She hadn't been rash, urging this flight to the plateau, had she? Nobody had questioned the wisdom of abandoning the house in Lyon. But was there somewhere nearer they could have gone? The convent? No. Too close. Sister Marie-Claude and Rosa were now known associates of the family: they'd helped at the delivery of Camille's babies. And she herself was already too much of a danger to the sisters. Thinking of Sister Marie-Claude reminded her she'd left Lyon without saying good-bye and thanking her for her help. She'd only known the nun for a few days, but she already felt a pang for her.

She looked back again at the babies, still sleeping in their cot. Paul was Bernhardt's second name and the name of his father. A little part of Bernhardt would live on through Camille's son. Paul would be his own person, but Sophie hoped he'd have some of Bernhardt's infectious charm and refusal to be downcast. Most of all, the tiny boy needed his grandfather's vitality. She wasn't much given to prayer, but fleetingly she found herself begging strength for Paul.

The traffic heading south seemed to speed up. From the back seat came a plaintive little cry. 'Louise,' Camille said. Sophie felt a mixture of relief that the girl wasn't so sleepy that she couldn't wake for feeds and concern that it wasn't Paul stirring. She couldn't wait for Erich Meyer to examine them thoroughly. He mightn't have the equipment, but he was ten times better a doctor than that brandy-stinking man last night. Erich would ensure she hadn't missed anything with these three souls she was tending. The thought that she would soon be with him was like a balm.

They were now driving through the industrialised area south of the city, guarded by Germans, checkpoints set up at factory entrances. Véronique pursed her lips at a German soldier glowering at them beside a barrier.

'I can feed Louise while we're on the move.' Sophie heard Camille reach over and pick the child up, Rosa murmuring words of encouragement, laughter passing briefly between them. The connection between the two young women, from such different worlds, seemed to be strengthening, even in a situation like this. Perhaps because of it.

'As long as nobody sees you,' Véronique said. Sophie smiled. The woman's insistence on propriety was almost reassuring at a time like this. They made faster progress now, the car running smoothly. Jean-Luc had kept it well tuned. Sophie silently commended her son-in-law for maintaining the Peugeot and reserving petrol for it. Perhaps he'd been thinking of Camille's confinement, wanting to be sure he could take her to a doctor. He couldn't have expected her labour to start so suddenly. Usually with first babies there was plenty of warning.

They passed the signs off to the Berliet motor works, catching occasional glimpses of the river, and carried on south towards Givors. The traffic had petered out. Along the Rhône, glimpses of barbed wire and sentries were a reminder of the German presence.

Ahead of them a truck made heavy work of a clear, flat section of road. Véronique sighed. They'd either have to over-take it or fall back. Why was it so slow? It carried no load and the tyres looked good? No signs of smoke billowing from the engine. Instinct screamed at Sophie to pay attention.

She looked over her shoulder and saw a black car, a Trac-tion Avant, coming fast towards them. Her heart gave an extra pump. She felt the cold sickness familiar to everyone in France at seeing that particular type of car, beloved of the Gestapo, sometimes used by the SS. 'Pull off the road,' she told Véronique.

Véronique looked in the rear-view mirror and cursed very quietly. 'There's nowhere to go.' Trees lined the road.

'There.' Sophie pointed at a narrow track on the opposite side of the road leading up to a boarded-up factory building. Heading towards them on the other side of the road came a horse-drawn wagon. Véronique would need to accelerate to make the turning before the wagon.

'Hold on tight to the babies,' she warned the passengers. 'Grab that bassinet.'

Her sharp left turn in front of the wagon propelled the bassinet into the back of Sophie's seat. She prayed Paul's head hadn't hit the wicker side with the same force. The horse neighed in panic. One of the babies screamed. Camille gasped. They'd made the track but the force of the left-hand turn skidded the car into muddy grass to the side. The Peugeot stalled, slowly rolling to a halt. For a moment nobody spoke. Paul cried on and on.

On the road they'd just left, brakes screeched, doors slammed. Guns cracked.

'We're fine,' Camille said. 'Bruised, but fine. And all three babies are all right.' Sophie turned to look at her. Camille clutched Louise in her left arm, her right hand still clinging to the bassinet, her eyes on her son. Rosa had wedged herself in against the door, Patrin still in her arms, her right hand holding the other side of the bassinet. 'What on earth happened?' Camille asked, letting go of the bassinet and stroking her son's cheek. 'It's all right, little one, you're fine now.'

'That black car was probably SS or Gestapo, going after the truck,' Sophie said. 'We would have been in the crossfire—'

'We're not safe here.' Véronique was trying to start the car again. She was right. Shooting off the road would have looked suspicious. 'If back-up comes, we don't want to be hanging around.' She cursed as the engine refused to respond. 'It's flooded. Jean-Claude says to wait a few minutes before trying to start the engine again.'

More gunfire cracked. 'Nobody's coming for us for a few minutes.' Rosa sounded as though she was trying to persuade herself.

Sophie got out of the car. 'Stay there, while I see what's happening.'

'Maman, non.' Camille sounded distraught. 'It's not safe.'

Nor was sitting in the car, if reinforcements came sniffing down here.

Sophie crept back along the side of the track. At the road junction, a tree's thick boughs gave her cover. She peered around the trunk. Two men slumped motionless in the front of the truck. Behind it the Traction's windscreen was shattered, the driver half-fallen out of the door into the road. Where were the others? Sophie's eyes scanned the road. The wagon on the other side of the road had stopped, the horse stamping in fear, rolling its eyes. The farmer clicked at it, driving past the truck and Traction. As he passed Sophie, he nodded back towards the vehicles. 'Dangerous game going on here. Get away while you can.'

The cars and cyclists behind moved on, too, nobody wanting to be on the spot when German or *gendarmerie* reinforcements arrived.

The smell of the fuel dripping onto the ground caught at the back of her throat. The truck's engine would blow. Her heart was beating fast. Time to go. She strained her eyes, looking for the passengers in the Traction. Just the one driver? It didn't seem likely, they never travelled singly. She could fight her instinct, wait a little longer and make sure no other Germans were prowling around, or they could rejoin the road and head off quickly before more trouble arrived.

Sophie waited another minute. Nobody else appeared.

She ran back to the car, keeping low, zigzagging in case a gun was trained on her. 'Do you think the car will start now?' she asked Véronique as she opened the passenger door.

Véronique shrugged. 'With luck.' Paul was still crying in the back.

'Pass him to me,' Sophie said. Somehow, the girls managed

to lift him through the gap between the front seat. If they had to run for it, they would manage better with a baby each. But how could Camille run anywhere? She'd given birth to twins less than twenty-four hours ago, she was bleeding and weak, still exhausted. She should be regaining strength, eating nourishing food with her family waiting on her. They needed to get her to the plateau as quickly as they could.

Véronique tried the ignition again, whispering a prayer. The engine caught. She put the car into gear and turned it round slowly. They bumped their way onto the track before the tyres gained purchase on the firmer surface. Reaching the road, she barely glanced over her left shoulder before rejoining the opposite carriageway, overtaking the immobile truck and car. It had been the Resistance, Sophie guessed, trying to lure Germans out somewhere so they could ambush them. Or perhaps genuinely trying to escape Lyon, unable to accelerate sufficiently. Jean-Luc's hidden workers flitted through her mind. Had he got them all safely away by now? She prayed he was hiding somewhere, preferably outside the city. Only twenty-four hours ago she'd harboured suspicions of her son-in-law. Now her heart was full for him, rushing off into danger for the sake of other people when he'd barely had time to welcome his new family members.

Something moved on the edge of the road. A man staggered out of a ditch, gun in hand. SS uniform. 'Put your foot down,' she shouted at Véronique. The man was raising his arm.

Sophie turned to check the road behind them, spotting two military trucks coming fast towards them, opening her mouth to warn the others, when the white flashes shot through the Peugeot on the driver's side.

A series of cracks, a scream, glass shattering. The car bounded forward and hit a milestone on the side of the road, the horn sounding.

Another bullet twanged against the metal bonnet. Not a

handgun, a rifle. The trucks were upon them. Too late, she realised that by driving off at speed they must have seemed as though they were part of the attack, quarry to hunt down and kill. Again, the guns fired. This time, the glass in the back window shattered.

Stay in the car and hope that when the gunman came closer he'd see that they were a car-full of women and babies? Or get out, hands up, call out for clemency?

Véronique was undoing the car door. She'd pulled a white lace handkerchief out of her sleeve and held it up as she stepped out, very slowly. 'Don't shoot, civilians,' she shouted. Camille hadn't spoken, hadn't made a sound. Sophie looked around. Her daughter lay slumped on top of Louise. Placing Paul carefully down on the seat, Sophie squeezed between the two front seats and shook her shoulder.

'Camille?'

Rosa, apparently unharmed, brushed off shards of glass and pulled Camille upright. Camille looked directly at her mother. Her lips opened. She sighed gently and her eyes lost their brightness. '*Liefje.*' Sophie shook her shoulder. 'Wake up.' She took her daughter's wrist and felt for a pulse. Nothing. 'Don't go.'

'The bullet passed right through her, madame,' Rosa said, very quietly. 'And then it went through Louise.'

'Non!' Sophie grabbed the baby from Camille. Louise was still warm, her eyes, still too new to have taken on more than the newborn blue, open. Sophie lowered her head so she could feel the baby's breath against her ear. Nothing. She couldn't lose her, too. She lay the child on her lap and pulled her arms up and over her head, lowering and raising them. No response. Louise's heart would not start. Turning her over in desperation, she saw a small red hole in the back of Louise's white cashmere cardigan, one Camille could only have finished knitting days earlier. Rosa was right. Louise's heart could never beat again.

One single bullet had killed mother and daughter. Véronique turned her head towards the car interior, gasping. She opened the rear door, reached over and touched Louise's forehead, whispering something intense. Some kind of improvised baptism? She touched Camille's head, too, whispering a quick prayer. Blinking hard, she looked at Sophie.

'Get out quickly. Take Paul. Crouch down in the drainage ditch, stay low until you reach the trees. I'll distract them here. They mightn't see you.'

'I'm not leaving them,' Sophie said. She'd abandoned Camille last year, never again. 'I just can't. I need to try, I...' She could lay Camille and Louise out on the road, try to get them breathing again. One of them would surely still live. Still clinging to Louise, she put a hand on Camille's wrist again. She'd missed the pulse, it was there somewhere. She tried her other wrist. She was shaking, she wasn't doing this right, the pulse was there, she just couldn't locate it. Perhaps it was beating in Camille's neck. Remember your training, she told herself, this is an emergency, stay calm, check vital signs again.

'Stop.' Véronique had reached over to shake her shoulder, her voice harsh. 'Our grandson needs you, Sophie,' she said, softer now. 'You're his only hope. We only have seconds. Hurry. I'll distract them.' She opened the window and waved her handkerchief. The response was another bullet ringing against the boot of the car. The male voice was telling them to come out, lie on the ground. 'Don't do that,' Véronique said. 'They'll shoot us all. Get away. Now.'

'Let me take Louise, madame,' Rosa said. 'See, I'll put her back with her mother, so they are together. You pick up Paul.' Sophie's arms tightened on Louise. 'Let me take her.' Very gently, wedging her own son under one arm, Rosa replaced Louise in her mother's arms. 'See, they're together again and nobody can harm them now.' Sophie could just glimpse the little gold and diamond pendant she'd given Camille, hanging with her engagement ring from its chain around her neck. She wanted to take the pendant, to feel the last of Camille's warmth on its metal surface in her hand. Reaching out, she tried to grab at the clasp and undo it.

'Leave that, madame,' Rosa told her. 'No time. Take the little boy.'

Sophie reached through to the front passenger seat and picked up Paul, who stopped crying. She checked him for glass. He seemed untouched.

'Open the door on the right side,' Rosa said quietly. Sophie tried it and managed to shove it open. Her body was stopping her, it didn't want to leave Camille. Her fingers clasped the door handle, clenching the chrome.

'I can't leave them.' Her body couldn't obey the rational part of her head, telling her to go. She had to stay, had to pull the two of them into her arms and cling to them. She belonged here in this car with the dead. Life was over for her now.

Rosa leant over and pulled her fingers off the handle, one by one, and shoved the door open with her right shoulder. Outside, the shouts and orders continued. Another bullet hit the back of the car. Rosa pushed her. Sophie all but fell into the ditch, instinct twisting her so that she took the brunt of the fall, shielding the baby in her arms. Rosa dropped down softly in front of her, holding Patrin above her, throwing objects out of the car, something dark crooked over her arm. 'Crawl,' the girl said. 'Keep your head down. I don't think they've seen us. If we can get to the trees, there's another track off the road.'

'I can't leave her.'

'You can. You must.' Rosa picked up the things she'd dropped. 'Follow me.'

Muddy water still lay in the bottom of the ditch, mixed with dead leaves and dirt from the road. Nobody could spare the manpower to clear them. Crawling on knees, holding the babies clear of the mud made progress difficult. Paul was silent, perhaps startled or even lulled into silence by this new form of movement. Or so weak he could no longer make a sound. Sophie's skirt felt heavy with mud. One of her shoes was about to come off. She had to stop to tug it back on. Moving further away from the car was like moving away from light and hope into a heavy darkness

A last shot fired. A gentle thud followed. Véronique, holding the Germans back for as long as she could to give them time, slumped dead or dying, to the ground. She'd done it for them, especially for her grandson, so small, so weak. Véronique believed Paul couldn't live, but she'd given up her life to give him the chance.

Sophie forced herself to keep up with Rosa, who was moving fluidly. The girl stopped abruptly, raising a hand. 'Keep quiet, even if you have to put a hand over his mouth,' she whispered. But Paul seemed to have dropped off to sleep in Sophie's arms. Boots tramped towards them on the road. Soldiers, probably SS, sent to liquidate the Resistance groups down here: trained, brutal men who had no qualms about killing civilians. Beside her, Rosa seemed to have made herself blend into the mud and grass in the ditch, lowering herself and Patrin and pulling the newly growing weeds around the two of them. Quickly, Sophie followed her example, praying Paul wouldn't make a sound. If he started to cry, what was she going to do? Babies could suffocate easily if you covered their faces to silence them, as Rosa suggested. Stories had reached her of people hiding in attics, putting a hand over an infant's mouth to hush it when the house was being searched. A woman could nurse a baby to silence. But Paul's mother could never again do that.

The men were coming towards them. 'Two more got out of the car, must have come along here... would have seen them... the other way,' she heard one say, in German.

A rifle barrel shoved its way into the grass, separating clumps, probing, searching. Sophie moved a fraction to the side, watching it pass just feet away from her. Paul's eyes opened. She dared not move to rock him back to sleep.

'...imagining it. Nobody here.'

The rifle was withdrawn. The boots pounded off back towards the car. The women stayed motionless. The trucks fired up their engines. What was happening back at Véronique's car? Were the three of them still lying dead and unattended to? Would the patrol call an ambulance to remove the bodies? Thinking of Camille and Louise lying inside the Peugeot, Véronique sprawled on the road, made Sophie want to run back, to lay them out in a row, wash their faces, find a blanket and cover them, pray for them. They couldn't just leave them. She felt herself move back the way they'd come.

Rosa's hand, black, dripping mud, caught her shoulder. 'No.' Her eyes blazed.

Sophie held out Paul to her. 'I might have made a mistake. They're not dead. I have to go back.'

'They were dead, madame.'

'Please take him.'

Rosa shook her head. 'I can't carry both of them. Your grandson needs you.'

'My Camille...'

'She has gone. Her son is all that's left of her and you have to save him. He's weak, you are the midwife, he needs your care.' Rosa leant towards Sophie and put a hand on her shoulder, shaking her gently. 'Think, madame. Where are we now?'

'I don't know. I can't...' She shook her head. She couldn't do this, couldn't move, couldn't plan, could barely even breathe.

'Where should we go?'

Continue south to Givors, then west to Saint-Étienne. Some memory was pushing into Sophie's thoughts, somewhere she'd been only days before, in a different world. Marianne's farm. 'There's a farmhouse where we can shelter and clean ourselves up. The other side of Givors.' Would there be checkpoints

ahead of them? Bound to be, on an important bridge over the
Rhône, just as there had been coming south only days ago.

'We can make that.' Rosa lifted herself and her child out of
the ditch, not looking back. 'Hurry, madame, we shouldn't
linger around here. They'll send the police to clear up the road
and tow the car away. They'll sniff around again to see if anyone
else was travelling in it.' Rosa's expression was that of someone
who'd been hunted down in the past, who knew to keep
running.

The thought of the *gendarmes* or the SS swarming the car
and its passengers, picking over Camille and Louise, and
Véronique, too, like dead meat made Sophie's stomach lurch.
She pushed herself out of the mud. Bernhardt's scarf hung
around her neck, sodden, but still useful. She wound it round
the child and tied him to her shoulder, wrapping the scarf end
round her waist. He needed feeding. Rosa was watching him,
too, seeming to know what she was thinking. 'I'll feed them both
when we're somewhere safer.'

They had no water and Rosa would need to drink. In the
car, there were bottles that Jeanne had filled for them. But Rosa
was right, they couldn't go back to the car. 'Come on.' Rosa
started to walk. No vehicles passed them from the Lyon direction. The road would be blocked while the incident was investi-
gated. *The incident.* Camille and Louise. Two people who were
Sophie's world were now part of an incident, along with
Véronique, in her smart driving hat, the white handkerchief
probably still in her motionless hand.

On the opposite side of the road, a few trucks drove past,
the drivers looking curiously at them. A man on a bicycle
laughed.

'What happened to you two? Fell in the ditch, did you?'

Rosa muttered something under her breath without stopping. Only a few years ago a man like that one wouldn't have
dared talk to Sophie like this. She'd been a well-dressed profes-

sional, who'd held herself proudly. As soon as you were bedraggled, downtrodden, you were fit for mockery.

As though sensing her emotion, Paul stirred, arching his back, head turning side to side, lips opening. He was strong enough to express his hunger. That was good, Sophie noted distantly. Patrin was making faint crying sounds, too. Rosa nodded at a run-down hut off a track leading away from the road. Looking over their shoulders, they left the road, trampling through the mud. 'I'll feed Camille's little one first,' Rosa said, sitting down on a section of fallen wall that was out of view of the road. 'Hopefully he'll remember me from before and know what to do.' They swapped babies. Patrin felt noticeably heavier than Paul. He was two weeks older and had been born at term, Sophie reminded herself. Paul was feeding well now.

Paul would survive. She would keep him bound to her own body, night and day, so that he wasn't cold, so that he could let her know if he needed milk or changing. If she had to steal milk for him, she would. She would do everything, anything, she could to keep Camille's son alive.

When Paul finished, Sophie returned Patrin to Rosa and took back her grandson. Even now, she could look at him with a professional eye. He was sleepy after the feed but in the moment before he drifted off again, he gazed at her face. Was he looking for his mother? Or did he miss the presence of his sister? She swallowed hard and rocked him in her arms. 'You're never going to lose anyone who loves you again,' she promised him. Rosa finished with the second baby and raised him gently to her shoulder, stroking his back.

'You must be thirsty, Rosa.'

'I took this from the car.' Rosa put a hand to her waist and Sophie saw there was something tied to the belt of her skirt. 'I didn't have time to grab much, but there was a water bottle I could reach just before we jumped out. I took your bag, too.'

Her midwife's bag. She must have seen the heavy brown

leather bag slung around Rosa but hadn't registered what it actually was. All her senses had been flooded with the horror of what had just happened. Sophie reached out a hand and touched the bag, hardly able to believe it could still exist, this link with her everyday world. Years either on the run or trying to escape from camps, Sophie guessed, had honed Rosa's instincts. Even when she was running for her life, she'd snatch something she, or others, might find useful a few minutes or days later. She'd carried the heavy bag all this way, along with Patrin and the water and her own bundle, without a word of complaint. Rosa handed her the bottle. Sophie shook her head. 'You need it.' She didn't deserve water, anyway.

Rosa stared at her for a moment before drinking. She took a long draught, wiped the mouth of the bottle on her sleeve and handed it to Sophie. 'You won't be able to walk as far if you're thirsty. Believe me, I've tried.' Sophie took a sip. Rosa studied her curiously. Sophie raised an eyebrow at the girl.

'What is it?'

'You're not like most French people.'

'I'm not really French,' Sophie said. 'I was born on the Dutch-German border. I've spent most of my adult life in other countries.'

Rosa looked at her with interest. 'You don't like to be tied to a place?'

'I used not to, no.'

The girl nodded. 'My people need to roam.' A faraway look settled over her. '*They* didn't like that. They said we were anti-social, spread disease, brought crime with us. But we harmed nobody. And we never hated other people like they hated us.' She looked down at Patrin. 'I want to take him where he will never have to hide again.'

'You'll have to hide on the plateau, if the Germans come looking for us. But the rest of the time, there are forests you can roam in with Patrin and somewhere safe to live in.' There'd be cowslips and primulas soon. She'd hoped one day to show Camille the wildflowers. Sophie blinked again. This wasn't real. Camille, Louise and Véronique were not really growing cold and stiff, the blood drying in their veins.

It's real and you need to pay attention so that you and our grandson survive.

She blinked. Bernhardt's voice had felt so real, so loud. 'We need to move. Get through the town.'

Sophie wrapped Paul back into the scarf, standing to tie it around her waist. Rosa fastened her blouse with one hand, holding Patrin with the other arm. The short rest seemed to have refreshed her: she looked as though she had slept for hours. The power of youth, Sophie thought, though she didn't know exactly how old Rosa was. A year or so younger than Camille—

Than Camille had been. Camille, whose daughter had never even made it to one whole day of life.

She should pray for the souls of her daughter and grand-daughter, and for Véronique, who'd given the rest of them the chance to escape. She was no devout believer but wanted to beg some greater entity to take the three of them into its care. As they tramped away, heading south again, she couldn't think of words to address to whatever deity might be listening. Paul gave a little cry against her chest. She murmured to him. His head nodded onto her and she felt his breath, warm against her.

She was carrying her bag again, she noted. Something, some deep part of her, was clinging on to her identity, even now, when almost everything had been lost. No longer a wife, or a mother. Still a midwife.

TWENTY-NINE

They crept through Givors, crossing the bridge when a convoy of food trucks occupied the sentries' attention, drivers waving papers, Germans barking orders, a single Vichy *gendarme* acting as intermediary and finding himself the object of both sides' fury. Nobody paid any attention to the two women carrying infants, heads down, passing through the checkpoint on foot. The *gendarme*'s brisk wave hurried them on as though they were inconveniences. The two of them walked on through the town heading west towards Saint-Étienne.

Sophie was physically there in the present, trudging along with Rosa and the babies. But part of her had been severed from her old self, left in that bullet-riddled car at the side of the road. She trudged along, head down, refusing to drink Rosa's water when the girl offered it to her.

The screech of brakes pulled her out of her trance. A truck driven by a woman transporting ducks and chickens had stopped for them. 'You're going where?'

Sophie couldn't remember the name of the nearest settlement to the farm but gave a rough distance along the road. The woman – in her forties, scarf wrapped tightly round her neck, her face witness to a hard life – nodded. 'Just tell me where to pull over.'

Rosa thanked her. She seemed to have taken on the role of leader. The woman asked no questions as they drove. Perhaps she understood that something had happened that was unspeakable, indescribable. When she pulled over to let them out, she muttered some kind of blessing at them.

Dusk was falling as they tramped up towards the farmhouse. It had been less than four days since she'd left the place. Marianne came to the door, her frown softening when she recognised Sophie.

'Is he still here?' Sophie asked, without preamble. What was she going to do if the German soldier was still billeted here?

'Ernst left us.' Marianne looked down.

'Can we stay a night here? Possibly two?'

Marianne was looking at the babies in their arms.

'Even a single night in the barn would help.' Sophie forced herself out of the void she'd fallen into.

'No barn.' Marianne opened the door. 'Come in.'

In the kitchen, she sat them down and heated water so they could wash themselves and the babies. Rosa still had some of the food Jeanne had packed for them and Marianne laid out plates for them to eat.

The little boy, Luc, came in, eyeing the hard-boiled eggs and slices of ham with interest. Rosa pushed the plate towards him. 'We don't take food from guests,' Marianne told him.

'Take it,' Rosa told him. 'Then we won't be guests.'

'I ask no questions,' Marianne said, looking at Paul, asleep in Sophie's arms. 'Would you like Luc's old cot for the two of them?'

'I have to sleep with him,' Sophie said. 'He needs to be warm all the time.' She'd curl up on a pallet of straw with Paul, if necessary, like an animal with its young. And it wasn't just maintaining his temperature that bothered her. Suppose he felt alone in the dark, away from the sister he'd shared the womb with? No longer able to hear his mother's voice, to pick up her scent? He might feel abandoned. Nobody was going to separate her from him. She could never replace Camille, but she'd open a vein in her arm if she thought it would save him.

Marianne found baby clothes and napkins that had once belonged to Luc and helped them bathe and change the infants. 'Take my bed,' she said. 'Sleep now.'

The four newcomers to the farm shared the bed, babies between them in the middle. Rosa fed them every two or three hours through the night, handing them to Sophie to settle.

In the morning, Marianne brought in an enamel mug of milk for Rosa.

'Can you spare it?' Rosa frowned. 'You have Luc?'

'We can spare it.'

Sophie sat motionless for hours at a time, with whichever baby wasn't feeding on her lap. She didn't like to put them down to sleep, not even for a few minutes, in case they had to move off again in a hurry. She was listening out for an engine, rough German voices, boots stomping up the track.

A day more here. No more than that. Even if they'd been spotted heading out of Givors, it would take time for any search to reach this farmhouse. But the locals would know they were here. Rumours of the two women with babies would spread. Half of her brain argued that nobody would be interested in pursuing them: two unarmed females with infants who'd been caught up in the middle of a gunfight? But if they did track them down and interrogate them, as *tsiganes* Rosa and Patrin were in danger of being returned to the internment camp. Her own Mireille ID would quickly be shown to be fake. They'd shoot her or deport her east to a camp. Paul would be taken, placed in some children's home where a frail infant wouldn't survive. She had to survive for him – she was his best hope.

She couldn't tell Marianne what had happened and why

they were on the run. Marianne didn't ask where Paul had come from. 'Surely they wouldn't take a baby away?' she asked, seeming to guess some of what was on Sophie's mind.

'It happens. If he survived, they could change his name to make him untraceable and foster him out.' Her arms tightened on her grandson. She'd failed Camille, hadn't kept her and her babies safe. She'd urged Véronique to drive back onto the road instead of staying on the rutted track where they'd been out of sight. Speeding away from the shooting at her urging had brought disaster down on them. She longed for Bernhardt's voice to tell her she was wrong, but he was silent. Perhaps she wasn't the best person after all to look after Paul. She thought of those sisters of Jean-Luc's. They were a close family. They'd treat Paul well. They had resources. But they'd bring him up to believe his father and mother had supported terrorists and enemies of the state. They hadn't opposed the occupation, hadn't done anything to help those terrorised by the occupiers.

An idea started to foment in her mind, the way she could keep Paul safe, at least for a while.

'I want to register his birth,' she told the other women. 'Tomorrow. As soon as the registry opens. I was the attending midwife and can make the declaration, as the baby's father's whereabouts are unknown and the mother is dead.' Dead. Even speaking the word made her heart ache.

'But going... down there?' Marianne said. 'If it's not essential? When you're hiding from the Boches?'

'Why?' Rosa's eyes blazed. 'Why would you do that? If the Germans stop you—'

'I know.' Sophie's eyes met hers 'But it's for his own safety.' The plan was almost absurd. But she couldn't see an alternative.

In the morning, she rose early, sponging her clothes and pressing them with the iron Marianne had heated on the stove for her, tying back her hair, applying the slightest hint of the battered lipstick still miraculously inhabiting her jacket pocket. Marianne found an old bicycle in a shed for her. Tyres pumped up and the chain oiled, it would take Sophie the five kilometres to the *mairie*.

The German flag was raised over the building's façade. Sophie tried not to look at it as she propped the bicycle up against a wall, observed by a German soldier.

The registrar was a man with a nervous tic, probably of an age to have served in the first war. She handed over the birth declaration she'd filled in for Paul as she always did for babies she delivered, according to the French custom, with the date and names of his parents filled in, half imagining some official or policeman would rush in, shouting a challenge. Her midwife's bag sat on the floor beside her. She didn't show any papers confirming her status as midwife, but the registrar eyed her bag and seemed satisfied.

'You don't have proof of maternal identity with you? No wedding certificate for the mother?'

She shook her head.

'It's irregular.'

'The boy was born in extreme conditions. I do not know if his father survived. The registration can be amended, can it not, monsieur, and a fresh certificate issued if details... emerge?' Sophie had seen how French registrars would add annotations to their records in the margins of the register. He looked at her, the tic seeming to cease for a moment. Then he lowered his head to the desk. The form was filled in quickly, the certificate completed in precise calligraphy. Paul was now registered.

She put the certificate he returned to her in her inner pocket.

'Madame,' he said quietly. 'These records are examined regularly.' She felt a cold shadow fall over her. 'We still have authority over registering births and deaths, but we are subject to scrutiny.' The words were said neutrally, but the way he looked at her was a warning.

She knew what he was saying. The Germans could order the authorities to hand over details of anyone they wanted to investigate. If they, or the French authorities, were on the trail of a newborn child as revenge against Jean-Luc, nothing would stop them. She herself had committed a crime by registering this birth as she had done. She'd just represented herself, not Camille, as Paul's mother. Did the official guess she was committing fraud? He'd probably seen it done before.

She and Paul needed to be away from here, hidden up on the plateau as Sophie Hansen and her son, Paul.

As she cycled back to Marianne's, the numbness that had fallen over her cleared. Her mind was running through the events of the last few days.

If he'd survived, Jean-Luc would eventually find out that the bodies of his wife, daughter and mother had been recovered. He'd come to find Sophie on the plateau to ask about his son. He mightn't know the name of the village, but eventually he would track her down. In the meantime, Sister Marie-Claude and Jeanne also knew there'd been two infants. Would they assume the smaller, weaker second baby had also died on the road or shortly afterwards, perhaps as a result of injuries, failing that from natural causes, not unexpected given his size at birth?

Sophie had just committed an act of deception here at the *mairie*, one she could barely admit to herself. If Jean-Luc tracked them down, would he ever forgive her? Cold resolve flooded her veins. She was doing all she could to throw the Germans off their trail for the sake of keeping the frail infant alive.

Rosa handed her Paul, sleeping quietly. She examined his tiny features. He still looked thin, but no worse than he had done when he'd been born. Perhaps he was holding his own.

Sophie nodded. 'Paul's got a family name now. One that

will perhaps throw them off the scent if they come looking for him.'

Rosa looked at her. 'I can guess what you did.' She frowned. 'Was it worth the risk of going down there?'

Marianne found clothes belonging to her husband's first wife: faded but still wearable, unremarkable, probably worn to Mass. Sophie pulled out a long navy coat and an old-fashioned wool hat that covered her pinned-up hair. Rosa chose a dark-green jacket and white cloche hat. The jackets they'd been wearing when they left Lyon were bundled up into a canvas bag. The next morning, Marianne harnessed her remaining horse to the cart. Sophie and Rosa hid under grain sacks with the babies until they were a few kilometres west of the house. 'I just picked you up on the road,' Marianne said, when they emerged, shaking dust from their hair. 'Don't know anything at all about you.' Sophie didn't like to point out that anyone could have seen them arriving at the farm the previous day or her cycling down to the *mairie*. Sometimes you had to trust to your luck turning. They were all owed good fortune, she thought bitterly.

At the outskirts of Saint-Étienne, Marianne pulled over.

'You'll be all right,' she told Sophie, looking awkward. 'It seems as if the world has ended, but you have Paul. So it hasn't.' Marianne blinked. Perhaps she was thinking of the baby she'd miscarried, a child that could have ruined her, but a link with Ernst, whom she had probably loved but could never keep. Sophie embraced her and Luc. Rosa put out a hand, still watchful but her eyes full of gratitude.

Marianne helped them down before remounting the wagon seat and clicking at the horse.

The two of them walked on to the station, carrying the babies. Sophie still had her return ticket, she discovered. She'd placed it in an inside pocket of her bag. Rosa was pulling something out of her skirt pocket. ID papers.

'Sister Marie-Claude gave me this when I was in the convent.' Rosa looked down. 'The photo doesn't look much like me.' The note in her voice wasn't fear, it was sadness.

'By now Jeanne will have told Sister Marie-Claude you had to leave. She'll know you didn't just run off.'

Rosa nodded, looking brighter.

'Come on, I'll buy you a ticket.'

The station was well-guarded, with papers being examined. 'No, not my own child,' Sophie told the German looking at her papers. 'I was the attending midwife.' He was looking at her copy of Paul's birth certificate.

'Where's the mother?'

'She didn't survive. Before she died, she asked me to take the child for her. I know of a family who'll foster him while we find his relatives.'

He nodded. 'And you're Italian, madame?' he asked Rosa.

'From Naples originally.'

'And your husband?'

'Haven't heard from him for months now.'

He smirked at her and nodded them through.

On the logging train, they sat silent. Sophie saw the same view from the windows she'd seen only days before. How could it be unaltered? How could the outline of the mountains remain fixed when Camille was no longer in the world?

Paul stirred inside the sling. Rosa had already noticed and was taking a prepared bottle from her bundle. Professionally, Sophie noticed that he was demanding feeds more frequently now, possibly actually gaining weight. She'd weigh him when they were home. Home. The word felt good. The hills were taking on a familiar outline. She started to breathe more slowly.

When they reached the terminus, she spotted a dray dropping off logs at the station. The man driving it was the father of a boy she'd delivered just before Christmas. She waved at him. 'Madame?' His face broke into a smile. 'How are you? Little Gaston is so big now. And Marie is doing well. You and your friend need a ride home?'

'We do need a ride home, *merci*.'

They passed through the village, with its buildings looking just as they had when she'd left. Nothing had changed, but everything was different. He took them as far as he could. They walked up the track to the house. Nina was standing on the terraced part of the garden, hanging out a sheet to dry in her lunch break. She saw Sophie and let out a gasp. 'You're back. And...' Her eyes took in the baby in the sling, Rosa and the second baby. 'What happened to Camille? Sophie...?'

She must have almost fallen because Rosa was grabbing her arm and the sheet was fluttering to the ground as Nina ran down to help.

THIRTY

SOPHIE, 1992

It's easy to tell yourself you can hear a voice guiding you. Often conveniently along a route you've already chosen. *I really could do with some guidance,* I say silently to Bernhardt, the one I'm longing to guide me. *What would you do this evening? Would you tell Paul? What would you have done back then?*

I don't hear an answering voice, but I hear my own darn common sense. Probably not spring something as momentous as this revelation on my son and his family when we're supposed to be having a relaxing and fun family ninetieth birthday celebration.

Bernhardt's voice finally speaks. It's been half a century, give or take.

Do it now, liebchen, *give them time to recover before tonight.*

I should have done it decades ago.

No use worrying about that now.

I thought he'd be furious, that he'd reject me.

Paul loves you. Tell him what he needs to know and trust that everything you've given him, all the life you've shared in the last half century will be enough for him to understand.

'I need to detour,' I tell the cab driver. 'Take the next left, please.'

Paul comes to the door with wet hair when I ring the bell, a towel around his shoulders, blinking at the sight of me. 'Did you need our serving platters after all, Mom?'

'I need to talk to you. Before the party. You might not want to celebrate once you know.'

'Know what?' He blanches. 'What's happened?'

I can hear Jill in the kitchen, talking to Milly. 'Can we go through to the lounge?' He senses I don't want them to hear and nods, probably thinking I'm coming to tell him I have a terminal illness. Frankly at this age, life itself is terminal.

We sit on the sofa overlooking the wintry garden. The snow's almost gone but the grass is still browned. I turn down offers of coffee and tea. No distractions. 'I'm not ill.'

He lets out a breath.

I close my eyes, propelling myself back to the Cévennes in the spring of 1944, when the sun was starting to warm the cold mountains, but we still cracked the ice in the jug in the mornings to wash. I'd built a new life for myself after leaving my only child in Lyon because I was fearful of the Gestapo. She wrote to me from Lyon, asking me to go to her. But it had all really started when I agreed to take the Jewish children to Annemasse, months earlier. I should begin there, but I'm drawn to our arrival in the States, when our new life started, based on a deception.

'I told you how we came here to America when the war ended in Europe?'

At first, he and I lived in a small town in Georgia where experienced nurses and midwives weren't plentiful and the local health board probably couldn't imagine the level of deceit a respectable middle-aged woman would go to. Some of the locals thought I was German and regarded me with suspicion for a few months, but they were good-natured people, naturally hospitable and I only had to tell them a little about my recent past for them to treat me kindly. More than kindly, generously.

It seems nobody distrusts the widowed nurse-midwife who delivers their grandchildren, tends to their husband's ulcers, attends church and is always happy to bake for community events. Sophie Hansen and her son, Paul, were a popular pair. I was respected for my medical skills and often found reason to bless Erich for what he taught me when we'd visited remote farmhouses together. 'Yes, I had my son very late in life,' I told anyone who asked. 'I've been truly blessed. Paul's been such a comfort since my husband died.'

The fact of the more than two years between Bernhardt's death and Paul's birth is something that nobody in America could ever have uncovered.

I loved our first American refuge in the South and would have stayed there for the rest of my life, tending to generations of the same families, sending my boy to the schools in the town. But Paul's real mother had craved the city. She'd have wanted her son to grow up in a metropolis with museums and libraries, concert halls and galleries. I owed it to her to take him somewhere larger when he was old enough to appreciate it. I pondered Chicago. Los Angeles. New York. Then I chose Boston, perhaps because it still felt European as well as American and because I couldn't think of a soul I knew there.

Paul and I moved when he was eight. Our first New England winter made me question my judgment, but I was still hardy from my time on the plateau and you can always buy warm coats and upgrade a furnace if you have money put aside. And I had enough of it to be comfortable in an unflashy way. I had a reliable car and replaced it regularly. Paul and I skied on weekends or took the train to New York to go to concerts or exhibitions. In the summer, we explored Atlantic beaches. I cheered him on as he adopted team sports and clapped when he performed in school concerts. Both of us dressed well and I kept a spotless house, something that would have amused Bernhardt. I didn't want anyone to be able to point at anything about us that wasn't good enough. I fought very hard against my instinct to protect him, to know where he was at all times, even when he was far too old to be coddled like this.

Paul's waiting for me to continue.

'I never said much about where I lived during the war. You once expressed interest in a family trip to the Cévennes and Lyon, but I wasn't keen.'

'Completely understandable. I know you had to hide up in the mountains from the Germans, that friends of yours were killed.'

'That wasn't the reason I didn't want to go to France with you. I didn't actually want you to go, either. I tried to hide it, but I was so relieved when you just visited Paris and the war graves in the north and didn't head to the south. Particularly not to Lyon.'

'Why not Lyon?'

This is it. No more stalling, but I can't do it brutally.

'Lyon is important in your family history.'

I've rehearsed this conversation a dozen times in the past, but I'm still not sure how to deliver the news. If I'm not careful it's going to come out like a badly presented baby in a labour. I need to start gently.

'You must have known that having a first baby at forty-two is unusual for a woman.'

He laughs. 'I'm hardly one to comment. I wasn't far off that when Melissa was born.'

'You had to wait to meet the right woman.' His first wife was a girl he married in his twenties. They were divorced by the time they were thirty, still in touch, still friends. Jill, ten years his younger, was the woman he was destined to start a family with. Sounds of her laughter ring through from the kitchen, where she's up to something with Milly. But yet again, I'm letting the moment slip away.

'In fact, *liefje*, I did have a child when I was younger, twenty-two. Her name was Camille.' Speaking it, I feel as if the walls are shaking.

He sits straighter, looking as if I've told him I went to the moon. 'Mom? You say "was"? What happened to her?'

'Camille died in 1944.' I can't look at him. 'Just south of Lyon. She was shot, caught up in crossfire between a Resistance group and the Germans.'

'I'm... I'm speechless.' He reaches over to put his arm around me. 'And so sorry. What a terrible thing to happen to you.'

'Don't feel sorry for me.' His sympathy and love will be the ruin of me.

'Why didn't you tell me?' His voice trembles.

'I'm coming to that.'

'Sorry. This must be distressing for you, Mom. Tell me in your own time.' His arm tightens around me.

I could just accelerate to the most important part, but I need to talk myself through what had happened on the road. 'When she died, Camille was fleeing Lyon with me and some... others. There was trouble. With the Germans.'

'Camille was involved in some kind of resistance?'

'Not directly. But her husband was helping people the Germans wanted.' Referring to Jean-Luc like this rather than saying 'your father' is so wrong, but I have to make sure everything comes out in the right order. 'I'd also put Camille at risk because of what I'd been doing with people who were in danger.'

'Jewish people?'

I nod. 'Stories for another day. Anyway, Camille had given birth just the day before she died.'

'That's dreadful. She left a newborn?'

'She'd had twins. A girl and a boy.' My throat seems to close as I say these words after so many years. 'She should still have been in bed. Safe. But she was in the car, escaping with her babies.'

'They'd have been my niece and nephew.' He shakes his head, before he works it out. 'But about the same age as me. So you...?'

'They weren't your niece and nephew. They were exactly the same age as you.' I let that sink in. His arm stiffens around my shoulder. 'Your mother, Camille, and your twin, Louise, were the ones who died then.'

There's such a long pause I wonder if he's actually struggling to understand what I'm saying.

'You're not my mother?' He's a middle-aged man, a father, respected in his profession, but he could be a bewildered child again as he says the words. The sting is just as painful as I'd feared it would be. I'm causing the pain I wanted to spare him. I shake my head. 'No. I'm your grandmother. Camille was your mother.' There. The words are spoken aloud to him. And even though it could be the end of our relationship, I'm glad for Camille that at last she's spoken of, properly acknowledged.

'So Bernhardt wasn't my father, either.' He shakes his head. 'I always wondered why you said so little about him.'

It has hurt me all these years not to talk more about Bernhardt, my beloved, long-mourned husband.

'Who then? Who was my real father?' The arm drops off my shoulder.

'His name was Jean-Luc. He ran a silk factory in Lyon. Very successful. He was a brave man who adored your mother. And you and your twin.'

'He actually got to see us? You said we left the day after we were born?'

'Yes. He saw you. He was thrilled with you both. Then he had to leave the house in a hurry to warn some Jewish people he was sheltering that their hiding place had been revealed. It wasn't safe for any of us to stay in Lyon, so we left, too.'

Paul gets to his feet. 'But why, M—? I don't even know what to call you anymore. Why would you keep up this deception?'

I've rehearsed answers to these questions so often but now my tongue is frozen. Staring down at the pattern on the rug I try to find answers in the weave. 'At first, when we were still in France and the war was continuing, I was afraid the Germans might take you as part of their revenge against your father or me, or both of us. You were also very small, very frail.'

'And you were an accomplished midwife. Best placed to look after me.'

'I did more than that. I officially registered myself, rather than Camille, as your mother.' I have regarded this deed of mine as a sin, but Paul doesn't look as shocked as I expected. 'I lied.'

'For a very good reason.' Perhaps he doesn't understand the extent of this deception. I need to explain more, but he's already pushing on. 'Then what happened? Where was my father?'

'There was no news of him. You and I were hiding out in a village that took in people the Germans were hunting, mainly Jewish children, but others, too. I was shaken by what had happened to Camille and Louise, and to your other grand-mother, Véronique.'

'Of course, you were in the car, too, when they were shot.'

'Yes.' I shudder, trying to expunge the memory of Camille, dying, still cradling her dead baby.

'My God.' He sounds appalled. 'I can't imagine. If some-thing like that happened to Melissa, I... I can't...' He looks destroyed by the image.

'Camille and Louise happened to be in the way of the bullet and the rest of us happened not to be.' It's hard to explain the sheer randomness of war, how seconds, centimetres, can mean the difference between living and dying.

'Rosa probably saved both our lives by insisting that I get

out of the car with you and run away.' I remember how she'd pulled my fingers off the door. 'Véronique acted as a decoy, to give us time. She was very brave.'

'Rosa?' His eyes narrow. 'Patrin's mother? And Patrin? He knew, too?' Patrin has visited us once, years ago, when he and Paul were in their late teens.

'Rosa never told Patrin.' Rosa would rather cut off a limb than break a confidence, even if only to her own child.

He looks relieved.

'Only a very few people knew who you were. Erich Meyer was one of them.'

'Erich knew?' He sighs. It probably hurts that others were aware of who his parents really were while he didn't.

'Other people in the village probably guessed. I'd gone down to Lyon to help Camille and returned with a baby, but it was a place of secrets guarded very carefully. Revealing children's real parentage could mean the *gendarmes*, the French police, coming for them, following German orders and placing them on transports to Polish extermination camps.'

'The French themselves would really do that? Even to babies?'

'Some wouldn't make any exceptions.'

'So you hid me away. You said I was very weak?'

I can't help but smile, looking at him now. Paul has always been a sports-mad, strong man and shows no signs of slowing down in his forties.

'I'd prided myself on being such a good midwife, but when it came to you, I doubted my ability.'

I doubted almost everything I'd taken for granted about myself. What had happened on the road from Lyon had shaken me so completely, I barely trusted myself to sleep at night in case Paul too was taken from me.

'If it hadn't been for my friends, I'm not sure I could have managed.'

THIRTY-ONE

SOPHIE, JULY 1944

Erich watched Sophie as she sat in the chair, cradling Paul. 'You could put him down just for half an hour and come for a little walk?' he suggested. But she'd lost Camille and Louise. No risks could be taken with Paul.

The pastor's wife had brought a cradle up to the house for the babies, but Sophie preferred to keep Paul close to her, convinced that only the warmth of her body and the sound of her beating heart would keep her grandson alive. This old rocking chair was where she spent most of the day. The motion soothed Paul to sleep.

'Look at Paul.' Rosa came in, carrying her own son. 'His cheeks are round now.'

'He's still so small in comparison with Patrin.'

'There's real flesh on Paul's legs and arms now. I'm no nurse or midwife, but can you not relax a little now the doctor says he is doing well?'

Rosa was the only other person she trusted to look after Paul. After Erich had examined the boy on their return here, she'd all but snatched him back from his arms. Paul was doing well now by every measure, Erich said. She didn't believe him.

She read any of his books she could find, racked her brains for what she remembered of caring for delicate babies in their first year.

To distract her, Erich found novels, usually humorous ones, sometimes in German, sometimes in English or French, all designed to take her mind away from that road to the south of Lyon where she'd left Camille and Louise. But still she returned to this chair with the baby, staring out through the open door at the mountains and trees. The mulberry leaves made her think of silkworms and silk led her thoughts inevitably to Jean-Luc. Was he still alive, wondering what had happened to his son?

'There's a case I'd like your advice on.' Erich sat down, breaking into her obsessive reverie. 'Older woman, forty-two. First pregnancy. Blood pressure occasionally a little high, but she's well enough otherwise. A second pair of eyes would reassure me.'

'Oedema?' She didn't know why he was asking her. He would have checked.

'None that I can see. No headaches. I just haven't come across many cases like hers and I might have missed something.'

'Were you able to test the urine?' She'd gathered from snatches of conversation between him and Rosa that a delivery of basic medical supplies had arrived at the surgery.

'No protein. No hint of diabetes.'

'Well then.' Paul murmured in her arms. She rocked the chair to soothe him. 'It sounds as though everything's going well. I'm not sure I can do anything else for her.'

'She feels she is the only woman in the world her age having a first baby. You must have cared for elderly primigravidas?'

She knew what Erich was doing, telling her gently it was time to re-enter life. 'Of course I have.' She stopped rocking the chair and looked down at Paul.

'Paul's dropping off,' Rosa said. 'I'm about to put Patrin

down for a sleep out on the terrace. If they're both asleep, I can finish the washing.'

'You won't go far? Perhaps it would be better if I stayed with them both and you went with the doctor?'

'I have my homework to do.' Rosa frowned at Erich. 'Dr Meyer has set me some very hard mathematics. I could actually do with a bit of peace in the house to concentrate.'

'Ah.' She'd been selfish, not thinking about Rosa. Or Nina. Or Erich. They'd been looking after her for weeks while she mourned and brooded.

'Your bag's under the stairs. I've kept it dusted.'

Picking the bag up made her feel almost dizzy, as though she was moving through time very quickly, back to where she'd once been. But it all looked different, changed for ever. 'Just let me have ten minutes. Alone.'

She took the midwife's bag into her bedroom and went through the items in it, removing a bottle that had broken. The instruments were still wrapped in the canvas, uncontaminated. Just as she'd stored them after Camille's babies had been born. The last notes she'd written in her book were those on Camille's labour. She found a paperclip and clipped the relevant pages so that they wouldn't open and she wouldn't have to see the record of that night. Perhaps in time she would want to read it again. She found the form she'd filled in for Louise's birth and didn't know what to do with it, so she placed it under her pillow, before going back to the others.

'I'm ready,' she told Erich.

By the time Paul was four months old, he was a curious, cheerful infant, reminding Sophie of his mother at the same age. He'd gained weight far more rapidly than she could have hoped. The problem now was keeping up with his appetite for milk.

She and Rosa were now taking it in turn to look after both

boys together, allowing one another time off for work or food hunting, although as Rosa's interest in midwifery grew, she was increasingly keen to accompany Sophie out to visit women. On these occasions, Nina, if she wasn't at the school, would mind both babies. Nina could be trusted not to let Paul out of her gaze. Otherwise Rosa strapped Patrin to her back and held Paul while Sophie rolled up her sleeves to examine a woman and check her blood pressure. Rosa would watch and listen attentively, asking questions on the way home. Erich Meyer had noted Rosa's aptitude, too, setting her ever-harder mathematics problems and insisting she read challenging books she found to improve her literacy.

'We'll move on to more hard science, but in the meantime you'll learn a lot by observing,' he told her. 'Don't expect me to coddle you, though. When you're out with me on my rounds, you'll be working hard.'

Sophie could never have expected Erich to be such a rigorous taskmaster. From somewhere, he'd found textbooks and dictionaries, even a book of logarithm tables the schoolmaster could spare.

'Any hint of condescension would put her off education,' he said, when she queried his approach. 'Rosa hates people feeling sorry for her.'

Some lunchtimes, Rosa returned from rounds, groaning. 'My head will explode. He tests me on all kinds of things: mental arithmetic, anatomy, Latin words.' She sat down and glared at Sophie. 'I don't know why you're laughing.'

'Probably because I know you'll pull those books out again as soon as you've fed Patrin.'

Paul became more of a positive distraction as he grew, and his smiles became more frequent. Erich took them out on walks to look at all the new things that were coming to life in the sunshine.

Sometimes, when they stopped to sit under the shady chestnuts, her head would drop onto Erich's shoulder and he'd take her hand as they watched Paul kicking his legs as he lay on an old blanket and gazed up at the boughs. 'Our days can still be good.' Erich kissed her hand. 'Not as we would long for them to be, but good all the same.'

And she'd imagine the summer going on for ever, holding them in a bubble.

The village saw increased traffic during that summer of 1944, as the Allies pressed the Germans from both the north and south of France. 'It will be more dangerous now,' Erich said. It wasn't just the Germans he was talking about. The Milice swept through villages, demanding loyalty, issuing punishment and reprisals for Resistance actions.

One morning, Sophie found herself at home. Nobody needed her to visit. She planned on doing the laundry, seeing whether any more of the lettuces could be picked.

Erich came inside. 'Your appointments must have gone very smoothly,' she said, surprised to see him. 'Or did they cancel?'

'You and Rosa need to hide. There's a patrol on the way.' Sophie had rehearsed herself and those she looked after so often in what to do, where to go, what to take. But on this occasion, she felt herself freeze. 'Come on, find blankets and food for the baby and yourself.' Erich was picking up Paul from the cradle. Rosa must have heard the exchange from her room, she'd already slung Patrin around her chest and was rolling up blankets, picking up an oil lantern and a box of matches.

'Come on, Sophie,' Erich said.

She seemed to have lost the ability to react, to move away from danger. Her head knew what it should do: move to the forest, to the hiding place deep within the trees, an old shelter that had half crumbled away, but she couldn't do it. It was as though everything was happening to someone else and she was looking on, powerless to act, back in the ditch on the side of the road. What was wrong with her?

'Do you have milk for Paul?'

'What? Yes. In the glass jug on the marble slab.'

'Sophie, we need to go.' He put a hand on her shoulder and gave her a light shake.

Finally, her senses were coming back to her. She stood up, blinking. Rosa was already waiting at the door for them. Nina appeared.

'A truck's coming up the road from the village.' Her voice shook. Nina, normally so calm, was pale.

Sophie grabbed a bottle and the jug of milk in the kitchen, managing to carry it all, as well as her shawl, which she pulled off the peg by the door. Erich followed her out, shutting the door carefully behind them, still carrying Paul. She wanted to grab the baby out of his arms. Suppose they had to run for it and she was separated from him?

The four of them took the track leading towards the forest, climbing it quickly, not looking back until they reached the ridge, where they turned. The truck was emptying, four soldiers and a man in plain clothes. The rest must be searching the other houses in the village. 'We should keep going,' Erich said quietly. 'You take Paul now, swap your things for him.' They exchanged a quick glance. He understood. She gave him a quick, apologetic smile. Relief flooded her as the baby was back in her arms.

If they were pursued, it wouldn't take the soldiers long to catch them. Their only hope lay in moving far enough, speedily enough to reach the deeper forest and the safety of the ancient shelter. Nobody from outside the village would know of its existence and only a few people within the village would remember where it was. They took the hill quickly, stopping briefly to draw breath. Only when they were in sight of the old hut did Erich's pace reduce. 'We'll need someone on guard.' He kept his voice low. 'There's a chance they might find footprints. I'll stay outside.'

In the hut, they sat on the blankets they'd packed. Something was niggling Sophie. 'One of us should have stayed in the village. They'll know people are living in the house and they've left. They'll be even more suspicious.'

'Could be working outdoors? Foraging?'

'Perhaps.'

Nina was scowling at her. 'You certainly can't go back. If that's what you were thinking.'

'Take Dr Meyer something to drink.' Rosa held out a water bottle. 'Paul's quite happy here. If he cries, I promise to find you.'

Suppose the soldiers reached the hut before Sophie could run back? Suppose they took Paul?

'My ears are very sharp,' Rosa said. 'I'll hear a twig snapping before Dr Meyer sees anything.'

Her face was innocent.

'What are they looking for?' Sophie asked Erich, going out to him with the water bottle. He was sitting back against a chestnut tree.

'I suspect they chased a Maquis group up the valley, lost them, but decided to sniff around the village while they were here. Opportunist, rather than a tip-off.'

Sophie thought quickly. The groups of Maquis, Resistance units named after the scrubby landscape they hid and fought in, had dispersed of late. She hadn't heard gunfire up here for weeks. He was probably right.

Erich was looking at her intently. 'It won't be much longer, probably only weeks before the Germans are driven out. But that can be the most desperate time.'

She looked at him, at his kind, thin face with its humorous eyes. He was five years younger than her, had grown up the German side of the border just kilometres from her childhood home on the Dutch side. They sometimes joked they must have been at the same Christmas markets as children. Skated on the same frozen water.

Erich had left Germany in the late summer of 1939, having put his ten-year-old daughter Lotte on a train to London. His wife had died a few years earlier.

'You might be able to write to Lotte before long.'

'I wonder if she remembers me much now.'

'She was twelve, not two, when you parted. She'll remember you.'

'But children that age change so much. And from what I heard, her foster family are kind people and she was settling in. I don't know—' He stopped. 'I don't know if it would be right to put her through such upheaval again. And where would I take her? Germany's out of the question.' His face tightened. 'I can never go back.'

'Could you work in England?'

'Not sure they'll be open to adult Germans, even Jewish ones. I was thinking of South Africa. But would Lotte want to go so far away with a father she barely even remembers? She'll have her own plans for when she leaves school.'

They'd both lost their daughters. But there was still hope for Erich to rebuild a relationship with Lotte, even if they never lived together again. 'She's your daughter, you must never let anyone take her from you.' Her words were fierce.

He took her hand and squeezed it.

'Sophie?' he asked her. 'Have you thought more about what you're going to do about Paul's family on, you know, the other side?'

'I can't do anything for the moment. I have to hope they buried my daughter and granddaughter somewhere I can visit. Assuming they accept Louise was actually baptised and can be placed in consecrated ground.' Her voice sounded harsh. 'I suppose they'll be entombed with Jean-Luc's family and

Véronique.' She softened, recalling what Véronique had done for them on the roadside.

'Would Jean-Luc know how to find you?'

'The convent in Lyon would pass on a message.'

It wasn't good that Jean-Luc had been silent since they'd all left Lyon.

'If he was arrested after we last saw him, sent to a camp somewhere, with no letters reaching him, he may not even know what happened.'

'He was in the Resistance?'

She shook her head. 'From what was let slip, I think he was hiding Jewish workers.' People like Erich, people who were enemies just because of their birth.

'You didn't like the sound of him when he first married Camille, did you?'

'I should have trusted my daughter's judgement.' Her voice shook. 'Poor man. To lose so much.'

'Everyone. Apart from his son?' He gave her a meaningful glance. 'Who is very much alive and thriving.'

She nodded. 'I know Jean-Luc may come for Paul.' She shivered, imagining herself placing Paul in Jean-Luc's arms and watching them walk away.

'Knowing something is the right thing to do doesn't make it easy.' Perhaps Erich was thinking about Lotte, about how he would disrupt the life she'd built for herself in England when he reappeared, even though he must be longing to claim her. And how could he not reappear, not claim his own child? He'd made such a sacrifice to keep her safe. Hope of reunion must burn hot.

'Where will you go?' he asked, perhaps trying to distract her. 'When it's safe for us to go wherever we want?'

She looked into the distance, to the tops of the mountains, blue-tipped in the warm air. 'I always thought I could live anywhere, work anywhere with all my languages and my oh-so-useful nursing and midwifery qualifications. But now.' She shrugged. 'I haven't lived in my homeland since I was a girl. Where Bernhardt and I lived earlier in our marriage in Berlin is probably rubble. Funnily enough the Nazis were always very keen on midwives, probably used them to spy on families in their own homes.'

He sighed. 'Unfortunately, who better than a midwife to keep an eye on what's going on in a family, listen in to any seditious talk?'

'Identify babies who don't fit their appalling physical and mental ideals? Fortunately, Bernhardt got us out of Germany as soon as they came to power.'

'So not Germany again for you either, Sophie?'

She shivered, for all the warmth of the day. 'It would take me a long time to trust people there again.' She stole a half look at him. 'I'd always wonder what they'd done, what they knew.' Or if they were the kind of people who thought it was acceptable to kill women and children.

'Sometimes I tell myself that my colleagues and friends in Germany would have tried to protect Lottie and me. But I'm probably being naïve.' He didn't often sound so cynical. 'I can't face them. If they even survived. Yet my family lived in that town for generations. My wife's buried there.'

'France is where my loved ones are buried.' Bernhardt, Camille and Louise, all dying within twenty kilometres of one another. 'Does that mean France is really home for me?' The air smelled of trees, fresh, growing. She loved it here, but was that enough to truly belong to a country?

In the valley below a gun cracked. They both started, muscles tensing, waiting for the next shot. Nothing. After a few minutes had passed, they looked at one another. Erich shrugged. 'Probably a car backfiring.' They both relaxed. A second passed. Erich smiled. 'Don't move. I wish I had a camera.'

The butterfly that had been resting on her shoulder flew away in a blur of cerulean and azure. She hadn't felt it. 'I've seen so many beautiful things up here,' Erich said. 'Even when we're starving, there's always been something.' He placed his hand on her shoulder where the butterfly had been. 'There was an eagle one morning when I was returning from a deathbed, floating above me in the dawn sky. And once I thought I spotted a wolf, though they say they left these parts before the war started. Perhaps it was just a large stray dog. But it was beautiful – just looked at me from a distance before it turned away.'

She'd never thought of him as being sensitive to his surroundings like this, though she remembered him marvelling at the blazing stars that night they'd attended Marta's delivery, just before she'd gone to Camille in Lyon, a million years ago.

'And you have been one of those things, Sophie, that have given me such solace all this time.' His words sounded choked. She moved in closer to him.

'Bedraggled in the middle of the night when we've trudged up to deliver a baby? Bossing you around at a delivery while wearing one of my most alluring outfits.' She held up a fraying sleeve.

'You always look beautiful. And you were never bossy, just confident, as your patients needed you to be.'

When their lips met, it was so gently that they wouldn't even have bruised the butterfly's wings. It wasn't a long kiss. It acknowledged what each of them had lost and hoped to regain, or dared to yearn for. It wasn't like the kisses she and Bernhardt had exchanged as youngsters, deep, furtive and excited, but it felt like coming home. Could they stay here, Erich and she, when the war was all over? They'd found contentment and companionship up here in the mountains. Love would follow naturally, in its season.

But it would be impossible. The village would want to reclaim its old rhythm of life. The inhabitants had been so brave, so hospitable, but resources were scarce, and at some point those sons and fathers who'd gone off to fight or sent as labour to Germany would hopefully return. Sitting in this sunny glade, the outside world felt a long way away and even the gunshot, if a gunshot it had been, seemed as though it couldn't harm them. But that same world couldn't be ignored for ever.

'I'll wait another hour and then go halfway down the slope to have a look,' Erich said. 'If the village sends a boy up to give us the all-clear, I'll meet him halfway. But if there's trouble coming, I'll have time to warn you all.'

They could go even deeper into the forest, hide out in there.

He reached for her hand, and they sat together in the sunshine, so quiet that all they could hear was the flapping of birds' wings and the gurgle of water from the nearby stream. Erich was right: nobody could come up here without a sentinel pigeon in one of the trees taking flight.

Footsteps pattered up the track. They jumped to their feet. It was the young lad who'd brought Sophie the note months ago, summoning her to Camille's side. 'The Germans have got back into their truck. They've all gone, it's safe for you to come down to the village,' he said, turning on his heel.

'We should tell them in the hut.' Sophie looked at Erich guiltily. As soon as they entered the hut, they'd be immersed in the world of babies, feeding, demands, questions. While they sat under the tree, they were in a world of their own.

'In a moment.' He looked guilty, too, but purposeful as well. Sophie felt she was stepping out of life, letting herself relax into the world of sensation.

They sat back down, looking at one another. The next kiss was just as tender but carried a note of urgency. If she was going to be happy again, happiness might look something like this, Sophie thought.

THIRTY-TWO

SOPHIE, SEPTEMBER 1944

The war was still raging elsewhere in the world but drawing to a close in France. People had been leaving the village from the end of summer as Lyon and then Paris were liberated. As Germany surrendered and officials from the Red Cross and other agencies began to reunite hidden children with any surviving family, Sophie, Rosa and Nina became accustomed to farewells. Sometimes, parents appeared, usually a single mother or father, haunted, thin, faces showing the signs of being on the run. The parents who'd been shipped out of France to eastern lands where fighting still raged were yet to reappear and probably never would. When mothers and fathers were reunited with their children, the very young ones were puzzled, not recognising them, sitting rigidly on laps or wriggling out of embraces. Sometimes, the older children were resentful. Even if they could understand in their heads that a mother or father had hidden them up here to keep them safe, something deep inside them still felt abandoned. It would take time for them all to find their way back to one another. Sophie had doubts that all of the children would ever settle back with their mothers or fathers. Some of them left books and toys behind, as though believing

that they were only leaving the village for a temporary holiday
from the families who'd sheltered them.

One day, Jean-Luc might come up the track to their house,
looking for his son. And Sophie would hand him over. And her
heart would shatter as she lost Camille all over again.

That early autumn of 1944, most of the adults who'd hidden up
here packed up their few possessions and made the rounds,
thanking families, taking a last look at the mountains and trees,
joking about never wanting to eat chestnuts or drink lime-
blossom tea again. Or perhaps unable to joke, still not believing
they'd survived, now facing the possibility of being the only
survivor of a family. A middle-aged Jewish woman heading
back to Paris deposited a record-player and collection of discs
with them, saying she couldn't carry them on the packed trains.
Nina was thrilled to have music again. The notes of *chansons*
and jazz filled their nights.

But from the day of Lyon's liberation, a cold shadow had
passed over Sophie. People would be free to make enquiries
now, to ask questions. That sister of Jean-Luc's, Vivienne, she
wasn't that far away. In her brother's absence, she might take it
on herself to track down her nephew. Perhaps her politician
husband had now been arrested for the help he'd given the
Germans. Sophie read the old newspapers that found their way
up here, looking for information, finding nothing.

Work was a distraction she welcomed. Each birth could still
give her that sense of worth. While the fighting raged on up
here, she'd crouched over young men's broken bodies knowing
this wasn't her realm: her role was to bring new life into the
world.

Erich seemed to sense her feelings: sometimes their eyes
would meet and she'd see despair in his face. The Allies were
winning, but nobody could bring back the dead.

Food was still scarce, but tins of powdered milk had started to make their way up to the plateau, often donated to the babies and children by American or French soldiers who probably didn't have much to eat themselves but who'd been moved by what they'd seen up here. Sophie patched up a young *maquisard*, a member of a Maquis group, with a scratch on his leg, who insisted on handing over his rations for the children. Yann's family came from Brittany. He hadn't seen them for years and thought they had been imprisoned or executed for reasons he wouldn't go into. 'I just want to leave Europe,' he told Sophie. 'America's the future. When I've found out what happened to my family, I'm getting on a ship to New York.'

'Will America take you in?'

Yann's gaze was intense as he turned to her. 'I wanted to go there even before the war. Every time I meet a GI, I'm learning more about the country, what they need, what I can offer. I'll do all I can to make myself seem valuable.'

'What did you do before you started fighting Germans?'

'I'm an artist. Cartoons and comic books.' He gave a self-deprecating shrug as he looked at the table, laid out with medical instruments. 'Not so useful, perhaps. Someone like you, madame, you'll always be essential.'

'You think so?'

'You're a nurse and midwife. The Americans must have women having babies and from what I've... seen, there'll be more babies than usual when the troops start going home.' He blushed. 'You know what returning soldiers are like, madame.'

She gave him a broad smile. Something about his optimism had cheered her up.

She waved him off from Erich's surgery, watching him walk towards the truck where his companions were waiting. So young, probably around the same age as Camille had been, and yet so sure of where he was going, where his future lay.

Restlessness afflicted her. The old patterns of life up here no longer engaged her as they once did. Did she have the determination to do anything about it? She'd have to wait a little longer, to know what had happened to Jean-Luc.

Erich had been restless for a week or so, too. She now knew him well enough to spot the signs: the fingers tapping on the table at meal times; the faraway gaze when they walked. They didn't live together, that would have brought down the pastor's disapproval and the even more terrifying rebukes of his wife, but they spent covert nights together when Paul slept through reliably and she could leave the backdoor unlocked for Erich to come to her. Nina almost certainly knew what was going on between the two of them. Rosa suspected, too, and her pursed lips at breakfast secretly amused Sophie. Erich always made sure to leave before anyone was astir, but the girl's ears were sharp.

'What is it?' Sophie said, her head resting in the comfortable spot on Erich's shoulder when they woke early on a fine early Fall morning. 'You're brooding.'

'No hiding anything from you, Sophie.'

'So?'

'So. I wrote to Lottie and she wrote back.' She sat up. 'The letter reached me yesterday.' He was beaming. 'It seems like a miracle that we can write to our loved ones again and reasonably expect them to reply.'

'It's peacetime. We've forgotten what it's like.' She ran a finger over his arm. 'And what did Lottie say?'

'She seemed overjoyed to hear from me, begged me to come to London, to find work as a doctor there as soon as the war is over. She said her foster family's contacts would help me register. Apparently, they're professional people, many of them doctors. I didn't know.' He sounded wistful. 'All these years they've been raising my daughter and they're strangers to me.'

She couldn't think of anything to say at first. 'You must be so desperate to see her.' That deep longing, visceral, unignorable. She understood that.

'I am, but...'

'But?'

'I can't bear the thought of another separation from Lottie. I'd almost rather not see her than have to say farewell again. When I waved her off at the station before the war, I...'

She stroked his face. 'You loved her so much you sent her to safety even though you knew you might never see her again.' She thought of what she'd done when she'd dashed down to Camille. Would it actually have been braver to have stayed away, to have urged Camille to find another midwife or doctor? Would Camille and Louise still be alive now if she'd never gone to Lyon? She pushed the questions away – she'd asked them of herself so many times already. Erich needed her attention.

'I didn't feel brave. I wanted to grab Lotte and take her home again.'

'But you didn't.' She took his hand and squeezed it. 'And she's obviously made the best of it and now' – she took a breath – 'it is time for us to do what is necessary to get you to London. So you and Lottie are together again.'

'I don't mind where in Britain I have to go. I've heard of Jewish doctors working in Edinburgh and Wales.'

'You'll need a good raincoat,' she said. 'I hear the food over there is even worse than usual. How about a bag of dried chestnuts to bribe any difficult officials?'

He laughed. 'I don't think that would improve my chances.' The smile left his face.

'What is it?'

'You've spent some time in London. You told me about the lecture you went to, dressed as a man. Come with me? You speak English. You'd be close to your old home in the Netherlands. We could all start again together.'

'London...?'

Something pulled on her heartstrings. A city she'd only known briefly, but had liked, big, bustling, full of possibility, even though the propaganda films had shown it bombed and grey.

That narrow channel of sea between France and England wasn't enough of a barrier. She needed to be an ocean away from France, just in case Jean-Luc didn't return and his sisters laid claim to Paul. She'd wondered if she'd soften towards them as time passed, but with every further piece of information about Nazi behaviour in Occupied Europe, the bile seemed to rise in her throat at those who'd helped them.

'There's been no word of Jean-Luc,' Erich said. 'I know you feel you should wait for him, but we could leave a letter with the pastor so that he can make contact?'

She could do that, yes. Just because they hadn't heard from Jean-Luc, it didn't have to mean what she feared. People believed dead had appeared on the plateau to claim children hidden up here. If he'd been sent to one of those terrible camps in German-occupied Eastern Europe it could still be months before Jean-Luc could make contact with them.

Erich was slipping out of bed. 'See you later,' he mouthed. 'Think about it.'

Sophie slipped on the old wool cardigan that acted as her dressing gown, relieved to distract herself. Being safe from the Germans had been enough for so many years, but she'd always known that the future would have to be faced.

Paul needed changing first. Thank god for the supply of towelling napkins the pastor's wife had somehow uncovered. When she'd changed the baby, she made up a feed for him, grateful for the tin of milk powder Yann the maquisard had left and gave him a bottle. Paul fed well, as he always did, kicking his legs gently in approval. 'You're a strong boy now, aren't you?' He gave her a gummy smile and, as always, her heart gave a little leap. Was there something of his grandfather Bernhardt in the way his eyes crinkled up? You could always see what you wanted to see in babies' features, she reminded herself.

Another day. No need to brood on the food situation. They'd been promised that supplies would improve now the fighting had stopped. No need to fear the sudden appearance of the police or Germans. General de Gaulle was in charge now. He'd told the French population that life was starting again where it had left off in 1940 – the years in between did not count.

Except that they did count. As she prepared for the day, Sophie was preoccupied with the future. She'd always believed herself to be a robust, resilient person, able to start again and again. Could she actually do one more time, though? Pack up and leave when pieces of her heart were scattered across this country?

In the next room, Paul gave a small call. Just a little one, reminding her that he was there. He beamed when she appeared, waving his arms and legs in pleasure. Every morning it was the same, she'd feel herself melt at his sheer joy in seeing her. She didn't deserve him.

If she went with Erich to London, they could recreate a little family with Lottie, perhaps. If Jean-Luc never came back, at least there'd be a father for Paul, someone to take him to football matches, teach him how to ride a bicycle and help with his mathematics. She could brush up her qualifications and practise as a midwife in England. Perhaps in time they'd accept Erich and her as medical professionals. The three of them would live a quiet and settled life. A *normal* life.

'Let's do it,' she told him, when he came back that evening. 'Let's go to London, the three of us. Either Jean-Luc's dead and nobody else is looking for Paul, or he's alive and, as you say, I don't need to be here to give him his son. He can come to London.'

Perhaps it would be easier to hand over the boy to his father if she was somewhere else, in a new life. It would never be easy, she told herself, but at least she'd still have a life with Erich to sustain her.

'But you know what I did when I went to register his birth?' Guilt about that lie she'd had formally written down still dogged her.

Erich nodded.

'They could prosecute me, prevent me from working again. They might even use it against you.'

She didn't even know who the 'they' was. The medical council in Britain?

'You'd take that risk, Erich?'

'Of course I would.' He pulled her to him. 'You and Paul are part of my world now. We belong together.'

A rush of joy flooded her. She could be happy again. God knows, perhaps she didn't deserve it, but there was a chance.

THIRTY-THREE

SOPHIE, 1992

'You were planning a new life for us, with Erich and his daughter?' Paul's nodding slowly, but there's still a question in his eyes.

'It seemed possible.'

'But then something happened?' my grandson asks, gently. 'When was this?'

'October 1944. The war was still raging on in other parts of Europe but had really come to an end in most of France. We were in a strange limbo, in a dream world where all kinds of things seemed possible.' A pause while I gather myself together. 'I was really starting to think that nobody apart from us up on the plateau knew about you. But then reality came to the village. It was just an ordinary morning, crisp and sunny. I wasn't working so I was looking after both you and Patrin.'

Sophie took both babies out in the large perambulator a refugee had left on departing the village. The fine autumn morning air was a tonic: the babies seemed to like it, too. Paul waved his hands up at the trees. Patrin blinked at the sky above. Both of them were happy six-month-old infants: smiling at everyone, keen to try any solid food they could grab with chubby fists. Both babies were used to being passed from lap to lap, seeming to thrive on having multiple people to care for them. This morning, Rosa was going out with Erich to look at a toddler with suspected whooping cough. On the walk up to see the little girl, Erich would be testing Rosa on anatomy and physiognomy. Sophie smiled, remembering how only that morning Rosa had accused him of being a heartless tyrant. Erich's eyes had twinkled. 'You haven't seen anything yet.'

The rumble of the engine made her blink. The car was motoring slowly through the village. A shot of adrenaline ran through her. It was peacetime, she reminded herself, and that automobile didn't belong to the police or any kind of military organisation. It stopped outside the pastor's house and a man in a black suit got out. Sophie stopped behind a clump of trees, hidden from view, watching the man as he approached the front gate. Patrin gave a little murmur. She rocked the pram gently until he fell asleep. Sophie stood watching the pastor's house. After twenty minutes, the man in the black suit came out. He looked up the road. She froze. He couldn't have seen her, standing as she was behind the clump.

Half her mind was telling her she couldn't know this man had anything to do with Jean-Luc's family. Plenty of people had come up here recently, looking for news of hidden relatives. But that black suit spoke of banker or lawyer to Sophie. She'd seen a few of them at the time of Bernhardt's death. And there was only one house in the direction he'd been looking. The pastor's door opened again. The girl who came in to clean a few times a week stepped out, heading back to the village for her lunch. Sophie waited for the car to turn around and drive away before pushing the pram down the hill at such a pace that Patrin stirred and emitted a wail of protest. She gained on the girl. 'Christine?'

Christine turned, face puzzled.

'That man, who was he?'

They were used to anxious conversations about strangers in this village. 'Don't worry, Madame Hansen, he wasn't the police.'

'He looked like an *avocat*, a lawyer?'

Christine picked at an invisible thread on her shawl. 'I believe so, yes.'

'What did he want?'

She looked embarrassed. 'You must ask Pastor Lefroy.'

'Was he looking for someone?'

Christine frowned. 'I didn't listen to the conversation.'

'No, no, of course. But was it concerning a child?'

Christine folded her arms. 'You've lived up here long enough to know we never talk about the children.'

Sophie had broken the unspoken code. 'I'm sorry.' She looked at Paul. 'I'm worried.'

Christine's face softened. 'You should talk to the pastor about the visitor, madame.' She muttered a farewell and walked on.

The lawyer, if that's what he was, might have been asking for information about any one of the children who'd been hidden up here. Yet Christine had told her to speak to the pastor rather than simply informing her that the visit had nothing to do with her.

She turned the pram around and walked back towards the house, moving briskly.

The babies were still sleeping by the time she reached home. She left the pram on the terrace, shaded and easily visible from the house. Inside her room, she pulled out the metal box she kept under the bed with the birth certificates and her passport in it, along with key pieces of official paperwork she'd acquired in her profession. She had no evidence they'd been tracked down, she told herself. For the hundredth time she ran through the events taking place in the twenty-four hours after the twins' birth, who exactly knew about the younger, weaker infant.

Once again, she counted on her fingers the people in Lyon who knew about Paul's existence. That drunken doctor who'd come belatedly to the house, Sister Marie-Claude and Jeanne might all have expected Paul to die. Rosa had been there too but she hadn't told a soul that Jean-Luc's frail infant son had survived.

Until today, Sophie would have sworn the pastor would never have spoken a word. She'd never directly told him Paul was Camille's son, but she knew he knew this. She'd left to deliver her daughter's baby and returned with an infant she'd guarded like a tigress, showing near hysteria at first if anyone came near him.

During the Occupation the pastor's conscience had allowed him to tell a falsehood to save an innocent life. But the Occupation had ended. Jacques Lefroy would have to admit to anyone official asking direct questions that he suspected Sophie Hansen was raising the heir to the silk business. He didn't even know the full extent of what she'd done, registering Paul as her own child.

Perhaps the black-suited visitor had simply been bringing news of Jean-Luc. Perhaps it was good tidings he'd conveyed. Perhaps. But Sophie sat on her bed, staring down at the papers in her hand, ears pricked for the sound of an engine.

The car didn't appear outside the house. When Erich and Rosa came back in the evening, she told them she needed to see the pastor, not giving a reason. Neither of them questioned her, perhaps seeing something in her face that told them not to ask.

'Ah, Sophie, I've been expecting you.' Jacques Lefroy took

her into his study, just as he had those months earlier when she'd told him of her plan to go to Lyon.

'You had a lawyer visiting you this morning.' She hadn't even sat down yet.

His gaze was steady on her face.

'Forgive me,' she said. 'I don't wish to intrude on private matters, but I've been...' Something was stuck in her throat. 'I've been half expecting enquiries from my son-in-law's family.'

He was still looking at her with his gentle yet penetrating eyes.

'Was that visitor looking for Paul?'

'Christine told me you'd been asking questions. How did you guess?'

She shrugged. 'Some kind of instinct. I shouldn't have put her on the spot. She was very discreet, but...'

'She's too honest to lie and tell you it was nothing to do with you. Yes, my visitor was making enquiries concerning your daughter's family. And about you.'

'What did you say?'

'I told him I couldn't be sure you were at home. I said he might try tomorrow evening. I thought you'd be in then.'

Tomorrow evening.

'I was about to come up to the house to warn you.'

'The family want Paul?'

'Yes.'

'Jean-Luc?'

The pastor swallowed. 'Sophie, I'm afraid he died, shot while helping Jewish employees escape from a warehouse. It sounds as though it was on the same day you lost Camille and the others.'

Jean-Luc was dead. She bowed her head, mourning him because Camille had loved him so much and because he had been a good man and would have been a loving father to Paul.

'I only knew him for such a short time.' And for most of that, she'd been masked.

'You must be proud that your daughter chose him. Her values were obviously sound.'

At the time of Camille's engagement, she'd worried that Camille had chosen a husband just to feel safe again. Yet Camille had instinctively known that Jean-Luc was more than just a handsome and rich man. She might not have known exactly what her husband was involved in, but her intuition had served her right.

The pastor cleared his throat. 'Camille's sister-in-law, Vivienne, has been made aware that Camille and Jean-Luc had not only a baby girl but a baby boy, who wasn't in the car with his mother's body...' He looked distressed. 'When the police searched the vehicle.'

She closed her eyes, still unable to bear the thought of those strangers moving Camille's body, touching her. 'How did they find out about Paul?' she asked, mechanically.

'The family's maid returned to the city when the Germans left. Vivienne questioned her about what had happened. The maid assumed that the second-born baby, the weaker, had died before or after the incident on the road. But Vivienne's lawyer has been unable to find any evidence of Paul's death. Or even of his birth in any registry in this part of France.'

Sophie took a breath.

'They're investigating anyone they can think of who might know what happened to Paul. They seem to have linked the midwife Mireille to Sophie Hansen.'

She nodded.

'At the moment they only have a suspicion that Camille's second twin could still be alive.' He leant forward. 'You have familial rights, too, Sophie. Paul's your grandson.'

'I'm not French.'

'That might not matter now. You saved his life at least

twice. You delivered him when he was born in what I gather was a perilous birth. Then you rescued him from danger. You've cared for him ever since.'

'I registered him under a false name.'

The pastor looked shocked.

'I made declarations that were untrue. Lies. I'd better not tell you more.'

'Sophie—' He stopped, looking at her.

'Best not say more,' she said. 'That's always been our way, hasn't it? Not to tell people anything that might harm them.'

'If you did it to save him from the—'

She shook her head. 'I told myself I was registering him as my son to protect him from the Gestapo. And then from Vivienne. That's all true in part. But I really did it because I wanted him. I'm not sure I'd even have been able to give him back to Jean-Luc. Camille had gone and I had nobody else but Paul.'

His eyes were full of understanding.

'Thank you.' Both of them knew she was thanking him for more than simply giving her twenty-four hours' grace. 'I owe you everything.'

'Think, Sophie,' he said. 'Reflect on what is best for the child. That makes a decision simplest, I've found.'

'That's what's on my mind. What does Paul need most?'

'Children need love more than anything else.'

She nodded.

'And people who will give them care and attention.'

She was forty-two. Was that too old to be the mother of a baby? She'd visited Erich's elderly primigravida back in early summer and told her about the sleepless nights, the relentlessness of laundry. But there was more: there were the years to come when a child became older, needing more. And you became older, too. But she was fit, healthy. She'd told the pregnant woman that she would be fine. She'd believed it. But was it true?

It would have to be. She wasn't leaving Paul with Vivienne, with a woman married to a collaborator, more than that, a politician who'd helped the Germans do appalling things.

'There are children running around who probably wouldn't have survived their births without you, Sophie Hansen. Mothers who might have bled to death in childbirth or died of infection. And those children you got to Switzerland when they would have been transported to their deaths if they'd stayed in Lyon. We will never forget what you did.' He was saying *au revoir* to her.

Blinking, nodding, she raised a hand, muttering another *merci* for all he and his wife had done, and walked out of the house.

'I can't stay here. I can't be in Europe. Not even London. Paul has to be further away.' She'd rehearsed what she was going to tell Erich, but it was flooding out, as though she'd pulled out a cork.

He was sitting at the kitchen table. She was watching all the hope fall from his face, the old anxious lines re-establishing themselves. The future they'd mapped out together was dissolving.

'The Channel isn't enough of a barrier between you and Vivienne?'

'We can't even get to London yet, not while the war's on.' Hitler's rockets were still falling on the capital of Britain.

'We could move somewhere else in France in the meantime, earn a living while we wait?'

'Where? We were lucky to come here, both of us strangers and foreigners. And to be able to work.'

A Dutch woman and a German-Jewish doctor. The two of them would be aliens again, probably distrusted, subject to bureaucracy and police checks.

'They might throw us into a displaced persons camp. God knows how long we'd be stuck there. It could make it harder for you to get to Lottie.' She didn't want to tell him what she feared, that the French authorities might even insist on sending Erich back to Germany.

Erich looked as though he wanted to argue the point but couldn't.

'You're better waiting for the war to end where you're known and trusted.'

'Surely the same's true for you and Paul, Sophie?'

She shook her head. 'Vivienne can get up here in a car in hours.'

'So you'll go further away?' His eyes narrowed. 'America?' Was he asking himself if he could bear going so far away, too? Her heart gave a little leap.

She shrugged. 'If I can get us there.'

'The French ports are wrecked,' Erich said. 'Piles of rubble everywhere, ships sunk and blocking the harbours. Priority's given to military supplies and troops. You might have to wait weeks, months for a ship out.'

'I'll find a quiet hotel in... some port for a few months.' The kind of shabby backstreet establishment in Marseille where nobody would question a woman and baby if they kept themselves to themselves.

Erich placed a hand on hers, stopping her from folding the sheet. 'Why are you so afraid of these people in Lyon, Sophie? Go to the courts and say that you want to adopt the boy yourself or have legal guardianship? You're his grandmother, you've cared for him since birth.'

'I'd have to tell them what I did when I registered him. That I broke the law.'

'You have a perfectly reasonable defence.' He waved his other hand to the window. 'Plenty of children here have been

hidden under false identities. It's moral to do whatever is necessary to save children's lives.'

She shook her head. 'But the reason doesn't apply now
we're not occupied any more. That family will want Paul back.
I can't fight them. They have resources.'

'Your place in Paris? Could you sell it?'

The property would be worth something, it was in a good
neighbourhood. 'I haven't seen it for years. It might be in a
terrible state. Or someone might have moved in and I'd have to
get them out first.'

'Taking Paul across the Atlantic doesn't mean Jean-Luc's
family can't find you. Even if you live in a cabin up on some
remote trail.'

She looked at him sharply. He gave a short laugh. 'I
remember you telling me about the Appalachians. Pretty
remote out there.'

'I wouldn't take him there.' Even now, she could smile at the
thought of the two of them living somewhere out up the hills.
'No more hiding in the mountains. Paul will need a different
life.' She wanted him to have the metropolitan existence
Camille had always craved and had chosen for herself when
she'd married Jean-Luc.

'Palestine has a healthy climate.' Erich's hand tightened
around hers, warm and strong. 'They'd welcome nurses. It's a
long way from Lyon, too. Let's try to go there together.' He
pulled her towards him. She felt the comfort of his embrace

'Are you sure Vivienne is what you think she is? Jean-Luc
was a good man,' Erich said. 'So was his mother at the end.
There's decency in that family. If Paul went to live with Vivienne, they'd let you be part of his life, surely?'

'Sunday lunches. A weekend or two in the summer. Maybe
Easter or Christmas, if I'm nearby.' She, Camille and Bernhardt
would become distant names to Paul.

She'd lost too many people. 'I don't trust them. I can't forgive them for what they let happen in France.'

'You've never told me much about the sisters.'

'Let me show you.' Sophie detached herself from Erich's arms and went to the bookcase. The newspapers and magazines had appeared in the village a few weeks earlier.

She brought a paper back to him, opening it up to a ringed article about arrests in Lyon. 'Vivienne's husband helped organise round-ups of Jews and anyone else he thought was a nuisance.'

Erich was reading the article in silence.

'Martine, the other sister, isn't much better. She's married to a man who seemed to spend the war selling automobiles to the Germans in Paris.'

She told Erich about the picture of Martine and her husband she'd seen in the house in La Croix-Rousse, the two of them standing in a gleaming showroom, with shiny automobiles and cheery Germans. He sighed.

'Jean-Luc was the best of them.'

'He and his mother had courage.'

'Is it possible Vivienne disapproved of what her husband was doing?' He held up a hand in surrender as she shot him a look.

'I'll never let Paul go to them.'

It made her sick imagining a future Paul believing that what had happened in this country didn't matter or had been justifiable. Or growing up to feel horror at what had happened, discovering that his grandmother had abandoned him to people who believed that it was justified.

Erich didn't argue. His hand tightened on hers.

'What about the silk business? You're depriving Paul of his birthright?'

Her sigh was a long one. 'Jean-Luc cared so much about the business, I know.'

'But that's not the only thing you're depriving him of?'

She looked at him. His eyes were very sharp.

'If you don't tell Paul about his father, you can't tell him about his mother, either?'

This was the part that would break her heart. For her plan to work, Camille would have to vanish from Paul's life. She met Erich's questioning stare. 'I'll tell him about Camille when he's old enough to understand why I took him away. I don't want Camille to be lost.' She put a hand to her throat, feeling as though it was full of stones. 'It would be as though she died twice.'

'We speak their names, and it keeps them alive.' Erich often spoke of his dead wife, Claudia. She liked to hear him talk about Claudia, how he and she had met, about the years of their marriage and their life with Lottie. She was part of Erich, just as Bernhardt was part of Sophie. And Jean-Luc was part of Camille. And of Paul.

There was a moment's silence. They were both waiting. She was still waiting to see if he'd tell her he'd give up Lottie to come with them and start again, a new little family in the New World. Erich was still waiting to see if she'd change her mind again, stay here with him and face Vivienne's lawyers together.

But neither of them could risk another separation from a child after so many losses.

She'd allowed herself to dream about the life she and Erich would lead: both tending their patients during the day, coming home each night to talk about the cases they'd seen, Paul chatting to them over supper about what had happened at school. Was it possible that telling the truth to the lawyers might mean they could still have this life together?

Who was she really doing this for? The baby himself, or for her own sake? She looked at the man beside her. His hair was sparser and he'd lost even more weight this summer, but his eyes were sparkling and he could walk for miles. Erich still had years and years of medical work in him and he couldn't wait to get back to a hospital.

Vivienne's husband, the prefect, would have seen Erich – the kind, gifted doctor – deported without notice to some terrible fate in the east without a moment's guilt just because of his race. As long as Sophie breathed, people like that would never have anything to do with Paul. She went back to Erich and held him close to her.

'We'd planned our future together.' His voice shook.

'It was a wonderful future.' She tilted her head to look up at him sadly. 'But you can't come with me where I need to go.' She melted into him. 'I need you, too, I really do. I don't know how I'll manage without you.' Her body was protesting at the separation to come, making her cling to him. Sobs, deep, painful, racked her. She couldn't leave him, it was unbearable. 'But our children have to come first.'

'When?' Erich asked, releasing her.

'Tomorrow.' It would give her long enough to pack their few possessions. 'The grocer's niece isn't due for another two weeks. She's doing well and her first baby was an easy delivery. There aren't any others due. Rosa's coming on well.' Tomorrow was heartbreakingly close. But she had to go before the lawyer returned. 'I'm not going to tell Rosa or Nina until I actually leave. Best not to have anyone else in the secret.'

'So tonight is our last night?'

She nodded. 'I'll ask Rosa and Nina to take the boys down to the square for a few hours. We can cook dinner. And be together.'

For the last night. The tattered but still best set of lingerie in her drawer. The silk blouse that had been darned but still showed off her figure. The last molecules of lipstick and rouge. A cracked record on Nina's wind-up player and a last slow dance.

'I shall bring up the bottle of Bordeaux I've been saving ever since Paris fell.'

She nodded, incapable of speech. She was turning to stone.

'One more night is still one night together.' He pulled her back to him. His body felt like lava next to hers. One of her tears dropped onto the front of his worn cotton shirt and dissolved.

In the morning, Rosa stared at Sophie without saying anything when she told her what she was going to do. She nodded. 'I knew. When I saw you dressing up for dinner last night with Erich, I knew.'

'I didn't say anything.'

'You didn't need to. Where I come from, there's a look in people's eyes we can read very clearly, a sign they feel in danger, that they're moving on, looking at people and places for the last time.'

'I'm not in danger.'

'Your soul is in danger if they take him.' Rosa looked at Paul, kicking his legs happily in the pram on the terrace. He was ready to travel. She just needed to change him for the last time, take his bottle from the cold slab, and walk down to the village with him wrapped around her in the shawl. 'Go where they can never find him, Sophie. You must not be separated.' The fierceness on her face reminded Sophie of how Rosa had reacted in the convent, when she thought Patrin would be taken from her. Rosa understood. A single tear rolled down the girl's cheek. She rubbed it away furiously.

The church bell rang. 'You need to go,' Sophie said. 'You're at the clinic this morning, aren't you?'

'With Erich, yes. You won't be here when we…?'

'I've already said goodbye to him early this morning. I don't want him to… I can't…' She couldn't see him again, go through it all once more, the last touch of his lips, his hand falling slowly from her shoulder. The last glimpse of him walking down the track, not looking back at her because it would be unbearable. She'd wanted to shout after him that she'd changed her mind, he should come back, she wasn't going to leave. 'I need you to take care of him for me today.'

'And Nina?'

'I told her at breakfast, but I think she guessed too when she saw me going through my things last night.' She'd wanted to leave something for Nina and had found a small silver mirror that had been in her pocket the day she'd fled Lyon in July 1943 to come up here. Nina hadn't wept. She'd sat staring at Sophie until Sophie wondered if she'd actually understood. Then she stood up and wrapped her arms around Sophie before picking Paul up from his basket and kissing him on the forehead and replacing him, murmuring about preparing for the school day, still holding the little silver mirror.

Rosa put down the basket she was carrying and embraced her, stroking Sophie's back. On her own back, Patrin was already wrapped up in his cloth sling. Sophie let herself touch his curling hair for the last time. He was a fine boy, strong, with a determined but easy-going nature. 'The first time I met you, you sprayed me. I'll see you again one day, little one,' she told the boy. 'And you can laugh about it.'

Rosa released her, saying something in her own language. 'May you and Paul remain with God,' she continued. 'You found us in a godly place, Sophie, with the sisters, and His blessings will remain with you always. I must give you something.' She went into the house and returned with Camille's pearl hair combs.

'They're yours, *liefje*. Camille would want you to keep them. You saved her son's life by feeding him.'

'They're valuable. People will only think I stole them. Your daughter wore them the night she had your grandchildren.'

Rosa pushed them into her hand. 'Keep them for Paul's daughter.'

'I want to leave you with something.'

'To remember you by?' Rosa snorted. 'You think I'd ever forget you, Sophie Hansen, with your bossy ways and that mane of hair?'

'I actually left you something else, too.' She went into her room and returned with her midwife's bag. 'Erich found me some leather polish only last week and I've buffed it up. It will do you while you train.'

'But I can't take this.'

'Why not?'

'It's part of you, Sophie.'

'That's exactly why I want you to have it.' She pushed it into Rosa's arms. 'I can't carry it with everything else I need for the journey. Now, *dépêche-toi*, Erich will be setting up the clinic and you know he'll scold you if you're late.'

THIRTY-FOUR

SOPHIE, 1992

'And all those years, you couldn't tell me who I really was?' Paul looks out of the window at the browned grass and patchy snow. 'We were safe in America, but you still said nothing?'

I kept hoping the moment would come when it felt natural to tell him about his father and mother. That he had family in France, cousins he might wish to get to know. But years and decades passed. 'There was always a reason why it wasn't the right time.' Important school years. The dog dying. Paul heading off for college. His first real job. His marriage. His divorce. My breast cancer twenty years ago, fortunately only requiring a small amount of surgery. My hand is cupping my mouth, as though it's too painful to admit to my failure.

He's shaking his head. 'Your insistence on me learning French. That was what it was about?'

Paul grew up as an American boy of Dutch ancestry when in fact he was half-French. As a sop to my conscience, I made him study the language, even employing a tutor for a few hours a week for a while. 'I wanted you to be able to communicate with your family over there.' But I'd done nothing to facilitate any coming-together.

'You wouldn't let me drop it.'

At sixteen he went on an exchange visit to Rennes in Brittany, at a very safe distance from Lyon, and fell for his exchange partner's Gauloise-smoking, moped-riding older cousin. I was forgiven the cruelty I'd inflicted on him when he returned to Boston and wrote to her in French every week for some months.

Erich and I were still writing to one another regularly, too. Perhaps a tiny part of me thought Boston might be a place he could visit, now Lotte was married and settled. But soon after her wedding, Erich himself met a cousin of Lotte's foster family, visiting from South Africa. They fell for one another and married in the Cape in 1954. I wept when I read his news, but I was pleased for him, too. My loyal and loved Erich, who'd devoted himself to other people for so many years, so deserved a happy second marriage and a sunny retirement.

We kept on writing to one another, of course we did. And I wrote to Rosa and Nina, too. Rosa managed to find a nursing school in northern France setting its own entrance examination rather than requiring the French school-leaving baccalaureate she'd never taken. Nina moved with her and took care of Patrin while she trained. Nina eventually returned to Antwerp, managing to scrape together the funds to buy a floristry business, which became very successful, and reuniting with the family who'd survived. I always think of her when I see the first blossoms of spring, and how she brightened our sparse breakfast table.

I've never seen any of them again in the flesh except for Patrin, on his trip to the States. I'd smile as I looked at him and Paul throwing a ball around in the yard, remembering how they'd once shared a perambulator – and Rosa's milk. I'm not mystical by nature, but sometimes I can't help wondering whether some of Rosa's vitality passed into Paul with her milk. He's always been a hardy sort: cheerful but dogged. Good attributes in a research scientist. With some struggle I managed to contain my over-caution with him.

'Bless your heart, he's your only child and you were older when you had him,' a neighbour in Georgia told me, when Paul started kindergarten and she spotted how reluctant I was to let go of his hand the first morning.

Despite my over-protectiveness in his early years, Paul has grown up seemingly at ease with life. The divorce was painful, but a year after he'd moved into the relationship with Jill. Marriage and the arrival of Melissa brought them both happiness.

I would have been content, too, even knowing that I had carried out such a huge deception. But someone so important had been cut out of our lives. Camille, unmentioned, unremembered. I have never even seen her grave. I do actually have a photograph of her which I obviously didn't hand over for the *This is Your Life* board. I keep it in my bedside drawer: Camille as a six-year-old, playing on a Normandy beach. Sometimes when Melissa's with me, I long to take it out of my night table drawer and compare the two of them now Melissa's the same age. Same dainty little nose.

'Didn't you worry I'd find out?' Paul asks.

'Of course I did. People are growing obsessed with genealogy. You could fly to Europe one summer and it wouldn't be hard for someone like you to find the discrepancies between the records and what I told you.'

Paul's research could lead him to discovering that Bernhardt, his supposed father, had died two years before his own birth. It could lead him to the births and deaths of Camille and Louise, to Camille's marriage to Jean-Luc. He could see the original birth register in a small French industrial town near Lyon naming Sophie Hansen as his mother, the birth registered by Mireille Leclerc, the attending midwife. He could have sought out Vivienne and Martine and they'd have told him of the missing infant son of Jean-Luc and how he and Mireille, or Sophie Hansen as she really was, had been traced to a Cévennes village before vanishing at the end of the war. If death had claimed me before Paul made such a trip, he'd have been hurt, angry, confused by my deception. Perhaps he wouldn't have understood why I'd been so hellbent on putting the Atlantic between myself and Lyon and between him and his father's family.

Approaching my ninetieth birthday was the clarion call to start writing down an account of what happened in France in 1944, but it wasn't a satisfactory way of explaining. It was cowardly. 'I wrote it all down,' I say. 'But it was better to tell you in person.'

He looks at me as though he doesn't know what to say.

It's an old, old story, the grandmother assuming the role of mother. I've seen it in my work. Usually, it happens because the mother is unmarried or very young. Often the real mother retains a presence in the child's life, perhaps eventually acknowledged as such.

Paul is staring out into the garden. I can't read his expression now. I want to babble on, begging for forgiveness, trying to explain, but I force myself to silence.

'My father's family?' he says at last. 'You think they may still be in Lyon?'

'One of Jean-Luc's sisters lived there. Her husband was a prominent local politician until his wartime misdeeds were exposed. I don't know if he's still alive.' I let out a breath. 'The sisters were another reason why I took you after your mother died. They were sympathetic to the Occupation. More than sympathetic.'

'But my father...?'

'Did something very brave.' I look down at my hands, still strong for my age, not as supple now. 'I worried your aunts would fight me for custody. In 1944 they seemed to represent everything wrong in France. They condoned or turned their eyes away from terrible things.'

'I'm glad you didn't let them have me.' The reply is instant and heartfelt.

'I believe your aunts sold the silk business, too much global competition.' I don't know more than this. When we came to the States, I purposefully avoided any news about French public figures, wartime history or the silk industry, not that much trickled through to us in Georgia or Boston.

'But the business was very profitable for a long time. You could have been wealthy.'

His eyes go round the spacious lounge with its well-chosen furniture, all earned by his own hand.

'Yes, but perhaps you didn't need family money behind you, Paul.'

He traces the pattern on a sofa cushion. 'When Camille died, she didn't know that my father had been shot?'

'Camille and Jean-Luc each died without knowing the other had been killed. Jean-Luc didn't know little Louise was dead, either.' I have always prayed that Camille, too, never knew she was cradling a dead baby but don't share this thought with Jean-Luc.

'I still can't believe I had a sister.' He shakes his head.

'Born just twenty minutes before you.' They weren't identical twins, sharing that level of intimacy in the womb, but they were together for nine months before birth. And then they lay together in the bassinet for that one day both were alive, curled up close.

'Louise and Camille.' He says the names musingly to himself, looking out of the window towards Melissa's climbing frame. 'You sometimes call her Milly. I always wondered why.'

'Milly for Camille. Her real grandmother.' My way of keeping a little of my daughter alive. Perhaps my way of throwing out a hint, half-wanting someone to ask why? Camille as a grandmother has always seemed a fantastical thought. In my mind, she's eternally twenty-two.

'Why now? Why today, Mom?' He shakes his head. 'I can't stop calling you that.'

'I could drop down dead,' I tell him. 'Sudden stroke. Pneumonia. Perhaps reaching this age has suddenly made me aware of my mortality.' You can't argue with ninety.

He snorts.

'Perhaps you knew there was something I was keeping from you?' I almost hope he did.

'The reluctance to visit the Cévennes or even talk very much about your time up there during the war, that puzzled me. But we thought it might have been very traumatic for you, so it seemed understandable. I even...'

'What?'

'Sometimes it crossed my mind that perhaps I'd been the result of something happening to you, something terrible.'

I don't understand for a moment.

'You were... older. It didn't seem that Bernhardt was living with you around the time I'd been conceived.' He shrugs.

'Oh god.' I feel nauseous, my hand going to my mouth. Paul had wondered if he was the result of something like a rape?

'Mom? Are you all right?'

I have no reason to be pathetic like this. I force myself to sit straighter. 'I'm fine. And I'm appalled I let that happen, that you might think something like that. I've been so selfish.'

He takes my hands. 'No, no, you haven't. I realised it couldn't be that.'

'How? Why?'

He doesn't seem to know how to answer. 'It seemed uncomplicated between us.' It was. I loved him from the moment I helped him into the world, very slowly – he was a breech baby and easing him into life had to be done with care. 'If there'd been something awful, I thought it would have shown.'

'How?' I ask.

A shrug. 'I saw how Jill was, is, with Melissa. And that's how you've always been with me. There's no... complexity. Is that the right word? You just seemed to love me and I loved you, too.'

'Yes.' I'm relieved. 'No complexity.'

'So I thought it couldn't be... that.' His facial muscles knot again. 'For a while I wondered if Bernhardt had been sent to a concentration camp and it was so traumatic you hadn't wanted to tell me.'

That happens. I know of families where Jewish heritage has been hushed up, the story of murdered relatives kept hidden. An attempt to protect children and grandchildren from any future persecution. Or from the psychological weight of such horror.

'We weren't Jewish. Your grandfather Bernhardt died of a perforated appendix. I should have urged him to go back to the doctor's again.' I tell him of Bernhardt's collapse on the street. 'Your mother was inconsolable. She adored him.' I look at Paul. 'Sometimes I see a bit of Bernhardt in you.'

He leans towards me.

'There's a glint in your eyes that was Bernhardt's. He had a mischievous sense of humour, but he could be dogged when he was on to a story.'

Silence. He swallows.

'Does Melissa really remind you of Camille?' He sounds wistful.

'There's a neatness to Melissa that's like Camille. A precision in the way she does things.'

'How do you mean?'

I struggle for an example but remember Camille's layette. 'Your mother was sewing and embroidering clothes for you and your twin just before you were born. Every stitch perfect, precise.'

And most of those exquisite baby clothes were left in the nursery of the Lyon house when we fled, I remember, with a pang. We thought we'd come back to that house at some point. But brooding is futile.

'I was reminded of your mother's sewing when I saw Milly's colouring in of the flags on my birthday card. Perfect. Neat. And the way she traced the letters. Bernhardt was like that, too.' On the face of it, very easy go lucky. But his desk was covered with balled-up sheets of paper he'd yank out of the typewriter because a single word wasn't right. He could have struck through the offending letters but preferred to start all over again.

We sit there together for a moment, silent.

'At least you know now.' A sense of relief is slowly flowing through me, tinged with sadness. Because no matter what happens, Paul will never know his mother, his father, his twin. 'I've written it all down for you.' I look at my watch. 'I should be getting back. Things to do. For this evening.' I pause. 'But perhaps we shouldn't go ahead with the party?'

Paul blinks. 'The party. Yes. Definitely we should go ahead with it.' He goes into the kitchen to use the phone and call me another cab home, just a few quick words muttered to Jill. I can imagine the looks exchanged: *Not now, you won't believe it...*

There's nothing more I can say to him.

Melissa bursts in, Paul trying and failing to stop her. 'Grandma, I think my blue dress is best, but Mom's making me wear the red one. It's your party, so you can say, can't you?'

'Sorry.' Jill's head appears round the door. 'Sophie, let me get you a coffee before the cab comes?'

'No coffee.' My bag is at my feet. 'I have something in here. I was going to give it to Milly later, but it might be better now.'

'My present!'

I take out the tissue-paper-wrapped parcel. It doesn't look much. 'Your father knows why it's special. Perhaps he can tell you later.' Jill and Melissa probably think it's just a family heir-loom. Of course that's true.

Melissa takes it, wide-eyed. 'Thank you.'

'It's a grown-up kind of present.'

She unwraps the pearl combs and her mouth opens. I think she's impressed. Jill certainly is. 'They look valuable, Sophie. Should we let her have them this young?'

'They've survived far more than a party. I was hoping she might wear them tonight.'

'Yes!' Milly is already dragging a chair over to the fireplace so she can stand up and look at herself in the mirror.

'Here.' Jill takes the combs from her. 'Let me.' She pulls back the sides of Milly's dark hair and pins the combs in. 'One in each side, like this?' She checks over her shoulder with me.

My daughter delivered Paul with those combs still in her hair because nobody had time to think about them. Camille's expression, triumphant, proud, looking down at her twins, one in each arm, seems written on her granddaughter's face, as Milly beams at being allowed at the grown-ups' party, with grown-up jewellery. Her hair is longer than Camille's was, with more of a wave to it. But her eyes, looking back at me from the reflection in the mirror, are Camille's.

'You're doing it exactly right. Milly, you look perfect.'

'Yes.' Paul puts an arm around me. 'She does.'

Rosa insisted the combs stayed with me. Rosa was perhaps prophetic. I must tell her that when we have our next biannual trans-Atlantic telephone call. She is never surprised at being proved right.

Paul squeezes me gently. 'This is going to be the best party, Mom. Relax. Prepare to have fun. All the hard work's been done.'

I let my head slip onto his shoulder. He's warm and solid, just like his grandfather Bernhardt was. I don't deserve him.

'You should go home and rest,' Jill tells me. I don't know

how much she has put together. Could she hear some of my story through the kitchen door?

I nod, though I have no need to rest. Jill is a kind daughter-in-law, easy to be with. I've never thought of her as a daughter – there can only ever be one of those – but when I'm with her, I'm reminded of my companionship with Nina all those years ago.

'Grandma doesn't look tired.' Melissa's reflection studies me.

I've put in many a night at a labouring woman's side. I've walked or cycled home, always weary, often hungry. But always, as dawn was breaking, I've felt the mystery of a new life entwined with the promise of a new day.

Dusk, not dawn, is falling outside now, but I still feel the same promise.

A LETTER FROM THE AUTHOR

Dear reader,

Huge thanks for reading *The Midwife's Promise*, I hope you were caught up in Sophie's journey. If you want to join other readers in hearing all about my new releases and bonus content, you can sign up here:

www.stormpublishing.co/eliza-graham

And if you would like to sign up for my regular newsletter, please click here:

www.elizagrahamauthor.com/newsletter

If you enjoyed this book and could spare a few moments to leave a review, that would be hugely appreciated. Even a short review can make all the difference in encouraging a reader to discover my books for the first time. Thank you so much!

Thanks again for being part of this amazing journey with me and I hope you'll stay in touch – I have so many more stories and ideas to entertain you with!

Eliza

facebook.com/ElizaGrahamUK

instagram.com/elizagraham1

ACKNOWLEDGEMENTS

My thanks again to Kathryn Taussig at Storm Publishing for her ongoing support, and to my editor, Emma Beswetherick, who wouldn't let me get away with anything less than my very best work – possibly the highest praise you can give an editor. My thanks also to Liz Hurst for her sharp-eyed catches on the manuscript. Marketing is always the lifeblood of a book launch and I owe much to Elke Desanghere and Anna McKerrow. A thank you also to Alexandra Holmes and Naomi Knox for their work on my behalf.

Covers are the first opportunity to grab a reader's attention. I love my cover art, the work of the talented Sarah Whittaker.

As always, Johnnie, Mungo and Eloise Graham have been huge supporters of my writing, especially this summer when much of my July was given over to unexpected surgery and recovery. The three of them plus Lewis Turner stepped in to help with 'rest of life' so I didn't miss important writing deadlines, and my previous book's launch was still fun, even if conducted in surgical stockings and gown. My thanks and love to them.

Researching *The Midwife's Promise* was such an enjoyable process, both in terms of subject matter and location. A visit in January 2023 to the museum at the Union Street headquarters of the Royal College of Obstetricians and Gynaecologists and College of Midwifes was a truly inspiring one. Thanks to Peter Basham, curator, and Clare Button, archivist, for giving me their time and sharing their knowledge with me.

Sadly, catching what turned out to be Covid while on a research trip to Lyon and Cévennes truncated what we could see, but was so helpful, if brief. There's much more of Lyon I want to look at and I am yearning for a return visit to the region.

Fortunately, Covid can stop you travelling but it can never stop you ordering up books to read for research. I found these ones particularly useful:

Vichy France: Old Guard and New Order 1940–1944
    Robert O Paxton
    An account of the government and governed under Marshal Pétain, the compromises and humiliations.

Village of Secrets
    Caroline Moorhead
    A moving description of how remote villages in the southern Massif Central of France saved several thousand mainly Jewish people from the Nazis.

Divided Loyalties
    Janet Teissier du Cros
    An account of a Scottish woman's isolated existence in the Cévennes during the Second World War, short of food and desperate for news of loved ones.

Call the Midwife
    Jennifer Worth
    It would be impossible to write about midwifery in the mid-twentieth century without somehow coming to Jennifer Worth's autobiographical accounts of her time in London's East End, and finding your way to the many BBC TV series. I started by thinking I'd watch one or two episodes, but here I am in September 2023 waiting for Series 13.

I had much to learn about the silk production process when I started writing *The Midwife's Promise*. Mulberries and Silk is a very informative website that taught me a lot about the process. I couldn't have written about Jean-Luc's attempts to keep his looms going without learning a little bit about the industry.

https://www.moruslondinium.org/research/mulberries-and-silk-john-feltwell